HOT FOR A COP

THE SINGLE MOMS OF SEATTLE, BOOK 2

WHITLEY COX

ISBN: 978-1-989081-37-2

For Kelsey.
I'm so glad my brother finally asked you to marry him.
Another sister in-law I love dearly.
Welcome to the family!

1

SOAKED TO THE BONE, pissed right the fuck off, and sweating like she was tap dancing on the surface of sun—even though it was a wet and windy December night— Lauren Green grunted at the same time the driver's seat of her Nissan Pathfinder squealed. She was attempting to wedge herself behind the steering wheel and was doing a shit job accomplishing it.

Her phone started to ring, and she let out a loud "MOTHER FUCKER" at the same time she wrestled with the wind to shut her door.

She finally managed to slam it closed, snatched her phone from her purse, put it on speaker on the cellphone holder attached to her dash and yelled, "What the fuck do you want?" as she attempted to fasten her seatbelt around her enormous baby-filled belly.

"To see if you wanted me to brew you some raspberry leaf tea," Bianca said quietly. "Get that Booty Call Baby moving on out of that belly."

"Fuck," Lauren muttered, immediately feeling like shit for

speaking to one of her best friends like she was a telemarketer trying to sell her diet pills. "Sorry."

"How was your doctor's appointment?" Celeste asked. They were on a three-way call, as they often were. Her two best friends. Her fellow single moms. Well, Lauren wasn't a single mom yet, but she would be soon. She needed to be soon. Otherwise, she was going to lose her fucking mind.

Besides hearing that steady heartbeat and being reassured that the baby was healthy and in the right position, she found her doctor's appointment rather unpleasant.

"Did they do a stretch and sweep?" Bianca asked. "I always hated those. Painful as hell."

Lauren shifted in her seat. She was told after the invasive, sometimes painful and definitely uncomfortable procedure used by doctors to induce labor she might have cramping, bleeding and be a little sore. She was. More than a little.

Grimacing, she buckled her seatbelt under her belly. "Yep. Not my preferred way to have a man's fingers inside me, but at this point in the game, the doctor could have stuck his dick in me if it induced labor."

Both her friends snorted in laughter.

It also sucked that it hadn't been *her* doctor. Dr. Finton, her regular OB-GYN was on call at the hospital delivering other lucky women's babies while Lauren got stuck with a locum, a man old enough to be judging her for her "condition" because it was unseemly for Lauren to be having a child out of wedlock with no father in sight. Clearly, she was a harlot. Not that he said these things to her, of course, but she could feel Dr. Judgy McJudgerson judging the shit out of her as he pushed two fingers into her cooch and scissored them around like her cervix had challenged him to a game of rock, paper, scissors, and kept throwing out rock.

She turned on the ignition, flipped on the defrost and let her vehicle warm up for a moment. The rain was coming in sideways because of the wind and hitting her windshield with a disturbing amount of force.

Starved, because she was always hungry these days, being forty weeks pregnant plus five days, she opened up a bag of dill-pickle-flavored mini rice cakes and started shoving them into her mouth three at a time.

"Did the doctor mention your dilation or anything?" Celeste asked.

The rice cakes had formed a gelatinous glob in the back of her throat, and Lauren struggled to swallow it down. She chugged water from her bottle before answering. "Yeah, still tight as fuck. Like two centimeters maybe. Cervix was hard as a raw carrot too."

"Damn it," Celeste said. "I'll bring over some spicy chicken wings."

"I'll bring raspberry leaf tea and dates."

Lauren wrinkled her nose. "Why dates?"

"Because they help ripen the cervix and decrease the need for Pitocin during labor. I ate dates like a fiend my last week of pregnancy with Charlie, and he came so quickly, with no need for drugs or anything. Barely made it to the hospital."

"And that wasn't because you had twins before him and they stretched the door as wide as a combine so he could just slide on out?" Lauren said, flipping on her windshield wipers and pulling out of the clinic parking lot. It was already dark out because, well, duh, it was five o'clock on a Saturday (thank God her doctor's office was open on the weekends). Add in the storm that had come in off the Pacific earlier that day, and she struggled to see ten feet in front of her headlights.

"Har-har," Bianca laughed forcibly. "Orgasms also help. You could just stay home and masturbate all night and not bring your crappy attitude over to my house."

Lauren turned off the side road and onto the ramp for the interstate. "Sorry. You know I'm not usually this big of a bitch. I just want this baby out of me so damn bad."

"I know, sweetie," Bianca said. "I'm just teasing you. Bring that crappy attitude over and we'll pour raspberry leaf down your throat and force-feed you spicy chicken wings. That baby will be out in no time."

She was just about to accelerate to the cruising interstate speed when a blur of red brake lights in front of her had her slamming on her own brakes hard enough to engage the locking mechanism of her seat belt and make her lurch forward. "What the hell?"

"You okay?" Celeste and Bianca asked at the same time.

"Traffic jam," she muttered. She tried to see around the vehicle in front of her, but it was a futile endeavor. They were in four lanes of traffic, and it was gridlock. Not to mention the sideways rain.

"I just brought up Google maps on my phone and yeah, major traffic jam on the I-5," Celeste said. "Any way you can take an off-ramp and do the side roads?"

"We're at a complete standstill."

Warm liquid pooled between her legs. What the fuck? She unbuckled her belt and shoved her hand down her pants.

Please don't let it be blood. Please don't be blood.

It wasn't blood.

She brought her fingers to her nose to make sure it wasn't urine. She'd started peeing herself a little at the slightest sudden movement. A lurch forward like she'd done when she slammed on the brakes easily could have made her empty her bladder.

It wasn't pee.

"Guys ..."

"You okay?" Celeste asked, panic in her voice.

"I think my water just broke."

"Fuck," both of her friends said at the same time.

"What do I do?" Lauren asked, craning around awkwardly into the back seat of her Pathfinder to reach for a towel.

"Don't panic." Celeste's voice wobbled. "Sabrina didn't come for another twelve hours after my water broke. So this may not mean anything more than the start of labor. And that's what you went to the doctor for, right? To *start* labor. So at least we know it worked."

"They had to break my water with the girls," Bianca added. "First babies usually take a long time to come. Hannah and Hayley were like thirty hours."

"Jesus fuck," Lauren muttered.

Attempting to breathe deep and stay calm, she put her vehicle in park and went to push her seat back farther when the mother of all cramps pierced through her abdomen and lower back like she'd just run belly-first into a hot poker.

She sucked in a deep breath. She rode out the pain, gritting her teeth and white-knuckling the steering wheel. "I think that was a contraction."

"I'm going to time them," Bianca said. "Let me know when the next one comes."

Lauren nodded. "Guys, I can't have my baby in my car in the middle of a traffic jam in the middle of a storm. I just can't."

"It'll be okay," Celeste said, her voice not the least reassuring.

"If you can talk through the contractions, they're not that strong. The baby isn't coming just yet," Bianca said soothingly. "Remember the breathing from your prenatal class."

"You mean the one I went to alone because I'm about to be a single mother?" Lauren blurted out, half laughing, half crying. "Because the guy I was seeing for three months, the guy who knocked me up, ran the moment I told him I was pregnant."

"We offered to come to the classes with you," Celeste said softly.

"You both have kids and lives. I need to be able to do things on my own. I'm on my own with this ki—" She squeezed her eyes shut and arched her back in her seat as another wave of nauseating pain hit her harder than the last. "Another—"

Fuck, she wasn't able to speak through it. Did that mean the baby was coming *now?*

"They're five minutes apart," Bianca said, sounding worried.

Lauren slumped back in her seat, panting. "What's the protocol?"

"Four-one-one," Celeste said quietly. "Four minutes apart, lasting one minute each, for one hour."

"That lasted just shy of a minute," Bianca added.

"Yeah, but they need to last an hour at that length and interval," Celeste said. "Her water *just* broke. Her contractions *just* started. She has time."

Lauren didn't feel like she had time. She'd been itching for this baby to make its debut for the last three weeks, and now that it was finally gearing up to do so, she didn't feel prepared at all.

"Do you have the car seat installed?" Bianca asked.

Lauren nodded. "Yeah. Took it to the fire station and one of the firefighters did it for me." And that man had fueled her rampant fantasies for a good two weeks afterward. Not that she could see her crotch anymore or get her fingers or a vibrator there. She'd resorted to showerhead, and it wasn't nearly as effective as some of her toys.

"What about your hospital bag?" Celeste asked.

"In the back."

"And towels or a blanket?"

"A few, yeah." She always had at least one blanket in the back of her car and usually kept one or two towels in case she got caught in a rainstorm or decided to go for a swim in some random river or lake when she was out for a Sunday drive.

Having grown up in Nebraska and Utah, now that she lived on the west coast in gorgeous Seattle, she loved going for Sunday drives through the mountains. All the twists and turns to the road. The beauty of nature and the sound of birds chirping and water burbling. She loved her family back home in Utah, but she'd never move back, not when she had the Pacific Northwest to call home.

About to open her mouth and ask if she needed to find boiling water—obviously a joke—another contraction ripped through her. Each one was worse than the last. Each one lasted longer and seemed to be hitting her harder and more concentrated in her back and between her legs.

"Was that another one?" Bianca asked.

"Uh-huh." She reached for her water bottle and took a long sip. Wasn't she supposed to be chewing ice chips or something? Wasn't that what women in labor on TV were always chomping on?

"Has traffic moved at all?" Celeste asked.

Not a fucking inch. "No," she whined.

"I think you need to move into the back seat," Bianca suggested. "Recline the seat to give yourself some space. You'll be more comfortable that way too."

"I ... I can't give birth in my car. I just can't." She'd always considered herself a strong person, an independent person, and yet right now, she felt helpless and weak and terrified of being alone.

"You might have to, honey," Bianca whispered. "I'm really sorry. But those contractions are strong, close and long. That baby is coming."

Tears sprang into Lauren's eyes, and she shook her head violently. "No! No! No!" She poked her stomach. "You stay the fuck in there, you hear me? You are not coming into this world in the back of a Pathfinder in the middle of a storm. That's not your story. That's not *our* story."

"Get into the back seat," Celeste said gently. "You'll be more comfortable there."

With tears of fear, pain and utter frustration burning tracks down her cheeks, Lauren braced herself for the onslaught of rain, wind and another contraction.

She opened her door, but the wind caught it, flung it open and took Lauren with it.

EVERY FUCKING YEAR. The closer to Christmas it got, the crazier people started to act. The more desperate they started to behave. Isaac Fox squeezed his eyes shut as he sat in his truck in the middle of the gridlocked bumper-to-bumper traffic in the plummeting rain and window-rattling wind. He was glad he'd decided to drive his truck today and not his motorcycle.

Even though his father had drilled into his brain since the day he was born that any other bike besides a Harley was for pussies, he loved his Ducati Enduro Pro and rode it to work whenever he could.

Fuck his old man.

Isaac was nothing like him and determined to keep it that way.

Right down to what rumbled between his legs.

Only now that winter had officially hooked her frigid claws into each and every day, he was grateful he had a vehicle to tuck into. He couldn't even imagine being trapped in this fucking mess of a traffic jam on his bike.

Goodbye nuts and any chance of having children.

And because he was a cop—but off duty for the next two days—he couldn't very well weave in between the cars on his bike. That was setting a bad example and showing his privilege. Though he knew countless other motorcycle-riding cops who would have swerved between the vehicles or ridden the shoulder to bypass the chaos.

But Isaac liked to stay aboveboard. He went into law enforcement for a reason. So he could uphold the law, not break it when it suited him.

Opening his eyes again, he checked to see if the traffic in front of him had moved.

Nope. Not a fucking inch.

Good thing he didn't have a wife and kids to get home to.

Not even a damn cat.

Normally, he liked his life. He had nobody to answer to, nobody to give him grief or a hard time for working late or staying three hours at the gym and then going out for a beer with his buddy. Nobody to pick up after. He could leave the toilet seat up without having to worry about being bitched out for it or some kid throwing his keys and watch into the bowl.

Yeah, he liked his life.

Except sometimes.

Like Christmas.

Like now.

He hadn't been home in ... fuck, nearly ten years. Because there wasn't really anything for him there anymore. He wasn't sure he had a *home,* per se. Certainly not a childhood home he could return to with memories carved out in every corner. A treehouse in the backyard and height measurements in the doorjamb. He'd never had a home like that. The only reason he knew those homes existed was because of television.

Originally from Nebraska, he, his mom and sister fled his

abusive father and moved to Phoenix when Isaac was eight and his sister, Natalie, only five. But now that he and Natalie were grown, neither of them lived in Arizona. His mother married a man from Ecuador two years ago and moved down there to be with him. Natalie was studying abroad in Germany, getting her PhD in some very specific kind of genetics, and even though six feet under would be ideal, he knew his father was back in prison. He'd been out on parole for a year, but then was put away again for money laundering, racketeering and possession of illegal firearms.

So Isaac really had no one.

Sure, he had friends. And he would call his mother and sister on Christmas, and he ordered them gifts online to be delivered directly, gift-wrapped and everything. But he didn't have anybody he could turn to in Seattle whom he could call *family*.

Which was why he volunteered to work Christmas Eve and Christmas Day. He took the long, ugly shifts because he could. So other cops with families and children could be with those they loved while Isaac raked in the overtime and kept the crazies from looting empty houses like those two crooks from *Home Alone*.

His stomach grumbled, and he went to reach for a granola bar from his bag on the passenger side of his truck when he noticed the person in the SUV next to him had opened their door.

What the hell? It was windy as fuck and raining like he'd never seen in his ten years living in Seattle. Who would leave their door just wide open? The wind was going to whip it clean off its hinges. That's when he saw the hand gripping the handle.

White knuckles.

The hand slipped, then scrambled to grab the handle again before finally failing and disappearing completely.

What the ...

Abandoning his granola bar, he unbuckled his belt and leaned over his bench seat to see what was going on. That's when he saw the woman on the ground, her face a mask of pure agony as she held one hand protectively over an enormous belly and struggled to make purchase somewhere on her vehicle with the other hand.

Holy fuck.

Before he could think twice about what he was doing, he was out of his truck and in the rain, running to the woman.

"I gotcha, I gotcha," he said, though he wasn't sure she heard him. The wind had probably carried his voice down to Oregon by now. With his hands beneath her arms, he helped her up. "Back in you go."

He made to place her back behind the wheel, but she screamed out, "No! I'm in labor. The baby is coming *now*. I need to get into the back seat."

What the fuck?

"Now?"

She nodded, her whole body soaked, blonde hair plastered to the side of her face. With cornflower-blue eyes, full of more fear than he'd ever seen in his life and brimming with tears, she dug her nails into his arm. "Help me, please."

He was a cop, not a paramedic. He didn't know how to deliver a baby. He knew basic first aid. That was it. He'd hardly even held a baby, let alone caught one shooting out of a person like a football.

But he was a first responder. And this woman needed his help. He would do what he could, even if it wasn't much.

"Okay, okay," he said gently, shutting the door to the driver's side and opening up the back passenger door. He folded the seat down so she could lie down through to the back hatch. The other seat already had a car seat installed. "You need me to call your husband or something?"

She climbed into the back on all fours, groaning and pausing as what was obviously another contraction hit her. He waited in the rain and wind until the contraction subsided and she climbed in the rest of the way.

"No husband. Doing this ... alone." She grunted as she flopped to her back.

Isaac climbed in, folded the driver's seat forward and sat on it. "What do you need from me?"

"Who's there?" came a female voice from inside the truck.

"Lauren, did you find a doctor?" asked another woman.

Isaac wasn't an idiot. There was no other person in the vehicle, so those voices had to be coming from her phone. "I'm not a doctor. I'm a cop," he said. "Who am I speaking to?"

"A cop? Well, it's better than nothing. We're Lauren's friends. Celeste and Bianca. Have you ever delivered a baby before?"

"No."

"Do you have your own kids?"

"No."

"A lot of good he's going to be," one woman muttered.

"Well, at least she's not alone now," the other replied.

"You need to help her get her pants off and place some towels beneath her. There is going to be a lot of blood. Her water already broke in the front seat."

"I should call 911. They can talk me through delivering the baby," he said, dreading the idea of being the first person a baby saw when he or she entered the world.

"You're not catching this baby," she said to him, her eyes wide in panic. "He's not catching this baby," Lauren cried out to her friends, her face twisting in more pain. "He's too hot to see me, to see *it* in such a godawful state. I watched those birthing videos. Everything swells and goes flat and nasty. No fucking way. I'll catch this baby myself. I think I've got a mirror on the compact in my purse."

"She's being ridiculous," one of the women murmured. He had no clue who was Celeste and who was Bianca, and at this point in the chaos, he didn't care.

"What's your name, officer?" the other woman asked.

"Isaac," he replied.

"Okay, Isaac, call 911. Let them know a woman is in labor on the interstate, then maybe go knock on some car windows to see if there is a nurse or doctor or paramedic in the jam. Somebody to help you."

"Should I leave her, though?" He was a cop. He should have known to call 911 first. This pregnant woman in such pain was making him forget all his training.

Lauren's face was once again scrunched up as she braved her way through another contraction. Her eyes were shut. Her teeth gnashed and bared as she squirmed where she lay. "Go!" she finally yelled. "Go find me someone who can catch this baby. But then you come back." Her eyes flashed open. "Please, don't leave me."

He nodded and opened the door again. "I'll be back as soon as I can."

Isaac had been through war. He'd been through shootouts and armed robberies, hostage negotiations and talking people off bridges. But none of that compared to the helplessness he felt right now as he wandered up and down the rows of vehicles knocking on windows.

After graduating college, he enlisted in the marines and was deployed to Iraq, where he served two back-to-back tours before returning to the U.S. and enrolling in the police academy. He'd never been to Seattle before, but a buddy in the marines had grown up in the Pacific Northwest and said there wasn't a better place to live. Stuart died before he was able to return home, but Isaac took his words to heart and decided to see what all the hype was about. Stuart had not led him astray.

The moment Isaac saw the sunset, the mountains and the trees, the ocean and the ferry boats, he knew he'd found his forever home. He found an apartment within a week and enrolled in the police academy a day later. And he hadn't looked back since.

Fighting the wind and rain, he attempted to shield his eyes and the droplets that felt more like shards of glass. It was to little avail. He should have grabbed his jacket from his truck, but he wasn't thinking about anything besides helping Lauren. Now, a ways away from her Pathfinder, he worried she and the baby would be in distress if he didn't return. He needed to get back to her, but he hadn't found anybody that could help her yet. And he needed to help her.

A woman in a blue Corolla saw him approach her vehicle, and she rolled down her window slightly. "Is someone hurt?" she asked.

"A woman is in labor. She needs help delivering the baby. It's coming now. Are you a doctor?"

She shook her head. "Midwife. I can help."

"Oh thank fuck. This way."

Nodding, she shut the lights off for her vehicle, reached for a bag from the back seat of her car and followed him through the cars, the wind and rain now at their backs, propelling them forward.

"Here, here," he said, pointing to her gray Nissan. "She's in the back seat."

The midwife nodded. "Is she alone?"

"Yeah."

"Are you comfortable staying to support her?"

No. But he'd do it anyway.

She didn't wait for him to respond and opened the door. "Hi there. I'm a midwife, and I hear you're having a baby in this storm."

"Where's Isaac?" Lauren shouted.

"I'm here, I'm here," he said, poking his head around the midwife to see her.

"Can you climb into the back seat through the hatch and go support her?" the midwife asked. "Maybe let her sit up between your legs. Rub her shoulders and hips. Let her squeeze your hand."

He nodded as the midwife climbed into the truck and shut the door.

Soaked through to his marrow and freezing, he knew he needed to get out of the rain, but he knocked back on the door before opening it. "I need to pull her vehicle off to the berm. Put her hazards on. Do the same for my truck. It's not safe the way we are now." Thank fuck his cop-sense was coming back. He was beginning to worry it might be gone for good.

Nodding, the midwife dropped the passenger seat the same way the driver's seat was and Isaac shut the door, popped the driver's seat back up and climbed behind the wheel.

"Might as well gimme your keys so I can pull your car off to the berm, too," he said, turning over the ignition. "Not safe where it is now."

The midwife made a "mhmm" sound in agreement and handed him her keys.

It took some finesse to pull over, as all vehicles were bumper to bumper, but eventually he managed, tossed on the hazard lights and shut off the Pathfinder. Then he went to do the same to his truck and the midwife's car, finally calling 911 as he did so. They were dispatching an ambulance to the scene, but given the gridlock, they would be severely delayed.

It felt like forever until he was climbing into Lauren's vehicle through the back. He was glad to finally be out of the rain but terrified about what was going to happen next.

Closing the hatch door behind him, he helped Lauren up to a sitting position and scooted in behind her.

She was wet too, but that was probably from rain and sweat. Her forehead felt warm, and she was limp like a noodle as he maneuvered his body around hers.

The midwife perched on the folded-down driver's seat and dug around in her bag. "All right, those were some big contractions. Do you think you can talk now?"

Lauren nodded.

"Good. My name is Nicki. What's yours?" She snapped on some purple latex gloves.

"Lauren."

"Hi, Lauren, nice to meet you. Now, while we're between contractions, I'm going to ask you a few questions. Are you okay answering them?"

Lauren nodded.

"Great. How old are you, Lauren?"

"Thirty-two."

"And how far along are you?"

"Forty weeks, five days."

"Oh, so this little one is overdue. Your first?"

Lauren nodded again.

"And the father?"

"A guy I dated for a few months. He ran when I told him I was pregnant."

"That fucker," Isaac blurted out.

Nicki's gentle gray eyes turned sad. "I'm sorry about that."

Lauren opened her mouth to say something, but another contraction came on first, and she wailed and groaned in Isaac's arms, her body twisting, face contorting in pain. The midwife was staring at her watch.

When Lauren finally relaxed, Nicki lifted her gaze. "And they've been like that for a while now?"

Lauren nodded. "My water only just broke like thirty

minutes ago. Contractions started right after that. But they've been long and intense."

"We've been timing them," said either Bianca or Celeste from the phone. "They're three minutes apart and lasting for a minute."

Nicki put a stethoscope into her ears and placed it on Lauren's belly. "Friends?"

Lauren nodded.

"How has your pregnancy been? Any concerns throughout?"

Lauren shook her head. "No. Doctors say I'm healthy. Baby is healthy. I was GBS negative."

What the fuck was GBS? Was it a good thing she was negative?

"Good. No need for penicillin." Nicki went quiet and stoic for a moment as she listened to the baby in Lauren's belly. "Heartbeat sounds good. I have my doppler too if this didn't work, but I can hear the heartbeat just fine."

Nicki pulled a blood pressure cuff from her bag, wrapped it around Lauren's arm, inflated it, pressed the stethoscope to the inside of Lauren's elbow and stared at her watch again as the cuff deflated.

Nodding, the midwife removed the cuff and stowed it back in her bag. "Blood pressure is normal. That's good."

"I had a stretch and sweep earlier today," Lauren said, her hands rubbing over the top of her belly. "Doctor said I was only two centimeters and hard as a carrot."

"Yes, well, that can change at the drop of a hat. And since you had the procedure, that probably got things moving."

What the fuck was a *stretch and sweep*? *Hard as a carrot?* Did he want to know what that meant? Probably not. He could only imagine, and that image did not sit well in his brain.

"We need to remove your pants so I can take a look," the midwife said. "Are you okay with that?"

Lauren nodded. "Whatever. I ..." But just like before, she couldn't get the words out before the contraction hit her hard.

Isaac had no clue what to do. He placed his hands on her shoulders and massaged, but like hell if he knew if he was doing any good.

When the contraction ended, Nicki helped Lauren remove her pants and underwear. She was wearing a long gray tunic dress thing, so at least she was able to keep her modesty.

Not bothering to look between Lauren's legs, Nicki put her hand beneath her dress.

"You're nine centimeters, Lauren. I can feel the head. This baby is coming now. How do you feel?"

"Like my body is going to be split in two," Lauren whimpered, her head slumping to the side and against Isaac's shoulder. "I'm already so tired."

Removing his hand from her shoulder, he wiped the hair off her face. "You've got this, Lauren. You can do this." His encouragement sounded hollow to his own ears, but he had no idea what else to say. "What a story for you and this baby. Born in a storm."

God, had he really just said that? Fuck, he was lame.

"Do you feel like you need to push?" Nicki asked.

Lauren barely nodded, but she did.

Nicki smiled. "All right. Let's bend your knees, and when that feeling comes again, let me know and we'll go for it, okay?"

"Okay."

Nicki glanced up at Isaac. "You ready?"

No. But he hadn't been ready for very much in his life, and that hadn't stopped him.

"ONE LAST PUSH, LAUREN," Nicki said. "The shoulders are out now. One more big push, and then you'll have your baby."

Gritting her teeth and holding on as tight as she possibly could to Isaac's hand, Lauren bore down, squeezed her eyes shut and pushed as hard as she could.

She felt the baby slide out of her.

The pressure was gone.

The pain a distant memory.

The relief was instantaneous.

Well, not quite. She needed to hear that cry.

Please, cry. Please. Oh God, just let me hear it cry.

And then she heard it. A beautiful lamb's bleat. She glanced down the length of her body, her belly already a fraction of the size it was a minute ago, to see Nicki with a soft green blanket. Little pink arms with five fingers on each hand flailed from the center of the quilt.

"He's perfect," Nicki said, bundling the baby more before passing him up to Lauren.

"It's a boy?" Tears stung her eyes as she accepted her son from the midwife and held him against her chest.

He was perfect.

Soft, light blond hair. Dark eyes that blinked unfocused but never not at her. His lips were puffy, his face round, and he was covered in goo, but he was magnificent. True and utter perfection.

"A boy!" Celeste and Bianca cheered over the phone.

"Oh my God, a baby boy!" Celeste was blubbering. "I'm so proud of you, Lauren."

Bianca sniffed. "We both are. I can't wait to meet him. Is she okay? Is Mom okay? Midwife? Nicki? Officer? Is Lauren all right?"

"She seems to be," Nicki said. "Mom, Lauren, good job. You were a trooper."

"Damn straight she was," Celeste said. "A fucking warrior."

"We'll let you go," Bianca said. "Call us once you get to the hospital. Let us know if you need anything. *Anything*. We mean it. We're so happy for you, honey. You did amazing."

"Bye guys. Sorry I couldn't make wine night," Lauren said.

"Yeah, but next wine night you actually get to *have* wine again," Bianca said before she and Celeste both said goodbye and hung up.

She loved those two women like they were her sisters. And she had a sister—a half sister, but she and Fiona had never been close. Not that she didn't love Fiona, but their age gap of ten years was big enough to make any significant level of bonding a challenge.

But Bianca and Celeste were her people, her bitches, and she knew that she could lean on them, count on them for anything. And even when she didn't ask, they would be there for her—and this baby.

"You're still attached via the umbilical cord," Nicki said. "I'll cut it in a moment, but I'm going to get you to push once more. Pretend to cough. It shouldn't hurt."

Staring at her son and the pure perfection that he was, Lauren did as she was told. She felt the placenta slip out.

"Do you have a name picked out?" Isaac asked behind her, his solid wall of muscle comforting, along with his warmth and that spicy, manly smell. She'd only just met the man, but she was damn glad it was him who had been behind her during this whole ordeal.

She shook her head. She'd gone through countless baby books and websites, and she just hadn't been able to find anything she could settle on. Because she didn't want to find out the baby's sex, it'd been twice as hard. She wanted to meet her child before she named it. Wanted to see his or her personality and features before she made that all-important decision of what they should be called.

She'd struggled the most with boys' names. She liked a lot of girls' names. But boys' names were tough. It didn't help that she'd had a fair number of boyfriends over the years, and all those assholes had sullied the baby name list for her astronomically. She liked Nate, but she'd dated a Nathan in high school, and he'd been a tool. She also liked Marshall, but her college boyfriend had been named Marshall, and he'd cheated on her. She liked Luke, but that was her half brother's name. She also liked Dereck, but that was her stepfather's name. Seriously, all the good names were taken by friends and family or sullied by some asshole she'd dated or who'd done her wrong in some way.

Gazing down at her unnamed son, she leaned back against Isaac. "I wanted to meet my baby first, but now that I have, I still don't know." Tucking her finger into her son's fist, she waited until he opened his palm and reached for her. His grip was strong. "Who are you, little man? What's your name?"

Nicki angled over Lauren's body and pried the blanket off the baby just over his belly. She snipped the cord and tied it off with a clamp half an inch from his stomach. "It'll fall off in a couple of weeks."

"Thank you."

"You also have time to name him. There isn't a rush. I think they give you thirty days." Nicki grinned and turned to grab a flashlight from her bag. She turned the powerful beam on and shone it between Lauren's legs. The woman's bag was like Mary Poppins's purse; it had everything in it. A baby blanket, garbage bags, you name it. The woman traveled prepared to deliver babies wherever and whenever. "A see a minor tear here. It can happen with such fast deliveries. I'm going to do a quick stitch with some local anesthetic. If we wait to do it at the hospital it won't heal properly. Are you okay with that?"

Lauren nodded. "Sure, whatever, just do what you gotta do."

Nicki's smile was warm and reassuring. "I'll do my best to minimize the pain."

Not wanting to take her eyes off her son but knowing she should, at least for a moment, Lauren glanced up at Isaac, with his thick red hair, blue eyes and strong chin. "Thank you. I don't know what we would have done if you hadn't found us." She tried to bite her lip to keep it from trembling, to keep the tears at bay, but she couldn't. The tears came, and they came on hard. "I was so scared. You saved us."

"Shhh," Isaac cooed, shaking his head and using his thumb to wipe away her tears. "You would have done the same for me, I'm sure of it."

Through the tears and blubbering, she laughed. "I would have helped you give birth?"

His smile was like a bolt of lighting in the sky. "Well, maybe not give birth, but ... you know what I mean."

And at that moment she knew the name of her son. Smiling up at the stranger, at the cop, at the man who had saved her and her child, she blinked through the tears. "I'm going to name him Isaac."

2

Two weeks later ...

IT WAS CHRISTMAS EVE, and Isaac had just finished a grueling twelve-hour shift. He also had to be back at work tomorrow morning at 5 a.m. Like Santa's elves, there was no rest for those who served. But for now, he was done. Barely able to keep his eyes from shutting, he pushed open the door of the men's locker room at the precinct and made his way into the lobby when he spied his friend and fellow officer Sidney.

"Hey, Sid. How goes it?" He fought back a yawn but was unsuccessful.

Sid lifted her chin in acknowledgement. "Oh, you know, never a dull moment on Christmas Eve in the city. What about you? Got any big plans tonight?"

He shook his head. "Nope. Heading home to sleep. You doing anything for Christmas?"

"Yeah, Mel and I did our Christmas with her family this morning and afternoon. Then we'll head to see my family tomorrow. We're both working Christmas Eve and Christmas

Day night so we can finally have that honeymoon for New Year's. Two weeks in Hawaii? Yes, please."

Sidney and her wife, Melody, another cop, had gotten married over the summer and were two of Isaac's closest friends on the force. The three of them often went out for drinks after work, hit The Rage Room or went ax-throwing.

He yawned again. "Oh, that's right. The honeymoon, that's exciting."

Sidney finished filling out the form she was tackling, then slid the documents back below the Plexiglas to the woman at the reception desk. "Whatever happened with that mom and the baby you delivered in the traffic jam and storm?"

"Funny you should ask," he said, his eyelids feeling heavy, brain foggy. "I was going to ask either you or Mel, since you're both aunts to a fuck-ton of nieces and nephews, but when is it the appropriate time to go visit after someone has had a baby? It's been two weeks, and I wanted to go check on her sooner. I just wasn't sure on the protocol. I'm not family. Not even a friend."

"But you are the guy who held her hand as she pushed a human from her body, so you do get a pass," she said with a chuckle. "But to answer your question, two weeks is a good amount of time. I mean, you should always call or text first. And *never* ring the doorbell. Always knock in case they're sleeping."

He'd called in the woman's Pathfinder to have it towed to the hospital for her once the ambulance finally arrived, so he did have her plates and found out her name was Lauren Cameron Green. He'd also gotten her phone number but felt weird calling her. What would he say? *"Hey, it's Isaac, you know, the cop who was there when you had your baby. You named that baby after me. Can I come by and see how you are?"* It sounded so lame and cheesy in his head.

"You like her?" Sid asked with a crooked smile.

He shook his head. "It's not that. It's just I don't want her to think I'm some weirdo with a single-mom fetish or something. I just want to see how she and the kid are."

"Do you know where she lives?"

He nodded.

"Hey, Isaac, this just came for you in the mail." A civilian worker in the reception area passed a small envelope beneath the Plexiglas.

The return address was in the top left corner for a Lauren C. Green.

He opened the envelope. It was a thank-you card and a small note.

Officer Isaac (because I don't know your full name or your rank—sorry if I'm offending you with the title "officer").

He chuckled. He'd actually made sergeant a couple of years ago, but he wasn't going to hold that against her. He continued to read the letter.

I feel like "thank you" is an inadequate thing to say to someone who saved me and my son. Who helped me when I was as helpless as I've ever felt and supported me when I needed it the absolute most. Without you, my son might not be here. So "thank you" seems insufficient compared to how I truly feel. But know that if there was a word that meant more, I would use it. I would scream it from the rooftops. You went above and beyond for us. My gratitude and appreciation will be forever endless and—oh shit, I'm crying as I write this, please ignore the teardrop stains, I'm crying a lot lately—anyway, thank you again. My son and I are happy, healthy and safe at home because of you.
Merry Christmas and Happy New Year.

Sincerely,

Lauren and Ike

"She named her baby Ike? As in Isaac?" Sid asked, having read the note over his shoulder. "Like after you?"

He nodded. "Yeah. Blew me away too."

Sid smiled. "I like her. She seems funny. But also kind." She glanced up at him. "You going to take a baby gift?"

He'd planned on it. He just had no idea what the fuck to buy. And seeing as it was late on Christmas Eve, he'd left it until the last minute, and a lot of places would be either closed or packed.

"I want to." He scratched the back of his neck. "Any ideas?"

She nodded, causing her dark brown ponytail to swish behind her. "Get her a sleeper for when he's twelve months. Then a toy for when he's six months. Something the baby can chew on when he starts to teethe. And a book. You can't go wrong with those items. And get something for her too. Wine. Flowers. Chocolate. One of those meal plans that comes to your door or a gift certificate for takeout."

All really good ideas. He'd seen a really cool-looking pair of baby sunglasses online—Babiators, they were called—but he wasn't sure if they were a gag thing or the real deal, so he hadn't bothered. Did babies wear sunglasses?

"One thing that bothered my sister after she had her first was that once the baby is out of you, nobody gives a flying fuck about the mother. People flock to see the baby, bring gifts for the baby, meanwhile the mom is an emotional, physical and mental mess who could use some attention too." Sid pinned a dark brown gaze on him. "Don't be one of those people. You supported her when she gave birth. Support her again."

He tossed his hands in the air. "I don't even know her.

We're not friends or family. I just happened to be stuck beside her on the interstate in the middle of a gridlock."

Her gaze turned skeptical and almost impatient. "Yeah, but you shared something really special with her. She had no one, and you became *someone*. To her, that means something. She went so far as to send you a thank-you letter. You don't have to offer to be the kid's godfather, but be the Isaac we know and love and show her that you care." She rested a friendly hand on his shoulder, squeezed and then shrugged. "Besides, it's Christmas."

"It's Christmas," he murmured.

Sid released his arm, and her lips pursed in thought. "Mel's sister-in-law owns that baby boutique on Fifth, next door to Flowers on 5th. I'll text Evangeline to see if she's still open and ask if the flower shop is open. It's only five minutes from here, and she'll be able to help you pick out the perfect gift." She brought out her phone and punched in a message. Seconds later, it vibrated. "She says she's open for another hour, and the flower shop is open for another half an hour. You can make it."

"YOU'RE SURE?" Celeste and Bianca asked for probably the tenth time as they stood in Lauren's entryway, all bundled up in coats and boots.

Lauren nodded and smiled at her two best friends. Ike was sleeping soundly on her shoulder after a good long nurse and an enormous burp. "I'm very sure, guys. But thank you. Ike and I are just going to hunker down, just the two of us tonight."

"Liam and Richelle said babies and kids are welcome at their party," Bianca said. "You can put him down in the master bedroom, bring the baby monitor, have some wine and talk to grownups. I think Mason and Lowenna will be there with the twins, and Zak and Aurora with little Dawson. Lots of babies. Lots of arms to hold them too."

Lauren's eyelids were heavy, and she smiled again at her friend. "At two weeks postpartum, would you go to a Christmas party filled with people, germs and noise?"

Bianca averted her eyes and twisted her mouth. "Good point."

"Not that I'm judging the other parents." She held up her free hand, palm forward. "You know I'm not judgy like that. I'm the last person to pass judgment on anybody, as I sway here with my Booty Call Baby. It's just ..." She shrugged and kissed her son for what was undoubtably the millionth time since he'd been born. "I'm good at home."

"We just feel bad leaving you is all," Celeste said, squeezing Lauren's upper arm. "Like we're abandoning you or something."

"You guys have been over here every day since Ike and I came home from the hospital. And you were at the hospital every day too. You haven't abandoned me. I appreciate all the meals and holding him so I can shower. More than you know. But I think I can handle tonight on my own. He's less colicky since the doctor put him on the anti-reflux meds, and we're both sleeping better."

Her friends' mouths formed grim lines.

"But it's Christmas," Bianca said.

"It is, but that's okay. I'm going to video chat with my mom, stepdad, sister and brother tomorrow. But tonight, I'm just going to pour a glass of wine, watch George Bailey realize he doesn't actually have it that bad, and gorge on a tray of nachos. If you ask me, I couldn't imagine a better Christmas Eve. Just me and my boo and that sexy merlot on the counter." She pecked Ike on the side of his head but left her nose there for an extra moment, inhaling that incredible, unique, addictive baby scent. How could she bottle it, so when it disappeared without warning, she could still have it when she needed it?

"I'll bring you over a container of leftovers tomorrow," Bianca said.

Lauren patted Ike's butt gently. "My freezer is full. You don't have to. You guys have been showing up with leftovers every day for over a week. I'm *one* person. A lasagna lasts me *days.*"

Both women looked like they were reluctant to go, so she scooted past them and opened the door. "Go. Your families are waiting for you. Ike and I will be fine."

Celeste and Bianca took deep breaths, finally seeming to accept Lauren's decision. Just as her friends turned to go, a sexy dark blue Toyota truck pulled into her driveway.

"You expecting someone?" Celeste asked with pinched brows.

Lauren shook her head. The few friends she had here in Seattle all texted or called before they showed up. For the most part, everyone she knew had been incredibly respectful of her and Ike's privacy and time.

All three of them watched and waited for the person behind the steering wheel to exit the cab of the truck.

Her friends gasped before she did.

"Who's that?" Bianca whispered.

"Gorgeous is what he is," Celeste said, her voice a quiet hiss.

She knew he was hot two weeks ago; it was part of the reason why she didn't want him catching her baby and seeing that nightmare between her legs. But she forgot just *how* gorgeous he was. Just how perfectly muscular, chiseled and masculine he was. The red hair, blue eyes and long lashes just added to what was already a spectacular specimen of a man. And in the gray knit cap and black winter jacket with dark wash jeans and black biker boots, he looked like the hottest thing she'd seen in a very long time.

With a gift bag in one hand and an enormous bouquet of flowers in the other, he cautiously approached all of them at Lauren's front door. His eyes turned more and more wary the closer he got to them.

Celeste, who was no longer single, and Bianca, who was still jaded and man-hating after her bitter divorce, watched Isaac approach with heat in their gazes and their lips between their teeth.

His Adam's apple jogged hard on a swallow. "Ladies."

"I recognize that voice," Bianca said. She turned to Lauren. "He's the cop from the delivery."

That he was.

Normally, Lauren was the one who completely lacked a filter, because honestly, life was too short to not say what you meant. But at the moment, she was really hoping her friends would activate their filters.

He came to a stop in front of them, his eyes focused on Ike, still sleeping soundly on Lauren's shoulder. "That's him?"

Smiling, she swayed and continued to pat Ike's butt. "This is him. All eight pounds nine ounces of him."

"We're going to go," Bianca said, her brown eyes gleaming. "But we'll be by tomorrow morning to bring Ike his presents. The kids insisted on each getting him something, so be prepared for an onslaught of gifts."

Celeste gave Isaac a final once-over before she and Bianca retreated down the driveway. Her friends lived in the same townhouse complex as Lauren, so they only had a few yards to walk to their own units.

Once they were out of sight, Lauren returned her attention to Isaac. "Come in. It's cold outside." He didn't look cold; he looked delicious. But she was cold, and her son was in nothing more than a cotton sleeper.

Nodding but not saying anything, he stepped over the threshold, and she closed the door behind him.

"I'm surprised to see you," she said, continuing on through her house into her living room. For a single mom with a newborn, she was proud of how tidy she managed to keep her house. Sure, there were a few baby items around, but it didn't look like a bomb had gone off. She wasn't embarrassed to have people over and for them to see the state she lived in. It was just her, and Ike slept a lot, so she had time to keep up with the cleaning.

Celeste and Bianca told her that wouldn't last, and she knew better than to get smug about things, so she was just grateful that so far, Ike was a good sleeper and a sound sleeper.

"I was surprised to get your note," he said. "I'm sorry I didn't come sooner. I'm just not sure on the protocol about visiting after a baby is born."

She sat down on the couch carefully so as not to disturb the baby. "I appreciate that you came. Two weeks is a perfect amount of time."

He sat down on the edge of her favorite recliner and shook his head. "I had to run your plates to get the tow truck to come grab your Nissan. That's how I got your address. I'm not a crazy stalker or anything, I swear."

"I just figured you could find anybody you wanted to since you're a cop."

His lip twitched. "I'm not a detective. The plates made it easy."

The man looked uncomfortable sitting there. Like he didn't want to be there but had come because someone had forced him to. He was still in his knit cap and jacket and looked too big for the chair. She knew he was a *big* muscular guy. Not fat, by any stretch of the imagination. But he was tall, like definitely over six feet, and had breadth to his shoulders.

She eyed him suspiciously before letting her gaze wander down his physique to the gift bag covered in jungle animals and the bouquet of flowers from Flowers on 5th. She knew they were from Zara's shop. Zara used the gold paper to wrap her flowers rather than plastic because it was better for the environment. And she also had a unique way of wrapping flowers that was easily discernible from lesser bouquets.

"Are those for us?" she asked, hoping to relieve him of some of his anxiety.

He nearly jumped in his seat before leaning over and placing the flowers and gift bag on her coffee table. "They are."

"You didn't have to."

He shrugged. "It's not much. I don't really know anything about babies, so I hope it's all okay." The unease in his eyes and the way his full lips twisted pulled at her heartstrings. She didn't take him for a man unsure of himself. He had an air about him that spoke of confidence, almost an alpha vibe. But at that moment, he looked anything but alpha or confident. The man was so out of his element, it would be funny if it wasn't sad.

She stood up from her spot on the couch and walked over to where he sat in the chair. "Take off your coat."

An adorable crease formed between his dark red brows. But he did as he was told, dropping the coat to the floor. He was in a long-sleeved, gray Henley, and it fit him like a glove. Muscles popped, and she finally got a true glimpse of those broad shoulders and chest. She quickly swallowed the saliva that pooled in her mouth and draped the burp cloth over his arm, then she placed her son in his arms.

The whole time Isaac looked like he was going to puke.

"I ..."

She rested her hand on his shoulder. "You'll be okay." Then she went back to sit on the couch and open the gift bag.

ISAAC STARED down at the tiny human sleeping soundly in his arms, and his chest tightened to a point of pain he wasn't sure he'd ever felt before. But even though his chest tightened, his muscles relaxed and his breathing evened out. Eventually, his chest relaxed too.

Lauren's throaty chuckle from the couch had him lifting his gaze to her.

"He has that effect on people. He's like a drug. The best medicine to calm the nerves," she said, eyeing him with a coy, knowing smile. "He's a good baby. Easy. The doctor has him on some anti-reflux meds, as he was spitting up a lot, which caused him some grief, but now that he's on them, he sleeps well, eats well, poops well. I'm very lucky."

It was like night and day, the woman who sat placidly in front of him with a calm, beautiful smile on her lips versus the woman who had been in a level-ten freak-out two weeks ago. But who could blame her? Two weeks ago, she was stuck in traffic alone and in labor. Now, she and her son were healthy, home and safe.

"How are you doing?" he asked, tucking his finger into Ike's fist until the little guy held on. He lifted his head again to her face.

"Thank you for asking that. Besides my best friends, who are also mothers, most people just want to know about Ike. Nobody really gives a damn about me."

Thank you, Sidney, for the words of wisdom.

"I'm doing okay, thank you. Tired, bloated and still a little sore. But all in all, I feel good."

"Overwhelmed?"

How could she not be? He certainly would be.

She nodded. "A little, yeah. But my friends have been

helpful. They come over and hold him so I can take a shower."

Having a newborn made it challenging to have a shower? Couldn't she just do it while he slept? But then, he had no idea. Maybe she had anxieties about leaving him alone or something. He had his own weird hang-ups about things, so he was no one to judge.

"Do you need to take a shower now?" he asked. The longer he held baby Ike, the more he was enjoying it. "I can hold him."

She smiled and chuckled. "I just did, thanks. The girls watched him for me." She opened the bag and pulled out the items Sid's sister-in-law, Evangeline, had carefully selected for him. She'd done all the work. He told her how old the baby was and then she did the rest. Set him back over a hundred dollars, but he didn't really have anybody else to spend his money on, so whatever.

Then the woman at Flowers on 5th made him the mother of all bouquets. He told her it was for a new mom and a single mom at that and she said "say no more" and went crazy grabbing various blooms and stems. She even gave him a discount—apparently. Though the thing still set him back over seventy bucks.

"This is adorable," she said, holding up the sleeper Evangeline had picked out. It was green with little orange and blue dinosaurs on it. The feet had dinosaur feet, and it also had a hood, which sported soft spikes that ran all the way down the back. When Evangeline had shown it to him, he'd nodded immediately. He'd always been a dinosaur buff as a kid—he still really liked them. "I plan to do his nursery dinosaur-themed. Did I mention that to you?"

He shook his head. They hadn't really talked much besides the necessary information, like she needed a doctor and was about to have a baby and the guy who got her pregnant was a fuckwad who should be castrated. Other than that, he knew very little about her. "No, I just really like dinosaurs and I thought it was cute."

"I love dinosaurs," she said, setting the sleeper aside to dig into the bag more.

After the sleeper, the rest of the gifts were a bit of a no-brainer. It was a dinosaur-themed gift, and now that he knew she liked dinosaurs and was doing a dinosaur-themed nursery, he had lots of ideas for future gifts.

Was he really thinking about future gifts? Where the hell did that come from?

She pulled out a T. rex-shaped teether filled with water that you put in the freezer, a matching dinosaur plate, fork and spoon, a couple of dinosaur bibs, a dinosaur stuffed animal and, of course, a dinosaur book. Once she'd emptied the bag, she looked up at him, tears in her eyes and an expression of wonder on her face. "You didn't have to get us, *him* all of this."

He shrugged before glancing back down at Ike. "I wanted to. I'm single, childless, petless. And this guy was named after me. Of course he needs to be spoiled." He lifted his head to smile at her, jerking his chin toward the bouquet. "The flowers and gift card are for you. I was told explicitly not to ignore the mom."

Chuckling through the tears, she reached for the bouquet and pulled out the envelope. She wiped the back of her hand beneath her nose as she opened it. He hadn't been anticipating the gasp, but it made him happy that she did. Her sky-blue eyes went wide before she started to shake her head, her messy topknot jostling on her head. "I can't accept this. It's too much. Isaac, I can't."

He rolled his eyes. "You can. You deserve to be pampered. When you're ready to leave him with a sitter, go and have a spa day. But for now, if there is a day where you're frazzled and don't feel like cooking, order something. Both the spa gift certificate and the pre-prepared meal gift certificate never expire, so use them whenever."

More tears filled her eyes, and her bottom lip and chin began to tremble. "I hardly know you ... this is too much."

"You named your son after me. We might not know each other well, but ..." He shrugged again. He'd never been good with crying women. "We have a connection."

Her throat wobbled on a swallow as she stood up and took the bouquet to her kitchen. He wasn't sure if he should follow her or not. Or if he even could follow her without waking up Ike. But he figured he had to. Had he gone too far with his gifts? He didn't have a clue if he'd bought too much. He actually thought, as he drove there, that he'd bought too little, that he should have brought more.

Adjusting Ike in his arms, he carefully stood up from the chair and made his way down to the kitchen. "Have I done something to upset you?"

She was filling a vase with water, but it seemed like more tears were falling from her eyes than water was filling the vase. He approached her gently, reached over and shut off the water. He'd shifted the baby to his shoulder like he'd seen Lauren do, cradling Ike's butt in his palm. With his other hand, he took Lauren's hand and turned her to face him.

"What's wrong?"

Her eyes were red-rimmed, her face a blotchy array of various shades of pink, but that didn't for a moment detract from her beauty. It was those eyes that got him. He had blue eyes too, but they were pale in comparison to hers. Her eyes were the color of a prairie sky in the dead of summer.

She huffed out a humorless laugh from her nose. "I cry over everything right now. Like *everything*. Commercials, music. I saw a three-legged dog the other day; it was alive and happy, but I still burst into tears." She rolled her eyes at herself and laughed again before hitting him with a look he felt deep in his solar plexus. "But you hardly know me and yet, these gifts ..." She shook her head. "They're all so *me*. It was like you knew me without knowing me. I already owe you so much gratitude for being there for me and Ike. For running through traffic to find a doctor, for holding me and supporting me when I literally had nobody. And now this ... it just feels like too much from a stranger."

Shit. He'd gone too far. He'd done too much. He needed to go.

"I feel like my thank-you card is"—she glanced away from him—"it's nothing compared to how much you've given us. And I can't very well just give you another card." Her eyes held such sadness, such unsureness, he wanted to do nothing more than take her in his arms and hold her. Wipe away her tears and let her know he felt her gratitude and didn't need another piece of paper to tell him she was thankful.

Still holding on to Ike's butt, he pulled her hand until she was against him and wrapped his free hand around her. "You don't need to thank me again. I get it. I feel your gratitude. I mean, you named your kid after me. I feel like I still owe *you*. The flowers will wilt. You'll use the gift certificates, and he'll grow out of and bored of the gifts. But he'll always have his name."

She shivered against him, her breath stuttering before she relaxed. "Do you want to stay for nachos?"

His chest shook on a laugh. "I'd love to stay for nachos. But then we're even, okay?"

She nodded against his chest, and he could feel her hot tears soaking through his shirt. "Okay."

3

THIS WAS NOT AT ALL how Lauren saw her Christmas Eve going, but as she stood in her kitchen grating cheese while Isaac held Ike and asked her about her life, she couldn't imagine a better way to spend her first Christmas Eve as a single mom.

A stranger had shown her so much kindness, and he continued to do so. Surprising her in all the very best ways.

"So I feel it only right for me to ask what you do for a living," he said, thanking her for the beer she offered him. "I mean, you don't strike me as a criminal. Not that they don't come in all forms." He made a show of crossing his fingers and holding them up. "I just would really rather not arrest you."

Smiling, she took a sip of her wine. "Law-abiding citizen, I swear. I'm a voice actor and narrator."

His brows scrunched. He'd done that a few times since showing up unexpectedly on her doorstep, and each time a deep crease formed above his nose that was absolutely adorable. "What do you mean? Like cartoons?"

She nodded. "Among other things. Radio ads, documentaries, video games—I do a lot of those lately. I narrate audio-books. I've done voice work for a bunch of different cartoons, animated movies. Pretty much anything that requires voice work, I've done it in some fashion."

His head cocked to the side like a puppy, and that crease between his brows seemed to grow even deeper. "I've never met a voice actor before. And there's good money in it?"

She nodded again. "There can be, yeah. I mean, I do well. I built a recording studio in my garage and work entirely from home. I make my own hours. I worked like a dog before Ike was born so I could coast for a few months."

Awe continued to fill his eyes. "Would I recognize anything you've done?"

Lifting one shoulder before she scattered the shredded cheese over the olives, jalapenos, tomatoes and nacho chips she said, "The Captain Fantastic movie franchise? I do the voice for Penelope the Magnificent."

The man's very chiseled jaw nearly hit the floor. "*You* are Penelope the Magnificent?"

She snorted. She hadn't expected him to know the chil-dren's animated phenomenon about a crime-fighting Labradoodle and his gang of trusty neighborhood pet side-kicks. And she certainly hadn't expected to land the part of Penelope the Magnificent, a tabby kitten with nerves of steel and a killer roundhouse kick. Normally, those starring or supporting roles went to big Hollywood names, and she was left filling in the blanks with background character voices. But she'd landed Penelope the Magnificent, and that gig alone was paying her mortgage every month and her car payments, not to mention her monthly subscription to Zara's bouquets and a few other luxuries she allowed herself.

"You know the Captain Fantastic series?" she asked, washing her hands before she started to clean up her prep station.

"I might not have kids, but I still love a good animated movie. *Toy Story, Shrek, Captain Fantastic.* I love them all. And I definitely think Penelope the Magnificent is one of the best characters." He was all sexy smiles as he casually bounced his body up and down and patted Ike's butt. He was a natural. Truly. With wide eyes and boyish excitement, he asked her, "Can you do Penelope's signature catchphrase for me? Just once. I won't ask ever again, I swear."

How could she refuse when he looked at her like that?

Clearing her throat and wiggling her lips, she donned her best Penelope the Magnificent face. "Another crime solved *purrrfectly.* Time to celebrate with a saucer of milk!" His cheesy, pleased smile made her buoyant, so she decided to say one more line. "I don't know about this, Cap, seems awfully *fishy* to me. And I know fish."

Laughing, he clapped his hands quietly over Ike's back. "Bravo. Just like the movies."

She nodded once and twirled her fingers sideways in the air like she was doing some flamboyant bow, smiling from ear to ear until her son made a noise of discontent and squirmed in Isaac's arms. Ike began to lift his head, only to slam it back down against Isaac's shoulder. He was searching for food.

"Whoa, little man. That's gonna hurt your face. Careful." He leaned forward and cupped the back of Ike's head in his enormous palm, letting the baby lay back against his forearm. "I didn't wake him, did I?"

She dried her hands on a dish towel and took her son from Isaac. "You did not. His stomach the size of a chicken's egg woke him. He's hungry."

"Oh!"

In what was already old habit, she snagged a new burp cloth off the clean and folded stack she kept in a basket on her kitchen counter and made her way back into the living room. Only instead of taking a seat on the couch, she went to the chair that Isaac had been sitting in. "You're okay if I nurse?" she asked, settling in and resting a rooting and whimpering Isaac on her thighs.

He'd followed her into the living room but didn't sit down. His hands in his pockets and the gentle shrug to his shoulders said he didn't mind, but the deer-in-the-headlights look on his face spoke otherwise. "I can go ... get the plates organized if you want," he said, hooking a thumb over his shoulder back toward the kitchen.

She shook her head. "You don't have to. I set the timer for the nachos, so when the oven beeps, just go pull them out. Unless you're uncomfortable being around a woman nursing?" She made sure to hit him with a lifted eyebrow and challenge in her eyes. As nice of a man as he was, if he couldn't handle being around a nursing mother and child, then the man had to go.

He cleared his throat and took a seat on the couch. "I'm not uncomfortable at all." For good measure, he cocked an ankle on his knee and tucked his hands behind his head. "Go for it."

She rolled her eyes but proceeded to get her breast out and begin feeding her son. She didn't *whip it out* though. She discreetly maneuvered her clothing in such a way that only a small part of her breast was revealed, and that part was instantly covered by her son's little head. Once Ike latched on and began to guzzle, she sat back in the chair and closed her eyes. "You left your beer in the kitchen."

"Oh, that's right."

She heard him get up from the couch but didn't bother to open her eyes. "Grab my wine while you're in there, please."

His deep, throaty chuckle faded as he headed to the kitchen.

Moments later, the stemless glass was placed into her hand, and she opened her eyes. "Thank you."

He nodded and sat back on the couch, taking a swig of his beer. "You're allowed to drink wine while nursing?"

As she took a sip of the delicious merlot, she nodded. "Yeah, thank God. Like I can't get shit-faced or anything. But I can have a glass or two. It takes a while to work through your bloodstream and into the milk. Two glasses of wine over the course of a few hours shouldn't have any effect on him."

He took another pull on his beer, his head bobbing in earnest. "So how'd you get into the voice acting stuff?" The genuine curiosity and eagerness to listen and learn that he came by so honestly was refreshing. He was probably a good three or four years older than her, maybe more, but the way he gave her his full attention and seemed to hang on her every word lent him a boyish charm she found equal parts endearing and attractive.

Letting another mouthful of wine sit on her tongue for a moment, she closed her eyes, inhaled deep through her nose and swallowed. "I was in college and in need of some extra cash. I used to sing in the choir in high school and was always told I had a nice voice."

"You do. Particularly your laugh. But your voice is nice too."

She opened her eyes, her cheeks growing warm from his compliment and the way he was studying her like she was some rare painting hanging on the wall.

With her head tilted down toward her son, she peered up at Isaac through her lashes. "Thank you."

He shrugged. "Do you still sing?"

"Not much. Only in the shower, when I clean the house or to Ike."

"Not for your jobs?"

"Not really. I have, but I prefer not to. I make enough just speaking. Anyway, I was in my sophomore year of college, doing a communications degree, and I was perusing the help-wanted bulletin board because I was getting close to living on an all-ramen diet. Things were tight."

"Shit. Been there."

"Yeah, well, I saw a notice for voice actors needed. I did up a demo recording, sent it in and started making money. It was slow going at first. I didn't get many contracts, only worked when I had time in between classes and my part-time job as a cashier at a drugstore. But then I started doing voices for video games, and that's when things really took off. I moved into audiobooks and started making even more money, and then radio ads. I mean, I do ads for radio stations all over the world now. Not just here in Seattle. They send me the script. I read it, record it, send them the bill, and they use it."

His head shook slowly in bafflement. "That's really cool. And Captain Fantastic, how did you get that gig?"

"I've made enough of a name for myself now that my agent came to me with the offer. I actually read for a smaller part in the movie, but they liked me enough they gave me the role of Penelope the Magnificent."

"That's so cool. I'm going to have to tell my colleagues that I met *the* Penelope Magnificent. They're not going to believe me. Mel and Sid are enormous animation nerds. And they own them all. Like buy the DVDs and watch the director's commentary. *Huge* nerds."

She snorted and rolled her eyes. "I have to say, I've never actually met a *fan*. I don't go to premieres. I prefer a low profile and my privacy. And my friends' kids can't wrap their heads around a human voicing a cartoon. Either that or they don't want to ruin the magic. What about you? How'd you become a—"

She was about to say *cop* when the timer in the kitchen began to beep and Isaac stood up.

At the same time, Ike popped off. A small dribble of milk ran down the side of his cheek out of his tight pout, and once again, his eyes were glued shut. She lifted up one of his arms to do the noodle limb test Bianca taught her, and sure enough, it flopped right back down. He was full, content and out.

Propping him up on her shoulder, she began to pat him at the same time she headed into the kitchen.

"We can eat in the living room if you want to grab plates, three bowls and three spoons. Sour cream, salsa and guac are in the fridge." She grabbed a couple of hot pads to protect her coffee table and a handful of napkins. That was all she could manage, and she made her way back out to the living room.

Isaac followed her and placed the big casserole dish of chips and melted cheese on the hot pads before he retreated back to the kitchen to grab the rest of the stuff. Before long, they were sitting side-by-side on the couch, with Isaac snoozing in the bassinet beside her, *It's a Wonderful Life* on the television and nachos in their mouths.

"This is a really great Christmas Eve," Isaac said, leaning back into the couch and finishing his beer. "I was just going to go home and go to bed, as I have to work at 5 a.m. tomorrow. But this is way better. Thank you."

She had to agree. She was content to spend Christmas Eve with just her baby, but having another person around who was actually awake and could hold a conversation was nice too. She smiled with nachos in her mouth, chewed and swallowed before speaking. "Thank you for staying, but don't feel like you have to. If you have to work so early tomorrow, I understand if you want to get home to bed."

Why did saying the word *bed* cause her insides to quiver? She was two weeks postpartum, bloated, bleeding and barely keeping it together. She should not be thinking about sex.

And yet, she was.

A lot.

But those thoughts were probably just leftovers from

when she was pregnant and hornier than a bitch in heat. She would have jumped anything and ridden it until her thighs chafed by the end of her pregnancy. And since she hadn't gotten laid since shortly before she found out she was pregnant, told the father and he ran, she'd been itching for some *D* for a *long* while. And something about the way Isaac's jeans hugged his thick thighs told her the man had an impressive *D* between his legs.

Was she drunk? Or was the way he was looking at her not just all in her head? His expression changed, his eyes darkened, and his nostrils flared.

She hadn't even had an entire glass of wine, so she definitely wasn't drunk.

Tired? Of course.

Hungry? All the damn time.

But drunk? Not for the last ten months, she hadn't been.

Horny? Despite how exhausted she was, yes. Lauren had always had a high sex drive, so to take a break for the last nine months had been pure torture.

She knew she was an oddity. Celeste and Bianca had told her so. Most new mothers were too tired, sore and emotional to even think about sex. But not her.

Maybe it had to do with how much time she spent alone, thinking about all the things she missed in her old life. One of those things being a decent man with a good tongue and a nice, long, thick lead pipe between his legs.

She hadn't had a man like that in a long time. Ike's father wasn't even a man like that. He was a filler. Somebody to scratch an itch with until somebody better, somebody with more substance came along.

But it wasn't simply that Isaac was a walking, talking, good-looking guy. There was definitely something else about him that struck a chord inside her and had her temperature rising.

"What are you up to tomorrow?" he asked, turning his attention back to the television.

She cleared her throat and sipped her wine to abolish the cobwebs from her mind. "Same as tonight, probably. I bought a turkey breast that I'll cook up. I'll make a small batch of stuffing and mashed potatoes, but I can't really go crazy. It's just me eating it. If the weather holds up and is pleasant like it was today, I'll pop him in the stroller and go for a walk. But other than that, no plans. Video chat with my family. Bianca and Celeste will come by with the kids, and we'll exchange gifts. Low-key. Just like I like. You?" She studied his profile, and damn if it wasn't almost better than his face straight on. His jaw was strong, his features pronounced, but not in a weird way. Just masculine and perfectly sculpted.

He'd removed his knit hat several hours ago, causing her to wonder if he always had that messy look to his red locks or if it was just from a long day at work and the hat. Either way, she liked it, and it suited him.

"I work tomorrow morning at five," he said, pivoting his gaze back to her. "Until five. But then I'm free."

Was that a hint at an invitation?

He lifted a shoulder. "You know, if you need someone to help you eat all the food and hold Ike while you cook." The sparkle in his eyes liquefied her insides and made her smile until her cheeks ached.

"That sounds great."

He nodded, stood up, and made a manly noise as he stretched his arms above his head, causing his shirt to ride up enough for her to see he had that delectable *V* line at his hips, disappearing into his jeans. A line she wanted to run her tongue across like it was a Popsicle.

She had to keep herself from purring, so she drank more wine.

"Not that I want to, but ..." He glanced at his watch and

whistled. "Almost eleven. I'm normally in bed by now when I start at five. I should get going."

Was it almost eleven? Where on Earth had the time gone? She waited for him to move out of the way and stood as well, following him to the door.

He slouched into his coat and pulled his knit cap back on his head.

Mesmerized by the way he managed to ooze sexiness no matter what he did, she leaned against the wall in her entryway and rolled her bottom lip in behind her top teeth.

Once his jacket was zipped, he lifted his head and chuckled. "You okay?"

Lauren blinked a bunch of times and shook her head. Once again, like a horny moth, she was caught in the cobwebs of depravity that seemed to fill her mind. "Yeah, just ... tired." That last word was said on a sigh.

"You should go to bed too." His big hand landed on the door handle, but he still faced her. "Thanks for inviting me to stay. I had a really nice time."

Swallowing, she pushed off from the wall and crossed her arms in front of her suddenly aching breasts. She could feel herself beginning to leak as well. Ike would be up any minute. "Thanks for staying. It was nice for some company."

He lifted his brows. "See you tomorrow after Santa's been by?" He opened the door, and a gust of frigid winter air whooshed inside. He stepped over the threshold and onto her front stoop.

She followed him and clung to the door. "I'll see you tomorrow."

With a wink that made her entire body clench, he took off into the dark toward his truck. The deep, throaty rumble of the V8 filled the silent night moments later.

She thought about waiting for him to pull away and do a final wave, but her nose was beginning to tingle from the cold, and the grunts of a famished infant down the hallway had her breasts gushing.

She closed the door and beelined it down the hallway to her child, the whole time, despite the pain of her hard breasts, smiling. She didn't even know Isaac's last name, and yet she already felt this connection to him. He helped her when she had no one, and even though she'd never admit it, he'd helped her today too.

She'd started to feel some fleeting moments of sadness over the last week—which she knew were probably just her hormones going bonkers—but either way, they were there. She'd put on a brave face for her friends with her conviction to spend Christmas Eve and Christmas Day alone, but to be honest, she was lonely.

She knew being a single mom would be tough—she wasn't in denial about that—but she was lonely nonetheless. Isaac staying tonight and coming back tomorrow filled her with more hope and happiness than she'd felt in a long time.

Shushing Ike, she sat down in the recliner in the living room and put him to her breast.

Could she have feelings for a man she hardly knew but who had already saved her in so many ways? Was this why Snow White and Sleeping Beauty married their princes after only knowing them for a few minutes? Because they saved them?

She was so used to being independent and strong, not relying on anyone—let alone a man—for anything. For as long as she could remember, she'd provided for herself, comforted herself, looked out for just herself. So much so, that it was almost impossible to admit, even to her friends, that she was lonely and sad. Celeste and Bianca came by when they could—which was a lot. But they had jobs and lives and children. Lauren would have liked to bring someone with her to her prenatal class, but the thought of inconveniencing anybody made knots form in her stomach. So she braved the class alone.

But Isaac seemed to know exactly what she needed without even asking. He showed up that night in the rain and gridlock to help her, and he showed up again tonight.

It also helped that the man was nice to look at. His hands alone and the way they wrapped around a beer bottle would be something she'd be adding to her spank bank—when she could spank again. Not that women spanked. Or did they?

Her buzz bank? Her vibe vault?

Whatever. That wasn't the point.

Idris Elba—the name she'd given her vibrator (its real name was Tracy's Dog, which is just a horrendous name for anything but a canine owned by a woman named Tracy) sat lonely in her nightstand. She hadn't been able to effectively use him for the last few months of her pregnancy, her belly had gotten so big. And now that she was bleeding, he sat in the purple satin bag pining for her and she for him. Like two star-crossed lovers.

But soon (hopefully), she and Idris could be reunited, and she'd think of Isaac and his hands and that *V* that disappeared into his jeans as she spoke with God and smelled colors and found her G-spot once again.

She silently rocked in the chair, her eyes closed and Ike guzzling away. Her mouth dipped into a frown the longer she thought of Isaac. From a painful smile to a frown of disappointment in under a minute.

Postpartum emotions were a wretched beast.

Because as much as she liked Isaac and found him hot, found him sweet and exactly what she needed when she needed it, she knew that they had no future.

At the most, maybe they could have a little no-strings fun, but as far as dating and love went, that was off the table.

She didn't date cops.

Never had.

Never would.

Not when there was a curse haunting the women in her family and taking away the heroes they loved.

Her father had been a cop, and he'd died on duty. His death was senseless, preventable, and tragic. Even though she'd only been five when he died, her mother had drilled it into her from the day of his funeral forward to never date a cop. To never marry a cop. Their family was cursed.

Every day of their life together, Lauren's mother had waited with fear in her gut and a dull ache in her heart when Lauren's father would leave for work, and she wouldn't relax until he returned home. Only to put herself through that torture the next day and the next.

It explained a lot about why Lauren's mother was such an anxious person by nature. Lauren didn't get that from her, but her half sister, Fiona, certainly did.

She'd only been five, but she'd had a nightmare and was in her parents' bed with her mom when there was a knock at the door and two officers appeared on their doorstep. It was eleven fifteen on Saturday night. October twelfth.

And it was that day she knew she could never fall in love with a cop.

4

IT WAS four forty-five on Christmas Day, and of course, Isaac got dispatched to a "kerfuffle" downtown. Two homeless men were fighting each other—and by the time he arrived it looked like a death match—in an alley because one guy stole the other guy's tarp. Then one of them set fire to the other guy's stuff, and it escalated from there until one was swinging a rusty old ax and the other brandishing some prison-grade toothbrush shank.

Both he and Sid had been sent out on the call, and Sid had carted both men away in the back of her squad car. They were in for a warm bed and a hot meal in a cold cell. Not the best way to spend Christmas, but given how they looked and how they lived, Isaac would take a day—hell, a week—in the slammer over living on the streets of Seattle in the dead of winter.

He managed to put out the fire without calling the fire department—those guys were busy enough this time of year —and was collecting what remained of the one guy's stuff, the stuff that didn't get torched, when he heard a faint but very distinctive *meow*.

But it wasn't your typical cat *meow*. This was the high-pitched, sharp mewl of a kitten.

He didn't have to pack up the guy's stuff. That wasn't his job, and he wished he had more than gloves in his car, like a full hazmat suit, but it was Christmas, and most likely, the contents of that grocery cart were the man's entire life.

He finished packing up the stuff into the back of his car when he heard the meow again.

Cardboard boxes and trash bins lined the alley, along with the torched remnants of the man's belongings. He couldn't see a cat. Or a kitten.

And if there was a kitten out here, it wouldn't survive for long given the way the temperature had been continuously dropping over the last week. They were expected to get snow in the next few days—and lots of it.

As he tossed the latex gloves into a trash can, he heard the mewling louder and closer than ever. There was definitely a kitten around there somewhere.

Pulling his leather gloves out of his back pocket, because it was really fucking cold out, he pulled them on and began searching among the garbage for the little beast.

It didn't take him long to find a tabby kitten, fluffy but filthy and terrified, hiding in a microwave box on its side. A few rags had been made into some makeshift nest, and there was a lot of fur. The kitten also didn't look old enough to be without its mother.

Was the mother around somewhere? Off gathering food?

He made a *psst psst* noise and crouched down, rubbing his thumb and fingers together to attract the kitten or hopefully draw out its mother. Should he take the kitten to the shelter? Or was its mom coming back for it?

It was dark now, and the streets were practically empty. He scanned up and down the alley and the sidewalks for a cat, but she was either hiding on purpose or not around.

He was about to turn back to go and check on the kitten again when he spotted a mound in the middle of the road less than a hundred yards away.

It wasn't moving.

Jogging to stay warm, he went and confirmed his suspicions.

The mother. She'd been hit by a car and most likely recently.

Fuck.

That kitten was now alone in the world, without a mother, without a food source and would not make it to morning.

Using one of the homeless man's blankets and a shovel from the back of his car, he scooped up the mother and wrapped her, then he went and gathered up her child, tucked the kitten into his coat, climbed into his cruiser and called Sid.

LAUREN KNEW he finished work at five, and she knew from being a cop's kid that off at five didn't necessarily mean your shift ended. Sometimes a case, a call, or paperwork forced you into overtime. So she planned dinner for six thirty. Not that re-heating the meal would be a problem. But there was nothing so delicious as fresh cooked turkey and all the trimmings.

Like the good man that he was, Isaac had texted her when he got off work. They'd exchanged phone numbers last night while eating nachos. He just figured it made sense, and she liked being able to enter him into her phone as *Sergeant Big Hands*.

But his text had been cryptic as hell though. *What's your opinion on cats? I'm running late. Should be there for seven.*

She understood the latter portion of his message. But the former baffled her. What was her opinion on cats?

For starters, she loved them. She'd always been a cat person.

She'd had her beloved Genevieve since she was thirteen, and the darling had only just passed away that previous March. She hadn't been able to bring herself to get a new cat. Her Genevieve had been irreplaceable. But she still had all of Genevieve's stuff.

She texted back as best she could. *Love cats. Had a cat most of my life. Why? Okay, I'll plan dinner for seven.*

But then she never heard back from him.

Did he have a cat and was worried she might be allergic to the dander?

With Ike wrapped up in the stretchy wrap—the way Celeste and Bianca had shown her—she swayed to the Bing Crosby that played on her computer over at her desk. The stove boiled with potatoes, the pan sizzled with brussels sprouts and the house smelled like turkey and stuffing, so in other words—incredible.

Ike had been a little fussy in the morning. Celeste figured he had gas, so she kept him upright a lot in the wrap and he seemed to settle right down. She'd even figured out how to nurse in the thing. But that success was short-lived when she shot her kid in the eye with her milk and he couldn't maintain a latch that wasn't painful.

"You'll get it," Bianca had said with an understanding smile. "It's only week two. My kids were months and months old before I figured out how to nurse while wearing them. Don't beat yourself up."

Her friends and their children had come over around eleven that morning, all of them with oodles of gifts for Ike. Bianca's twins, Hannah and Hayley, who were six, kept fighting over who got to hold Ike, until Sabrina, Celeste's fifteen-year-old daughter, stepped in and took him from the girls.

"Nobody gets to hold him if you're going to fight over him." She pressed her forehead to Ike's. "Nobody but me, that is." Then, as she said, nobody else was allowed to hold him. She sat in the recliner with him for the rest of the visit, both of them happy and staring adoringly into each other's eyes.

Sabrina was already a well-seasoned babysitter for Bianca's kids—which was why she was able to go all authoritarian on them like she did—as well as many others. Lauren was looking forward to the time she felt comfortable enough to leave Ike with someone else—even just for an hour so she could go for a run.

But with only two weeks of being a mother under her belt, she felt weird not being in the same room as her kid, let alone not in the same house.

By the time her friends left, both she and Ike were exhausted. They took a Christmas siesta from one until three, and then she started cooking while Ike snuggled into the wrap for a post-nap nap.

It was five minutes after seven when there was a knock at her door.

She liked that he was a punctual person. Or at least appeared to be.

She glanced at herself in her hallway mirror. She'd been living in maternity leggings and baggy T-shirts with nursing bras underneath for the past two weeks, but tonight she decided to dress up. Black yoga pants and a red and white checkered flannel over a black tank top.

It was new-mom chic, as she told herself.

She'd also showered while her friends visited and styled and blow-dried her hair so it curled around her shoulders. A far cry from the messy mom-bun she sported every day.

Feeling less than sexy, but not as much like the hot bag of

trash she'd felt like last week, she opened the door and plastered on a big smile. "Merry Christmas!"

That smile. Jesus, it was going to make her orgasm on the spot if Isaac wasn't careful. "Merry Christmas!"

She stepped to the side so he could enter, but before she was able to close the door, he paused, stepped toward her and reached out. She held her breath. What was he doing?

But he innocently pulled back the part of the wrap that was covering Ike's head and smiled again. "Looks pretty cozy in there."

She swallowed. "He's actually snoring."

Isaac snorted and continued on into the house. "Maybe I should get one of those carrier things."

For who, Ike? Why?

"I've just been using my coat." That's when he unzipped his jacket to reveal the most adorable, the most cuddly, the most *purrfectly purrfect* kitten Lauren had ever seen. "I found her in the alley under some trash bins. Her mother was hit by a car."

Ah, fuck. Tears immediately sprang into her eyes. "Her mother's dead? On Christmas?" Now she was blubbering. Damn hormones. Would she ever have control over her emotions again?

The man looked like he was ready to puke. Or at the very least find a quick exit. "I ... I'm sorry. I didn't mean to upset you." He went to zip the kitten back up into his jacket, but she reached out and grabbed his hand to stop him.

"No. No. I told you, I cry over everything, remember?"

He nodded. "But I don't want to *make* you cry."

She smiled through the dripping tears and sniffed. "I'm okay, really."

He didn't seem so sure. "My friend, Sidney's brother, is a vet. He runs his practice out of his home in an adjacent building. That's why I was late. I called up Jim and asked him if he could give her a checkup. I didn't want to bring her over to where Ike was if she had worms or something."

It'd been a long time since she'd met such a considerate man. Did he also remember to put the toilet seat down?

"She's about six weeks old. So she's really young. Was filthy. We gave her a bath. She got her shots and some deworming stuff. I know it's a lot to ask of you with a baby and all, and feel free to stay *no*, but I was wondering if when I'm at work, for the time being until she's litter-trained and able to be alone, if you wouldn't mind cat-sitting for me?"

Lauren coughed. "Cat-*sit?* As in you're keeping her?"

She figured for sure when he started his whole "*I know it's a lot to ask,*" he was going to ask her to *take* the kitten. And about ninety-five percent of her wanted to. But the other five percent was telling her to be practical. She had a newborn. That was enough work for now.

But he wasn't asking her that. He was asking for her help. He was asking her to cat-sit for him. He was becoming a cat dad, and that just made her want him all the more.

"I've never owned a cat," he went on. "I wasn't sure owning a pet would be fair to the animal, given my busy work schedule. But the shelters aren't open today, and they're always so overrun after Christmas because so many idiots buy people pets for Christmas only for those pets to be dropped off at a shelter a couple of weeks later." He shrugged, his expression turning boyish and innocent. "And besides, I kinda like her."

Goddamn it. Her ovaries were about to explode.

"It's a her? I mean *she's* a her?"

He nodded. "Penelope the Magnificent, or Penny for short."

Kaboom! Pow! Blamo! Both ovaries went off like fireworks. She was probably dropping eggs worse than a broody barnyard hen.

She knew the house was warm from all the cooking. And with Ike on her in the wrap, she was even warmer. But now? Now she was a nuclear reactor. She needed to cool off. She needed to get some air before she went into a full-on meltdown. And by meltdown, she meant attacking Isaac's mouth with hers.

Nodding but not saying anything, she took off toward her garage.

It was cool in there, and the space away from the man muddling her brain was welcome. Ike began to stir in the wrap, his head bobbing around in search of food. Her breasts started to ache as well, and when her little man whimpered, her breasts actually throbbed.

It still amazed her how in tune and connected she and her baby were. Even outside the womb, her body still responded to his needs almost instantly.

Wincing from the painful letdown of her milk, she quickly located the bin she'd been searching for and hauled it off the shelf.

Returning to the living room, where a nervous-looking Isaac stood with a drowsy-looking Penny, she plopped the bin on the coffee table. "Everything you'll need for her is in there. It's already washed. You'll need to get kitten kibble and mix it with wet food until she's older. I think that's adult or even geriatric adult cat food in there. But for now, I can give her some canned salmon and crumble up a little bit of adult food over top. There should be a water dish in there if you'll get that out for her."

She left him there and went to check on her food in the kitchen. Meanwhile, Ike began to bash his face against her chest and grunt like a little bear cub.

"Yes, yes, I know, sweetheart. I just need to turn off the potatoes and the oven."

A squawk she'd never heard from him before made her

jump. She glanced down at her son, and he was blinking up at her with big dark eyes full of hunger.

She could feel her nipples leaking. By the time she got them situated, both she and Ike would probably be soaked. Oh well, she was already doing an inordinate amount of laundry. Between spit-up, blowouts and receiving blankets, it was at least a load if not two a day. When she lived alone, she did two loads twice a week. Another thing she'd hadn't anticipated to accompany motherhood.

Not bothering to explain herself to Isaac, she took off down the hallway toward the bedrooms.

Ike was wailing and flailing by the time she got him out of the wrap, in her arms and her nipple in his mouth. The guzzling that followed and the relief she felt nearly brought her to more tears.

She shut her eyes and began to rock in the glider in the corner of the nursery, humming a tune she had no words for, but since the first time she felt him kick, she'd hummed it and it settled him right down.

Unlike Bianca and Celeste's townhouses, which were two floors, with another set of stairs going down to the garage behind and beneath their homes, Lauren's townhouse was one story but deep. Her garage was in the front of her house, and the bedrooms were down the hallway from her kitchen and living room. She preferred her layout to that of her friends' homes. At least when she put Ike in the bassinet in her room, he was on the same floor as her. She wasn't sure she could put him down for a nap upstairs and then be on a different floor or in the garage working. Even though she had a kick-ass baby monitor, she just wasn't sure she could do it. Not yet anyway.

"You want me to carve the turkey?" His voice so nearby made her jump and her eyes flash open.

He was standing in the doorway to Ike's nursery, his jacket

and knit cap off his head but a fluffy little Penny in his hand. He reminded her of one of those Australian firefighters on the calendars. Only Isaac wasn't shirtless—unfortunately.

"I didn't mean to startle you. I just wasn't sure how long you were going to be, and I can take over in the kitchen if you want. I know I already made you delay dinner for me, and not that I know much about pregnancy or nursing, but I know you should never make a pregnant or nursing mother wait to eat." That smile was going to be the end of her. It was sweet and sexy, and even though she could tell the man had confidence, there was just a slight bit of shyness there too. The way he dipped his head and glanced up at her had her whole body reacting in very primal way.

Clearing her throat, she nodded. "I would appreciate that, thank you. Newborns tend to take forever to drain the tanks."

Pink colored his cheeks, and he chuckled. "Anything special you want me to do to the potatoes besides mash them?"

"There's roasted garlic, already peeled, in a bowl next to the stove. If you wouldn't mind adding that to the potatoes, as well as salt, pepper and, of course, butter and heavy cream." She could not remember the last time a man had helped her in the kitchen.

Maybe it was because she hadn't had a serious boyfriend in a while—just a bunch of hookups, booty calls and men who she knew she had no future with so she didn't accept a second date. But even her old boyfriends, the ones she dated for months and some a few years, were never interested in helping her in the kitchen. Her last serious boyfriend, Ken, would actually go to bed without eating if she didn't put a meal in front of him. The man could not boil water. That, among other things—mainly the man's gross inadequacy with his tongue—were why she ended it after four months.

But Isaac was offering to help. So she was going to put him to work.

"The gravy is on the stove. Give it a taste and let me know if you think I need to add anything. I feel like I always under-season my gravy and then end up adding more salt once it's on the table."

He nodded before clapping his heels together and saluting her. "Chef, yes, Chef. Anything else?"

That had her smiling like an idiot. Then he was smiling like an idiot too.

"Turkey can rest before you carve it, if you want to take care of the potatoes first. Stuffing can rest and be covered like the turkey. Foil is in the second drawer next to the fridge."

He nodded again, flashed her another big smile that made her arms, legs, belly and lady parts tingle, and then he was off down the hallway.

He wasn't a quiet man in the kitchen. A lot of bashing and crashing, banging and clanging. But as long as he didn't destroy the place or her meal, she didn't really care. It was just nice having someone else in the house with her. It was just nice sharing a meal with another person, spending Christmas with another person.

She switched Ike to the other side, and he latched on like a leech again. She checked her clothes and his, and sure enough, they were both drenched.

After about twenty minutes of staring lovingly into her baby's eyes, he finally popped off, made a face, went beet-red and shat himself.

Because of course he did. In one end and out the other.

Hoping that her dinner was still in safe and capable hands, she changed Ike's diaper, put him in a new sleeper and then changed her own bra and shirt.

The house smelled even more incredible than it had

earlier when she finally entered the kitchen, and what she saw had her jaw practically hitting the damn floor.

He was in one of her aprons—the yellow one with pink flamingos on it—and Penny, the kitten, was in the front pocket of the apron, fast asleep, her little head peeking out, paws clinging onto the pocket lip.

"Fuck," she muttered. "This is fucking torture."

Pulling his finger from his mouth with a wet *pop,* he gave her a curious look. "Torture? Have I done something wrong?"

She nodded. "Yeah, kept your shirt on. Jesus, man." Shaking her head, with Ike on her shoulder and out of the wrap, she opened the cupboard beside the stove, pulled out a stemless wineglass and filled herself up from her bottle of merlot. She sipped it instantly. Normally, she would have decanted it, but she needed to take the edge off pronto. Otherwise, she would be taking Sergeant Big Hands' pants off instead.

He laughed. "You want me to take my shirt off?"

Showing him her back, she murmured into her wineglass, "And your pants and your underwear ..." Holding Ike's butt in one hand and sipping her wine with the other, she slowly turned around and studied his face over the rim of her glass. "You do know how attractive you are, right? Like, let's just get this all out of the way. You do know you're sex on a stick."

His lips twitched as he tried not to smile, but it became impossible, and he hit her with another one of those grins that soaked her panties. "I've been told I'm nice to look at. But I'm not sure *sex on a stick* has ever been used to describe me, no."

She rolled her eyes. "Self-deprecation is not a good look for you."

Laughing again and turning away from her, he rinsed his hands under the faucet. "I don't know what you want me to say. Okay, I know I'm not a troll. I work out. I take care of my body, but ..." When he hit her with that look, like the one from earlier, his head down, gaze lifted, she thought she heard her ovaries sigh. They were still recovering from the explosions earlier. But that didn't mean they weren't paying attention.

"But what?" she challenged, not ready to let this go. She'd never had a very thick filter. If you don't say how you feel when you feel it you might not get the chance next time. Not a day went by she didn't wish she'd told her father she loved him one more time before he died or how much he meant to her. Sure, she was only five, but she knew what love for a parent was and she'd loved her dad more than any other person in the world.

His chuckle was forced and uncomfortable. "But I've never had anybody say to me the things you've said just now."

"You're kidding, right?"

Like hell he didn't have women throwing themselves at him twenty-four seven.

He shook his head. "I've had girlfriends and hookups, but nobody has ever been as—"

"Lacking a filter?"

He nodded. "Yeah."

She shrugged and sipped more wine. "Filters are over-rated. But it's not that I don't *have* a filter; it's that it's very thin. Life is too short not to speak your mind."

"And you're speaking yours?"

Setting her wineglass down on the counter, she brought Ike off her shoulder and propped him up in her arms so he could see out. "All I'm saying is that you're very attractive. And seeing you in my kitchen with an apron on and a kitten in the pocket is orgasm-inducing."

His brows flew up nearly to his hairline. "Did you?"

"Not quite. But just know, it's a *good* look."

"Okaaay ..."

Scoffing, she reached for her wineglass again.

"Are you *interested* in starting something? Is that where we're going with this conversation?" He reached into her cutlery drawer and pulled out the big carving knife and fork.

Leaning against the counter, she shook her head. This conversation was not going as she expected.

How exactly DID you expect it to go?

She ignored her inner thoughts and stared down into her wineglass, suddenly unable to look at him. "I'm two weeks postpartum. I ... I'm not looking for ... I'm a single mom now. I'm damaged goods. I just ... I've always had a very high sex drive, and it's been since just after this little bug was conceived that I've gotten any. My libido is in overdrive. You're like window-shopping."

He paused before slicing into the turkey breast. "You're wanting something casual? Purely physical?"

YES!

His face held no hints as to what he was thinking. None.

Damn it.

Now her face was on fire, and it wasn't just from the wine or the warm kitchen. Swallowing the wine in her mouth, she gathered her wits. "I'm not saying I *want* anything." *Besides your cock in every one of my holes.* "I'm just thinking out loud is all. Just admiring what I see."

He returned his focus to the turkey. "Grab me a couple of plates, please."

She did as she was told, and he expertly sliced the turkey and plated it.

"You a cranberry sauce person?" he asked.

"No. Gravy all the way."

"Me too. You want me to make you up a plate as you're holding the wee man?"

Now she *really* couldn't get a read on the guy. He was acting all casual, like she hadn't just told him to take off all his clothes and that her sex drive was currently running at hyper-speed.

"Uh, sure. But I'm going to put him in his bouncy chair." Frazzled and confused by the way his attitude had shifted, she ducked into the living room and popped Ike into the slingback chair that vibrated and had a little mobile hanging from it.

She returned to the kitchen to find Isaac holding a plate full of dinner for her. "For you."

"Thank you." She took it, but of course, their fingers touched beneath the plate and another zap of lust struck her between the legs like a bolt of horny lightning. She grabbed her wine from the counter, as well as the bottle, and went to go sit at her two-top bistro table. From there, she could see Ike in his chair. He was transfixed by the sparkly sunshine toy on the mobile that had a mirror in the center.

Isaac joined her at the table with a beer. He'd ditched the apron and put Penny in one of the small plush cat houses from the bin of cat stuff Lauren had pulled from the garage.

For a moment, they ate in silence. But unlike yesterday, when they ate and were quiet and it felt companionable, now it just felt awkward.

Why oh why didn't she tighten her filter?

Tucking food into his cheek, he lifted his beer bottle into the center of the table. "Merry Christmas, Lauren."

Swallowing her mashed potatoes, she lifted her glass and clinked it with his bottle. "Merry Christmas, Isaac."

His grin as he took a sip was diabolical. "May you get everything you asked Santa for and then some."

5

"You're sure you don't need any help in there?" Isaac asked, sitting on Lauren's couch and playing with a sleepy-eyed Ike. The baby was like a noodle. Pliable and bendy. He seemed to like it when Isaac made him do sit-ups or bicycle legs.

"Nope. Just play with the baby. I'm almost done anyway."

He made faces and noises at Ike, who ate it right up. He wasn't smiling, because two-week-old babies didn't smile—as Lauren educated him—but the baby wasn't getting angry either. He simply stared at Isaac like he was the most entertaining and interesting thing in the world.

The little guy's eyes began to droop, and even as Isaac did bicycle legs with him, Ike fell asleep. Penny was asleep on the arm of the couch, curled up in Isaac's sweater. Both babies were out.

The warm house, delicious food and good company, not to mention the tryptophan from the turkey, had him yawning as well. Leaning his head back against the couch, with Isaac on his lap, he let his eyelids drop.

It wasn't until he felt the couch cushion beside him shift and he smelled Lauren's delicious scent that he lifted one lid.

"It would seem like the Christmas festivities wiped out everyone," she said, curling one leg under her body and resting her arm on the back of the couch, her wineglass in her hand.

He lifted the other eyelid but didn't shift or move in case he woke up Ike. Though the way that baby was passed out with his arms above his head and his lips open, it would take a shitload of fireworks to rouse him. "Good food will do that. Thank you for dinner. It was excellent."

Her smile was small as she sipped her wine. "Thank you for helping."

She'd been quiet since her little confession earlier in the kitchen. A confession that had thrown him for the mother of all loops. He would have thought sex, relationships and intimacy of any kind would be the furthest things from her mind at the moment. But then, he didn't know Lauren very well. And she did say she had a high sex drive and hadn't gotten laid since just after Ike was conceived so ... Nine months was a long time to go without if you were used to always going with.

He went to say something, but she spoke first. "Listen, about earlier ..."

He held up his hand. "You don't have to explain."

"No, I do."

Shrugging, he gave her the floor to continue speaking.

"I think you're very handsome. And the kindness you've shown Ike and me over the last couple days, and when you helped us two weeks ago, just adds to your appeal. But I'm only vocalizing my observations. I'm not asking you for anything. Call it the harmless flirtations of a hormone-rampant, postpartum, sleep-deprived single mother. I'm delirious. But I'm sorry if I made you uncomfortable. I'm really liking this budding friendship of ours, and I wouldn't want to do anything to jeopardize it."

Her throat bobbed on a sexy swallow as she sipped her wine, a bead of the merlot getting caught on her bottom lip. He wanted to lick it off or at the very least catch it with his thumb, but he resisted. She'd just put a barrier back between them, one he thought she'd torn down earlier. He needed to respect her boundaries.

But when her mouth twisted in such a way and that droplet clung to her lip, just calling to him, he said "fuck boundaries," reached forward and swiped his thumb over her lip. "For the record," he said, popping his thumb into his mouth, "you're not *damaged goods,* as you said earlier. When my mom finally left my dad, I would have punched any person in the face who dared to call her damaged goods."

Heat flashed in the blue of her eyes, and her bottom lip dropped open.

"I'll respect your decision," he said. "But just know, it's not off the table for me ... if you're interested."

She did nothing more than stare at him. But the flare of her nostrils and the widening of her eyes did all the talking for her.

Sitting up, he adjusted Ike on his lap. The baby didn't so much as flinch. "But I'm okay with just a friendship too. This isn't an ultimatum."

"I'm only two weeks ..." she whispered. "We can't ..."

Shifting again, he turned to face her. Ike remained deep in REM, his eyes behind his closed lids the only things moving, save for the rise and fall of his little chest. "And if it *is* something you want to explore, we can take things slow. I'm not a horny teenager that needs to jump into bed right away. We can get to know each other."

She nibbled on her lip. "You're saying all the right things, Isaac." Her laugh was more of a throaty chortle as she turned her head. "I don't even know your last name. Besides the fact that you're a cop—a sergeant—you are single and childless and just adopted a kitten, I know nothing about you. And yet we're discussing—sort of—the idea of becoming ..."

"Fox."

"Huh?"

"That's my last name. Isaac James Fox."

"You're Foxy Sergeant Big Hands?" She shook her head and averted her eyes. "Of course you are."

"Foxy Sergeant Big Hands?" he murmured. Did he miss something?

She sipped her wine. "Never mind."

Okaaaay.

She shook her head and looked away from him, the pink blooming in her cheeks only adding to her beauty. "I can't date a cop anyway, so maybe we should just stay friends."

She couldn't date a cop? Why?

"Are you a secret felon? A kingpin?" Chuckling, he asked, "Why can't you date a cop?"

"Because I saw what it did to my mom. And there's a family curse."

A family curse?

"You're going to need to elaborate for me."

She exhaled through her nose, her expression turning equal parts irritated and disappointed. "My dad was a cop. And I saw what it did to my mother, how she worried every day when he left for work, wondering, stressing if he'd ever come home. And then one day, he didn't."

Fuck.

"She told me to never marry a cop, to never fall in love with a cop because when my dad died, so did a piece of my mom, and she didn't want that for me. She couldn't bear to see me go through what she did. And frankly, I'm not sure I could."

He raked his fingers through his hair and scrubbed his

hand down his face. "Ah, fuck. I'm really sorry. How long ago?"

"I was five. So ... twenty-seven years ago."

"Fuck."

"My mom remarried when I was nine. But she married an accountant. She said she wanted a man with a boring, safe job and said I should too. Less heartache, less loss." Her eyes turned misty. "Even though she's happy with my stepdad, Allan, who adopted me—and had two more children with him—my half sister and half brother—she was never the same after my dad passed. To this day, she still says he was the love of her life, her soul mate, and when he died, so did a piece of her soul."

Yeah, if that wasn't enough to convince Lauren to stay the hell away from cops, he didn't know what was. Fuck.

"How did he ..." He shook his head. "Never mind. You don't have to tell me."

"He went to a call about a domestic dispute. Husband was beating up the wife and kids."

A prickle formed at the back of Isaac's head. He cleared his throat and cracked his neck side to side to dislodge it. "Those are some of the scariest calls. We never know what we're walking into."

"I know."

"Was it the husband?"

She shook her head. "I don't know. I was five. I don't remember much, and they kept me pretty in the dark about everything. My mom hates talking about it, so I'm ignorant to the details."

He nodded. That was probably for the best anyway. "You mentioned a curse ..."

She shrugged, her body language telling him she wanted to get off this topic. He could see that even now, over twenty years later, it still hurt to talk about her father's death. Understandable. There were still things in Isaac's past that he'd rather not think about, and most definitely not talk about. "When women in my family get involved with cops, things for those cops don't end well. Let's just leave it at that. The Russo women are cursed. A lot of death—and not ours."

Well if that wasn't ominous and creepy as fuck.

He'd never been an overly spiritual person, so he wasn't sure if he believed in that hocus pocus curse talk, but the look in he eyes said she'd seen enough heartache to not want any of it for herself, curse or no curse.

"So then *we're* off the table?" he asked, overwhelmed with how much he disliked the idea of not being able to turn this into more than a friendship.

Not that he was a dick like that, though. If she decided she only wanted a friendship, he'd be fine with that. But he'd enjoyed their little *whatever* it was earlier. The sparkle in her eyes, the color in her cheeks. He'd been afraid to admit to his attraction to her because he thought there might be something inappropriate about it.

He'd never been a single-mom chaser. He knew a few guys who were. Guys who liked dating women with baggage —but who the fuck didn't have baggage these days? If he wanted someone without baggage, he'd have to date *well* below his own age, and he wasn't interested in that. He liked women his own age. Women with substance. Women with maturity and who knew what they wanted out of life.

At least *now* he did.

"I think so," she finally said, the lack of conviction on her face giving him hope. "My mom would kill me, first of all, and second ... I have another little heart to consider now. Not just my own. And the thought of potentially breaking his ..." She reached for Ike off his lap and held her son against her chest. The spot where her fingers had touched his thighs still tingled. "I think a friendship is best."

He nodded. "Then a friendship it is."

ISAAC HAD the next two days off from work, so he spent them litter-training Penny, stocking up on cat food, and Googling "how to train your cat not to be an asshole." He hadn't done that much intense research on anything since college, but he learned a lot.

He didn't see Lauren, but they texted periodically. Mostly he had cat questions for her, but sometimes, he used a cat question as an excuse to just message her.

Her revelation about her father had rocked him more than he'd like to admit, as did her pledge to her mother and herself to not fall for a cop.

He got it. He did. But it still fucking sucked.

It was his first day back to work after his two days off, and the first day he planned to leave Penny with Lauren.

Thankfully, he had four day shifts in a row, so Lauren wouldn't have to cat-sit overnight.

He felt like a bit of a tool asking her to kitten-sit for him, particularly when he went online later and found a little mesh and canvas dome tent that he could leave Penny in, complete with a litter box, food dish, bed and toys. But taking Penny over to Lauren's gave him an excuse to not only see her but Ike as well. For a baby that slept ninety percent of the day, Isaac had fallen for him nonetheless. Maybe it was because Ike was Isaac's namesake so he felt a bond with the little guy or it was because Isaac had been there when Ike came into the world. But either way, not only was he drawn to Ike's mother, but he was drawn to Ike as well.

He packed up all of Penny's stuff into his truck, tucked the kitten into his coat and headed over to Lauren's. His shift started at six, and he thought a five thirty drop-off would be unwelcome, but she said she was up at that time feeding Ike anyway so to bring Penny by.

He crawled his truck through Lauren's complex, careful not to wake any of the dark houses. It had snowed and rained off and on over the last several days, so although there was white stuff on the ground, it hadn't amounted to very much. Slush filled the streets and gutters dripped, but it was easy to navigate through with his truck and four-wheel drive.

There was a light on in the front window of Lauren's place, so she'd either left it on or she was up. His guess was on the latter.

He parked in Lauren's driveway, made sure Penny was tucked up snug in his coat, grabbed her stuff and headed to the front door.

His fist was lifted and he was about to knock when the door swung open.

Damn, even in a fluffy light purple housecoat and a topknot on her head, she was beautiful. Tired blue eyes blinked as she stepped to the side so he could enter.

"Ike asleep?" he whispered.

"*Just* got him back down."

The woman looked exhausted. "Rough night?"

She nodded and her eyelids drooped. "He was up *a lot.* Doing some fucked-up thing called reverse cycling where he sleeps all day and then is up and wanting to party at night. It's killing me. He started it two days ago, and I'm already totally over it."

Isaac chuckled as he took Penny out of his coat. "Well, hopefully this little baby doesn't give you much grief. She's been excellent for me over the last few days. Mind you, she hasn't left me alone. Follows me everywhere. I feel like a mother duck. Like she's imprinted on me or something."

"She probably has, in a way. She's still very young."

He handed her to Lauren.

"Come here, sweet baby," she cooed, nuzzling Penny and closing her eyes. "Oh, I miss kitten snuggles."

"Well, you'll be getting a lot of them. She slept next to my head all night. Meows uncontrollably from her bed on the floor until I pick her up and put her on the pillow beside me."

Kissing Penny, she murmured, "I'm okay with that. Ike's in the bassinet, so it can just be us girls in the bed."

Not letting the thought of being in Lauren's bed cause him too much agony in his pants, he cleared his throat and zipped up his jacket. "I'll be by just before six if that works?"

She nodded. "We'll be here."

He turned to go, opening the door and getting struck in the face by a harsh, icy wind. But he hooked a glance over his shoulder at her standing there with his kitten. "Thanks again."

Her words that followed hit him like a sledgehammer to the chest.

"Just come back home in one piece."

Well, if that didn't make his heart crumple, his gut churn and his fingers itch to lock the door with all of them behind it and never step foot outside again.

6

IT WAS NEARLY seven o'clock by the time Isaac pulled back into Lauren's driveway. After her parting words that morning, he made sure to text her at five on the dot to let her know he would be late. He also followed that up with a note that he wasn't in any dangerous situation, he was just dealing with a pretty nasty accident beneath the Alaskan Viaduct.

She responded with a selfie picture of her cuddled up on the couch with a snoozing Isaac in her arms and a curled-up, zonked-out Penny on her lap.

That made him want to get back to them even sooner. He was missing out.

He made that image his wallpaper and pushed through the next two hours in the freezing sleet and glaring headlights of oncoming traffic.

Despite his gloves and boots, his fingers and toes were like Popsicles by the time he climbed into his truck back at the precinct. He put the heat on high and blasted it through the cab until he was sweating beneath his jacket.

When he pulled into Lauren's driveway, he was no longer

freezing but seriously considering giving himself a facewash in a snowdrift to cool off.

He hated winter. It was dark when he started work and dark when he finished. It didn't matter that he worked out in the daylight all day and wasn't cooped up in an office or in the filthy, black depths of a coal mine. It just sucked starting and ending work in darkness.

Knocking on her door, he attempted to stem the tingling feeling in his gut, but it was only amplified when the door opened to reveal Lauren, Ike and Penny. His smile hurt his face as he stepped over the threshold and shut the door behind him. Was this what fathers felt like coming home to their families? Was this the kind of joy they felt every day seeing people they cared about waiting for them?

His own dad probably never felt anything but contempt when he came home from work as a bounty hunter. His family was just another reminder of all the mouths he had to feed, all the people dependent on him, squeezing him dry of all his hard-earned money.

Every time he thought of his old man as a bounty hunter, he shook his head and laughed in pained disbelief. Steve Fox was the ultimate hypocrite, holding others accountable to their crimes while he committed dozens of his own.

Lauren put Penny on the floor, and she began to weave in between Isaac's legs, meowing until he scooped her up. "Hey, Penelope the Magnificent, how was your first day of daycare?" He kissed her head as he toed off his wet boots and followed Lauren into the rest of the house—which smelled amazing.

"How was your day, *dear*?" she asked. He wanted to wipe off her sassy grin with his lips.

"Grueling," he replied with an exaggerated groan. "How was your day with the wee ones?"

She draped the back of her hand over her forehead and

closed her eyes. "Grueling. You saw the picture I sent. If that's not hard work, then I don't know what is."

"Hey, I'll trade you any day. You go to work, and I stay home with the kids."

She glanced at him with a lifted brow and a smirk. A look he couldn't figure out but knew meant she was thinking hard about something. "Hungry? I made a turkey potpie with the leftovers."

He was starving. He'd missed lunch and had only had a smoothie for breakfast. His body was devouring him from the inside out. A painful, demanding grumble rocked his stomach.

"You don't have to feed me," he said. Though his stomach and heart were both telling him to shut the fuck up and eat all the potpie. The house smelled just as good as it had on Christmas, and he already knew Lauren was one hell of a cook.

Even if she hadn't offered him food, the reluctance he felt to leave the house, even despite his fatigue, caught him off guard like a snowball to the face. Coming *home* to Lauren and Ike warmed him, made his heart soar and his feet take root where he stood. He liked being with Lauren and Ike. Even if nothing romantic happened between them, he liked being with her and her son. It made him feel a part of something. It was far better than returning to his cold, dark condo and making a frozen pizza for dinner as he binge-watched something on Netflix until he passed out.

She turned around to face him, a plate with a giant slice of steaming potpie in the center, with cut-up cucumber and bell pepper beside it. "Go eat. I heard your stomach rumbling."

Dipping his head and murmuring a thank-you, he took the plate and went to sit at her two-top bistro table.

He put Penny down on the floor, and Lauren buckled Ike

into his bouncy chair before she joined him at the table with her own plate.

"You haven't eaten yet?" he asked, shoveling the food into his mouth like he hadn't eaten in days.

She shrugged and nibbled on a piece of cucumber. "I had a snack around four thirty. But I figured I'd wait for you. I hate eating alone anyway."

"This is amazing. You're a really great cook."

She tucked the food in her mouth into her cheek so she could speak. "It relaxes me. In college I lived in a big house with six other roommates. It got to the point where they all paid me forty bucks a week plus money for groceries and I made dinner for everyone. I also made sure there were always baked goods around, like muffins, cookies or scones, and every Sunday morning all seven of us would sit down and have a huge Sunday breakfast. They were all too busy and stressed out to cook, plus some of them sucked at it, and I made a bit of extra cash while doing something I enjoyed."

"That's an awesome idea. I *can* cook—albeit not this well—but I don't do it very often. I'm just too busy or tired. A lot of frozen pizzas, cold-cut sandwiches or takeout passes across this tongue, I'm afraid. I make a mean Szechuan stir fry, but I probably only get to do it twice a month." She'd already set water glasses out for them on the table, and he took a huge sip. "I'd pay you more than forty bucks a week to cook for me like this." Hell, he'd pay her five hundred bucks a week if she fed him, watched his cat and let him hang out with her and her kid.

She snickered. "We might be able to work something out."

He nodded as he shoved more food into his face. "I'm serious. Let me know your fee and let's do this."

He allowed the flavors of the potpie to sit on his tongue for a moment as he watched his new friend eat her meal. It was going to be a struggle not to fall for this single mom. He already knew that. But if her friendship was all he could have, then that would have to be enough. His life already felt a whole hell of a lot fuller having Lauren and Ike in it.

"Any plans for New Year's Eve?" he asked, swallowing what was in his mouth and sitting back in his chair. He wasn't finished, but he'd satisfied the beast in his belly enough to take a breather.

"I've been invited to a party, but I'm not sure I'm going to go. I'm just not sure I'm ready. You?"

"I've been invited to a party too. A friend from the gym is hosting one. Should be a pretty big thing."

"Yeah, same with the one I've been invited to. And the couple hosting it has a new baby as well. He was born two days before Ike was. There will be lots of kids and people. I'm just ... they're not *my* friends." She wrinkled her nose. "I mean they *are*. But they're not. They're friends of friends—you know what I mean? And even though I see them all the time at gatherings, I'm worried it might be weird."

He cocked his head to the side and wiped up a dollop of gravy from the side of his plate with his finger and popped it into his mouth. "Weird how?"

She shrugged. "I dunno. I think most of the people there will all be coupled up. I probably wouldn't last until midnight anyway, so I don't have to worry about not having anyone to kiss."

"You'll have Ike."

Smiling, she glanced at her wide-eyed boy in the bouncy chair. "And his kisses are da bomb, but you know what I mean."

He did. Truth be told, he wasn't entirely on board with going to the party he was invited to either. Like Lauren's party, it was going to be mostly couples. It was one thing being the third or fifth wheel—which was still really fucking awkward.

But it was another thing being the twenty-seventh wheel or whatever. Where the room was full of kissing people, and the only thing he had his mouth on was his beer bottle.

No, thanks.

He narrowed his gaze and sipped his water. "You said the couple hosting the party just had a new baby?"

She nodded. "Yeah, Dawson."

"Are you friends with Zak and Aurora Eastwood?"

The blue in her eyes darkened and her face turned serious as she slowly said, "Yes. Why?"

"Because that's whose party I was invited to. I know Zak from the gym. In fact, I know all the guys. I hang out with Aaron a fair bit. We both served, me in the Marines, he in the Navy. And I go to Prime Sports Bar at least once a week for lunch to hang out with Mason while he works."

What a small world.

She shook her head, the seriousness in her eyes fading but replaced with another look he couldn't quite put his fingers on. "You know Liam and Scott, then?"

He nodded. "Not as well as Zak, Aaron or Mason, but yeah, I know all of the guys. They all go to the gym."

"Okay, so Liam and Scott's little sister, Bianca, lives in this complex. You met her on Christmas Eve—she was the brunette. And Scott's girlfriend, Eva, is the older sister of Celeste—who you also met on Christmas Eve. She was the redhead. I'm the interloper in all of this. But they usually invite me to their parties and barbecues anyway."

Yeah, Isaac had been invited to a few parties and barbecues, but he always seemed to be working when they happened, so he hadn't been to a big shindig with all the men and their families yet. It was strange to think that if he had managed to make it to a get-together, he might have met Lauren sooner.

"Well, now that we know we'll both be there, we can go

together," he offered, diving back into his meal. He might have to hint at her sending him home with a care package. The potpie was midnight snack material for sure.

Her lips twisted as she chewed. "Maybe. Though I honestly don't think I'll last until midnight, and I wouldn't want to pull you from the party before you were ready to leave. Maybe if we took separate vehicles."

He shook his head. "Naw, I'll leave when you want to leave. And I won't drink. I'll be the DD so you can let your hair down with your friends and enjoy the party."

"What's the price of you being the DD?" The woman's expressions were hard to decipher. Was she teasing? Was she being serious? Coy? Suggesting something? He was having a hard time figuring Lauren out but loving every minute he spent trying.

He finished his last bite of the potpie and pointed at his empty plate with his fork, waggling his eyebrows. "Leftovers. I'll drive your tipsy ass home safe if you send me home tonight with the rest of the pie."

Her hand reaching across the table surprised him, and the twinkle in her eyes made his body temperature reach an uncomfortable level, though that was nothing compared with the heat in his jeans when he grasped her hand and shook it.

"Deal," she said, squeezing his hand. "Joke's on you though. We each ate half the pie."

***

THIS TIME ISAAC refused to take no for an answer and cleaned up the dinner dishes. Not that there were many to clean because she'd done most of them before he arrived and she had a dishwasher, but she appreciated the gesture none-theless.

While Isaac did the dishes, she nursed Ike and was just

tucking her breast back into her bra and getting ready to burp him when thunder rumbled in his diaper and then the sound of a Super Soaker water gun being sprayed at full blast filled the living room.

"What the hell was that?" Isaac asked from the kitchen.

"If I were to guess," she said, pressing her nose to her son's sleeper, "he just had an enormous crap and ... yep, it was a blowout. Fuck." Careful not to break his noodle neck but also not get any of it on her, she held Ike on his stomach over her forearm and headed for the bathroom.

"Need help?" Isaac called after her, his voice already following her down the hallway.

"I'm going to have to bathe him. I can already tell it's up his back. Babies shit with such power. Like a rocket booster in his pants."

His warm, whiskey-thick chuckle was close, and when she turned around, he was right behind her. "Here, gimme him and you get ready what you need to."

She passed off the wide-eyed Ike, who, despite being covered in his own crap, didn't seem to be put out by it, and proceeded to get the baby bathtub ready.

"You want me to strip him?" Isaac asked, holding Ike toward the mirror and making goofy faces at him. Lauren's heart constricted.

"Sure, if you want to brave it. Otherwise I can do it in a moment. I'm just checking the water temperature."

She placed the baby bathtub on the floor in the bathroom after filling it from the large tub and reached for the all-natural lavender-scented baby soap from the counter.

She hadn't expected Isaac to actually brave the poonami in Ike's pajamas and strip him, but when she reached for her baby, he was wearing nothing but a diaper and what she could have sworn was a big grin.

"I didn't take off the diaper, as I wasn't sure what was

waiting for me under there, but I relieved him of his first layer." Isaac crouched down next to the tub at the same time she did. "Put me to work. What can I do?"

She'd never met a man like him before. He just jumped right in, despite the fact that Ike wasn't his kid and he could have just cracked a beer and sat on the couch while she bathed her son, or he could have taken off completely. But he didn't. He came into the shitstorm and was eager to help her weather it.

Whoever Isaac Fox's mother was, wherever she was, she'd raised her son right.

Lauren relieved her baby of his diaper and brought his dirty little butt under the warm spray of the shower to hose off the majority of the mess. Once she knew he was clean, only then did she plop him into his bath. She dipped a soft washcloth into the water and then laid it over his exposed belly to keep him warm.

"So far, he loves baths. Hasn't gotten upset once. Not that I've bathed him much. I think this is the third time, and only because he keeps having big blowouts."

With another washcloth, she pumped a dime-size amount of soap onto it and began to wash him. Ike watched them both with wide-eyed wonder, his arms and legs flailing and splashing. The noisy fountain he created only encouraged him to flail more and soon the floor was soaked.

"I hope this doesn't sound pervy," Isaac said, sitting on the floor next to Lauren, Ike's fist wrapped tight around his finger, "but the little dude is *blessed,* if you know what I mean?"

Lauren snorted and rolled her eyes. "A bit too soon to tell, but yeah, he is. Didn't get that from his father though."

He appeared to be fighting a grin but failed. "Well, it comes with the name, really. Isaacs, pretty much all of us globally, are well-endowed gents. It's all in the name, right, buddy?" With his free hand, he fist-bumped Ike's free hand, making the baby's legs kick even more.

"So big hands ..."

"Big gloves," he replied, that smile so big, so cocky, so damn panty-soaking she had to reach out and hold the wall to stop herself from swooning. "Big shoes. Big jock strap too."

Laughing, she shook her head. "Are Isaacs this cocky too?"

He nodded. "Yeah, because we've got big cocks so we can afford to be."

She rolled her eyes, but the heat between her thighs and the throbbing of her pussy said *make him drop his pants and prove it.*

She splashed him playfully with the water from Ike's tub, the baby smiling back at them, his eyes wide and watching. "Go pick out some pj's for your *blessed* namesake. Top drawer of his dresser."

He stood up from his spot beside her, his knees cracking just a bit. "I hope you got something roomy for the little guy between the legs. We need to let our *blessings* breathe. Full range of motion. No constriction." All smiles, he disappeared around the corner. "I might have to get the little man some boxer briefs."

Chuckling, Lauren continued to run the soft washcloth over her son's even softer skin. "Do you like him?"

Ike's legs kicked double-time.

She hunkered down close to his head and kissed his damp little nose. "Yeah, Mommy likes him too."

As HE KNEW it would be, Isaac's house was cold, dark and empty when he and Penny finally walked through the front door. He set her down on the floor, and she scampered off to go sniff things while he juggled all of her stuff, his duffle bag and the whole potpie Lauren sent him home with.

Oh, she was a sneaky thing, making the deal when she knew there was no pie left, only to surprise him on his way out the door with a duplicate. Her smile had been electric, the glimmer in her eyes brighter than the stars in the clear sky.

She'd bounced on her heels and giggled when he took it and called her a wily wench.

"I'm making turkey soup and biscuits tomorrow," she said, the hope on her face that he'd stay for dinner again making it impossible for him to refuse.

"I can't wait."

He put the potpie in his fridge and unloaded all of Penny's stuff. She was under his feet as he walked, meowing, so he scooped her up, unzipped his hoodie a bit and plopped her inside, tucking his hoodie into his jeans so she didn't fall out.

She clawed at his stomach a little before settling down, the rumble of her purr like the muffled roar of a lion cub.

He liked his condo. It was spacious and southwest-facing so it got a lot of sun. But at thirty-five years old with no woman and no children, he was beginning to feel like his place was *too* big for just him. It was feeling emptier than usual. He had a futon in the guest room, along with workout gear, but the people who owned the unit before him had used that room as a nursery.

Before he moved in, this had been a family home.

He hadn't bothered to paint over the light green color of the walls. There was even a bunch of white decals on one wall in the shape of jungle animals. He hadn't bothered to peel those off either.

Was a family supposed to live here? Should he have gone with a one-bedroom, or was that giving up the dream that he might be able to use that spare room as a nursery one day as well?

Once he got Penny's stuff all sorted in his room, he pulled her out of his hoodie and plunked her down in her bed. She protested at first, jumping at him and trying to get back into his hoodie, but when he tickled her head, she settled down into her bed and closed her eyes.

He needed to have a shower. It was only nine o'clock, but he had to be back at work again at five, so he needed to get to bed.

A lot of people said the heat zapped their energy, but Isaac had always felt like the cold zapped his energy more than anything. And he'd been stuck out in the cold most of the day. The wet and snowy weather always seemed to bring out the city's worst drivers. He'd been called out to four different accidents, all stupidity-related. And he'd frozen his nuts nearly clean off standing there taking statements and dealing with idiots who didn't think they needed winter tires or who thought they'd be able to make the yellow light if they gunned it, even though the icy slush in the middle of the intersection proved them wrong.

Double-checking that his bedroom door was closed so Penny didn't escape, he put her bed on his floor and stripped out of his clothes.

Turning on the shower, he let it get hot before he hopped in. Growing up how he had for the first several years of his life, where he was never sure if his dad had paid the heating bill or spent that money on booze instead, Isaac loved his showers as hot as he could fucking stand it.

He also took long showers.

His dad had always limited him and his sister to two-minute showers each. Though, when the water was ice-fuck-ing-cold, he could scrub the bare minimum of his body in under thirty seconds when he needed to. That skill had come in handy as a marine.

But now, he could afford to heat his place, have hot water and food in his belly every day. He allowed himself only one luxury—his bike—and the rest of his paycheck went to bills and savings.

Even though he'd only lived with his dad until he was eight, he remembered going to bed cold and hungry enough times that he never wanted to live that way again. He would never be without a job, never be without a roof over his head, food in his fridge or clothes on his back. And if he was ever lucky enough to have kids of his own, those kids would want for none of life's basic necessities either.

You didn't have to give your children the moon to show them that you loved them, but you did have to show them that they were more important than a bottle of Wild Turkey.

He washed his hair and scrubbed his body. Then he took himself in his palm.

With his eyes squeezed shut, his forearm against the wall and his head down, he stroked his cock until it was hard and throbbing.

Was it wrong that thoughts of Lauren were what fueled him? Probably. But nobody would ever know.

The image of her in her housecoat that morning, all sleepy-eyed with her messy topknot and pillow-creased face, brought him close. Even in the morning, after a rough night with the baby, she was gorgeous. Sexy. The epitome of the girl next door, but with a killer sense of humor and a smile that brightened up any room. She also had a killer rack and an ass that refused to quit.

It made sense why she was a voice actor. She could read him the back of a cereal box and he'd grow hard listening to that sensual rasp. Deep yet still feminine. Not that he'd ever called a phone sex hotline, but that was the kind of voice he guessed those women (or men, because let's be honest here, they could be men pretending to be women) sounded like.

And her laugh. Oh fuck, her laugh. Even her giggle was deeper than most women's, and it made his cock jerk in his jeans every damn time.

He tried not to be a perv and look while she nursed Ike, but damn it if he didn't swing his gaze across the room and catch a glimpse of those soft, creamy mounds. He had no issues with nursing. That relationship was between a mother and her child—so none of his fucking business—but given his stirring feelings for Lauren, and how adamant she'd been *not* to get involved with a cop, that just made him want her more.

And it wasn't that she *didn't* want him, it was that she didn't want to get involved with a cop, which he understood.

It also made it ten times harder.

The mutual attraction was there.

She wanted him.

He wanted her.

And yet anything more than friendship between them was forbidden.

By her of all people.

He hated it.

But he also understood it.

But seeing, even just for a moment, Lauren's breast out left him feeling the need to take himself in his hand and imagine his hand was her hot little mouth.

She said she had a high sex drive. Well, so did he. Very high.

He used to sleep around a lot in his twenties and early thirties, but a pregnancy scare with a one-night stand, followed by a fun case of chlamydia with another one-night stand, had him smartening the fuck up. He was clean now, but he also hadn't been with anybody in months. His celibacy was a self-inflicted punishment for his man-whorish ways.

Sid and Mel had knocked some sense into him after the chlamydia debacle. It'd actually run rampant through the precinct. A female rookie had only slept with Isaac and one other cop, but that other cop gave her chlamydia, and she gave it to Isaac. The other cop—Shawn—was a massive slut, and he gave it to nearly a dozen people in the department—both cops and civilian workers.

He was also growing tired of the meaningless fucks. Sure, sex was better than rubbing one out on your own, but there came a point where the sex became less and less satisfying and more of just a way to kill time and get your rocks off without developing carpal tunnel.

But as Sid and Mel pointed out, he wasn't getting any younger, and at a certain point, his man-whoring days would catch up with him. He was lucky the pregnancy scare had been just that—a scare—and that he only caught chlamydia.

They told him to smarten the fuck up, not have sex for at least six months and really figure out what the hell he wanted.

And he'd done that. He could honestly say that he had not had sex with anyone since May 31. He was at seven months celibate and counting.

And in those seven months, he'd learned a lot about himself. About his wants, his dreams and his desires.

A woman.

A family.

A future.

He knew now those were the things he wanted most in life. No more of these meaningless, hollow hookups. He wanted one woman—one *good* woman—for the long haul. Until they were both old, gray and wrinkly.

He wanted the picket fence, the house in the suburbs and

matching rocking chairs on the porch so they could watch their grandchildren play in the yard.

And after getting to know Lauren, he knew she wanted those things too.

She just didn't want them with a cop.

But what about what he wanted?

What about his intense, unrelenting desire to study the arch of her throat with the tip of his tongue, taste the tight peaks of her raspberry nipples? He'd caught a flash of her nipple yesterday, and he hadn't been able to stop thinking about it since. He wanted to feel her pulse quicken beneath his lips, kiss her, explore her mouth with his, suck and bite her lips until her pout became puffy. Stare into those incredible blue eyes when he buried himself deep in her slick heat and came.

What about his wants?

For now, he was left with his imagination. And the more time he spent with Lauren, the more rampant and wild that imagination became.

Tonight, in his fantasy, he popped out of Lauren's mouth, hoisted her up and spun her around. She grinned back at him as she hinged over and pushed her ass into the air. With the hot water pummeling their bodies, he dipped his fingers between her thighs from behind, drew her wetness up her crease and pressed the head of his cock against her tight rosette.

She puckered at first, but smiled, her teeth caught between her lips at the same time she pushed back against him, welcoming him into her tight, forbidden channel.

They both moaned as he seated himself deep in her ass. She shut her eyes and hung her head between her arms. He began to move. Slow at first, then faster. But it wasn't fast enough for his sexually charged woman, no. She bucked and slammed back into his hips harder and faster than he ever imagined. He didn't want to hurt her, but the noises she made were anything but pain.

He was close. Really. Fucking. Close.

Holding on to her hip with one hand, he leaned over her body, reached beneath her, cupping her breast with the other. She shivered beneath him when he pulled her nipple.

"Harder," she groaned. "Fuck me harder, Isaac."

Yes, ma'am.

He pistoned his hips as hard as he could, his dick like an iron bar and as deep into her ass as he could go. She reached beneath her body and between her legs, cupping his balls and tugging down.

Fuck, yes.

"Gonna come."

"Me too," she mewled.

He tugged hard on her nipple again. She gripped his sac and yanked, and they both came. Explosions. Dynamite. A powder keg in a fireworks shop.

He filled her ass with cum and dug his teeth into her shoulder as the orgasm rocked through him. His toes curled in the water that circled the drain and his balls cinched up when she released them.

Her walls tightened around his cock as it pulsed, each throb a streak of pleasure through his veins so intense he thought he might black out.

When he finally opened his eyes, she was gone.

His thick load disappeared down the drain, and his cock lay spent in his palm.

He slammed his eyes shut again to see if he could bring her back. But she was really gone. All he saw as black.

"She wasn't there to begin with," he muttered to himself as he shut off the water and stepped out of the shower to dry off. He shook his head at his stupidity. He'd let his fantasy run rampant to the point where it felt more real than any other fantasy he'd ever had. His hand really did feel like Lauren. He could have sworn he heard her. Smelled her. Tasted her.

But she was a phantasm of his reverie. And that's all she ever would be.

Because as much as she wanted him and he wanted her, Lauren didn't date cops.

And all Isaac ever wanted to be was a cop.

7

.

IT WAS SATURDAY NIGHT, and Lauren was headed over to Bianca's for wine night.

Finally.

She needed her girls to help her sort through the confusing and wanton thoughts in her head. Because after spending as much time with Isaac as she had been, she was more wanton than ever. She stared longingly at Idris Elba in her nightstand drawer the previous night after Isaac left. Wishing, praying, willing her body to be healed enough that she could take matters—and needs—into her own hands and rub one out to release the stress.

No such luck.

She was a new mother, and her body was hell-bent on reminding her of that for another few weeks.

Once again, they enjoyed dinner together, this time soup and biscuits. Isaac helped her bathe Ike again after another blowout—her kid was a serious shitter—and then he took Penny home around nine thirty. It wasn't a routine yet, but she could feel it starting. The comfort level between them was growing, as well as the friendship.

But she wanted more.

She wanted to jump his bones and grind them to dust, sit on his face until he struggled to breathe and have him pull her ponytail so hard her scalp burned.

But they couldn't.

At least not in real life. Her fantasies were another story, and the longer she went without Idris Elba between her thighs, the more depraved and filthy her fantasies about Isaac became.

Was she in over her head, pursuing a friendship with the hot cop? What if he started to date someone else? Would she be jealous? Would he stop coming over?

Eventually, Penny would be old enough she wouldn't have to kitten-sit. What then?

Was this friendship destined to be short-lived anyway?

She hoped not.

As much as she wanted to see the man naked and feel his muscles beneath her fingertips and his cock between her legs, she didn't want to lose his friendship, more than anything else. It was a fast and furious friendship. One born almost out of necessity at first, but overnight, it had grown into something so much richer.

With Ike in the stretchy wrap and her big puffy coat over top of them, she heaved the diaper bag over her shoulder and balanced the plate of peanut butter cookies she'd baked that morning on her one hand and held a bottle of wine in the other.

It was tradition that they each brought a snack to share, as well as a bottle of wine. Though Bianca always had more than enough booze, the polite thing to do was to not drink your friend and a single mother of three out of house and home.

Grateful that it was only a two-hundred-yard stroll across

the complex, she bowed her head to battle the wind and kept her eyes peeled for any slippery spots on the road.

In no time she was using the back of her hand and one knuckle to rap on the door. Bianca's kids were most likely already in bed, and as a new mother herself, she knew better than to ring the doorbell.

One of the gifts she received from a friend back home was a sign to hang on her door. It read: *You wake the baby, you take the baby. Text, call or knock, but do NOT ring the doorbell under any circumstance.*

She'd yet to put the sign up, but she could only imagine that in a few months, when Ike's naps became more routine and more cherished by her, that sign would be super-glued to the front door.

Bianca swung the door open, looking as lovely as ever. She made the *gimme gimme* motion with her hands, and Lauren handed off the wine and tray of cookies.

"I meant for you to hand me the baby, but wine and cookies are a close second," her friend said with a quiet laugh, closing the door behind them both.

Lauren ditched her coat and wet boots and followed Bianca into the house. The flush of a toilet and running of the faucet in the bathroom off the kitchen said Celeste was already there.

Bianca set the cookies and wine down on the counter, then went for Lauren's wrap, pulling a warm, curled-up and snoring Ike from inside.

Rolling her eyes but grateful to be relieved of her child for a bit, Lauren handed Bianca a blanket from the diaper bag. Not saying a word, Bianca draped it over Ike, who was still sound asleep on her shoulder, and began patting his bum. "I miss this stage," she finally said, pressing her nose to the top of his head. "They smell so freaking good."

Lauren smiled and went about opening the wine bottle.

Soft rock played gently in the background, and the women maneuvered around one another in companionable silence.

That was one thing she'd quickly come to learn and love about her two best friends. They didn't always need to be talking or making noise.

A mother of three, Bianca relished any silence. And Celeste had a moody—albeit sweet and lovely—fifteen-year-old, so she too took solace in the quiet and peace.

It'd taken Lauren a bit of getting used to when they started having these wine nights, the lack of talking, but she soon came to enjoy it.

It wasn't always like that either. Sometimes they were cutting each other off nonstop because they had so much to say. But other days, they just sat together and enjoyed the peace. Those were the days when Bianca had had a more challenging afternoon with the kids. They could always tell when Bianca was having a tough go with her children because she made fried food for a snack, had two wine bottles sitting on the counter and stayed quiet.

It seemed today was one of those days.

"What'd you bring?" Celeste asked.

Lauren slid the tray closer to her redheaded friend. "Peanut butter cookies. You?"

"Crab cakes. They're in the fridge."

Lauren scooted around her friend, opened Bianca's fridge and pulled out a plate of nine crab cakes. Her mouth watered. She was born in Nebraska but moved to Utah when she was six. So she hadn't eaten a ton of seafood growing up, let alone fresh-caught. But since moving to the Pacific Northwest, she could not get enough fresh-caught everything. Salmon, cod, halibut, crab, prawns, scallops, oysters, mussels. If it came from the ocean but didn't squeak like a dolphin, Lauren would eat it and love it—guaranteed.

"I made deep-fried shrimp wontons, which are on that plate over there, and I have a spinach and artichoke dip in the oven," Bianca said softly, kissing Ike on the side of the head. "And those melba toast crackers on the counter are meant to go with it." She closed her eyes and swayed, her expression serene.

Even though Lauren hadn't known Bianca long, the woman had quickly become one of her best and closest friends.

A Seattle native, Bianca moved back to the Emerald City from Palm Springs after her husband cheated on her with his secretary and got her pregnant. She was starting over. Her and her three kids. Thank goodness she had her parents, brothers and their women in Seattle to help.

"Lauren, bring the food to the coffee table when you can," Bianca said with almost a hum to her voice. "I'm busy with baby snuggles." Not bothering to glance back at either Celeste or Lauren, Bianca took off to the living room with Ike.

"Rough day, I take it?" Lauren asked Celeste as they piled everything into their arms.

Celeste nodded, and her green eyes went wide. "Winter break gets longer and longer the older your kids get. The first few days are fine and even fun. And then they turn into little sugar-buzzed monsters. She says they've been fighting with each other a lot."

That explained the already half-finished bottle of wine on the counter and Bianca's almost catatonic state.

They joined their friend in the living room and set everything down on the coffee table.

Bianca's eyes were closed, her lips pressed against Ike's head.

In the six months that Lauren had known Bianca, the woman had done a true transformation. Not only physically but also mentally. Emotionally.

When they first met, Bianca was hot off her separation and was struggling to get her kids situated in Seattle and in their new townhouse. She was also damn near skeletal.

She'd confided in Lauren and Celeste that during everything going down with her husband and their divorce, she'd developed an eating disorder. She said what she put in her mouth felt like the only control she had left in her life. She was also too stressed out to eat, and it showed. Not a big woman, Bianca had weighed less than a hundred pounds when Lauren met her. It was frightening.

But as she and the kids began to adjust to their new life, and the wine nights started, Bianca began to gain weight. Now, she looked amazing. She had curves again. Tits and an ass. And her dark brown hair had a shine to it Lauren hadn't noticed before.

Taking their seats on their respective couch corners, Lauren and Celeste curled their legs under their bodies, balanced their wineglasses in their hands and waited for Bianca to open her eyes.

"Any time now," Celeste said with a chuckle. "Unless this is all you want to do tonight. Sit in silence, get drunk and eat until we explode."

Lauren chuckled and sipped her wine.

Bianca slowly peeled one lid open. "I'm meditating. Give me a break. You have one child, she's perfect, and she doesn't argue with herself."

Celeste snorted. "Yeah, but she argues with me."

Bianca's gaze swiveled to Lauren. "And you have one child and *he's* perfect and his head smells like heaven and miracles and *he* doesn't argue with himself ... *or* you."

Lauren pursed her lips to keep herself from smiling. This was Bianca's way of saying she'd had a rough day and just needed a minute.

She could have all the minutes she needed.

"Fair enough. But I thought you guys might like to know that Isaac is friends with Zak and has been invited to the New Year's Eve party tomorrow night. We're actually going together." Lauren took another sip of her wine before leaning over to scoop a bunch of piping hot spinach and artichoke dip onto a cracker.

That got Bianca's attention. Both brown eyes popped open, and her friend sat up, causing Ike to grunt in protest. "Are you two seeing each other? Are you going to the party *together together?*" Lauren went to reply, but Bianca shook her head. "Does that mean I will be the only single person at this party?" She made a face. "Ugh. All the more reason for me to just stay home and get super drunk by myself and ring in the new year with Jason Momoa upstairs."

Just like Lauren's vibrator was named Idris Elba, Bianca had named hers Jason Momoa. Celeste called her battery-operated boyfriend Henry Cavill.

"We are not going together *together*," she said. "We realized we were invited to the same party, and he offered to be the designated driver so I could enjoy the evening with my friends and wine."

"That was really nice of him," Celeste said, nibbling on a cookie. "But you still plan to suck his face at midnight, right?"

"I doubt I'll make it to midnight and no."

Her friends rolled their eyes.

"He's a cop. I don't—I *can't* date a cop."

More eye rolling.

Bianca switched Ike to the other side of her shoulder and resumed patting his little butt. "Last time I checked, you weren't the leader of some crime family. Why can't you date a cop?"

"Because of the family curse."

"You date a cop, you turn into frog?" Celeste snorted.

"No. You fall in love with a cop, the cop dies."

Brows narrowed at her in both skepticism and confusion. She rolled her eyes. "My grandfather, my mom's dad, was a cop. He died on duty. Was stabbed in the neck from behind during a raid on an outlaw motorcycle club that was running illegal firearms. My dad, another cop, was killed on duty. He was called out to a domestic disturbance and was shot in the head. And then finally, my aunt, or my great aunt." She paused and wrinkled her nose. "My mom's cousin's husband. What does that make her to me? We just called her my aunt."

"Works for me," Celeste said. "But I think the correct term would be your first cousin once removed."

Bianca nodded. "Yes, that's correct."

Lauren shrugged. "Anyway, my mom's cousin's husband was a police officer too. He was an undercover cop in the gang unit. He went into prison alive and undercover but came out in a body bag."

Celeste and Bianca both blew out long, loud breaths.

"Jesus," Celeste said. "That's a lot of dead cops."

"Right? The Russo women are cursed. That's my mom's maiden name. I just can't live my life wondering if it's a family curse and I'm dooming the man I fall in love with to death. Are the women in my family jinxed? If I marry an office supplies salesman, would he die from a gangrenous paper cut? I don't know. But being a cop is a dangerous job and just increases the likelihood." Plus, she'd promised her mother.

"You're being a touch dramatic here," Celeste said gently. "I don't think your family is cursed. Cops are first responders. Their job is not easy or safe."

"Exactly. I saw what my dad's death did to my mother. It destroyed her. She lived every day in fear that he wouldn't come home, and then the day he didn't, she nearly died herself. I was only five when my father was killed, but I still remember him. My mother may have remarried, but Bruce Cameron was *the* love of her life." She finished off the rest of her wine and took a deep breath. "It just sucks that I want him as badly as I do."

Understanding and sorrow filled her friends' eyes, particularly Celeste's. She was a widow. Her husband, Declan, had been her high school sweetheart. They got pregnant with Sabrina while still in high school but married and were happy until he had a horrific construction accident eight years ago. She'd only just put herself back into the dating pool, where she found Max, Sabrina's math teacher, and the two seemed perfect for each other.

"I get it," Celeste finally said, her green eyes damper than before. "I *really* get it. But as we all know, the heart wants what the heart wants."

"It's too soon to know what my heart wants. It's my clit and vag that are doing all the talking."

Bianca made a guttural noise in her throat. "Amen, sister. Jason Momoa has been *pretty* damn busy lately. Poor bugger gets little reprieve these days."

"So what are you going to do about New Year's Eve, then?" Celeste asked Lauren. "You want us to duct-tape your panties to your skin so you're not tempted to run off into an empty room with him?"

"Baby chute is still mending, thanks," Lauren said dryly. "I don't know what to do. I just know that I *can't* date him. I *can't* fall in love with him. But I don't want to stop spending time with him. I also know that the more I spend time with him, the more likely I will want to date him and I will most definitely fall in love with him, and then ultimately into bed with him, because let's face it, I have very little willpower when it comes to a man with big hands, nice traps and a talented tongue."

"Don't we all," Bianca muttered, sipping her wine with one hand while her other hand cradled Ike's butt.

"What about a no-strings thing?" Celeste asked, but then

she waved her hand in dismissal. "Never mind. That would be torture. You'd inevitably fall in love with the man like you said, and then you'd be right where you don't want to be."

Exactly.

"Oh, the pickle," Bianca said. "To bone the hot cop or not bone the hot cop."

There was a little more to it than that, but yes. That was the gist of her problem. Though it was more like, to continue a friendship with the hot cop or sever ties completely before she gave in to her baser instincts and straddled his face, ultimately falling in love with him in the process.

Leaning forward, she grabbed a deep-fried wonton and a napkin. "Just a day in the life of yours truly." She bit into the wonton. It was greasy, savory, spicy and delicious.

"So what's his name?" Celeste asked.

"What do you mean, *what's his name?*"

"Well, you call Max 'Professor Washboard.' What's Isaac's *name?*"

Grinning more to herself than her friends, she finished her wonton. "Foxy Sergeant Big Hands. Because his last name is Fox and he's a sergeant and his hands are fucking huge." Her eyes went wide as she remembered just how enormous Isaac's hands were and just how tiny her son's head looked cradled in them as he helped her dry him off after his bath.

Bianca shook her head. "Sergeant Foxy McBigHands."

"Oooh," Celeste purred. "I like that better. Sergeant Foxy McBigHands reporting for *duty.* Is there a crime in your panties you need solved, ma'am?"

"Ma'am, please turn off your vibrator and remove it. This is a crime scene and police investigation and we can't hear anything over all your moaning," Bianca added, before she and Celeste burst into laughter. "Poor Idris Elba, he must be collecting dust by now."

Lauren scowled at her friends, but it was all in jest. "I

swear I heard it turn itself on the other night just to taunt me."

Bianca and Celeste both chuckled and Celeste leaned over, grabbed the bottle of wine from the table and topped Lauren up. "Ah, cheer up. Before you know it, your vag and Idris will be reunited and you can forget all about Sergeant Foxy McBigHands. Or you can get him to babysit for you while you go on a date with an insurance broker or baker— you know, men with safe careers."

Lauren rolled her eyes and sipped her wine.

Ah, but there lay the problem.

She didn't want an insurance broker or a baker or any other guy for that matter. Safe job or a dangerous one.

She wanted Isaac. But Isaac was a cop, and curse or not, women in her family needed to stop falling in love with cops because it only ended badly—for everyone involved.

8

It was New Year's Eve, and Isaac had shown up to Lauren's house at six o'clock looking drop-dead fuckable. He knew he was early, but he also claimed to have a plan.

"Go shower, get ready and do your thing," he said, taking Ike from her arms before she even offered the baby to him. "I'm here early so you can get ready without any interruptions."

Smiling up at him, she tucked a strand of hair behind her ear and let her gaze roam his body from top to toe, pretending to not enjoy what she saw. "And then I'll hold him while you get ready." Her lip curled up, as if he didn't look like a model for J. Crew but rather a hobo on the train tracks.

His head reared back and he glanced down at his black dress shirt, brown loafers and dark wash jeans. "I thought I was ready. Is this not okay? Zak said it was casual."

She turned and headed down the hallway toward her bathroom. "Ah, I guess you'll be fine. Lipstick might help."

He was more than fine. He was delicious, and the scent of him when he'd walked in made her knees nearly buckle.

She was about to close her bedroom door when a meow at her feet had her stumbling.

"Oh, Penny, you little ghost."

Heavy footsteps down the wood floor hallway had her turning around. "Sorry," he said, holding Ike against his shoulder like a pro and scooping Penny up in his other hand. "She got away from me. She's getting fast."

He'd slid into this cat-dad role like a pro. And she had to admit, a baby against his chest was a good look for him too.

"Mallory and Sabrina are so excited to kitten-sit tonight. We'll pop by Celeste's on the way out and drop Penny off."

The concern in his eyes was endearing. "They know what they're doing with a kitten, right?"

She tried not to smile but failed, reached out and cupped his cheek. "Your baby will be safe with them, I promise."

His brows furrowed before he rolled his eyes and glanced at Ike. "Your mother is a smartass."

Chuckling, she jerked her chin toward the living room. "Go watch sports and scratch your balls or something. You know, manly shit. Let me get ready in peace."

His eyes went wide in mock disbelief. "That was the whole plan for coming here early." Shaking his head, he retreated down the hall. "Ungrateful woman we've got there, Ike. Telling us to go scratch our balls and watch sports. Sexist is what she is. What if we want to watch a baking show instead? Is there something wrong with that? Something *un*-manly?"

With a laugh that filled her heart near to bursting, she closed her door and stripped out of her housecoat and pajamas. There was no point getting dressed when she didn't go anywhere all day.

She hopped into the shower and let the warm water sluice over her body. Even though she hadn't fully recovered from childbirth, she was *feeling* healed. Not Idris Elba or a real man healed yet, but healed enough to let the scent of Isaac just now and the image of him in that dark shirt all confident and in full-on dad mode push all her right buttons.

Tilting her head back beneath the spray, she dipped two fingers into her pussy and spread her lips, finding her clit. It throbbed beneath her fingertip, and she flicked it, making her entire body spasm and her free hand reach out to the wall for support.

He'd started showing her his cocky side recently, particularly with that comment earlier in the week about big hands, big shoes, and that all Isaacs had big cocks. Was it in jest, or was there actually a biological correlation between big hands and endowment?

She hoped there was.

But then again, he was off limits, so maybe she hoped there wasn't.

Either way, in her fantasy, Isaac was well-hung and had the tongue of a god.

She imagined him surprising her in the shower, coming in behind her and cupping her heavy breasts. His thumb and forefinger twisting and tugging her nipples until she gasped and arched her back, letting her head fall to his shoulder. He was rock-solid behind her. A pillar of strength and safety.

One hand slid down her torso from her breasts and a finger dipped between her lips, touching her clit but not staying there. He explored deeper, pushing one finger and then two into her channel, where she contracted around him and bucked into his hand, forcing his fingers deeper.

His thumb pressed against her clit and she shivered, her knees threatening to give out. "Stay with me, baby," he murmured against her ear, releasing her breast with the other hand and bringing it up to the front of her neck. He kept her head tilted back and raked his teeth along her jaw and the side of her throat.

His fingers pumped, his thumb flicked and his teeth scraped. But she wanted more. She wanted all of him inside her. She wanted to straddled his face, taste him as she took him in her mouth and milk his cock as he came inside her.

"You're going to come hard for me, baby," he whispered, pushing her head back even farther. "Squeeze my fingers. Feel me fuck you with them. You like that?"

"Yes," she panted.

"Say my name, Lauren. Say my name as you come."

"Isaac ..."

His fingers sped up and curled inside her, his thumb twiddled double-time and she brought one hand to her breast and tugged on a nipple. That did it.

She exploded around him.

"Oh God, Isaac."

"That's right, baby. Come for me. Come hard."

She pulled even harder on her nipple, and her hips shot forward at the same time her chin tilted to the ceiling. She squeezed her eyes shut and rode out the waves as they crashed through her from her center outward, rippling along her arms to the tips of her fingers and down each leg until she felt it in her toes.

And just as each wave hits the shore only to be tugged back out to sea, the orgasm retreated, settling between her legs once more until all that was left was a pleasant throb.

Lauren opened her eyes and blinked through the spray.

Isaac was gone.

Those were her fingers between her legs, her hand on her breast, pulling at her nipple. She scraped her thumbnail over her engorged clit and trembled before pulling her fingers free and beginning to wash her body.

She forgot how good an orgasm by her own hand could be. It'd been a while since she'd done that. A while since she'd been able to reach. And imagining that her fingers were

Isaac's fingers was even better. Too bad that was all she could ever have of him—the fantasy.

By the time she shut off the water, Lauren felt like a million dollars. Clean, warm and in post-orgasm heaven.

Could she talk Isaac into blowing off the party with her? Just curling up on the couch together, drinking wine and eating nachos as the ball dropped?

Was she being selfish, pursuing a friendship with him when she knew he wanted more?

Absolutely not. Give your head a shake, woman.

She tossed a towel around her body and wrapped one around her hair before she strode out into her bedroom.

What an asinine thought. She was not stringing him along. She wanted his friendship. She also wanted his dick, but that was off-limits. Friendship would have to do. But if that wasn't enough for him, if he *had* to be more than just her friend, than that said more about him than it did about her, and she didn't want that kind of a person in her or her son's life anyway.

She'd laid out an outfit for that evening on her bed earlier that day but was already having second thoughts about it. Isaac was in jeans. Did she need to be all uncomfortable in a skirt? Did the skirt even fit? She hadn't had a chance to try it on yet.

This new body of hers was going to take some getting used to.

Tossing her skirt into the pile on a chair she'd designated as the "Don't throw away but unsure if it fits" pile, she dug through her drawer until she found her favorite pair of stretchy black velour pants. They were cute, they were comfy and they were soft. Dressed up with a sparkly gold top that was loose where she needed it to be, minimal makeup, and her hair blow-dried and in chunky curls around her face, she looked every bit ready for a New Year's Eve party. Now, whether she would last until the new year was debatable, but at least she was ready to ring it in if she was able to stay awake.

She didn't bother with lipstick. Bianca and Celeste told her not to bother with lipstick for the next two years. Mothers kiss their babies way too much, and the kid just ends up looking like a leper if you've been wearing lipstick.

Her knee-high black leather boots were already by the door. She just needed to grab her men, pick up the cat and their host gift of some cool artisanal soap she bought at an outdoor market earlier that summer, and they were good to go.

Careful not to let them know she was ready, she gently opened her bedroom door and crept down the hallway toward the living room. The television flickered light and the sound of sports highlights drifted toward her.

She peered around the corner, remaining out of sight.

God, how she wished she had her camera.

Both Isaacs, big and little, were sitting in front of the television, watching sports, and they each had a hand between their legs.

Ike was facing forward toward the TV in the crook of Isaac's arm, his eyes wide, almost unblinking.

"Was this what you wanted?" Isaac asked, not bothering to look at her. "Us being manly, watching sports and scratching our balls?" He gave his junk an extra healthy over the pants rub.

Her body tightened in response.

Rolling her eyes, she stepped out of she shadows. "How'd you know I was there?"

"I'm a cop. I'm trained to have bionic hearing."

She wandered around to stand in front of them, her hands on her hips. "Really? They can train that into you?"

He lifted one brow at her. "No, but there's a floorboard

next to the kitchen island that squeaks when you step on it in a certain place. I heard you."

She rolled her eyes again. "I'm going to assume my son put his hand there on his own?"

Isaac shrugged, and his lip lifted on one side. "I didn't do it. Kid's just doing what his mom told him to do."

Snorting, she stepped around the other side of the coffee table and scooped up her mesmerized son. "Come here, baby."

"Quite the shower," Isaac murmured, turning off the television and picking up a sprawled-out Penny from the other side of him on the couch.

Lauren nearly dropped Ike. "What?"

"These walls aren't sound-proof." He was having a hard time keeping a straight face. In fact, he wasn't even trying. His grin was massive, his attitude cocky as hell. "Unless that was your neighbor having an early New Year's Eve celebration next door and her husband *also* happens to be named Isaac?"

Propping Ike against her shoulder, she stood in the center of her living room, wishing that a hole would open in the floor and swallow her up.

He'd heard her?

He'd heard her doing *that?*

Had she actually said his name out loud?

She didn't think she had.

She thought that'd all been part of her fantasy. Just like when he told her to say his name and to come. He hadn't been there in the shower with her, and yet she'd heard him. Her words were in her head too, right? RIGHT?

He grabbed his jacket off the back of the recliner and put it on, shifting Penny to either hand until she could take her place in the front of his coat. "It's okay. I'm not *mad.*" He was still fucking smiling. Laughing, actually. "I mean, you've already told me you think I'm sex on a stick. It's nice to know

I'm getting some somewhere with you, even if it is in your shower fantasies."

Without hesitation, he took Ike from her and went about putting the baby in the bucket car seat. They'd never gone anywhere together in a vehicle before, and yet he was already taking over the duty of getting Ike ready.

She hadn't moved from her spot of mortification.

Her face was on fire. Her skin prickling. Her gut in tight, tangled knots.

He grabbed the blanket from the bouncy chair and tucked it around a buckled-in Ike, then found a knit cap with owls on it and plopped it on the baby's head.

Lauren still had not moved.

"Get your coat, woman," he said, glancing around the living room like he'd lost something. "I think he needs another blanket. Is there—never mind. I see one." He grabbed the green one Ike was given by the midwife and tucked that around him too. The baby looked as snug as a bug.

Ignoring her, Isaac went to the foyer and slid into his shoes.

"Okay, well, I guess Ike and I are going to go party. You can stand there and ring in the new year with your embarrassment. But we're going to go get our dance on." He walked back into the living room and grabbed the bucket seat. "Would it help you to know I've jerked off like four times in the last week to thoughts of you?"

Lauren's bottom lip nearly hit the damn floor.

Isaac rolled his eyes. "I guess not."

Now all she could picture was him. Naked, hard and touching himself as he thought of her.

Oh my God. This was torture.

The cruelest, most painful, most outrageously awful form of torture she'd ever experienced. Not that she'd experienced a lot of different forms of torture, but this was brutal.

Rolling his eyes, he set Ike's car seat down on the floor and gripped both her shoulders. "Lauren, it's okay. I'm sorry if I embarrassed you. I'm not embarrassed. I'm flattered. And I figured since I now know I was the leading man in your reverie, it was only fair that you knew you were the leading woman in mine. All harmless. This doesn't have to change anything. We're still friends, right?" He blinked at her in earnest.

Yeah, they were still friends. But he was making it harder and harder for her to keep her resolve and remain *just* friends.

Grumbling, she jerked his big, warm hands from her shoulders and stomped around him to go and grab her boots and coat. "You could have just *not* said anything."

He was behind her, holding the car seat again. That big, stupid, gorgeous smile was back on his face. She wanted to smack it off him. "Yeah, but where's the fun in that?"

"Happy New Year!" Zak and Aurora cheered as they stood in their foyer and welcomed Isaac, Lauren and Ike into their home.

Isaac had only been to Zak's house a couple of times before, but never for a big party. He knew most of the guys, as they all went to Zak's gym and Zak helped them train, as he did Isaac, but he hadn't met many of their women.

Aurora drew him in for a hug. "Didn't know you were dating Lauren," she whispered into his ear, her dark blonde hair tickling his chin. "Is this new?"

He pulled away and smiled down at the woman who was nearly a foot shorter than him. "We're just friends."

Aurora's brown eyes glimmered. "Sure, you are." She peered down into the bucket car seat, where a wide-awake Ike looked like he wasn't sure if he should lose his shit or shit himself.

He had that look a lot.

"Hey, Ike. Dawson is really excited to finally meet you." She glanced at Lauren, who was shedding her coat and hanging it up with the rest of the guests' jackets. "Zara glommed onto my kid about an hour ago and has refused to give him back." She stretched her arms above her head and yawned. "Not that I'm complaining.

Zak glanced down at his wife skeptically.

She rolled her eyes. "Okay, not that I'm complaining *that* much."

Isaac and Lauren chuckled, and Isaac hung up his coat, grabbed the car seat by the handle and hauled it toward the living room, where all the noise was.

The house was packed. They appeared to be the last to arrive.

Not waiting for Lauren's permission, he unbuckled Ike from his car seat, propped the baby on his shoulder and went off to mingle.

"Beer? Scotch? Gin?" Zak asked, slapping Isaac on the shoulder.

"One beer," he said. "I promised Lauren she could let her hair down tonight and I would be the designated driver home."

Mitch, Mason and Adam all narrowed their brows at him. "You're seeing Lauren?"

He wished.

"We're just friends."

"Are you the cop who delivered her baby on the interstate?" Liam asked, wedging his way into the circle.

Zak returned and handed Isaac a bottle of San Camanez Ale.

Taking a sip, Isaac nodded. "I was there to help her deliver her own baby, but yes, that was me."

A bunch of his friends all shook their heads in disbelief.

"I don't know why I didn't put two and two together," Mason said, his heavily tattooed arms bunching as he switched one of his twin infant sons to his other arm before lifting his beer bottle up to his mouth. "That's crazy, man. And now you two are *friends*?" He waggled his eyebrows playfully.

"We're friends."

Smug, knowing smiles drifted around their group.

"Sure," Liam said. "Richelle and I were *just friends* for a while too."

"You were not. You were enemies, then friends with bene-fits, and then you wore her down until she finally relented and married your sorry ass," Liam's brother Scott said, nudging his way into their group by elbowing his brother in the ribs.

Liam shrugged and sipped his tumbler of what was undoubtably scotch. "It worked. She's mine. That's all that matters."

A hard slap on the back, followed by a squeeze to his shoulder, had Isaac moving over and making room. Aaron, another dad, gym-buff and redheaded with tattoos, gave him a nod. "Hey, buddy, how's it going?"

Aaron, who had served in the Navy and as a SEAL, was a regular at Zak's gym as well, and he and Isaac had hit it off pretty quickly. However, unlike Isaac, who had seen some shit in Iraq that still gave him nightmares, Aaron had seen a lot more shit and *done* some crazy shit during his time as a SEAL, and that kind of thing stayed with a man. He was usually pretty quiet and always seemed to be stewing about something. But once in a while, he let his guard down and relaxed enough to have a beer and crack a smile—once in a while.

"Where's Weston?" Isaac asked, taking in both Aaron and his fiancée, Isobel's, empty arms.

"Iz's parents offered to watch Soph and Weston for us for the night," he said, his deep voice a rough grumble as he took a long pull from his beer.

"Nice."

Aaron jerked his chin toward Ike. "Whose kid?"

"Lauren's."

Aaron's blue eyes widened. "Lauren Green?" He turned his big body around to scan the living room until he found Lauren. She was off in a corner chatting with Celeste, Bianca and Aurora. "You guys together?"

"Not yet," Liam said. "But give it time."

"Who are you?" Scott asked, turning to his brother. "You used to be the love cynic. Now you're the love guru?"

Liam's smile was placid. "What can I say? I'm a changed man. Love will do that to you."

Several of the men shook their heads and laughed. Apparently, before Liam and Richelle got together, Liam had been the biggest cynic about love, relationships and happily ever after. Now, however, it appeared that the leopard had changed his spots and believed everyone had a fairy-tale ending in their future.

"I hear Mallory and Sabrina are watching your cat?"

Isaac turned around at the familiar voice.

Max, another guy from the gym who Isaac didn't know very well and who wasn't a single dad, was grinning.

Isaac gripped his beer bottle between two fingers while still cradling Ike and shook Max's hand. "I didn't know you were coming. Good to see you."

"Lauren hasn't told you I'm seeing Celeste?"

They all made room for Max. The space in front of Zak's fireplace next to the enormous Christmas tree where they were all standing was getting tighter and tighter.

Isaac shook his head. "No, she hasn't mentioned it."

Then again, neither had Max. Isaac didn't know he was seeing somebody. Relationships weren't something any of them really discussed at the gym. They talked about sports, weights, food and, once in a while, politics. Though that could be a dangerous topic if they weren't careful about eavesdroppers. Zak had his own political views, but he sold gym memberships to everyone no matter who they voted for.

"I just moved into the complex, too," Max said, sipping a clear liquid from a glass similar to Liam's. "Had to get out of my old place."

Scott shivered. "Yeah, man. Snakes should not be pets. I don't blame you one bit."

They had all heard the story about Max's neighbor with the giant-ass python that kept escaping and wound up on Max's motorcycle. Just the thought of finding something like that gave Isaac the willies. He didn't have a fear of them like Max did, but he also didn't have a penchant for things with scales either.

Liam elbowed Isaac. "If you move in with Lauren, you and Max will be neighbors. Hey, hey."

Every one of them rolled their eyes.

"You're a dork," Aaron said to Liam.

Up until that moment, Ike had been happy as a clam to just hang out on Isaac's shoulder and participate in guy-talk, but he must have either smelt, heard or noticed his mother, because the kid's attitude shifted and he began to mewl. Then the face smashing on Isaac's shoulder started.

"Uh-oh," a bunch of the dads said together.

"Kid's hungry. Must have heard Lauren laugh a second ago," Mason said. "Warren and Wyatt do the same thing."

Zak nodded. "Dawson too."

Like a ghost, but more like a mother penguin in a rookery who heard the cry of her chick, Lauren appeared at his side. "I can take him."

Reluctantly, he passed Ike off to his mother, but not before pressing his lips to the little guy's head. He glanced down at Lauren. "Bring him back when he's full."

Her gaze turned curious.

"What? I like hanging out with him. I'm the *strong* male presence he needs in his life."

Snorts echoed from the men around him.

Lauren's mouth twisted, and she lifted one brow. "Is that so?"

He nodded, giving her a grin that made her pupils dilate and her nostrils flare. He hadn't had a chance to tell her how beautiful she looked that night, not that she didn't look hot all the time, but she looked exceptionally hot tonight.

Glancing at her empty wineglass, he took it from her. "Go find a quiet place to feed him and I'll bring you a refill."

Her smile turned demure, but she nodded.

"The study has a great recliner where Aurora likes to nurse Dawson," Zak chimed in. "It's just off the dining room."

Lauren thanked him and took a grunting and hungry Ike toward the kitchen.

He made to head after her to the kitchen to fill up her wineglass but was stopped by a hand on his shoulder.

"Bro, you are in deep. You sure you want this?" It was Mason, with Aaron beside him.

Mason shifted the twin he had into the crook of his arm.

"Sure, she's hot and the kid is cute, but do you really want to take on *all* of that?" Aaron asked. His blue eyes held a skepticism Isaac couldn't place. Was Aaron testing him? Looking out for Lauren?

"I've been a single parent to a newborn," Mason said. "It's

not easy. I know what Lauren is going through as a single mom. She's grasping at any and all help offered to her because most of the time she's doing it all by herself. But I also know that if Lowenna hadn't been all in with me, I wouldn't have kept her around. You can't have casual relationships the way we once did when there are kids involved. It's not possible. Too many hearts are at play. Ike will fall in love with you and you with him. You need to consider the kid too."

Aaron grunted in agreement.

Isaac shifted back and forth on his feet, gauging the two men in front of him. Two men just as big as he was, two men who had found love and had families—something Isaac wanted.

He knew that now.

"I'm whatever she needs me to be. She's already said that anything more than friendship is off limits, that she doesn't date cops. And I'd rather be her friend than nothing at all."

Aaron gave Mason the side-eye, which Mason returned.

Clearing his throat, Isaac continued on through the kitchen to refill Lauren's wine.

"Why doesn't she date cops?" Mason asked, he and Aaron following Isaac into the kitchen. They replenished their own drinks.

He topped up Lauren's wine and then popped a canape into his mouth. "Her dad was a cop, and he died on duty. Says there's some family curse involved and the women in her family can't date cops or they die. She also says she can't do that to herself or her kid. Always worrying if I'd come home from work or not."

Aaron grunted again. "Fair enough. Some chicks flock to guys with dangerous jobs. We called them army groupies."

"We call them badge bunnies or holster sniffers," Isaac

confirmed. "But Lauren's like the total opposite of that. My job is *too* dangerous, and she wants no part of it."

"Can you blame her if her dad died on duty?" Mason asked.

No, he couldn't. But it still sucked.

"And you can do just the friends thing?" Aaron asked, turning his head when Isobel approached.

She wrapped her arm around his waist, the top of her head barely reaching his shoulder. "What are we talking about, gentlemen?" she asked, pinning a look on Isaac that immediately made him squirm. He liked Isobel. In fact, he liked all his friends' wives and girlfriends—at least the ones he'd met so far—but there was something about Aaron's woman that made him a little anxious. Like she was looking past your exterior and straight into what made you tick, directly into your heart and what—or *who* resided inside. Was she trying to draw out all of your secrets?

Probably.

And that freaked him the fuck out. Because Isaac had a lot of them.

He'd heard the jokes from some of the other guys—and women—not to let Isobel shake your hand because she wouldn't let go until she'd uncovered every hidden compartment of your soul.

He believed it.

Only he, God, and his therapist knew all the dark corners, the painful memories and horrific moments in Isaac's past.

He kept them hidden for a reason.

His mother and sister knew the big one, the one that still haunted him, that followed him like a noose around his neck, because they'd been there too. But the rest of the memories, the terrors, his tortured past and necessary evils, were his burden and his burden alone.

They never spoke of that night after it happened. His

father had gone to prison, his mother, sister and he to Arizona. He went to therapy and was expected to talk about "the incident" there. He did because he had to. But his mother never once spoke of it, and Natalie had been too young to remember. He wished he'd been too young to remember too.

"We're talking about Lauren and Isaac," Aaron said, pecking Isobel on the top of her head. "He wants her. She won't date a cop. Something about a family curse." He rolled his eyes. "Sounds hokey to me."

Isaac blinked away the dark thoughts and cleared his throat, shooting Aaron a glare. "So much for the bro code of secrecy," he muttered.

Aaron smirked.

Isobel nodded. "Ah, yes. I've heard the murmurs."

What murmurs? There were murmurs? Was Lauren murmuring about him to her friends?

"Is she nursing Ike in the study?" Isobel asked.

Isaac nodded. "I'm just refilling her wine."

"I can take it to her," she offered.

He shook his head. "I'll do it."

The three people staring back at him exchanged smiles.

"Be careful, Isaac," Isobel said, dipping a crab puff into dip before popping it into her mouth. "It's not just Lauren and Ike's hearts you need to worry about." With a final glance and a genuine but still disconcerting smile, she steered her and Aaron back toward the living room.

Mason gave Isaac a final grimace and shrug before catching the eye of Lowenna, who held their other son, and he went to meet her near the stairs.

Rolling his eyes, Isaac filled a small plate with food because she was probably starving and went to find Lauren.

LAUREN FOUGHT BACK another yawn and leaned her head on the back of the couch.

"Uh-oh," Richelle said next to her, snuggling a snoozing Ike. "That's like your tenth yawn in the last hour. Are you going to make it to midnight?"

Lauren blinked a bunch of times and sipped her wine. "What time is it?"

Richelle glanced at the clock on Zak and Aurora's mantel. "Ten thirty."

"Shit."

"It's how warm it is in here, and the wine," Celeste said, patting Lauren on the knee. "A potent combination for an already tired mama."

All Lauren could do was nod.

It'd been great party so far, with lots of laughter, incredible food made by Paige, and a few entertaining games. But as much as she wished she could last until the clock struck twelve and ring in the new year with her friends, she knew she wouldn't be able to.

"Isaac seems great," Bianca whispered, sitting on the coffee table in front of Lauren and cradling a stemless glass of white wine. "And he loves Ike."

"I had to wrestle the baby away from him," Richelle put in. "Possessive fucker."

Lauren smiled but didn't bother to open her eyes. "He's really taken to him."

"And have you?" Richelle elbowed her.

She had. So damn much. But they just couldn't. She couldn't.

"Family curse has her keeping her distance," Celeste said.

Violet was sitting on the other side of Richelle and leaned forward. "Family curse?"

Thankfully, Bianca could tell Lauren wasn't interested in explaining things again and took over for her. By the time she was done, all the women at the party were sitting around Lauren with sad faces, shaking their heads.

"That's tough," Isobel said, resting her hand on Lauren's arm.

Lauren knew better than to let Isobel touch her for very long, otherwise, Iz would use her freaky voodoo empath powers to learn all of Lauren's secrets. Not that she had very many, but still.

Lauren pulled her arm from beneath Iz's hand and reached for her wineglass off the side table. "Yeah, we're cursed. At least my mother thinks so."

"But the heart wants what the heart wants," Celeste whispered.

"Right now, my heart isn't the one doing the talking," Lauren said plainly. "Sure, we've become close over the last week, but it's *only* been a week. My heart has no voice in the matter."

"Your clit and vag, on the other hand ..." Richelle said with a wry smile. "Those ladies are screaming, aren't they?"

Loudly.

"And harmless fun is off the table too?" Eva, Celeste's sister, asked. She looked an awful lot like her sister: red hair, green eyes, killer smile.

Lauren nodded. It was too much of a slippery slope. She knew it would be. Isaac was too great a guy. The lines would blur so fast, she'd be in love with him before she could stop herself. And that's when the curse took hold.

Celeste shook her head. "She's worried she'd fall for him."

Isobel's sister, Tori, was holding her infant daughter, Grace, who appeared to be sleeping. She had perched herself on the arm of the chair her sister was in. "Maybe we can figure out a way to break the curse. Like a séance or conjuring or a spell of some kind."

All eyes fell to Isobel.

"What are you all looking at me for?" she asked, her expression disgruntled.

"You're the resident witch," Richelle said. "Don't you have a spell or something up your sleeve?"

Isobel actually managed to look hurt. "I'm not a *witch*."

"Wiccan. Sorceress. Voodoo Mama. Can't you lift the curse?" Lowenna, Mason's fiancée, rubbed Isobel's back from behind. "We're teasing, Iz. You know we love you."

Isobel grunted. "There's no way to break this curse." She glanced at Celeste with sorrow in her eyes. "I mean, Celeste's husband had a dangerous job too. He wasn't a cop, but it was still dangerous."

Celeste nodded. "That's true. Even if I knew the future and that Declan would die, I still would have married him. We had eleven amazing years together, as well as a beautiful daughter."

"My fiancée died of a tumor in his back," Violet chimed in. "And he was a ballet dancer. Nothing dangerous there, besides gnarly toes."

"And Mitch's wife died in a car accident," Paige added, holding one of Lowenna's twins on her lap. Zara held the other one.

"Atlas's wife died of cancer. I don't think it's a curse. I think it's just really bad luck," Tessa said. She was Atlas's wife and a trauma therapist.

Lauren hadn't spoken much with Atlas at the parties she'd attended, he seemed rather the stoic type and typically grunted his replies. But Tessa was lovely and warm and someone Lauren really enjoyed spending time with.

Tessa tossed her long blonde hair behind her shoulder. "I mean my dad died trying to rescue hikers on a glacier. He was a helicopter pilot. I know what your mom went through, because my mom and I went through the same feelings every time he went to work. He was in the air and flying in some pretty rough weather. But he'd also been born to fly. He'd never wanted to be anything but a helicopter pilot. Before he could spell helicopter or even say it correctly, he would tell people he was going to fly them when he was older. And he did. He died doing what he loved. Even though I miss him, it's knowing he died doing what he loved and trying to save others that keeps me from spiraling. My dad was a hero. Just like Isaac is."

9

Even though he'd only "known" her for a week, he knew Lauren better than she thought he did. It was closing in on eleven, and just based on the way she'd been yawning during their group game of charades an hour ago, he was sure she was close to nodding off completely wherever she was now.

He found her and Ike surrounded by the women in the living room. They seemed to be having some kind of serious meeting of the minds, and all of them eyed him suspiciously when he broke through their circle.

"Excuse me, ladies," he said, stepping in to take Ike from Richelle. She'd had him for nearly an hour, and he wanted the little guy back.

Richelle glared at him, but it wasn't a death stare, more of a curious, almost wary look. "What makes you think I'm ready to give him up?" she asked, holding on tight to Ike and leaning away from Isaac.

He glanced at Lauren for a moment. She seemed to be enjoying the hard time Richelle was giving him. "How are you feeling?" he asked her, ignoring Richelle's attitude.

"I'm having a hard time keeping my eyes open, to be

honest," she said.

"Ready to go?"

Her gaze drifted across the faces of all her friends before she found his eyes again and nodded. "Yeah. I'm ready to go."

A few of the women whined and asked her to stay, but most of them were mothers and several of them new mothers, so they understood her fatigue. She wasn't the only woman who had ducked away on several occasions to nurse or change a diaper, and she certainly wasn't the only mother there with a severe case of the yawns.

"I'm sorry to be such a party pooper," she said, standing up and turning to all the women. "But chances are I'd be asleep before the ball drops anyway. Passed out on Zak's expensive couch with a big string of drool coming out of my mouth."

Isaac snorted, gave Richelle the *don't mess with me* look, and took Ike back.

"He's not *yours*," she said sassily.

"He's not yours, either," he shot back. "But I'm his ride home."

Richelle's lips twitched before breaking into a big smile. She faced Lauren. "I like him."

Lauren yawned again and stepped through the women, following Isaac and Ike to the perimeter of their women's brain trust. "Yeah, he's all right. A bit cocky. But I hear most cops are. A bit of a god complex, too." She glanced at Isaac and gave him a cheeky grin he wished he could kiss off her lips. "He's good with my kid though and sober right now, so I keep him around. He has his uses."

She had no idea how many *uses* he had. If only she'd let him show her.

They said their goodbyes, which took them another twenty minutes, and were shown out by their hosts, Zak and Aurora.

"We'll have to do this again soon," Aurora said, propping Dawson up on her shoulder.

"Definitely," Isaac said, gently swinging a bundled-up Ike in the car seat. The little guy had barely roused when he took him from Richelle and plopped him in his seat. He'd just stretched, made a goofy face, squeaked and then settled right back down.

If only Isaac could sleep that deep.

They waved goodbye and headed out to Isaac's truck. He had an automatic starter on his fob, so it was already running and toasty when they hopped in. The sky was clear and the stars out. It was going to freeze hard. He hoped everyone inside had sober rides home.

They all seemed responsible though, and he remembered hearing Atlas mention his co-worker's daughter, Kimmy, and a bunch of her high school friends were going to be making mega coin off their party by acting as a bunch of designated drivers.

Driving through the dark, quiet streets of Seattle, he glanced over at Lauren. Her head was on the headrest, her eyes closed. They hadn't spent much time together at the party, which bummed him out. He mainly chatted with the guys, and she was always surrounded by at least three women. Except when she ducked off to nurse Ike.

That seemed to be the only chance he got to get her alone.

He thought back to when he found her in Zak's study, alone, her eyes closed, humming softly to her son.

Not that anybody cared if the women nursed in front of everyone, but apparently with all the commotion, several of the babies became too distracted by all the people and wouldn't nurse, so most of the mothers preferred to go somewhere quiet and *boring*.

That first time she'd glanced up at him when he entered

Zak's study with her replenished wine and a plate of food, he thought his ribs were going to crack, his heart swelled so much.

"How did you know?" she asked, her smile magnetic and tears brimming in her eyes. "I'm absolutely starving."

He set the plate down on the side table next to her and handed her the wineglass.

She took a sip and shut her eyes. "Damn, these people know good wine."

"They know good food too. I hear Paige catered. The crab puffs are going like crazy, so I snagged you four in case there aren't any left when you go back out. Liam was going all chipmunk and filling his cheeks, the greedy fucker."

She glanced at the plate beside her, then up at Isaac. More tears filled her eyes.

Oh shit. Had he done something wrong?

"Are you allergic to crab?" he asked, reaching for the plate. "I had no idea. I'm so sorry. I can get rid of these."

She shook her head and laughed, touching his hand. "No, no. I'm not allergic to anything. It's ..." She swallowed and glanced up at him with glassy eyes and pink cheeks. "It's just like Christmas Eve. You bring me what I need before I even know I need it. I don't know what I did to deserve you ... to deserve your friendship, but ... thank you."

A plump tear slid down the crease of her nose and hung on her lip. He reached out and caught it with his thumb. "It's not entirely selfless," he said. "I'm getting something from you and Ike too. I like spending time with both of you."

Her chest rattled as she inhaled, her smile small, grim and thin.

"You're making it very hard for this to just remain a friendship."

Yeah, that was also his plan. That might be selfish, but he was going to do his damnedest to prove to Lauren that what they had, what they were building was worth taking a chance on. He was in this for the long game. Friendship or romance, he was in this to be a part of her and Ike's life.

His life had already become so much richer for knowing them both.

Chuckling, he grabbed the footstool and sat down on it. "Are you enjoying yourself tonight?"

She nodded. "I am. I'm glad you pushed me to come. I've been so cooped up in my little cocoon that I forgot how nice it is to chat with adults. Particularly other mothers. To hear that I'm not the only person awake five times a night and getting puked on is comforting, albeit also slightly depressing."

"It won't be forever, though," he said, resting his hand on her knee. An act that did not go unnoticed by her.

He didn't remove it, and the slight lift to the corner of her lips as she popped a crab puff into her mouth said he didn't have to. He pulled her socked foot into his lap and began to massage it, working his thumbs into the balls and the pads of her toes.

A groan of pleasure bubbled up her throat. She shut her eyes and leaned her head back in the recliner. "Damn, that feels good. And you're right, it won't be forever. I know that this time is fleeting. I mean, he's already three weeks old. And in that time, he's changed so much." She opened her eyes again and hit him with a look that he felt in the depths of his soul. Her tangible loneliness caused the air to grow dense around them. "But when I'm in the thick of it, up alone, covered in spit-up, exhausted and unable to console him for whatever reason, I feel alone. I feel like I'm failing at this whole motherhood thing. Like I'm failing at life. This wasn't how it was supposed to be."

"How was it supposed to be?"

She shrugged and glanced away, the blue in her eyes appearing extra dark. Tears brimming. "I dunno. Me *not* having to do it alone. Married to the father of my child. Or at the very least raising my son *with* him. With someone else. I was raised by a single mom for a time, and I know how hard it can be."

"I was raised by a single mom too. And it *is* hard. But you know what?"

She only gave him the side eye.

He had to push back his urge to laugh and tugged on her baby toe instead. "My mother is the strongest woman I have ever met. She was dealt a shitty hand with my dad, and then she got out. She got us all out, moved to another state and started over. It was hard on her. I know it was. She worked two jobs, raised two kids, and sometimes she had to make the choice between food and electricity because she couldn't pay both. We'd have peanut butter and jelly sandwiches for a week until we could use the fridge, stove and microwave again. But as hard as all of that was, I know that our lives were better than if we'd stayed with him."

She reached for his hand. He released her foot and took it. "I'm sorry. Now I feel like an idiot. My life is a bed of roses in comparison. Here I am complaining about being alone when ..."

Shaking his head, he pressed his lips together and squeezed her fingers before letting them go and resuming her foot massage. "Hey, no. Don't say that. You have nothing to be sorry for. Everybody's Everest is a different height, okay? And I'm sure, if you'd been dealt the same kind of cards my mom was, you'd handle them with the same grace and strength that she did. Because you are a strong woman, Lauren."

"And you're an incredible man, Isaac."

They sat there for a moment in silence. Staring into each other's eyes. His hands massaging her feet as she fed her son. It rattled his brain to think that he'd only really known this woman for a week, and yet he already had such strong feelings for her. For her son. For this friendship, this life, this *relationship* that they were building. And how completely right and natural it felt. He wasn't Ike's father, and yet sitting there with Lauren as she nursed Ike, rubbing her feet, bringing her food and something to drink, felt more natural and made him feel more whole than he'd felt in a long time —if ever.

"*Knock, knock.*" A female voice at the door broke the spell, and he sat back and removed his hands, setting her feet down on the floor. Lowenna appeared, holding a baby in her arms. "Mind if I join you? Mason is changing Wyatt, so I figured I'd nurse Warren down here with you."

Lauren cleared her throat and wiped away another tear that had formed in her eye. She sipped her wine and smiled brightly at Lowenna. "Not at all. The more the merrier."

Isaac stood up from the footstool, lifted Lauren's legs and propped her feet up on the stool. "I will leave you ladies to feed your wee ones in peace." He tapped his phone in his pocket. "If you finish your plate and want more, just shoot me a message."

She hit him with another one of those smiles, and he disappeared back into the rest of the house.

It was eleven forty-five by the time he pulled into Lauren's driveway. She was asleep in the passenger seat, and when he hopped out of the truck and opened the back door to grab Ike, his namesake was sawing logs as well. Like mother, like son.

She'd already given him her key to the house, so he left her in his truck, carried Ike inside, popped him out of his car seat and put him to bed in his bassinet in Lauren's room. Then he went back to retrieve Lauren.

It'd always baffled him how deep some people could sleep. His sister was one of those people. Even now, if she fell asleep in the car, Isaac could unbuckle her and carry her inside without so much as an eye flutter or a pause in her bear-like snoring.

Lauren appeared to be the same. She draped her arms around his neck but didn't open her eyes. Her head lolled against his shoulder, her breath tickling his jaw as he carried her over the threshold of her house and closed the door. She was right when she said she wasn't going to make it to midnight.

The hallway was dark, but he had no difficulties navigating it. He'd made his way through worse without stubbing a toe. He entered her room and laid her down on the bed, grabbing a blanket from the foot of it to drape over her. She'd probably wake up cooking, seeing as she was fully dressed and in her winter coat, but he didn't dare try to remove it in case he woke her.

He turned to go when a hand reached out and grabbed his, curling into his fingers and pulling. His heart began to thump wildly in his chest as he turned back to face her.

She blinked up at him, dozy-eyed and gorgeous. "Thank you for tonight, for everything."

A hard wad of something akin to stale bread became lodged in his throat, and he fought to push it down. He squeezed her fingers and nodded. "I had fun."

She propped herself up on her elbow and glanced around her dark room in a state of surprise. "Did you carry me to bed?"

"No, you've been here the whole time. Did you think we went to a party?"

Her smile grew until her nose wrinkled and she squeezed his fingers. "Smartass."

"I'm going to go. I'll go grab Penny if you think the girls will still be up?"

She swung her legs over the side of the bed and made to stand, but she still hadn't released his hand. "I think they're probably still awake. I'll text Sabrina to make sure." She grabbed her phone from her coat pocket, and her thumb began to fly across the screen. She still held onto him with the other hand. "She says they're still up."

He nodded. "Okay. I'll let you get back to bed."

"I'll see you out," she said, following him. Still holding his hand.

He led her down the hallway toward the front door, loving the feel of her hand in his, her warmth, her softness. He wished he was leading her back to her bedroom rather than away from it, where he would then peel her out of her clothes and show her just how much she was coming to mean to him.

He reached the door and opened it, the icy breeze from the clear night making his cheeks tingle. Only then did she release his hand.

"When do you work again?" she asked, her fingers twisting around each other. "When do you need me to take Penny for you?"

"I work the night shift for the next two days, then I'm off for four. Are you okay taking Penny overnight?"

She nodded, dipping her head and tucking a strand of hair behind her ear. "Of course. Whatever you need."

Whatever you need.

That was a loaded statement.

He inhaled deeply through his nose, allowing the frozen air outside to fill his lungs and cool him off.

He took another step out into the night, away from the smell of her. Her heat, her everything. The more he was around Lauren, the harder it was becoming to stay away, to keep his distance. Their moment in the study back at Zak's house had rocked him more than he wanted to admit.

She'd called him an incredible man.

Most days he just tried to be good, let alone incredible. He tried to prove to himself, to the world, that he was one of the good guys.

He saved people.

He helped people.

Lauren thought he was incredible. What would she think of him if she ever found out the truth? That he was incredibly awful and she never wanted to see him again? Probably.

"I'm glad you had fun with your friends tonight," he asked, clearing his throat and pushing away the dark thoughts that had started to creep in.

"I did. Did you?"

He nodded. He did had fun. But he would have had just as much fun staying in with Lauren, watching a movie and eating nachos on the couch, just the two of them.

He glanced at his watch. It was midnight on the dot.

A new year.

"It's midnight."

Her eyes widened, and she leaned against the doorjamb, crossing her arms over her chest, a sleepy, serene smile curling her lips. Lips he wanted to kiss. Lips he wanted to see wrapped around his dick. Lips he wanted to see part in a perfect *O* as she squeezed her eyes shut and came with his dick buried deep inside her. "Happy New Year, Isaac."

Clearing his throat again, he bobbed his head. "Happy New Year, Lauren."

"I'll see you tomorrow?"

More head-bobbing. "I start work at six, so I'll be by around five thirty to drop off Penny."

"We'll be here. Unless you want to come early and have dinner?"

Abso-fucking-lutely.

He stowed his eagerness and simply nodded again and thanked her. "That sounds great, thank you." God, why did this all seemed so forced, so awkward?

Because you want her.

Right.

It was him who was making it awkward. She seemed normal. Easygoing. Lovely and kind. She wanted his friendship and only his friendship, and she'd made that clear. Now he just needed to put his feelings aside and be the friend she needed, the friend she wanted. Their connection felt natural. Him being a part of her and Ike's life felt natural. He needed to stop forcing their relationship to be more.

He could do that. He'd done harder things in life than that. Way harder.

With a grunt, he gave her a half smile. "Okay, then, I'll see you for dinner."

"Have a good night."

"You too."

He turned to go but then stopped.

It wasn't that she didn't want him.

She did.

She'd said so.

It was that she was afraid.

Afraid of him dying because of some ridiculous family curse and a promise to her mother.

It was a new year, a new day, and he needed to at least show her what they could be, if she just gave them a chance.

Whipping around, he stepped into her space, cupped her face and kissed her. He took her mouth. Possessed it. Captured her gasp and fed off her moan. She didn't push him away. Thank fuck, no, she did not. She uncrossed her arms and wrapped them around his neck, tugging him down to her, opening her mouth and accepting him. Giving him what he'd come to her for and so much more. She slipped her tongue into his mouth and stroked it against his, tasting him, teasing. His cock pressed against the zipper of his jeans until it throbbed.

He wasn't her dad or her grandfather. Sure, his job was dangerous, but these days, so was being a bus driver or a teacher. Threat lurked everywhere, not just for the first responders, and you couldn't live your life in fear. He needed her to know what they could be if she didn't let fear run her life. If she didn't let the past, other people's pasts and tragedies influence her future.

Because they were good together. It'd only been a week, but it'd been an intense week, and he knew they were good together.

A cry from down the hall had them pulling apart as if their tongues had suddenly caught fire. She touched her puffy lips and blinked up at him wide-eyed. "I, um ... I need to go."

His chest heaved, and he took a step back toward the driveway. "Yep."

"I ..." She stumbled backward but caught herself on the wall. "I ... I ..."

Smiling, he shoved his hands into his pockets and adjusted his tight jeans. "Good night, Lauren."

She nodded. "Yeah. Night, Isaac."

The crying down the hall intensified, and panic filled her flushed face.

"Go tend to your son. I'll see you tomorrow."

She was still nodding. "Right, tomorrow. Okay."

He turned to go. "Happy New Year, Lauren."

"Right. New Year."

"Go."

She did as she was told, shutting the door before he'd turned the corner. But he didn't mistake her pulling back the living room curtains a second later and her wide doe eyes watching him leave.

Tomorrow was certainly going to be interesting.

10

Lauren's lips still tingled as she sat in the glider in the nursery and nursed Ike. She touched her mouth with her finger for probably the hundredth time since Isaac had left.

The man could kiss. Holy Hannah, could he kiss.

She hadn't been kissed in a long time, and she wasn't sure she'd ever been kissed like that.

Her body was electrified. It was like up until that moment, she'd been dead, and Isaac's lips were the paddles that jolted her back to life.

And of course, her brain went immediately to the gutter. If he could kiss like that, that had to mean he was a savant at other things as well.

His tongue inside her mouth had her core tightening, her pussy throbbing and her nipples beading to the point of pain.

And all from a kiss.

No, not *a* kiss.

The kiss.

The kiss she would compare all past and future kisses to. The kiss that would go down in the history books as her greatest kiss of all time.

They'd only been spending time together for a week, but because of everything they'd shared, it felt like so much longer. He'd helped her deliver her son. He'd checked up on them, brought them gifts. They spent Christmas Eve and Christmas Day together, and now they welcomed in the new year together as well. Those were not things you did with someone when you just started to date them. Those were things you did with someone you loved, who you'd been with for a long time, who knew all your secrets, all your quirks.

And yet, sharing those moments with Isaac felt right.

They shared an intimate, monumental moment together.

The birth of her son.

And he seemed to be holding that connection between them with as much value as she did.

Ike popped off. She tested his arm. It fell like overcooked spaghetti. He was down for the count.

Carefully, she placed him back into his bassinet and went about undressing and washing off her makeup. One glimpse in the mirror at the shower behind her had her cheeks going red.

She still couldn't believe he heard her earlier or that she'd cried out his name.

She'd never been a quiet person during sex, but she certainly knew when to keep the volume at a respectable level.

Apparently, her fantasies lacked that wisdom.

Then, he'd gone and divulged that he touched himself at least four times since they'd met, all to thoughts of her.

Combined with his attentiveness all night, their talk in the study, his magical hands massaging her feet and how he'd carried her to bed, he was making it impossible for her not to fall for him.

Ah, who was she kidding? She was already halfway there.

By the time she crawled into bed, it was nearly one

o'clock in the morning. Ike had taken forever to nurse, and her movements as she brushed her teeth and removed her makeup were sluggish and filled with fatigue. Glancing at her phone, she thought about texting Isaac and mentioning the kiss.

But what could she say?

Thanks for the kiss. Let's do more of that, but I can't fall in love with you. You know, family curse and all.

Or *To hell with the curse, come back over and let's suck face.*

Or *Maybe we shouldn't be friends if you can't follow the rules.*

God, no. That was the last thing she wanted to send.

Because as much as she knew she shouldn't, as she'd promised her mother she wouldn't, she didn't want to just be friends with Isaac. She wanted to be so much more.

She didn't end up texting him at all.

She fell asleep with her phone in her hand, a picture of Isaac holding Ike up on her screen. She'd taken it earlier that night when he wasn't looking. He had Ike in his arms and was staring down at him, making faces. Ike was eating it right up, gazing at Isaac like a son gazes at his father.

Her heart had practically exploded from her chest when she saw them together, and she definitely felt her ovaries heating up. Several of the women around her had swooned too, all of them mentioning how good Isaac was with Ike and how natural he seemed to be with him.

Her son loved him. And Lauren knew if she wasn't careful, it was only a matter of time until she loved him as well. And then what?

Could she ask Isaac to take a safer job?

No, that was selfish and impractical.

Could she ask him to wear extra protective gear, including a bulletproof helmet and vest?

No, that was impractical too.

The selfless thing to do would be to stay away from him.

Sever ties, sever the friendship and let him live his life without the burden of a single mom and her family curse.

But the thought of that just brought tears to her eyes.

Tears she fell asleep with as she stared at Isaac with her son and tried to come up with a way to break the family curse, a way that they could all be together.

11

WITH PENNY in the front of his coat, Isaac strode up to Lauren's front door. It was four-forty in the afternoon on January first, and it was already dark outside. He could not wait for longer days and warmer weather. That was one of the things he missed most about Arizona. He never had to deal with the slush, sleet and slippery-ass roads.

With one knuckle, he rapped on the door.

Were things going to be awkward now?

He'd replayed that kiss over and over in his mind last night. He hadn't been wrong to do it, had he?

Was their situation a *no* means *no* situation? Or were there shades of gray and crossable lines? Had he stepped over a line he shouldn't have? She'd told him no, but everything about her, about *them* said yes in a million different languages.

She'd deepened the kiss, wrapped her arms around him and pulled him down to her. If she hadn't wanted him to kiss her, she would have shoved him away.

But he already knew she wanted him. She just couldn't have him, wouldn't let herself have him.

Family curse bullshit and the like.

How could he prove to her that danger came with the job but that didn't mean they couldn't plan for a beautiful future?

Jesus fuck, he'd known the woman for less than a month and he was already talking about a beautiful future? Did he leave his balls at home? He needed to give himself a face wash in the snow to clear his head. Knock some sense into him and start thinking with something besides his dick.

The door swung open, and he steeled himself for any kind of a welcome.

Warm.

Frosty.

Aloof.

He was ready.

Or a least he told himself he was.

She had Ike back in the stretchy wrap thing and was bouncing her body and patting his butt. She didn't say a word but simply ushered him in with a jerk of her head.

He pulled Penny from his coat before he hung it up, and she quickly scampered off to the living room. She'd come to know Lauren's house well and was getting braver each day.

"He's been screaming all day," she whispered, continuing to bounce. "I *just* got him down like this."

Oh shit.

The longer he looked at her, the more frazzled he could tell she was. Dark circles hung like purple half moons beneath her eyes. She'd also been crying.

He hooked a thumb over his shoulder and whispered, "I can go. Take Penny to Sabrina or something?"

Her head shook, and fresh tears brimmed her eyes. "No. Please, don't go."

Oh fuck.

She swallowed hard. "This whole mom thing is way harder than I ever thought it would be. He was up so much last night and then has only had catnaps all day. I'm so tired. And gross. I haven't even brushed my teeth. I keep forgetting why I'm in the bathroom and then turning around and leaving without doing it. He has a horrible diaper rash. I think he's allergic to something I'm eating. The websites say to start cutting out things like dairy and chocolate and all the best kind of food." She buried her face in her hands. "I'm just fucking all of this up."

Her shoulders shook, and Ike squirmed and made a lamb-like noise.

Laughing at the situation, she began to bounce and sway again. "I can't even stop to cry without pissing him off."

Normally a man of action, a man with a plan, Isaac stood there like an idiot, feeling helpless, not the first time with Lauren. He'd been helpless that day on the interstate too.

And yet, you figured it out.

He found a midwife. That was it. She did all the work— well, besides Lauren. He'd just been a delivery boy.

You were more than that, and you know it.

But crying women were not his wheelhouse.

When his sister, Natalie, would cry, he'd kiss her "owie" and hug her until she stopped. And that seemed to do the trick. When she was older and her problems were no longer a scraped knee or a paper cut but more of the boy variety, he would take her to the park and they'd shoot hoops and talk about what was wrong until she felt better.

It was too cold outside to go shoot hoops with Lauren, and she had no visible "owie" for him to kiss. The only thing he could think of didn't seem like enough, but he did it anyway.

Taking her by the shoulders, he drew her into his arms, careful of Ike, but holding her tight enough to hopefully absorb some of her heartache.

"You're an amazing mom," he said softly, shushing her.

"Ike is so lucky to have you. You're just having a hard day. Hard days are allowed. Even non-parents have them. But I bet my hard days are nothing compared with yours." He pressed his lips to the top of her head because it felt like the most natural thing to do. "What can I do to make things easier for you?"

Her fingers bunched in the fabric at the back of his shirt, and her breathing evened out. "You're doing it," she said.

They stood like that for a little longer before Ike made another barn-animal-like noise and they were forced to pull apart, both of them glancing down at the mood-killer the size of a watermelon. His eyes weren't even open. He was protesting in his sleep, the bugger.

With his arm still wrapped around her waist, Isaac squeezed gently until she lifted her gaze to his.

Her hand fell to his chest, and she blinked damp lashes at him, her complexion a mottled red but no less beautiful. Blue eyes sparkled, damp but full of something that both excited and scared him. Terrifyingly exhilarating. She pushed up onto her tiptoes and pressed her lips against his, cupping his cheek with her other hand.

He tightened his grip on her and pried her lips apart with his, deepening the kiss, going in for more. She allowed it. She welcomed it.

Was she finally going to give the idea of them a chance? Or was this just a sad, tired mom saying thank you?

A grunt from Ike had them breaking their kiss. The little guy started to smash his face against her chest and root around like a truffle pig.

She opened her eyes, and her puffy lips dipped into a sad frown.

Without saying anything, she stepped out of his embrace and went into the living room, taking up residence in the recliner and adjusting Ike in the wrap until he was quiet.

"I made a pot of chili. It's on the stove. There is shredded cheese, sour cream and jalapeno biscuits there as well," she said, watching him cautiously as he entered the living room. Even though they'd just kissed and they'd kissed last night, he still could not get a read on her.

Did she want to explore their attraction? Or was she regretting what they'd just done? Did she regret last night?

He regretted nothing.

He wished they'd done more. Kissed more. She felt so right in his arms. She belonged there. He knew it. Now he just needed to convince her to take the leap, too.

And by the way she moved into his body, melted against him, he knew she—at least at the time—wanted more too.

Her back hadn't stiffened when he held her. No, it'd relaxed. Her entire body had relaxed against his. He would love to see that back arch as she tossed her head into her pillow, the feminine lines of her throat tremble as she cried out during an orgasm. He would love to hear his name on her lips—puffy from being wrapped around his dick—as he buried his face between her thighs.

But he was a patient man, and he was in this with Lauren for the long game.

His stomach rumbled as he inhaled the scent of chili and spied the biscuits on the counter. "You had time to cook?" he asked, standing where she left him.

She shrugged and glanced up at him, her eyelids heavy, expression sullen. "What else was there to do? He didn't want to sleep, got angry if I sat down with him in the wrap. Standing up, wearing him is the only way he stays happy, so I may as well be productive."

Damn. That had to be hard. She couldn't lie down even if she wanted to.

"Go eat," she ordered. "You don't have much time." Her brows pinched, and she flicked her hand toward the kitchen.

"We can talk about what just happened and what happened last night if you want, but I'm also cool just sweeping it under the rug."

His jaw dropped.

She lifted one eyebrow. "I know that's why you're acting all weird."

"You're sure it has nothing to do with the crying new mom I just walked in on? Crying women are not my expertise. I'd rather negotiate a hostage situation than deal with a crying chick." He hit her with a look similar to the one she was giving him. Sassy, impatient, but also still slightly uneasy.

Her tired eyes widened, but her lip lifted at one corner. "You mean to tell me you'd rather deal with a terrorist who's threatening to blow up a bank than show a bit of compassion to a sad, exhausted woman?" The twinkle in her eye said she was joking—mostly—but there was also a glint of challenge there too.

"Did I not show you compassion right there?" he asked, pointing toward the entryway. "I think I showed you a lot of compassion. I think I compassioned the hell out of you."

Her lip twitched, and her gaze softened. "You did. Thank you."

Disgruntled, he nodded once. "Damn straight I did, woman."

Smiling, she glanced down at Ike. "Go eat, Mr. Compassionate."

He gave her some serious side-eye. "You want a bowl?"

Continuing to gaze down at her son but smiling, she nodded. "Yes, please."

CAREFUL NOT TO DROP ANY chili on Ike's head, Lauren ate her dinner in the recliner while nursing. It was an art form, truly, learning to eat over your kid's head and not drop anything on them. She couldn't say she'd never dropped anything on him, but she could say she'd never dropped anything hot on his head—yet. Just lettuce from a turkey sandwich, a few crumbs from a muffin, and then a chunk of banana that fell out of the peel and landed on a sleeping Ike. He didn't even wake up when it happened, so unless she decided to tell him when he was older, he'd never know he was beaned by a rogue banana.

"So," Isaac started, sitting across the room from her on the couch, leaning back casually with his ankle on the opposite knee, "let's discuss last night and earlier."

Groaning, Lauren rolled her eyes.

Of course, he wanted to discuss their kiss. Correction —*kisses*.

"You kissed me last night," she said, chewing her food.

"And you kissed me today."

Right.

She had.

And she'd enjoyed every damn second of it.

She went to say something, but he held up one finger to stop her. "Let's just speak in hypotheticals for a moment, can we?"

Could they?

Shrugging, she gave him the floor.

"Say we give this burning, animal attraction between us a shot."

She snorted and rolled her eyes again, which made him smile.

"Admit it, it's burning and it's primal," he said, grinning even bigger. "You can't deny it. Your cheeks are the color of a tomato right now."

Curse her ghost-like complexion. She was like a glass house.

"There's an attraction, I'll admit it," she said coyly.

"There's more than that. You said I was sex on a stick. One does not forget such a compliment. I'm actually thinking of getting it embroidered on a pillow for my couch."

"I would pay to see you keep an *embroidered* pillow with anything on it."

He lifted a brow in an oddly sexual way. "Would you now?"

Now she wasn't so sure. Did he have some weird fetish for embroidered pillows and secretly had a stash of them at his house?

She didn't really know much about the guy. Except that he was wonderful, smart, sweet, sexy and ... a cop. She couldn't forget that last part.

"Back to your insatiable desire to jump my bones," he said, shoveling another spoon of chili into his mouth. "I know you say you're cursed and can't date cops, but what if I told you I'm cursed too, and if I don't date a woman who can't date cops then I will surely perish?"

She added up the negatives in her head. Can't. Don't. Can't.

Oh, he was a sly Fox.

His smile turned as wily as the rest of him. "Hmm?"

She grumbled. "Okay, just for a second, *say* we gave *this*, whatever it is, a shot. I'm still recovering. I'm a single mom. I'm frumpy and hormonal and sleep-deprived. Do you really want to take this on? I mean, right now we're friends, but you're not *invested*. You can turn and go whenever you want. But if we started something ..."

A look she didn't recognize darkened his face. He set his unfinished bowl of chili down on the coffee table and leaned over, resting his elbows on his knees.

A tremor of something wriggled inside her.

"First of all, you're not *frumpy*. Don't ever say that again.

Second of all, who says I'm not invested? Just because I'm not sticking my dick into you doesn't mean I'm not invested. I like Ike. And I like you. Can I not be *invested* in a friendship? And third, I don't *have* to stick my dick in you tomorrow. We can take this slow if you need to. I already said that. It seems to me you're just making up excuses because you're scared."

Her mouth dropped open. Here she'd been willing to discuss their kisses but secretly preferring to ignore them altogether, and now Isaac was pulling out some serious therapist psychobabble from his well-toned ass.

Ike popped off, so she set her chili down on a side table and propped her son up on her shoulder to begin burping him.

Isaac hadn't looked away. She wasn't even sure he'd blinked.

"Admit it, Lauren," he said, his tone holding an edge that excited her. "You're scared."

Growling, she began patting Ike's back. "Of course I'm scared. My dad was a cop. He died. My grandfather was a cop. He died. My first cousin once removed's husband was a cop. He died. The women in my family are cursed. Marry a cop, he dies."

He shrugged and sat back into the couch, resuming eating his dinner. "So we don't get married. We live a wonderful life in sin and have oodles of bastard babies. Loads of people are doing it these days, and nobody bats an eye. It's not a scandal like it once was."

"You just have all the answers, don't you?"

He nodded confidently. "We're doing this. We're going to give it a shot. We'll take it slow, at your speed, but as of right now, Lauren C. Green, you are my girlfriend and I am your incredibly sexy, well-endowed, *patient* boyfriend."

Her body began to heat up, and her heart started to

thump heavily in her chest. Could Ike hear it? Could Isaac? Her breathing was also getting ragged.

"Calm down," he said, pushing his palms down toward the ground. "I can see you're on the verge of a panic attack."

Panic attack? Not quite.

But her body was reacting to Isaac's words—to his authoritative side and that he'd pretty much just decided they were going to be a couple.

She swallowed the pool of saliva in her mouth and took a few deep, fortifying breaths.

"We'll go slow," he said again. "You set the pace."

That was a bad idea. If she wasn't in recovery, they would have rounded home base at least a dozen times by now. Her pace was warp-speed. Or at least she wanted it to be with him.

"Now I'm going to worry even more than before with you heading off to work," she said softly. Her arousal wasn't the only thing increasing her temperature. She really did worry about him being out there on the job. Putting his life on the line. It was as admirable and honorable as it was terrifying.

His lips pressed together, and his eyes glanced down between his spread legs for a moment. Ike burped, and she pulled him from her shoulder, stood up and took him, fast asleep, to his bouncy chair. She held her breath as she set him down. Would he wake up the moment she took her hands away? He'd done it every time she'd tried that day. The kid would not let her out of his sight. They always had to be touching, and as much as she loved her baby, she needed some space.

Like a bomb technician cutting the right wire, she tossed her free hands up into the air and backed away in triumph, only for Isaac's fingers to lace through hers. She found herself on his lap.

His big hands splayed across her back and held her in

place. The look on his face was dark, serious and thrilling. "My job is dangerous. I know that. But if you're actually in this with me, if we're going to give it a shot, then I will be extra vigilant when I'm on the job. I know you think you're cursed. But a curse has to break sometime, right?" He pressed his forehead against hers until they were nose to nose.

More tears threatened to spring free, but she nodded. "Okay. I'm in this."

The smile he gave her was boyish and sexy and robbed all the air from her chest. "Good."

She thought for sure he was going to seal the deal with another one of his incredible kisses, but he didn't. He took her hand, helped her up and led her down the hallway.

"Isaac, I can't ..." Didn't he say he was going to let her set the pace? Was he lying? Was he trying to get the *deed* over with before his shift started?

Sure, she said her pace was turbo, but not *this* kind of turbo.

He didn't even bother to glance back at her but just continued on into her room. Her bed was unmade, her laundry hamper full. Not a room that said *take me now, big boy*. Not that she wanted him to take her anyway—well, she did, but she didn't. They couldn't.

God, it was all so confusing.

But he passed the bed and flicked the light on in her bathroom. "Go have a nice, long, hot shower. I'll watch Ike. I have a bit of time before I need to be at work. Take some time for yourself, regroup. We'll be okay."

Now she really did want to tackle him to her bed and grind his bones to dust.

But hormones, fatigue and an overwhelming melee of emotions took over, and she burst into more tears.

Isaac's hand fell to her back, and he drew her against him again. She huddled into his warmth and strength without hesitation, tucking her forehead against his broad chest and inhaling that incredible, fresh and manly scent.

He rubbed her back. "These tears aren't from something I did, are they?"

She shook her head but didn't lift it. Emotion clamped her throat, making her words come out in a croak. "No. But yes. I'm just ... so tired. But also so grateful for you."

He kissed the top of her head like he had earlier, and it made her entire body begin to hum. "I'm your boyfriend now, baby. I'll take care of you."

Chuckling through the sobs, she pulled away and blinked up at him. "You're my boyfriend."

He nodded with a sexy smile. "Damn straight. Now have a shower, woman, because you stink." Wrinkling his nose playfully, he released her, slapped her butt and pushed her deeper into the bathroom. "I'm going to go make sure it's okay with Ike that I date his mom. I think he's going to be okay with it, though. The kid loves me."

That he did. And his mother felt the prickling of love too.

Pulling her shirt over her head, she wiped away the last of her tears. "Don't you dare wake him up," she called, caught off guard by her enormous smile in the bathroom mirror.

12

THEY WERE NEARLY two weeks into their "relationship" now, and Isaac had had dinner at Lauren's house nearly every single night. He'd offered to give her a "night off," but she insisted he stay, said she hated eating alone and it gave them more time to get to know each other since he'd forcibly made himself her boyfriend.

But based on the way she greeted him at the door with a kiss every time he showed up, she didn't much mind that he'd declared her his girlfriend. She fell into the role pretty seamlessly.

Sid and Mel had both laughed their asses off at him when he told them he didn't give Lauren a choice and simply told her he was now her boyfriend and she didn't have a say in the matter.

"And she didn't kick your butt to the curb? This woman's either crazy about you or just plain crazy. I'd have told you to hit the bricks if you ordered me around like that," Mel said, bouncing up and down on her heels and blowing into her hands to keep them warm as the three of them stood in line, in uniform, outside the very popular Wicked Sister Chocolates downtown. Lowenna happened to own the place, and she sent out a mass social media blast whenever she was debuting a new dessert. Which usually resulted in people trampling each other to get in line and get one.

Sid and Mel were big fans of Lowenna's chocolates and dragged him there on their lunch break, promising to buy him "whatever his little man heart desired" if he went with them. They were nearly inside the store, and already the scent of chocolate had his stomach growling.

"I think she's just crazy about him," Sid said, rubbing her wife's back.

Isaac felt like a pasty-faced ghost standing next to the beautifully tanned newlyweds who had just returned home from their honeymoon two nights ago. They'd brought him back some macadamia nuts from Hawaii, but he'd eaten those on his drive home from the gym already. Need to feed the muscles to keep them growing.

They kept up with the line, and all three of them sighed as they entered the warm, chocolate-scented store.

"I can't believe she has *two* new flavors," Sid said, shivering and sending her brown ponytail swishing. She licked her lips and brought up her phone. "I mean, listen to this: yuzu-infused white chocolate ganache with Japanese curry-infused ruby ganache." She held up her phone so Isaac could see. "The bonbon looks like fire. *Fire!*"

"And I bet it tastes like heaven," Mel crooned. Her closed-mouth smile was accompanied by clasped hands beneath her chin and closed eyes. Like she was swooning about a lover and not food.

Isaac rolled his eyes.

"Okay, and what about this one?" Sid grabbed her phone again and started to read. "PB and J raspberry caramel with roasted peanuts, house-made peanut butter praline, peanut duja—whatever that is—with a blend of Nicaragua origin chocolate." She trembled. "I may have just peed a little, I'm so excited."

Mel and Isaac snorted and stepped forward with the line.

Things could get a little hairy when Lowenna debuted a new chocolate, but she usually managed to maintain order in her shop and keep her patrons happy in the process. Everybody had to wait their turn and follow protocol. No budging, no gloating, no whining, no scalping. She actually had that sign up on the wall in a big, bold font. Apparently, people used to camp outside her store before a new chocolate debuted, buy up a bunch and then sell them for double the price to people farther down the line.

It was worse than Black Friday shopping.

But Lowenna was off with her newborn twin sons, so Mason said she was only going into the shop two half days a week to work on new creations and check in on the staff. But she was always there on debut day, apparently. Because she was *The Wicked Sister*, she had to show her face when she put up a new chocolate.

They stepped up to the counter.

"Well if it isn't Sergeant Foxy McBigHands." Lowenna's smile was warm, bright and earnest, just like he knew Mason's woman to be.

Isaac rolled his eyes. "Is that what you're calling me now?"

She shook her head. "Not just me. All the women. News travels fast, and I hear you held poor Lauren down and demanded she accept you as her boyfriend despite her saying she's cursed."

Sid and Mel snickered beside him.

"Such a gentleman," Sid said under her breath.

Glaring at Sid, whose smile wasn't getting any smaller, and Mel, who looked like she was ready to come out with her own one-liner and barely able to contain it, he rolled his eyes. "I didn't *hold her down*. I just made an executive decision, and she didn't refute the decision in the time allotted to her." He was all grins despite the snickering females around him, as was Lowenna and her staff bustling around behind her.

"Well, I'm happy for you," she said. "Lauren deserves a good guy."

Sid slapped him on the back. "And Isaac is the best. Forces women to be his girlfriend. Can't get a better guy than that."

"I don't like what's in his pants, but he has nice hair," Mel chimed in, earning a snort of laughter from her wife.

"And bossy as hell," Sid added.

"I happen to like an alpha." Lowenna's gray eyes twinkled. "What can I get for you?"

"I have *got* to try the new creations," Sid said, her dark brown eyes widening. "How many are we allowed each?"

Lowenna's smiled turned coy. "I'll see what I can do."

Sid bounced up and down on her toes and clapped her hands. "I'm so excited."

Mel lifted her chin at Isaac. "What can we get you?"

Rolling his eyes again, he shook his head. "I can take care of myself, thanks." He waited until Lowenna returned from the chocolate case to the register. "Do you happen to know Lauren's favorites?"

Sid and Mel made *ooooh* noises, but Lowenna was all smiles.

"I do," she said, grabbing an empty bonbon box off the stack and heading back to the case.

"Keeping your woman at home eating bonbons." Mel guffawed.

He handed Lowenna's staff member his credit card. "You know it. As long as she's happy."

Lowenna returned and folded the box, placing it on the counter. "Tell Lauren I say *hi*." There was a glimmer in her eye that wasn't necessarily ingenuine but had a mischievous glint to it. "We should get the kids together for a playdate soon."

He took back his credit card and wrinkled his nose, picking up the boxes. "Can newborns have playdates?"

"No. They just lie next to each other on a blanket or awkwardly stare at each other during tummy time. It's more for the moms. But the boys will be friends before we know it, so we might as well start now. Get Aurora to bring Dawson over too."

"Lots of babies in this group of yours," Mel said, opening up her box and staring longingly at her chocolates.

"It just keeps growing," Lowenna added. Her eyes widened. "Though, we're done. Not that we can have an *oops* anyway, but we're still done. Three is enough."

Sid and Mel finished paying, and they said their goodbyes. Neither of his friends made it to the front door and back outside before their mouths were full of chocolate.

"You're really upholding the image of stoic and respectable officers of the law," he teased, glancing down at his friends, whose cheeks were puffy.

"Shut up. You're ruining my high," Mel said, stopping in the middle of the sidewalk for a second and shutting her eyes. "I think the yuzu one is my favorite."

"I think they're all my favorite," Sid said, popping another one into her mouth.

They continued on down the sidewalk. Not that Isaac would consider them an intimidating image, the three of them, particularly since Sid and Mel were gorging themselves on chocolate, but either way, people on the street gave them a wide berth. A few women gave him a second glance, but he was used to it. He smiled, nodded, said hello and kept on his merry way.

He might be a big guy and capable of taking down a man twice his size during a chase, but he'd seen Mel and Sid in action, and even though they were no more than five feet six each, they had strength and stamina like he'd never seen before. Both of them were going out for the SWAT team later in the year, something Isaac was sure they'd both excel at. He'd thought about applying himself, for a time, but he didn't like the idea of always being on call. He still wanted a family, and being on the SWAT team was no way to live if you had a wife and children at home who could never rely on you sticking around to finish a movie or stay to the end of a soccer game.

His captain had approached him about taking the bomb-tech training, and he was still considering it. But again, it was another thing to be on call for, and he liked his down time to be *his*. And when the time was right, to be his and his family's.

"So, you and interstate mama done the deed yet?" Sid asked as they all approached their side-by-side parked squad cars. "Have you broken that—what, eight-month dry spell?"

"I happen to think the dry spell did him a world of good," Mel said, stepping down off the sidewalk to her vehicle. "He's more focused. More in tune with the world around him and not just what's going on in his pants."

Rolling his eyes, he unlocked his cruiser. "Aren't you just the sweetest."

Mel's toothy grin had a glob of chocolate on her lip. Her wife stepped down next to her and wiped it off. "All I'm saying is, it was nice getting to know the *real* Isaac and not just the man-whore Isaac looking for his next set of legs to slip between."

Sid's look was surprisingly motherly, if not a bit judgy. "Admit it, you were sticking your dick into anything willing with two sets of lips. It was getting gross."

Well, when she spelled it out like that, it was.

Shrugging, she kissed her wife on the cheek and walked

around to the driver's side of her own car. "I'm not saying you shouldn't or that you *can't* with interstate mama—"

"Lauren. Her name is Lauren."

That earned him an eyebrow twitch and an impish grin. "Sorry, *Lauren*. I'm not saying that you shouldn't or that you *can't* with Lauren, but if things go south between you guys—"

"They won't."

Her lips pressed together tight. "But if they *do*, don't turn back into the slut you were before. You're looking for the real deal now, right? Someone you can settle down with."

He didn't say anything. He didn't have to. They were two of his best friends. They knew he wanted a family.

"We say this to you because we love you," Mel said, her tone softer than Sid's, her green eyes gentle. She'd come back from Hawaii with a shorter haircut—a bob, she called it—and blonder highlights. It suited her. "And we want to see you happy."

He glanced at her. "I know."

"We'd like to meet her," Sid went on, her earlier look of an authoritarian mother with the wooden spoon in her hand having dissolved. "When you're ready for that."

"You two are a lot to handle," he said, tossing back the jabs. "Maybe we'll have you over next Christmas and you can meet her then."

Sid and Mel stuck their tongues out at him.

At that moment, all three of their radios began to chatter.

"All right, back to the salt mines," Mel said, opening up her car door. "Don't get shot, guys."

"You too," they both said before swinging into their own vehicles.

It was their go-to goodbye for each other. Morbid, but it kept the gravity of their jobs and what was on the line at a level they could handle.

Mel pulled out, then Sid, each of his friends giving a

whoop with their siren as a goodbye before they entered traffic.

Isaac turned on his cruiser but didn't put it into reverse. He sat there for a moment, grabbed his phone and brought up his wallpaper. It was of Ike and Lauren. He'd taken the photo the other day when she was holding him on her lap and reading to him. Ike stared up at his mother like she was the universe—because she was his, technically—and she had the most beautiful, serene look on her face. It was that moment there that he knew those two were the real deal for him. They were his family. His happily ever after.

He wanted what they were creating more than he'd wanted anything in a long time. Now he just had to make sure Lauren didn't get spooked and let this *curse* ruin the forever they were building.

LAUREN WASHED her hands in the bathroom sink, dried them and reached for her phone from the pocket of her hoodie.

She sent a message to Celeste and Bianca. *No more blood. Stitches are healed. Do I need to get "checked" before I jump the Sergeant?*

Her friends' responses were almost immediate.

Bianca: *Woohoo! Hallelujah! And no. Not if everything "feels" okay. You know your body best.*

Celeste: *Maybe invite Idris down there first. Get him to scope out the scene before you let in the Sergeant.*

Lauren snorted but paused in her bedroom, her eyes focused on her nightstand drawer, where Idris sat fully charged and probably very lonely.

Ike was asleep in the bouncy chair out in the living room, and Isaac wasn't supposed to be back to get Penny for another few hours. Could she?

The last thing she wanted to have happen was for her and Isaac to finally be together and things be painful for her. She knew she could still orgasm—she'd done that in the shower a few times now—but Idris was bigger than her fingers, and Isaac was definitely bigger than Idris.

Biting her lip, she slid the drawer open and pulled out the purple satin bag.

Months ago, during a wine night with Eva, Bianca, Richelle, Zara, Paige and Celeste, they came across the reviews for the vibrator to rival all other vibrators—Tracy's Dog. A horrendous name if ever there was one, but the reviews did the trick, and Bianca, Lauren and Celeste all ordered themselves one. The other women said they didn't need it because they had men in their lives—so what? Lauren still used vibrators when she had boyfriends. Sometimes you just needed a quick *zap* to fall asleep but you weren't interested in cuddles or waiting for him to get his *zap*.

Celeste claimed to be able to hear colors, Bianca swore she met God, but Lauren knew for a matter of pure fact that the first time she turned Idris on, she died for a second only for him to revive her back to life with his clit-suctioning powers.

Not long after that, all the women had one. Men in their beds be damned.

She opened the bag and pulled out Idris.

He looked just as wonderful as the last time she'd used him. Sleek and smooth. A deep dark purple in the shape of a squished *L* with a bulbous, ribbed node on one end and another node on the other that had a hole the perfect size for a clit hood—with ten suction speeds.

She turned on the suction and pressed her finger to the hole, her body quivering when he began to make noise and tickle her fingertip.

Could she?

Should she?

She didn't like being this far away from Ike for so long. But she also didn't want to masturbate in the living room or in front of her child.

#SingleMomProblems?

She set Idris down on her bed, went and carefully picked up the entire bouncy chair and carried it down the hallway. She placed it in front of her door but turned it around so Ike couldn't see her. Not that his eyes were open.

She closed her door halfway, so as to block her own view of her son but not inhibit her from seeing the seat or hearing him if he woke.

She just didn't want to be able to see her kid or for him to see her. But she also didn't want to be deep in the throes of ecstasy, momentarily dead, chatting with God and smelling colors while her kid was losing his shit in the living room.

Once she figured out the baby dilemma, she dimmed the lights, pulled off her yoga pants and underwear and slid into bed between the sheets.

It was like reuniting with a lover after months apart. Only Idris hadn't sent her love notes or sonnets. He'd waited patiently for her, silently.

She slipped him down her body. She and Isaac had only made out on the couch so far. High school stuff. Not even hand stuff. She'd tried a few times to take it further, put her hands down his pants or sink to her knees, but he'd stopped her.

"I'll only take when you can take too," he said, his hand on hers. "I told you we can take it slow."

Well, if a line like that didn't get her lady juices flowing, she didn't know what would.

The man had made it absolutely impossible not to fall for him. Impossible. He was perfect. Kind, attentive, caring, but also dominant in all the right ways. When he kissed her, he kissed her fully. Like it was his mission and he could not, would not fail. He gave it his all.

What would it be like to make love to a man who kissed like that?

Would she die for a moment? Chat with God, smell and hear colors?

Probably.

Hopefully.

She hit the button for the first speed of the vibrating node and inserted it into her pussy.

So far, so good. No pain.

Once she had it in position, she turned on the suction.

Oh yes.

Idris knew exactly what to do.

Squeezing her eyes shut, she increased the speed on both the vibrator and the suction. Speed three usually did the trick in no time.

Idris was efficient. That's what she loved most about him.

Her hips rocked and jerked off the mattress, and her fingers bunched in the sheets. Richelle told her that using the vibrator while letting your partner in your ass was like having an out-of-body experience. She'd have to see if Isaac was up for it.

She'd died, spoken with God and knew what purple sounded and smelled like, but she'd never been out of her own body before.

With her eyes still closed, she replaced Idris with Isaac. With his tongue, his fingers, his cock. She ground herself against him and tugged on her nipples. He hovered above her, gazing down at her with a blue intensity that caused her entire body to quiver.

"Don't come yet, baby," he purred, reaching behind her to grab a knee and press it into her chest, changing the angle.

She shook her head. "Not without you," she whispered.

Her head flew back into the pillows, and her chin lifted to the ceiling. She wouldn't last much longer.

As she increased the suction speed to five, her body thrashed violently in the bed and a moan burbled up from her throat. "I can't wait," she whimpered. "I can't." The glorious, familiar hot prickle worked its way up her spine, settling between her legs. Like a struck match, it lit the fuse, and her world exploded. A powder keg of pure pleasure radiated out from her core to every nerve ending in her body.

Lauren tensed and lurched up off the pillow, only to crash back down in a boneless state of euphoria.

She lay there limp, satiated and relieved as the bliss began to recede back to her center. The suctioning became too much and she turned it off, as well as the vibrations, pulling the toy from her body. With tired limbs, she swung one leg and then the other over the bed and went to go wash up in the bathroom. Just as she was remaking the bed, Ike began to make noise in the hallway.

She tucked Idris back into his bag and in her nightstand, grateful that she wasn't broken and excited to share her news with Isaac.

13

Isaac let himself into Lauren's house, since she gave him a key a week ago. It was just easier than her having to get up from the chair while nursing Ike to let him in. Also, he was her boyfriend now, apparently, so boyfriends and girlfriends did that kind of thing. Right?

It felt weird that she'd never even seen his condo. They'd spent all their time indoors at her place. But then again, she wasn't going out much. She had her groceries delivered, and the weather had been considerably foul, so why would she take her and her son out in it just to get drenched? They went for a walk every day to get fresh air, but flu season was upon them, so she had no desire to go to any baby groups and expose herself or Ike to unnecessary germs.

Maybe she needed to push to see Isaac's place though. Even just so she knew what kind of a guy she was dealing with.

He found her in her recliner nursing Ike. His lips rested against her forehead. "Hey baby, how was your day?"

It amazed her how seamlessly they'd fallen into their relationship. He called her baby, grabbed her butt, kissed her. It felt as natural as breathing.

She glanced up at him and smiled. "Good day. Bianca found her baby-wearing jacket in storage, so she gave it to me. I bundled Ike up and we went for a nice hour-long walk with Celeste."

His thumb brushed across her cheek, and she closed her eyes, leaning into his touch. "You still have a bit of color from that icy wind. How'd Ike fare?" He ducked his head in lower toward her chest to get a better look at a guzzling and dozy baby.

"He slept through the whole thing." This man was making it impossible not to fall in love with him. The way he adored her son, cared for her, took care of both of them. And he hadn't pushed once or even asked if she was ready to take the next step in their relationship.

He said she had the reins and was in the driver's seat, but now she wondered what it would be like if she handed those reins over to Isaac and let him take control.

Idris had helped her earlier that afternoon, and now she knew she was good to go.

Was tonight the night?

Isaac straightened but cupped the back of her head, threading his fingers into her hair and tugging just enough to send a jolt of something exhilarating down to the apex of her thighs. "Dinner smells great. What's on the menu?"

"Chipotle chicken wraps," she said, tucking her nipple back into her bra when Ike popped off.

Isaac didn't even ask, he just swooped in, scooped Ike up, propped him on his shoulder like a pro and began to burp him. His lips fell to the side of her son's head, and he murmured something to him that Lauren couldn't quite hear.

She stood up. "You've really taken to this whole *dad*

thing," she said, heading into the kitchen to begin dishing up their meal.

He shrugged and followed her into the kitchen. "It's not so much a *dad* thing as it is just liking the kid, his mom and doing what feels right."

She smirked and pulled a couple of plates from the cupboard.

"Speaking of liking this kid's mom," he went on, "I was at Lowenna's shop today with Sid and Mel. I got you something."

She whirled around, her eyes wide, taste buds gearing up. She spied the bonbon box on the edge of the counter. "Oh my God. Are her new ones in there?"

One shoulder lifted. "Probably. That's why we were there. Mel and Sid follow her on social media and she sent out a big blast announcing two new flavors, so we stood in line with the rest of the cocoa-bean addicts." His cheek twitched, the start of a smile curling at his lip. He didn't meet her gaze, but she could feel the warmth blossoming between them. In her thirty-two years on Earth, the only man to ever buy her chocolates had been her dad. He brought a box for her and a box for her mother at least once a month, just because.

"That yuzu one sounded amazing. Thank you." She tilted her head, studying the man who was quickly capturing her heart. "What's the occasion?"

Another shrug. "No occasion. Just because."

Hot tears pricked her eyes, and she quickly swatted them away, swallowing down the emotion that threatened to clamp her throat. "I used to be among the cocoa-bean addicts waiting in line before I became with child."

"With child?"

"Sounds less crass than *knocked up,* don't you think?"

"How about 'before you became a mom'?"

"You just know all the right things to say, don't you, Sergeant Fox?"

"Apparently it's Sergeant Foxy McBigHands," he said, his eyes two dark blue flames.

Grinning like an idiot, she didn't say anything but opened the box to find one dozen shiny, colorful bonbons all nestled in their molds. Each one was a different color, each one a different morsel of decadence. "I'm not sure I can wait until after dinner," she said, wiggling her fingers as her hand hovered over them. "Hmmm. Maybe just one."

"They're yours. You could eat them all right now and I wouldn't bat an eye."

"I intend to savor them," she said, finally settling on one of her favorites—dulce de leche. She popped it in her mouth, squeezed her eyes shut and moaned deep in the back of her throat as she crushed the candy between her teeth. Flavor burst across her tongue and sugar flooded her bloodstream. She felt the rush right down to her toes.

She reached out and gripped the counter, unable to open her eyes, unable to keep the second moan from rumbling up from her chest. By the time she swallowed it, she was exhausted. It was like her afternoon with Idris all over again.

She opened her eyes to find Isaac staring at her. His mouth hung open. His eyes were wide, his cheeks red, nostrils flaring. But it was where his hands were that surprised her the most.

Covering Ike's ears.

"Did you just ..." he whispered, removing his hands from the sides of her baby's head.

"Did I what?"

"Did you just ... have a *lady* moment?" He mouthed the last part and turned Ike so he couldn't see Isaac's mouth.

"A lady moment?" she asked, putting the lid back on the box and setting it on the counter. "As in an orgasm?"

He nodded, almost appearing embarrassed. "Yeah."

"No. But even if I had, why were you covering my son's ears?"

He turned Ike away again, his concern for her son adorable if completely unnecessary. "Because his mother looked like she was in the fits of female hysteria, and I wasn't sure that was something he should hear."

Lauren tossed her head back and laughed until tears pricked the corners of her eyes and her sides ached. She glanced back at Isaac, who was standing there, talking to Ike, mock irritation pinching his brows. "Your mother is a wingnut, kid, you know that? Climaxes when she eats chocolate and then doesn't have the decency to go and do it in another room. You're going to be traumatized, I bet." He clucked his tongue and booped Ike on the nose. "Don't worry, I'll set her straight. I got your back, man."

Rolling her lips inward, she stepped toward her men and rested her hand on Isaac's arm. "Ike's mother did not just climax. I was close, because Lowenna's chocolates are that good. But I didn't. However, your concern for my child is adorable."

He lifted his eyes to hers. "Can't be doing that in front of your kid. Just doesn't seem right."

Her lips pinned together so tightly, they ached in an attempt not to laugh. "Well, he seems no worse for wear after hearing me this afternoon."

He nearly dropped the baby in his arms. "He what? You what? With who?"

Men were such easy marks. They were all the same.

She returned to the counter where the plates were and began putting together their chipotle wraps.

"You can't leave me hanging, Lauren. What—or should I say *who*—did you do today?"

She didn't look over her shoulder, but she knew he'd

stepped behind her. His heat, his scent, his strength, it filled a room. Filled her space and her senses. "I stopped bleeding, so I wanted to make sure everything was in working order. That I could still ... without any pain."

"So you ..."

"Idris Elba came off his sabbatical and did me a solid." Did he ever.

He whipped her around so fast, she nearly sent lettuce flying across the kitchen. "Idris Elba? Who was over here today?"

He was so cute when he was jealous and confused. She could see it was taking every ounce of his strength not to go completely green-eyed monster on her. He was protective of what was his. She liked that.

"It's the name of my favorite *toy*," she said. "The name it came with was awful, so I renamed it after another sex on a stick."

The color in his cheeks began to fade. "Idris Elba?"

Grinning, she nodded. "Yeah. Celeste named hers Henry Cavill, and Bianca named hers Jason Momoa. It sounds better to say we spent the night with Henry, Idris or Jason than Tracy's Dog, which is what the toy is really called."

He snorted, glanced away, but then jerked his gaze back to her. "And you did *that* in front of Ike?" Horror filled his eyes. "You're going to traumatize him."

It was her turn to snort. "I am not. I put him—asleep—in his bouncy chair, set it in my hallway and then partially closed the door. I also faced him into the hallway and not into my room. So I could see the chair, but not him, and hear him if he woke up. No traumatization happening in this house."

He didn't seem convinced.

She tapped his cheek twice. "All's well *down there*. Thanks for asking. Idris and I had a wonderful afternoon." His reaction had her turning back around to hide her smile.

She felt him press up against her back. "Does that mean ..."

Wiggling her butt against what she could already tell was an iron bar, she hummed, "Mhmm."

Then he was gone.

She finished plating dinner, only half wondering where he'd gone off to but mostly just fantasizing about finally getting to see Isaac naked, when warm, strong, long fingers wrapped around her bicep and hauled her out of the kitchen.

"Come on."

Wiping her hands on her pants, she stumbled after him. "Where are we going?"

"To town on each other."

Giggling, she followed him, unable to keep the skip from her step. "Now? What about dinner?"

"Dinner can wait. We can't. You want this. I want this. We need to do it."

"But ..." She wanted to shower before they did it the first time. Get waxed. Maybe set the mood with some nice lingerie. Something that hid her post-partum pooch of a tummy. She knew she wasn't going to look like she did before she got pregnant, but she hadn't counted on looking five months pregnant either. The squishy lower belly was going to take some getting used to. It was also going to see some crunches and sit-ups when she found some energy again.

"No buts. I mean, chances are, you're going to be bad in bed anyway, and I'm going to be riddled with anxiety as I figure out a way to let you down easy. You're going to want to jump my bones every day afterward, and I'll want none of it. But I need to take one for the team."

"What team?" She could feel her resolve deflating like a botched soufflé.

"I don't know, *the* team. That's just what they say." They passed Ike in the hallway, who was fast asleep in the bouncy chair, facing away from her bedroom door. Isaac half closed the door like she had earlier, made sure he could see the chair but not the baby, and he tossed her to the bed.

He reached behind him and pulled off his shirt, revealing, finally, after long last, the torso of all torsos. The body to upstage all other bodies. Isaac was pure. Fucking. Perfection.

The last granule of her resolve to not fall into bed with this cop was crushed like a cookie crumb beneath the heel of a shoe, and she raced to tear off her pants. He did the same. They were both frantic. She reclined on the bed undressing while he stood at the foot of the bed, tearing off the layers one by one until he was in nothing more than black boxer briefs.

Her mouth pooled with saliva as she let her gaze sweep across the hard planes of his chest, down his tapered abdomen until her eyeballs stopped and froze in her head at the enormous tent between his legs.

Big hands, big ...

Whoa.

He'd dropped his boxers and whoa ... just, whoa.

The man had not been lying when he said Isaacs were blessed. Nor had his large hands and big shoes been false advertising.

It was as if his body had been molded by the gods, all but his cock. That was the work of none other than the devil himself.

Without waiting for her to relieve herself of her own underwear, he crawled up the bed, pinning her beneath him. His heat surrounded her, the damp, silky head of his cock knocking the top of her thigh.

"I thought you said we'd go slow?" she whispered with a teasing smile. "That *I* could set the pace."

Hovering above her, all long, muscular and smelling

fucking amazing, he slid his mouth into a salacious grin that made her pussy throb. "Do you want to slow down?"

Fuck, no, she did not.

His smile grew. "I didn't think so." His head dipped, and he took her mouth, his kisses gentle at first but becoming more and more hungry as he lowered himself, pressing her into the mattress. She grappled at him, raking her nails down the length of his back, scoring him, marking him as hers. She dug trenches into the rock-hard globes of his ass, enjoying the ripple and clench of every muscle beneath her fingertips.

He broke the kiss and lifted his head, his pupils dilated, cheeks ruddy. "You'll tell me if it hurts, right? If I'm too heavy or you want to stop?"

Emotion gripped her throat, an unexpected consequence of giving in to the passion. All she could do was nod.

"I want you, Lauren. So fucking badly."

She nodded again. "Me too."

Dipping his head again, he pressed warm, wet kisses down her cheek, jaw and neck, over her chest and the swell of each breast.

His brows furrowed as he glanced down between them. "Why aren't you naked?"

Ah, right. She was hoping he wouldn't notice that she'd kept her tank top and nursing bra on. She typically wore a nursing tank top with the built-in bra, or a nursing bra, a tank top and a loose T-shirt over top. She liked to layer so if she had to nurse Ike she could do so without flashing whoever was around either her breast or her puffy tummy.

"I, um ..." She swallowed and rolled her lips inward.

Growling, he sat up on his knees, his cock bobbing with every movement, a bead of precum dangling precariously from the plum-hued crown.

He reached for the hem of her top, but she stopped him. "No. Please."

His brows pinched together even more. "What? Why?"

Unable to meet his intense, scrutinizing, layer-stripping gaze, she glanced off into her room. "I just had a baby. My body ..."

"Created life. Grew a brain, feet, a spine, internal organs, eyeballs, a nervous system, bones. You did that. And then you delivered that life into the world in the back of a Pathfinder on a gridlocked highway in the middle of a winter storm." He made to lift her tank-top hem again. She resisted his efforts.

Sighing, he sat back on his heels. "If you're worried I'm not going to like what I see, then you're dead fucking wrong, Lauren." He pointed at his cock. "Does this look like the cock of a man who doesn't think you're hot as fuck? Who doesn't want to stick it in you, mommy tummy, stretch marks and all?"

Emotion clung hard and heavy in the back of her throat, and she blinked back hot tears that slipped down her temples.

"I know your situation, and it's not a deal-breaker for me." He tugged at the hem again, and she allowed him to lift her tank top up just past her belly button. "This isn't a deal-breaker for me either. I think you're beautiful. Let me see all of you."

Air escaped her barely parted lips, and she nodded, wiping away more tears as they fell with abandon and dripped into her ears.

He relieved her of her tank top, leaving her in her nursing bra.

"You can leave your bra on if you want," he said, climbing back up her body and settling over her. He pulled one breast free from the cup, glanced up at her with a lifted brow.

She nodded. She was a nursing mother, yes. But she was still a woman. A woman with needs. A woman with passion and desires. And she'd always loved her nipples played with.

Tugged and tweaked until the snap of pain ricocheted through her, a zap of lightning to her clit and right down to her toes.

He laved at her nipple and cupped her breast in his palm, kneading it. Teeth raked across the sensitive bud, followed by a hard tug and suck. She groaned as he drew the other breast out of her bra and tweaked that nipple. Her hips shot off the bed, knocking his cock into her thigh.

"Are you wet?" he murmured, switching his mouth to the other nipple, scraping his teeth over it until she gasped.

"Why don't you find out yourself." She shoved her fingers into his hair, giving his head a gentle but direct push.

His gaze flicked up to her, and although there was a grin on his face, his eyes held a look of unease, but it was only a flicker and vanished before she could question him. His lips curled up even more, giving him a wolfish look. "With pleasure."

He continued on down her body, his lips covering every inch, his fingers peeling back the elastic of her white cotton briefs. She'd been waxing since she was a teenager, so she didn't have a ton of hair left anyway. But she still wished she had time to tidy things up.

His nose pressed against the top of her mound, and he inhaled.

The groan in her chest took on a life of its own and wormed its way up her throat. She arched her back and pressed up, desperate to feel his tongue on her. To have him taste her.

She lifted her head to find his eyes tipped to hers. He was watching her. The wicked gleam in his eyes and the triumphant grin had need tightening to a painful knot in her belly. She felt a trickle of arousal seep out from her pussy. His tongue came out and he snaked it downward between her folds, only stopping right at the very top of her pussy, right above her clit, which was swollen and throbbing and oh so ready for his touch.

Without lifting his head, he grabbed her ankles gruffly and placed her legs over his shoulders so her feet draped over his back.

"That's better," he murmured, the warmth of his breath over her throbbing clit making her shudder. With two fingers, he spread her lips and swept his tongue up her slit, ending at her clit, which he sucked hard into his mouth.

Her heels dug into his back. He sucked harder, both her clit and swollen folds, making her cry out and causing her hips to shoot off the bed again. She rocked into his face. A thick muscular forearm rested across her lower belly to pin her, while one finger from the other hand and then another pushed into her slick channel and began to pump. She rode his fingers and his face, gripping his hair and tugging when he took her to the edge but didn't kick her off.

"You need to fuck me," she panted, her head thrashing on her pillow. "Please. Inside me, Isaac. I need it. I need you."

With a final long sweep up her cleft, he wiped his face with his hand and hovered over her. She glanced down between them and gulped as his dick, leaking precum like a faucet, bobbed between them heavy-headed and veiny.

"Condom, babe," he breathed, his biceps bunching next to her head.

Nodding, she pointed to the nightstand. "In there."

He shifted, and she heard him rummaging around. "Is *this* Idris?" He twisted and brought out her afternoon companion.

Unashamed, she nodded. "It is. Isaac, Idris. Idris, Isaac."

Snorting a laugh, he put Idris back into his bag and into the nightstand. "Any chance we can double-team you?" he asked, returning to the bed and standing on his knees to roll down the condom.

A shiver raced through her at the thought. "I think we might be able to work something out."

Grinning, he finished rolling down the condom, lifted his gaze and crept back up the bed, hovering above her. "You're okay?"

She was better than okay.

Bending her knees, she planted her feet on the bed, relaxed her body and nodded. "Ready."

With a hand between them, he notched himself at her center and began to slowly slide in.

Isaac was definitely bigger than Idris. Perhaps bigger than any guy she'd ever been with. But he wasn't uncomfortably huge.

Well hung, but not a monster cock.

Blessed, not cursed.

A grower and a shower, but not a tripod.

Every inch he pushed in, her body relaxed deeper into the mattress, allowed him to take control, consume her. With a final thrust and a grunt, he sank balls deep.

He filled her, stretched her.

"You okay?" he asked, glancing down at her.

She blinked and nodded, trembling when his pubic bone grazed her clit. "I'm so okay."

"You'll tell me if you're not?"

"Isaac, you really need to start fucking me, like seriously. I'm not going to break. But you've met Idris, so if you're unable to get the job done, I'll have to bring in the ringer."

Growling, he lunged forward and bit her lip, at the same time beginning to drill into her with deep, heavy plunges and long, luxurious pulls.

"Bring in the ringer," he said, scraping his teeth along her jaw. "No fucking way."

She made a noise that shocked even her. Something both feminine and animal. She clenched her teeth as he palmed her breast in his big, warm hand. His teeth raked down her neck. She grabbed at his flexing hips, bringing his body closer to hers, and she hooked a leg around his waist, the heel of her foot notching in the crease of his ass.

Lauren's body arched, and she tossed her head back, her blonde hair splayed out over the pillow. Levering up onto one elbow, he lifted his palm from her breast to her hair and splayed his fingers through the long tresses. His thumb moved in circles over her temple; his fingertips kneaded her scalp. It wasn't rough, but he held her where he wanted her.

She blinked up at him, and his blue eyes hit hers and held.

Gathering her hair into his fist, he tugged until her chin tilted toward the ceiling, exposing more of her neck. He tucked his head and nipped at her throat, scoured his teeth over the hollow and sucked.

She trembled as he withdrew nearly all the way to the tip, only to mewl when he plunged back in with a hard slam that had her seeing stars. Her eyes had trouble focusing, even as they remained locked with his. Their mouths parted as he pounded the breath out of her with each glorious slam. His groan rumbled out of him like rolling thunder, making his lips vibrate against hers. She squeezed her internal muscles, but they weren't as strong as they once were. She'd have to work on that.

Drilling into her over and over again, Isaac broke his gaze and dipped his head, sucking a nipple into his mouth. He wasn't gentle this time, which was all the better. Her back bowed and her head tossed to and fro on the pillow until that divine, warm tingle deep in her core began to blossom outward.

She dug her nails harder into his ass cheeks as everything washed over her: his masculine scent mingling with the sweat of their exertion; the relentless rhythm of him, pushing into her over and over again; the feel of him filling her in a way that she knew only Isaac ever could. In just one time together, he had ruined her for all other men.

She cried out, the fireworks of euphoria erupting hot and brilliant behind her closed eyes. And then finally, a guttural groan and a gruff "fuck" filled the room as he came.

He lifted his head and pressed his lips to her forehead, their chests heaving against each other. Nobody spoke. Nobody moved. They lay there, breathing the other in, taking in the moment. That beautiful splice in time where the Earth seemed to slow down, heart rates normalized and wits were regathered.

His warm breath across her skin had her closing her eyes, enjoying his weight and the feeling of being full. Full of Isaac. They were caught in a quiet reverie it seemed neither of them wanted to leave.

But alas, all reveries must come to an end, and theirs was interrupted by a grunting and squawking cockblocker in the hallway.

With a manly grunt of his own, Isaac sat up and pulled out of her. He tugged off the condom, tied it and headed to the bathroom.

"Spend the night," she said, slipping off the bed and tossing on her robe from where it lay draped over a chair in the corner.

He washed his hands in the sink, smiling at her. "I planned on it."

14

NEITHER OF THEM had been able to keep the smiles from their faces or their hands off each other as they sat on Lauren's couch, watched television and ate dinner.

Thankfully, Ike seemed none the wiser to what Isaac had done to his mom. In fact, once they redressed and exited her bedroom, they found Ike grunting hungrily in his bouncy chair, while a snoring Penny was curled up next to him.

They fed their children, then fed themselves, sharing smirks across the kitchen, heated glances and looking for ways and reasons to touch each other.

Sex with Lauren had been just as he knew it would be.

Pure. Fucking. Heaven.

And they'd only just started.

She asked him to stay the night, which meant they had hours to explore each other's bodies, learn the other person's likes, dislikes and tells.

He'd only tasted her briefly, but he was already an addict. Her flavor was one he craved. One he would go back to for seconds, thirds and fourths. Hell, Lauren was a dish he'd gladly have as his last meal, or his one and only meal for the rest of his life.

She'd been a little bossy, giving him the ol' head push, but he liked that.

Could she take as well as she gave?

He needed to be the one in control in the bedroom.

Would she be okay with that?

He fucking hoped so.

He'd allowed her to take the lead that first time. Because she was still recovering, and he didn't want to hurt her. But she said she'd felt nothing but good when he slid his dick into her. Her body relaxed beneath his. She squeezed her pussy around him and lifted her hips up, asking for more. She demanded harder and faster from him. Which he gave her and then some.

But next time, she wouldn't be the one calling the shots.

It needed to be him. Control was necessary.

It wouldn't work between them if they fought for power and she kept telling him what to do. He'd never push her too far, would always check in, make sure she came, but he needed to be the one giving the orders.

To Isaac, there wasn't anything sexier than a woman submitting and taking what he gave her without an ounce of hesitation. It showed trust. It showed respect, and it allowed him to be the one in control.

She certainly hadn't balked at the mention of double-teaming her with Idris.

He snorted as he did the dishes. She'd named her vibrator Idris.

It was better than Tracy's Dog for sure, but did she have to pick a good-looking man who was probably as well hung or more so than Isaac? A man with an accent. A celebrity.

Couldn't she name it something like Craig? Craig was just a dude who worked in a random accounting firm—he was sure of it. Craig was five-eight, slightly overweight, and he brought the same ham and cheese sandwich to work every day.

Yeah, Craig wasn't intimidating at all.

Not like Idris.

She'd called him her ringer.

Had Isaac outperformed *the toy*?

If he hadn't, he was going to make sure that by tomorrow morning, he most certainly had. He'd have Lauren walking bowlegged and tossing Idris in the trash can if there was anything he had to say about it.

"What's with the face?" She wandered into the kitchen and ran her hand over his back, her touch electrifying and sending a sharp zap to his balls.

He shook his head. "Just thinking."

"About?"

Side-eyeing her, he continued washing the dishes. "Did I outperform Idris?"

She had a sleeping Ike cradled in her arms, so her laugh was more of a whisper that shook her body, but her smile and glittering eyes helped soften the blow to his ego.

"I'm not kidding here, woman. Did I outperform Idris?"

Crushing that plump bottom lip between her teeth, her lips curled up at one side. "Tenfold, baby. You have nothing to worry about. Idris and I have an agreement. He's there for me when I have nobody."

"But you have me now. You can toss him."

"And you can cut off your hand," she teased.

He pulled the drain from the sink and dried his hand on the dish towel. Careful not to disturb Ike, he hooked his hand roughly around her head and tugged her close. He ran his thumb over her lips, prying the bottom one out from between her teeth. "You're a smartass."

Her pupils dilated, and her breath quickened. "Yeah?"

He nodded. "Yeah. I think you'd be mighty unhappy if I cut off my hand. There's a lot I can do with these fingers that you haven't experienced yet."

Lauren's nostrils flared and her throat worked, his eyes following the movement. He'd already tasted her there, but he wanted to do it again. Scrape his teeth along the delicate line, swirl his tongue in the hollow, grip his fingers around it as he captured her gasps with his mouth, feel every undulation as she swallowed when he came down her throat.

A deep flush rose into her cheeks, and he pried her bottom lip from the top. He was tempted to stick his thumb in her mouth and see what kind of suction power she had, but he wanted his cock to be the first thing to experience that.

"Isaac ..."

Dropping his hand from her head, he took Ike from her. "Go have a shower. I'll finish up here, get this little man settled in his bassinet."

Her T-shirt tightened across her breasts, chest rising and falling on a strained breath.

Smirking, he lifted a brow. "That wasn't a request."

Heat flared in the brilliant sky blue of her eyes and her throat bobbed. Her cheeks were even ruddier, her pupils growing larger, just as his dick was.

"Lauren ..." He made sure to add an edge to his tone, one he could tell she didn't miss.

With that lip back between her teeth, she turned and left the kitchen. It wasn't long before he heard the water in the bathroom turn on. By that time, he had already finished tidying up the kitchen with one hand and turned off all the lights in the living room.

He grabbed Ike's rolling bassinet and gently set the little guy down in it, then he wheeled him out to the hallway. Just like earlier, he kept the door open a touch, but this time, he set up the baby monitor, with the camera clamped onto the side, poised directly on Ike's face. Then he turned on the receiving end of the monitor and placed it on the bathroom counter before he stripped naked and opened the shower door.

She didn't turn around, but the snapping of her spine said she knew he was there.

With his cock already hard and ready, he bracketed her body against the wall with his hands on either side of her. How perfectly did his cock nestle against the crease of her ass? Like it was meant to go there. To explore, plunder and pleasure.

The thought of double-teaming her with Idris popped into his head, and he groaned at the thought of taking her ass as a big vibrator fucked her pussy. He'd feel it all too.

With his mouth next to her ear, he tugged the lobe between his teeth. "Want your mouth."

Her only response was the gentle tilt of her head, inviting his teeth. He obliged, raking her soft, creamy flesh. Scoring it, marking it.

"Mouth, Lauren," he repeated, removing his lips from her shoulder and spinning her around. Water dripped from her lashes, but the enormous smile on her mouth was unmistakable.

She dropped to her knees and took him between her lips immediately.

He was forced to reach out and grab the wall again, her suction power was so strong.

Jesus fuck.

He'd already come once that evening. But if he let her go much longer, he'd come again before he was ready.

With her right hand, she worked his shaft, up and down, her lips following, only for her hand to pull away on every other stroke so she could bottom out. She didn't even gag. Not even a flinch.

He refused to think that it was because she'd had practice. Nope.

He wouldn't go there.

She was just made for him. Built to take him everywhere. In every hole. Designed for him. And he for her.

It wasn't long before the prickle at the base of his spine had him tapping her on the head. He didn't want to come. Not yet. He'd come in her mouth another time. Many *other* times.

But first, he wanted to feel her hot silk wrapped around him again, feel her quiver as he drove up into her, whimper when she thought he was withdrawing, only to sigh in relief when he filled her again.

She stood up, blinking the water from her eyes, and he took her mouth hard, slamming her wet, slippery body up against the wall of the shower, claiming her mouth—because it was his now. He'd claimed her. Lauren was his. And he was hers. There was no going back now.

With one hand holding her wrists above her head, he cupped and kneaded her breast with the other, ducking his head to tug a nipple between his teeth until it grew diamond-hard and made her squirm against him. Her cry was sharp and sudden, but the way she pushed her breast into his face rather than away said she wanted more, not less.

He gave her what she wished.

He captured her cry with his mouth, tangled his tongue with hers, not letting her take control of the kiss. He kissed her harder, drove his tongue deeper, releasing her nipple, sliding his hand down her stomach. He slipped his fingers down her body and between her legs to where hot liquid silk dripped down her inner thigh, getting washed away with the water. He found her clit, and she gasped through their kiss. She responded by driving her tongue more frantically against his. He pressed, circled and teased her swollen nub before sliding his middle finger lower, through the sparse, damp hairs.

She wriggled, her body bowing away from the wall, but his knee between her legs kept her open to him. His hand kept her and her wrists against the wall. She was at his command. At his disposal to do as he wished.

And he wished to hear her come.

With his fingertips, he tickled and explored her entrance. Teased her folds. She ground down against him as best she could, groaned into his mouth. She wanted his fingers inside her.

But *he* was in control, not her. He'd fuck her with his fingers when he was good and ready, and then he'd fuck her with his cock.

Which would be really fucking soon.

Wet. Soft and oh so fucking hot. He was struggling not to blow his load all over her belly as she gyrated up against him.

What he needed was to shove his face back between her legs. Use her thighs as earmuffs to drown out the din of the rest of the world.

Focus only on the good.

Lose himself in her scent, to the sounds she made as he drilled into her.

Lose himself in Lauren.

He slipped a second finger inside of her, and she lurched against him as he didn't let up, not for a second.

His cock throbbed. His head—not the one on his neck— was telling him to take her. To fuck her hard. But they had time. He needed to take his time.

His thumb circled her clit, and she moved against his fingers, trying to break free of his kiss. But he didn't let her go. Her mouth opened, but no words came out. She rode his fingers, bucked against him, slammed her body down onto his hand. Every muscle on her tensed, and her gasp came like a gust of wind at the same time her body stilled and her pussy pulsed around him. Warm honey flowed down over his fingers, getting lost in the spray. He wanted to lap it up, not waste a drop.

When her climax receded, she slumped against the wall, her eyes closed, body lax. Her hair lay slicked back against her head, darker than her normal straw-colored blonde, and her body held a beautiful pink hue from the warm water and hopefully his attention as well.

He pulled his fingers from her and popped them in his mouth, sucking off her flavor.

He found her watching him with hooded eyes and a placid smile. "Can I suck you off?"

He shook his head. "Not yet, baby." Gripping her arms, he whirled her around and bent her over. She planted her hands on the shower wall and spread her legs. She knew what was coming next.

He gripped his dick and worked it up and down her plump, juicy folds. She was still engorged from her orgasm, and pink peeked out at him. He fought back a groan and the urge to drop to his knees and bury his face there. Suck those folds, stick his tongue in her ass and tease her clit until she came all over his face.

But they had time. After they showered, he'd dive face-first into her pussy and stay there most of the night. He'd waited a while for a woman like Lauren to come into his life, a woman who embodied strength, humor, intelligence and motherhood, and now that he had her, no way was he going to fucking let her go.

She pushed back against him and removed one hand from the wall, dipping it below and spreading her pussy lips with her fingers. "In case you forgot where to put it," she said, craning her head around, smirking at him over her shoulder.

Growling, he slapped her ass and slid inside her, both of them sighing when he hit the end of her sheath.

Pure. Fucking. Perfection.

She fit him like a damn glove.

Her nails beneath her raked his shaft as he began to move in and out of her. Soon he was moving too quickly and with a force that surprised him enough that he needed to pull in his own reins a bit. She braced both hands back on the wall. Her head hung low between her arms, her hair a damp curtain shielding her face.

He was close, but so was she.

Pistoning in and out of her with a rhythm he knew would take him to the edge quick, he reached beneath her and pinched her clit. Thumbed it, raked his nail over the hood until her snap of an inhale followed by a deep groan had him giving it to her double-time.

She broke first. Her hot fist of a pussy convulsed around him. Her body shuddered with each wave as he continued to pound into her, sending her ass cheeks jiggling, her thighs quivering. He could only imagine her glorious tits were swaying beneath her. They'd have to fuck like this in front of a mirror next time so he could get the full view.

When she finished, he pulled out of her fast, gripped her hair and forced her to her knees again. She seemed to know the drill and opened her mouth wide, taking his load on her and her lips. Did he wish it was her pussy milking his cock? Of course. But he didn't have a condom on, so this would have to do.

The sight of his cum on her face was a beautiful thing though, and when she opened her eyes and smiled before licking her lips, Isaac knew he was in fucking love.

FIGHTING ANOTHER YAWN, Lauren smiled into the dark and inhaled Isaac's delicious, manly scent. After their shower fun and another orgasm involving Isaac's face between her legs, they lay in Lauren's bed, a hand from each of them intertwined above them as they listened to the sound of Ike snoring in the bassinet next to the bed.

"You're sure it's okay if I just sit up and nurse him in bed?" she asked for probably the third time.

He squeezed her fingers and brought the back of her hand to his lips. "Totally okay with it. I know what I'm getting into here. You're a new, nursing mom. If I plan on spending the night—which I do—I'm going to have to adapt to your routines."

"I tried doing the co-sleeping thing, but it just freaked me out too much. I wasn't able to sleep. I was worried I would roll on him. I can't even side-nurse—at least not yet. Maybe when he's bigger we'll figure it out. But right now, he wakes, I pick him up, nurse him, burp him and then sometimes change him. Then I pray he goes back to sleep. Sometimes he does. Other times he wants to discuss world events, the fragile economy and the rising price of oil."

He snorted. "Smart kid."

"He also scratches himself in the face and starts to cry because he has no control over his hands," she whispered.

Isaac chuckled and turned his body to face her. She did the same.

It was dark in her bedroom, but they'd been in bed long enough that her eyes had adjusted to the light and she could make out his beautiful features perfectly. With her free hand she traced the outline of his jaw, his nose, his brow line, his lips. "Have you ever modeled?"

Snorting, he began to trace her face with his finger as well. "No. Have you?"

That made her want to laugh. She could maybe be a foot model. She always thought she had nice feet.

"I want to see where you live," she said. "It feels weird that we've only ever spent time at my place."

"It's where you're most comfortable, isn't it? Where Ike's stuff is."

Was he deflecting? "Yeah, it is. But if we're going to do this, I think I need to see your place. See what kind of a *bachelor* you are. Are you a slob? A neat freak? Collector of embroidery pillows?" *Or doll heads?*

His lip twitched beneath her fingertip and slowly curled up into a smile. "You're more than welcome to come to my house and see how I live. I have no secrets. No weird fetishes."

Now she felt like she was pushing and prying. But it was important for her to know who she was with, who she was bringing into Ike's life. Before it had just been her heart, her life that she was turning upside down when she'd fall for a guy. Now it wasn't all about her anymore, and she needed to be more cautious. She needed to vet people harder. Not just let the first pretty face with a wicked tongue and magical hips blind her to the rest of the guy's less favorable qualities. If she'd done that sooner in her life, she wouldn't be a single mom right now.

Not that Tucker had a wicked tongue or magical hips. There wasn't much magical about Tucker besides his ability to vanish, perhaps.

"I work a night shift tomorrow, but then I'm off for four days," he said. "Why don't you and Ike come over on one of those days and you can go through my medicine cabinet?"

"I don't need to—"

"Lauren, it's fine. I want you to see where I live. I pushed for this, and I'm willing to do whatever you need me to do to make you comfortable. Besides, it'll give me a reason to finally clean my bathroom. It's been months."

She made a face of horror, but his smile said he was lying. Then he rolled on top of her and smothered her disgust with his mouth.

They were naked—besides her sleeping nursing bra— and her legs fell open so he could settle between them comfortably. His cock was like a steel pipe against her belly, and she shifted until it knocked her hipbone.

Breaking the kiss, he levered up onto one arm and stared down at her. "We don't have to again if you're tired."

"I am tired." She reached up and cupped his cheek, her thumb grazing across the prickly stubble. It was less than a day's growth, but it was already rough to the touch. She'd certainly enjoyed it between her legs, though her inner thighs and pussy lips were perhaps a little raw. "But I can nap when the baby naps tomorrow."

Hooking her ankles around his back, she pressed her hips up until the head of his cock found her center.

"Are you on any kind of birth control?"

She shook her head, the responsibility of things hitting her square between the eyes.

"I'll get a condom."

He leaned over and opened the nightstand just as Ike began to grunt and squirm in the bassinet.

Isaac's body froze over hers. "Never mind." He closed the nightstand drawer again and flopped over to his back beside her.

Without even turning on the light, she reached for the bassinet, pulled it over to the side of the bed and lifted Ike out. He was swaddled up but had broken free of his confines, and his limbs were thrashing about as he grunted like a small pig.

Her breasts began to leak, and she hurried to get him

latched while putting the milk collection cup onto her other breast to catch the leaking milk.

Ike was quiet in moments when he settled and began to feed.

Leaning back against the headboard, she glanced down at Isaac. "Sorry."

He stroked a knuckle over Ike's cheek, tipping his eyes up to her. "Don't be. Don't ever apologize for being a good parent. There are too many shitty ones out there that should apologize and don't. The good ones—like you—definitely shouldn't be apologizing."

Heat swam through her from his kind words. He'd mentioned before that he'd been raised by a single mom. That his dad was abusive or something. But just how bad had it been? Where was his dad now? Had he hurt Isaac?

"Besides," he said, turning over to his back again and tucking his hands behind his head. "Joke's on Ike if he was trying to cockblock us. I already boned his mom three times today, and as soon as he falls asleep, I'm going to bone her again."

15

THEY WERE NEARING the end of January now, and things between Isaac and Lauren could not be going better. He spent all his free time with her and Ike, unless she told him to get lost. Then he hit the gym or spent time with Penny. Otherwise, he was with his two new favorite people as often as they would allow it.

It was a particularly ugly day filled with wind, rain and just a constant dark grayness that didn't seem to lighten at all. He had the next three days off, so where better to spend the day than in his happy place? Ears-deep between Lauren's legs.

Her whimpers and hip lifts told him she was close. She'd already come once from his efforts, encouraging him to climb up her body and "impale" her, as she put it. But he'd ignored her and continued with his lunch.

A liquid lunch.

He drank her down, not willing to waste a drop.

Ike was passed out in the hallway in his bouncy chair after sucking Lauren's tits dry, and when he made sure the little guy wouldn't rouse, he'd scooped Lauren up over his shoulder and run full-tilt into the bedroom, tearing her yoga pants off with one swift jerk.

Then he set up camp.

His face was coated in her juices, his fingers wrinkly from being inside her damp channel, and his tongue was starting to cramp, but fuck if he wasn't happy as could be.

Lauren couldn't make up her mind between bunching the sheet in her fists or tugging on her nipples. She kept alternating, growling out in frustration when he'd nudge her close to the tipping point, only to haul her back down by removing his tongue from her clit and sucking on her plump folds.

"What is your angle here, Sergeant?" she asked, her hips churning when he pushed two fingers deep inside her and pressed up hard on her anterior wall. That soft, spongy button made her pelvis shoot up extra high when he pressed it.

"No plan," he murmured, moving his lips along her inner thigh, following it with a drag of his tongue, then a blow of cool air. "Are you not enjoying this?"

"Ike's going to wake up soon if we don't get a move on. I need you to fuck me." She lifted her head and glared down at him. "As much as I love getting eaten to within an inch of my life, I *do* love getting the D too. Been a long time since I've had it. Now I'm making up for it."

Fuck, he loved her lack of a filter. She said what she wanted and didn't give two shits about diplomacy.

But she'd have to wait a bit longer, because once he slid inside her, once he slid home, he wasn't going to last long. Being inside Lauren was unlike anything he'd ever experienced before. The way her hot pussy squeezed his dick so perfectly, the noises she made when he let her be on top and set the pace.

Fuck, when she rode him, like *really* rode him, it was the most glorious sight he'd ever seen. The way she moved, bobbing up and down on his shaft, her incredible tits bouncing, nipples so peaked and dusky.

He'd managed to get milk out of them once—not that he was trying—and it hadn't tasted bad at all. It wasn't his thing. He knew some men liked to drink breast milk during sex, but it certainly didn't turn him off.

"Isaac!"

Her little squeak of authority drew him from his thoughts of her tits jumping in front of his face, and he lifted his eyes to where she was glaring at him down the length of her body. "I need the dick."

"Soon," he purred, sweeping his tongue up the center of her cleft. "I want you to come one more time for me, then I'll fuck you good, baby. Promise."

Rolling her eyes, she put her head back down on the pillow and began to tug on her nipples again. He fought the urge to chuckle and hunkered down to get the job done. He could get her to the precipice in seconds once he found that sweet spot beneath the hood of her clit. When his tongue hit it, her whole body spasmed.

He hit it once.

Twice.

He was about to hit it a third time, which he knew would probably push her over the edge, when her phone on the nightstand began to vibrate and ring quietly.

"Leave it," he growled, drawing one of her labia between his teeth and tugging.

She'd already grabbed it. "It's the girls. They're three-way calling me. I have to answer it."

Now it was his turn to roll his eyes. He made to roll over so he could wait for her to talk to "the girls," but she glared, squeezed her legs against the sides of his head and pinned him. "You can keep going," she whispered, waving with her hand to indicate he should continue. "I can multitask." She answered the phone and put it on speaker, resting it back on the nightstand.

With a headshake accompanied by a snort, he waited for her to release him from her vice thighs, and then he dove back in.

"Hey," she answered, knocking him in the head with her knee on purpose when he teased her anus with a finger.

"Hey!"

"Hey!"

"We still on for tonight?" Lauren asked, thrusting up against his face and pulling on a nipple.

"We better fucking be." He'd only met her friends a few times, but he could tell that was Bianca. "I'm already drinking."

Were her kids at home?

Lauren had the same thoughts he did. "Where are the kids?"

"With my parents. I'm in a bad place right now. I'm drinking and cleaning my house." Her words were slightly slurred, but it sounded more like she was trying to keep herself from crying than puking.

"What happened?" Celeste and Lauren asked at the same time.

"My husband fucked his secretary, got her pregnant with twins, and she gave birth to those twins yesterday."

Fuck.

"Fuck."

"Fuck."

"Yeah," Bianca went on. "So I called my parents and asked if they could take the kids. Sabrina and Mallory are going to go over and help, as they also take Freddie and Jordie for the night because it's poker night."

"Right, poker night," Lauren breathed. He could tell she

was having a tougher time multi-tasking than she thought she would. Her words were choppy, her breath ragged.

"You guys can come over here," Celeste offered. "That way we don't dirty up your freshly cleaned house. And oh, that reminds me, is Isaac there?"

"He's ... *around*," Lauren said. He opened his eyes to find Lauren glancing down at him. He stared back at her, his tongue paused on her clit. It wasn't like they were making any noise or they were on video chat, but he also hoped he didn't have to stop what he was doing and talk.

"Max wants to know if he wants to come over for a beer while we're doing wine night. Apparently, they talked about motorcycles and stuff on New Year's Eve, and Max needs some help with his Bonneville."

She lifted a brow at him.

He nodded and shrugged, then shut his eyes and went back to task.

"He said that sounds good."

"What are you two doing?" Celeste asked, suspicion in her tone.

"Nothing," Lauren snapped. He would have been suspicious after a response like that.

"You're not having sex, are you?" Bianca asked. "Because I honestly couldn't take it if you were. I haven't gotten laid in *forever,* and if you're getting boned by Sergeant Foxy McBig-Hands right now, I will literally drink myself to death."

"We're not having sex," Lauren said, crossing her fingers, a guilty expression on her face.

"See you guys at my place at seven," Celeste said. "I'm making chicken satay and Vietnamese salad rolls."

"I'll bring brownies and popcorn," Bianca said. "I need junk food. I also think I'm going to have a smoke before I come over. I'm stressing the fuck out right now."

He lifted his brow at Lauren. Did Bianca mean a smoke as in a *joint*?

Lauren read his mind and nodded. "It is legal here," she mouthed.

He knew that. He just never would have taken Bianca for someone who smoked pot.

"I have an artisan pizza in the oven right now," Lauren said. "I'll bring that and wine. Should I bring tequila too, Bianca?"

"Bring all the alcohol," she said. "Opal named their children—and I'm not shitting you—Garnet and Emerald."

"Two girls?" Celeste asked. That had been Isaac's first thought too. Followed quickly by: horrible choices.

"Boy and a girl. Garnet Zircon Onyx Loxton and Emerald Amethyst Diamond Loxton. Like what the fuck?"

"Jesus." Lauren whistled. "That's rough."

"Like are these kids not being set up for a world of hurt later on in life?" Bianca asked.

"Do you care?" Celeste asked.

Isaac's thoughts exactly.

"No," Bianca said softly. "I need more wine."

"If you need it now, just walk over," Celeste said. "Don't drive anywhere. I have lots."

"I have enough until I see you guys," Bianca said glumly. "I'm going to go pour myself more wine, clean my bathroom and cry." The line went dead.

"You still there?" Celeste asked Lauren.

"Yeah."

"She's going to need us tonight."

"Yeah."

"I'll run out and buy some ice cream."

"I'll see if I can whip up a voodoo doll in the likeness of Ashley."

Isaac glanced up at her and lifted a brow. She was all sexy, sassy smiles.

Celeste snorted. "Okay, sounds good. I'll see you tonight."

He lifted his head. "How long will wine night last?"

"A while," she said with a pout. "But I promise to let you and Idris double-team me when we get back. I'll have been drinking, and if you think I'm *adventurous* now, just wait until I'm tipsy."

The steel pipe in his jeans that was pressed up against his zipper began to throb.

"Uh, guys, I didn't hang up," Celeste said, her voice a whisper.

"Shit!" Lauren grabbed the phone. "Sorry, Celeste. See you tonight." She hung up quickly, barely able to contain her laughter, then she reached down, grabbed his ears and hauled him over her.

Isaac's body shook with laughter too as he allowed her to pull him up from her center. He wiped his hand over his mouth and hovered over her.

"Ditch the jeans, Sergeant," she said, the huskiness of her voice making his balls tighten.

' Grinning, he did as ordered, kneeling up and dropping his jeans down enough to reveal his cock. With a move that made her squeal, he fell back against the pillows and tugged her roughly over him so she straddled his thighs. She dripped down on his cock, and he fought back the urge to take her without a condom.

He'd done so in the shower, which had been risky, even though he'd pulled out. It'd be fucking life-altering, but they couldn't make a habit of it. He'd had a pregnancy scare once, and he never wanted to do that again.

Reaching into the nightstand, he pulled out a condom, tore it open and rolled it on, the entire time with her full, creamy tits just inches from his face, just begging to be licked, sucked and worshipped.

Once the condom was on all the way, she lifted up and slid back down until he was sheathed to the hilt, each of them sighing in unison when they were finally connected. When the world finally righted on its axis.

He buried his face between her tits, pulled on her nipples with his thumbs and forefingers and shut his eyes, inhaling deep through his nose. "I could die right now and I'd be happy as fuck about it," he said, his words muffled by the milky cushions.

She chuckled, the sound a sexy rumble in her chest. "Yeah, but I wouldn't be. I'd like to get off again first."

He pinched her nipple, making her yelp. "Then start moving, woman."

***

He saw Lauren and Ike to Celeste's door before making his way down the sidewalk to Max's unit on the corner. How convenient for Max and Celeste to live so close to each other. It must make booty calls easier than ever.

The scent of snow lingered in the air, and dark gray clouds covered the sky. Were they in for another dump of the white stuff? He sure as hell hoped not. The snow always brought out the worst drivers—those who thought they were invincible and didn't have to carry chains or buy proper winter tires. He'd already witnessed enough travesties this year alone because of idiots going out in the blizzard because they *needed* smokes or to meet their Tinder date.

You *need* to live.

You *want* the rest.

Big fucking difference.

Pulling his coat tighter around himself, he approached

Max's door. It swung open before he even had a chance to knock. "Saw you coming up the walk," Max said with a grin. "Plus, Celeste texted me and said you were on your way. Come on in."

Max stepped to the side so Isaac could enter. He hung up his coat on a hook and went to remove his wet boots, but Max told him not to.

"We're just going to head down to the garage anyway."

Nodding, Isaac followed him down some stairs to a doorway where classic rock could be heard from the other side.

"Beer?" Max asked, opening the door to reveal an enormous double-wide garage.

Isaac grunted a yes.

Max's Toyota truck was parked on one side, and his motorcycle, a couple of black leather club chairs, a beer fridge and a work bench took up the other.

Max reached into the bar fridge and pulled out a bottle of San Camanez Lager and handed it to Isaac. "I take it you heard Bianca's ex had the babies?" Max sat down in one of the club chairs.

Isaac took a seat in the other and twisted off the cap of his beer. "Yeah. Horrible fucking names."

Max blew out a breath. "I've been teaching high school math for over fifteen years. I have heard some pretty awful names, but those two might take the cake."

"I just hope Bianca doesn't overdo it in her reaction to it," Isaac said, taking a long pull of his beer. "She was already drinking when she called Lauren earlier and then said she was going to smoke a joint."

He had no problem with people who smoked pot or who drank. It only became a problem when they got behind the wheel after smoking or drinking or became disorderly or violent.

Particularly toward their spouses and children.

At least Bianca's kids weren't home to see their mother and the way she chose to handle things.

Not that he was judging. Everyone had their own ways of coping with things.

Isaac battled his demons with sex and working out. And when neither of those worked or were doable, he and Sid would hit The Rage Room, go throw some axes or take their guns to the shooting range and fire off a few rounds in the bullseye.

"Lauren and Celeste won't let her overindulge," Max said, sipping his own beer. "I can't imagine going through what Bianca is going through. And with three little kids to boot."

Nodding along, Isaac took another sip.

"You put your Ducati away for the winter?" Max asked, thankfully changing the subject.

"Yeah. No sense riding it right now. I like my nuts. Don't need 'em freezing off."

Max snorted and bobbed his head. "Yeah, only downside to living where we do. You from here?"

"Originally from Nebraska. Moved down to Phoenix when I was eight, then Seattle after my second tour."

"Army?"

"Marines."

"Nebraska, huh?"

"Yeah, a town called Quaint, just outside of Omaha."

He wasn't sure why he was telling Max all of this; he never spoke about his time in Quaint, not to anyone. If anybody ever asked, he was from Phoenix. That place felt more like *home* anyway. Not that he had anybody left there. But the memories in Quaint weren't ones he wanted to keep. They were more like nightmares that he couldn't shake no matter how old he got, no matter how much he tried to move past the things he'd done, the things his father and grandfather had done.

But Max had a certain way about him. He was easy to talk to. Relaxed and nonjudgmental.

"You ever been back to Quaint?" Max asked. "Got any family left?"

If he never stepped foot back in that town, back in that state for the rest of his goddamn life, he'd be better for it. Everyone who he'd loved had fled the state too. Too much history and devastation resided in Quaint for anybody with the last name Fox to ever make a go of it there.

He shook his head. "No need to. Family all left."

Because his dad and grandfather had forced them to.

Max nodded. "You got a place to store your bike? You're welcome to keep 'er here if not. I've got plenty of room."

Smiling around the mouth of his beer bottle, he shook his head. "I've got a garage at my condo. I'm not *supposed* to work on my bike in it, but I have. But I appreciate the offer. I might take you up on it if the homeowners' association climbs up my ass about working on it there. Not that they'd ever know. I lay down cardboard to catch any oil."

"I do that here," Max said. "Just let me know."

"Appreciate it."

They continued on through the evening, chatting about various shit. Max's time in Vietnam teaching, Isaac's time in Iraq. Motorcycles and the fact that both their fathers were bikers as well, so they came by their love of bikes honestly.

He never went on to say that his dad was part of an outlaw motorcycle club back in Quaint, though. The True Destroyers were dead now anyway. And those that didn't die were either in prison or had fled. There was no need to rattle bones and crack open headstones. He was already worried that he'd talked too much about his dad and time in Quaint that it was going to affect his sleep. It usually did. Even though he knew he needed his therapist to talk through the shit in his head, both from his past, his time in the Marines and his life as a cop, dredging up his life in Quaint always fucked with his sleep more than anything he'd ever witnessed in Iraq or on the force.

Then they worked on Max's Bonneville a little before heading upstairs to watch the football game Max had recorded on the PVR.

"You a Seahawks fan?" Max asked, tipping up another beer.

Sucking air through his teeth, he smiled and shook his head. "Cardinals fan, man. I can't just ditch my team because I moved. I'm loyal that way."

Max laughed. "You need to be loyal to where you live *now.*"

"I'll root for the Hawks if the Cards aren't playing, but the Cards are my team. Always will be."

"And to think, I was going to see if you wanted to catch a game at CenturyLink field with me next season. My dad knows a guy who's a season ticket holder, sells his seats for a decent price. Lower bowl and everything."

"Ah, well, for lower bowl seats, I might be able to suffer through wearing blue and green for an afternoon."

Grinning, Max turned up the volume of the game. "I'm going to see if I can get tickets to when they play the Cards."

Isaac's smile fell, which only prompted Max to laugh even harder.

IT WAS past midnight by the time Lauren texted Isaac and he came to collect her and Ike from Celeste's. Max was with him, as he was staying the night at Celeste's.

Always out to serve and protect, even on his days off,

Isaac walked a very drunk Bianca to her door before coming back to get Lauren and Ike and walking them home as well.

She was tired but also excited for what she had promised Isaac. He and Idris were going to double-team her tonight.

She only hoped she had the energy and Ike cooperated. He'd been awake a fair bit at Celeste's house, having to endure being passed around among the three of them like a football. So hopefully, that meant he'd sleep well and long after she topped him up.

Isaac unlocked her front door with his key and held it open for her, but he didn't step inside. She had Ike in the stretchy wrap, so she turned to face him. "You coming in?"

The man in front of her seemed a million miles away. His head shook, his eyes sad, mouth in a flat line. "I can't."

"But ..."

"I just think I need to spend tonight at home, okay?"

She reached for him, and thankfully, he didn't step away. He looked as reluctant to leave as she was to see him go. So why was he leaving at all?

Her fingers wrapped around the front of his coat. "Have I done something?"

Now he just looked broken. "Baby, you have done *nothing* wrong. I just ... I talked about some stuff with Max, and I probably shouldn't have, because when I talk about that stuff, it fucks with my sleep. I toss and turn forever, and then when I finally do fall asleep—*if* I finally fall asleep—my dreams are fucked up. I don't want to put that on you or Ike. Your sleep is already so broken up as it is."

"Wh ... what did you talk about with him?" She'd have to message Celeste to find out what kind of questions Max had asked him. What the hell was Max's angle probing into Isaac's life like that?

He shook his head. "It doesn't matter. I just know myself, I know my head, and I think it's probably best if I sleep at home tonight, okay?"

Flurries began to drift down behind him, the wind pushing them into the house and his hair. "Will talking with me about it help?"

His head shook again. "No. I'm sorry."

"Was it your time in the Marines?"

She could tell he didn't want to talk about it, but she was so confused, there wasn't much else she could say or offer besides a nonjudgmental ear and a shoulder to cry on if he needed it.

"I don't want to talk about it." His long, warm fingers wrapped around her hand, and he peeled it from the front of his coat, bending his head to brush his lips over hers. "I'll be by tomorrow, okay?" She squeezed her eyes shut as his warm breath coated her lips.

Confusion and sadness hung thick and heavy in the back of her throat, like a wad of stale bread that just refused to go down. She clenched her molars tight, blinked back the tears and smiled up at him, though the struggle to lift the corners of her mouth was almost unbearable. "Okay."

She made to pull away, but he hauled her back against him, sandwiching Ike between them. His lips crushed hers, and his tongue forced its way into her mouth, claiming every contour, every corner. She melted against him and moaned, lifting her arms to rest on his shoulders and wrap her hands around his neck.

Her attempt to pull him into the house was futile. He was so much stronger than she was, it was like trying to move a marble statue.

When he broke the kiss, she was left panting and more confused than ever. He released her hand and stepped away. "Tomorrow, Lauren. Have a good night." Then he disappeared down her driveway toward his truck, the beep of the door opening, followed by the rev of the engine like thunder echoing through the quiet complex.

She waited on her doorstep until he drove away, tears in her eyes, a crushing ache in her heart, and frustration heating up inside her veins.

Once he drove away, she shut the door, pulled out her phone and called Max.

She could have texted or called Celeste, but why not go straight to the source? The man who had been the curious little cat asking all the questions.

It rang four times before Max answered. "Everything okay, Lauren?"

"What the hell did you ask Isaac?"

"Huh?"

"He just left here saying he couldn't spend the night because the shit you two talked about would give him nightmares. What did you talk about?"

"I ... I asked him where he was from. If he ever went back there. About his time in the Marines and Iraq. His job as a cop. And then we talked about motorcycles and football. He seemed fine with it all. What did he say?"

"He said that the things you two talked about—his past—when he talks about it, it ends up affecting his sleep. He tosses and turns and has nightmares, and he didn't want me to be burdened with that, so he left."

"I ... I'm really sorry, Lauren. I had no idea. I was just trying to be friendly and get to know the guy. Give him a place to hang out while you women did your wine thing. I never intended to pry and upset him or you."

Whispers over the phone distracted Max before she was put on speakerphone and Celeste's voice came on. "Did you ask him what it was they talked about that triggered him?"

"I did. He wouldn't say." She was at a loss right now. More helpless, confused and hurt than she'd been in a long time.

Did Isaac not trust her enough to let her see all his sides? The good, the bad and the scary? If they were going to do this, for real, she needed to know what his triggers were. About his past and the things that haunted him. She didn't want to be blindsided five years from now when he was all of a sudden triggered by something and went off the deep end or tried to strangle her in her sleep.

Or would they need to sleep in separate bedrooms if he was triggered?

She could handle that. But she deserved to know what those triggers were and how she could help him.

"I don't know what to say, Lauren," Max said, his voice laden with remorse. "I'm really sorry if I messed things up for you guys. That wasn't my intention at all."

Exhaling, she stepped out of her snow boots and headed down the hallway to her bedroom. Ike had fallen asleep in the wrap—great! Now she had to hope he didn't wake up when she peeled him out of it.

She sat down on her bed, defeated. "I know you didn't, Max. And I'm sorry for jumping down your throat."

"You're just worried," Celeste said.

She was more than worried. She was scared. Scared she'd started to give her heart to a man who had more skeletons in his closet than she was prepared to deal with.

"Yeah. I'm worried."

"Call me tomorrow," Celeste said. "We'll talk more then."

Nodding, she plugged her phone into the charger and began to unwrap Ike. "Okay. Sorry again, Max. I hope I didn't wake you guys."

"No worries, Lauren. We're always here," he said, before disconnecting the call.

Yeah, she knew her friends would always be there for her, but she wasn't so sure Isaac would be.

16

THEY WERE a week into February now, and although Isaac's unwillingness to open up to her still hung like a noose around Lauren's neck, he proceeded to act like nothing happened.

Which just bugged her even more.

He also hadn't been back over to Max's.

He'd shown up to her house the next morning after bailing on their night together, all smiles, kisses and hugs, and when she brought up his talk with Max or asked him how he slept, he either changed the subject, kissed her or downplayed everything.

Were they at a point in their relationship where she could push him to open up? Or would he shut down even more and end things?

She knew getting involved with a cop was dangerous because of the curse and all, but she hadn't anticipated how hazardous it would be to her heart. She was falling for him. Hard. The way he was with her son, how he treated her. Isaac was an impossible man not to fall in love with, and knowing that had her terrified.

She was transitioning Ike to sleeping in his bassinet even for his naps, and so far, the kid hadn't put up a colossal stink about the change. While she and Isaac were on the couch, Ike had managed to sleep a solid forty-five minutes in there before the grunts and squeaks on the baby monitor had Isaac lifting his face from between Lauren's thighs to go and get the little cockblocking beast.

"It's a beautiful day, Mommy. What do you say we bundle up and all head downtown for a walk along the water? Go watch the guys throw fish in Pike Place, get some Beecher's mac 'n' cheese." He handed her Ike and wandered into the kitchen to grab a glass of water.

She put Ike to her breast in the recliner and gauged the man standing at the sink in the kitchen. "When are you going to open up to me?"

The playfulness in his blue eyes disappeared, replaced with a wariness that made her stomach spin. He set the empty glass down on the counter. "What do you want to know?"

Exhaling through her mouth, she glanced down at Ike for a moment to ground herself. "Whatever you're willing to tell me. I feel like I hardly know you, Isaac. I don't want to push, but if you have triggers—*demons*—I think I deserve to know what some of those are. You're sleeping in my bed, spending time with my child ... is there a *danger* that I should know about?"

Like you were kidnapped by the enemy while in the Marines and then reprogrammed with a trigger word? If she said "molybdenum" five times fast, would he go into kill-mode and start strangling everything that breathed? Was she falling in love with an assassin?

Swallowing, she clenched her molars to keep her chin from trembling. "I've seen your house, which I appreciated.

Nothing out of the ordinary, no doll heads in a China cabinet, but I still don't feel like I *know* you."

With purposeful strides, he was around the island and into the living room, sinking down to his knees beside her and taking her hand. "I would *never* ever hurt you or Ike. Ever. *Ever.* You got that?"

Dragging the corner of her bottom lip between her teeth, she nodded. A hot tear slid down the crease of her nose.

His somber expression matched the heavy lift and drop of his chest. He was in distress. "I grew up with an abusive father. One who liked to hit. Not just my mom but me too. I wouldn't let him touch my sister though. When he went after Natalie, I took every swing intended for her. Took a lot intended for my mom too."

Oh God.

"My *demons* have a lot to do with that. I don't like to talk about my dad or that time in my life because none of it was good. Life did not get even remotely bearable until that bastard went to prison. Until we moved to Phoenix."

"Where did you live before that?"

He shook his head. "It doesn't matter. I don't like to think about it. I don't like to talk about it. But please know, Lauren, that even when I'm having a hard night, that will never spill over to danger for you. I toss and I turn. I cry out in my sleep. I have nightmares—bad ones. But I don't get violent."

She struggled to swallow, but her throat was too tight.

He cupped her face in his hand, his fingers threading into her hair behind her head. His warm thumb brushed her cheek, wiping around the tears. "Have I scared you?"

No. Her heart just ached for the little boy who'd been forced to grow up way too fast. Take punches for his sister and mother all because a man who was supposed to be his protector looked at him more as a punching bag than someone he loved.

"I don't want you to shut me out," she whispered, leaning into his palm. "I don't want to push, and I won't. But I hope, over time, you'll let me in. Tell me more. Just because I'm crying doesn't mean I can't take it. I cry over everything right now, remember?" Her laugh was choppy and broken by a sob.

Surging forward, he captured her mouth with his. "When the time is right, I'll tell you, okay? I'm just not ready yet. It's a lot to take in."

A lot to take in.

What did that mean?

Would her opinion change of him when she found out the truth? Was he waiting until she was head-over-heels in love with him, married to him, they were celebrating their diamond anniversary before he finally told her the truth?

Was that fair?

"It's not something that was illegal or hurt somebody else, was it?" she asked, unwilling to let it go, even though the expression on his face said he wanted nothing more.

The grim line of his mouth was back. "I killed in Iraq. You know that, right?"

No, she didn't. But she knew there was a possibility.

That was different though, wasn't it?

"Does that change your opinion of me?" he asked, his eyes narrowing, shifting slowly across her face.

She shook her head. "No."

A swift nod, a peck on her forehead and a smack of his hand against the arm of her chair was all she got as a response. "I'll go double-check we've got wipes, diapers and extra clothes in the diaper bag. Then we'll hit the road. I'm craving some mac 'n' cheese. I don't know about you."

He disappeared down the hallway, leaving her sitting there with her son, wondering what kind of a man she was with but also knowing there wasn't much besides cold-blooded murder that would make her leave him.

THAT EVENING they were back at Lauren's house; Ike was asleep in the bassinet, and Lauren was just finishing up with the dishes.

They'd had a great day downtown, exploring, eating and enjoying the weather, but even so, Lauren was distant with him.

He knew she wanted to know more about his past, more about what haunted him, but he just wasn't ready to pick back that scab and let it bleed. Because when he did, it bled like a motherfucker and didn't stop.

But he'd hurt her with his evasiveness. He could tell. She was all smiles, holding his hand, laughing at his jokes, but the spark was not in her eyes. The glitter he'd fallen hard for had gone out, and it pained him to see it vanish and know it was because of him.

He was in love with her.

He knew that.

Knew it with every fucking fiber of his being.

But as much as he would toss himself in front of a bus for her or Ike, he wasn't ready to tell her everything. To tell her his past, his failings and how he'd ultimately destroyed his family and others.

He needed to convince her he was all in this though and that he trusted her and she could trust him.

He'd never hurt her.

That's not how his triggers worked.

It was just the discussion of it that resurfaced the memories to the forefront of his mind, causing them to take over his thoughts and dreams. And then instead of dreaming about fucking Lauren in the shower, or arresting the carjacker in Emerald City Plaza, he was an eight-year-old boy again and everyone around him was screaming, crying, and there was a lot of blood on the floor.

After wheeling Ike into the nursery and setting up the baby monitor, he went about preparing Lauren's room. She already had candles set out on her dresser and nightstand, so all he had to do was find a match.

By the time she was done with the dishes, he was done in the bedroom as well. He intended to pamper her tonight. Show her just how much she meant to him, how much he loved her, and that even though he wasn't ready to talk about the things he'd done, it didn't mean he one day wouldn't or that he didn't trust her.

Because he did.

He trusted her completely.

Her back was to him in the kitchen, and he took a moment to just stand there and watch her. Appreciate her curves. Her ass. The flare of her hips and the way her blonde hair curled down her back and over her shoulders. She rarely wore it down—said Ike was in a grabby stage—but when she did, it took his breath away.

Walking up behind her, he cupped her ass. Two perfect globes that filled his palms and then some.

Brushing her hair over her shoulder, he pressed his lips to her neck. She tilted her head to the side to grant him better access, and a delicate feminine purr rumbled through her. At the same time, Penny began to weave her way in between his feet.

If it wasn't one of their "kids" cockblocking them, it was the other.

She meowed until he bent down and picked her up. "You're killing the mood here, kitten."

Penny meowed again.

Lauren spun around, her eyes soft, expression gentle. She rested her forearms on his shoulders. "She knows who the easy mark is. She wouldn't get away with that stuff with me."

"You saying I'm the easy parent? The softy?"

Her smiled warmed him. "I'm saying you might be *bossy*, but you're not *the* boss. She knows who rules the roost." She angled forward and pressed her forehead against Penny's. "Don't you, baby? Mummy is the boss and Daddy is just a big sof—"

"Second boss," he corrected.

Her throaty chuckle made his dick twitch.

"And I'm the first boss in the bedroom."

Smiling, she removed her arms from his shoulders and took Penny from him. "I'll put her in her bed. She's tired; she'll stay there." Without saying another word, she headed off with Penny down the hallway toward her room.

He followed her, but she beat him there, and he didn't get to see her gasp. He only heard it as he entered the room behind her.

She spun around, her eyes widening when he approached her, his intentions plain as day in the sizzling blue of his gaze.

"Take off your clothes, baby. Let me pamper you."

Nibbling that lip of hers, she set Penny down in her bed in the corner of the room and began to peel out of her yoga pants and T-shirt, her eyes never leaving his.

"Climb onto the bed on your stomach."

He'd pulled the duvet and top sheet all the way down to the bottom of the bed and arranged the pillows in a way that he hoped resembled the hole in a massage table.

After rooting through her nightstand drawer, he found a bottle of safflower-scented massage oil and intended to spend the evening—until either of the little cockblockers woke up, that is—showing her just how much she meant to him.

She climbed onto the bed as instructed and positioned

herself on her belly, resting her face between the pillows, with her arms extended over her head.

He dimmed the lights and shucked his shirt and jeans until he was in nothing but his black boxer briefs with a pitched tent.

Sex wasn't off the table tonight, but it didn't have to happen either. He knew Lauren was struggling with what he'd told her—but more with what he hadn't told her—and he wanted to ease her confusion and anxiety by kneading her muscles into butter. Hopefully, banishing any reservations she might have about him, and them.

Settling on the bed beside her feet, he took one and then the other on his lap, squeezed a bunch of massage oil into his palm and began to work it into the balls of her feet.

Her moan had his dick throbbing.

"God, you're good at that," she murmured, her voice already sounding distant and sleepy. "I had to pay people to do it while I was pregnant."

"Can you get full body massages while pregnant?"

"Yeah, and they're amazing. Some places have special holes in the table. Other places make you lie on your side, and they prop you up with pillows. But even the places with holes in the table will make you lie on your side when you're near the end. Too much strain to hang the belly like that for so long."

Made sense. He got a massage every now and then after a particularly grueling week at the gym with Zak. Did any of the tables he lay on have a hole in them?

His hands traveled up her calves, massaging the oil into her soft skin. She whimpered again as he tickled behind her knees, squirming on the mattress, pressing her pelvis down against it.

Adjusting himself on the bed, he straddled her legs and ran his hands up, focusing on her inner thighs and hamstrings. She had great muscle definition and strength; he already knew from the few times she'd mentioned it that it was killing her not to be able to hit the gym like she used to.

His middle fingers brushed her pussy lips, and she tilted her hips and spread her legs—not that she could do that much, because he was sitting on them. He continued on up over her ass cheeks, kneading them, caressing them, working his thumbs into the muscles he knew would be tight.

"Move those fingers back down," she murmured, shimmying on the bed again.

Smiling, he dipped one hand below and pressed his middle finger against her clit. "That's not what this is about."

"But it could be." She pressed down against the bed in an attempt to keep his hand beneath her. "I'm willing to forgo the massage if you massage my clit with your tongue."

With a laugh, he wiggled his finger over her clit again before pulling it away and working his hands into the small of her back. "If you want to after, we can, but I'm okay just taking care of you tonight."

She craned her head around, her expression worried. "You don't want to?"

Gripping his erection over his boxers, he shook it gently. "Does this look like the dick of a man who doesn't want to stick it in you?"

Her smile was illuminating, warmed his heart and forced the words out of his mouth. "I love you."

Her eyes went as wide as dinner plates, and she motioned to sit up, but he held her down with both hands on her ass, his body still straddling her legs.

"Stay down. Let me spoil you."

"But I—"

"You don't have to say it back. If you're not ready, that's okay."

"Isaac—"

"Just close your eyes. If you want, I can grab Idris for you and let him go to town on your front while I massage your back."

"Would. You. Shut. Up?" She held up a finger. "Though, let's pause for a minute, because that's not a bad idea. Let's do that. But now, unpause and back to what you said before and then when you kept cutting me off."

His lips wanted to do nothing but curl into a smile at her bossy tone. "I'm sorry. What did you want to say?"

"That I love you, too, you sexy, *annoying* beast. Only you wouldn't let me get a word in edgewise." She growled, but it was followed quickly by another giant smile.

She loved him.

He wasn't sure he'd ever heard anything so fucking wonderful in his life.

Abandoning her massage for a moment, he reared up over her body and stole her mouth, kissing her like he had that first night. With a need so strong, he had a hard time believing it was real.

But she was real.

She was the real deal.

With Lauren and Ike, he was going to build the family he'd always wanted. He would not let history repeat itself. He was going to be a good partner to Lauren and an amazing father—if she let him—to Ike.

Because he loved them both.

He already knew he was nothing like Steve, nothing like the man who had been a "father" to him for eight years of his life. Now he just needed to keep it like that. Not let Steve and the plague that he was on humanity, on Quaint, on Isaac's family affect his future with Lauren and Ike.

With his heart doubled in size and wanting to burst free from his chest, he pecked her once more on the mouth before returning to his task of massaging her. He didn't want to get sidetracked. She deserved to be worshipped without the expectation of something in return.

He'd never forget the way his old man thought anything "nice" he did or said to Isaac's mom should be rewarded with some sex act. When Steve would unbuckle his jeans after dinner, let out a loud belch and thank Joan for the meal, he'd then jerk his head toward the bedroom, slap her ass as she stood at the kitchen and expect her to follow him down the narrow hallway of their mobile home.

Even at seven and eight years old, Isaac knew what was going on.

He'd turn up the music on the radio in the kitchen and finish the dishes and cleaning up while Natalie played on the floor with her dolls. His room was next to his parents' room, so no way in hell was he going to go sit in there and listen to the headboard bang for ten minutes.

"You okay?" Lauren's voice drew him from his thoughts, and he found her staring at him over her shoulder, concern in her eyes.

"Yeah, I'm fine. Why?"

"Because you're massaging my back so hard, I'm going to have bruises."

Shit.

"Sorry." He eased up and moved his hands to her shoulder blades, finding a knot between them and using his thumbs to work it out. But she didn't let him stay there for long before she was rolling over to her back, concern back in her eyes.

She reached for him, and this time, he went willingly into her arms. She took his weight and didn't balk. His head rested between her breasts, and her fingers began to play with his hair. "I forgot to tell you, I have an appointment with the doctor tomorrow to get an IUD put in. They had a cancellation and called to see if I wanted the slot."

"No more condoms?" He closed his eyes and breathed her in, the sound of her heart beating next to his ear a reassuring, calming boon.

"Not if you don't want to."

"Up to you, babe. I've had a pregnancy scare in the past with a"—he let that last part hang—"and it was just that —*scary*. How was Ike conceived?"

Her fingers through his hair were magical. He would probably fall asleep there—between her breasts, between her thighs, if he wasn't careful.

"Ike was an oops. Tucker and I were sleeping together on and off for about three months. We weren't serious, but we did agree to be exclusive. I was on the pill, but I was having a lot of side effects from it, and I kept forgetting to take it. We went to a party at his friend's pool, got drunk and wound up in the pool house, the condom broke when he rolled it on, so we decided to do the pull-out method. Obviously, that didn't work."

"And then he split?" The thought of some person— because, let's face it, this Tucker was no *man*—abandoning Lauren and Ike made Isaac's blood bubble. He needed to find this Tucker fucker and keep tabs on him. Make sure he never bothered Lauren or Ike again. The last thing any of them needed was a year or five from now there being a knock at the door and Tucker Fucker suddenly wants to play house and play catch with Ike in the backyard.

Lauren hummed, the rumble a pleasant din next to his ear. "Obviously, it takes a few weeks for the signs of pregnancy to show up, so we continued to see each other for that month or so. Then I found out I was pregnant, told him. He went white as a sheet and left. I have not heard from him since."

"Did you try calling him?"

"Of course, I did. It went to voicemail for a while, then it said the number wasn't in service, so he obviously changed his number. We're better off without him anyway."

"Absolutely you are. You have me. You, Ike, you don't need him."

"No, we don't."

She didn't say anything, but he could tell by the way she squirmed beneath him that he was probably getting heavy for her. He rolled to the side, taking her with him and drawing her in front of him, her ass nestled against his cock. "Tell me more about this curse. If we're going to try to break it or navigate around it, I need to know what I'm dealing with."

He also needed to get off the topic of Ike's AWOL father and thoughts about his own deadbeat dad.

"Well, my grandfather died first. He was caught from behind and stabbed in the neck by the president of the True Destroyers during a raid on the club's warehouse where they trafficked illegal firearms."

Sharp shards of ice embedded themselves in the base of Isaac's spine.

"Luckily, the president was caught and sent to prison for the murder."

He needed to control his breathing, otherwise he was going to pass out.

Clearing his throat, he fought past the taste of bile on his tongue and asked the question he needed to ask. "I thought you were from Utah? The True Destroyers aren't in Utah. They're mainly in the Midwest and have a few charters in the east."

"How do you know that?"

"I just ... I just do."

She shrugged and continued. "I was born in Omaha. My dad and grandpa worked for the Quaint police department. Dad said it was always best to shit where you eat, so he didn't want to live where he worked. Grandpa too."

He swallowed past the harsh lump in his throat. "And you said you had an uncle who was killed too?"

"Uncle. Cousin's husband or whatever. I called her my aunt and Doug my uncle, even though I know that's not the proper terminology." She was starting to ramble. He needed to get her back on track.

"How did he die, Lauren?" Isaac asked, trying his damnedest to keep his tone light.

She snuggled in deeper against him. "Right. He was the last one to be killed, yeah. High up in the PD, he worked in the gang unit, so they brought him in from another county, and he went to prison undercover to try to get some more intel on the True Destroyers. At this point, the new president was also in jail, but they were still selling guns, and there were more drugs in Omaha than ever."

She wiggled her butt against his cock, but he'd gone soft. It was tough to stay hard when your world was slowly crashing down around you.

"My uncle was ambushed in prison. They say it was the MC president that killed him, but we never got a straight answer. This is also just information I garnered from over-hearing the adults talk over the years."

He couldn't breathe. There was nothing but a beautiful woman's naked back up against his chest, and yet it felt like an anvil was on it, slowly compressing his ribs until the bones snapped and pierced a lung.

"And your dad?"

He needed to know. He had to know.

She'd lived in Nebraska, just outside of Quaint. Her father had worked in Quaint. Her father had died on duty when he went to check on a domestic dispute.

With numb fingers, he pulled her tighter against him, her warmth and softness the only thing able to even remotely ground him at this point.

"Killed when he went to investigate a domestic disturbance. I'm sure my mom knows who killed him, but I was never told. Just that the husband was roughing up the wife and kids and my dad and another cop went to check it out and my dad was shot."

"How old were you?"

"Five."

"So that was ..."

Twenty-seven years ago.

But he needed to hear it from her.

"Twenty-seven years ago. October twelfth. I'll never forget the day."

No, and neither would Isaac.

17

HIS NUTS WERE GOING to freeze off soon if they didn't open the damn door. He pounded again and waited, his fingers trembling around his phone as he thought about calling them in case they slept with earplugs in or something.

But then a light came on through the window in the door, and he could see two dark figures approach.

Jamming his phone and hands into his coat pocket, he teetered back and forth on his boots in the cold as he waited for Sid and Mel to open the door.

Neither of them looked pleased when they did, until they saw it was him and that he was seconds from having a nervous breakdown.

He'd waited until Lauren fell asleep in his arms before he carefully untangled his limbs from around her and slipped from the bed. He dressed, grabbed his bag, checked on Ike, kissed him and left. He needed to talk to somebody, to sort out the cannoning thoughts in his head. There was no denying what he'd done, what had happened, but he still needed to make sense of it all. Figure out a way to tell her.

Mel turned on the kitchen light and Sid went about filling up the electric kettle. Isaac took a seat at their kitchen island bar and buried his face in his hands.

He knew it was late. Or early, depending how you looked at it. The clock on the stove said eleven minutes past two. But he also knew that Mel and Sid were two people he trusted more than anyone in the world, and they would help him figure this the fuck out. If the roles were reversed, he'd welcome them into his place regardless of the hour in a heartbeat.

That's what friends did.

"She dumped you?" Sid asked, pulling down a teapot from a cupboard.

He shook his head. "No."

"She tell you she loves you and you're just not there yet?" Mel asked. She grabbed a seat and swung it around to sit at the end of the island so she could face him.

He shook his head again. "No."

"Did somebody die?" Sid asked, swiveling around, a floral shoebox marked "tea" in her hands.

Not just somebody. Three somebodies. Three important somebodies. And his family had had a hand in killing each one of them.

Mel plopped her elbows on the counter and hit him with a no-nonsense look. The diamond stud she was forced to take out when she was on duty twinkled on the left side of her nose in the recessed kitchen lighting. "It's too early in the morning for me to play twenty questions, Isaac. Can you just cut to the chase and tell us what happened?"

"She thinks the women in her family are cursed if they marry cops. Her dad died, her grandfather and her uncle or cousin's husband or whatever. All of them were cops."

"That's silly superstition," Mel scoffed, batting her hand

in the air at an imaginary mosquito. "Yeah, we don't have the safest job in the world, but we're not crab boat fishermen in the Bering Sea either. Apparently, *that's* the most dangerous job in the world."

Sid gave her wife a dubious look.

Mel just shrugged. "I saw it on the Discovery Channel."

"That's not it though," Isaac went on. "I found out tonight that she was born in Nebraska."

"So? Are you going to hold that against her?" Sid asked, pouring loose tea into a silicon tea diffuser that looked like an apple. If he hadn't spent time with these women drinking tea in the past, he never would have known what the fuck she was doing.

"*I* was born in Nebraska."

Mel made an irritated noise and tossed her hands into the air. "Dude, seriously, cut to the chase already. Why is it such a terrible thing you were both born in the same state? What does that have to do with the curse? With you showing up in the middle of the night and disrupting our REM?"

"Because I killed her dad. My dad killed her uncle, and my grandfather killed her grandfather!"

The mug in Sid's hand slipped from her fingers and fell to the tile floor with a smash. Mel's mouth dropped open, and the air around them grew suffocatingly thick.

"Back the murder truck up just a little," Mel said, lifting her hands and pushing her palms forward. "How did you kill her dad?" Her words were slow, cautious, and the way she was looking at him said she wished she or Sid were packing heat in their Hers and Hers matching black terry cloth bathrobes.

Sid was already sweeping up the mess from the broken mug with a broom from the pantry.

He let out a slow breath. "I was eight. We lived in Quaint,

Nebraska, just outside of Omaha. My dad, just like his dad, was part of an outlaw motorcycle club. His dad went to prison for murder. Killed a cop—turns out it was Lauren's grandfather. I connected the dots tonight when she started telling me more about this *curse*."

"I still don't see how that means you killed her dad?" Sid said. Her chestnut hair curled down around her face in messy waves. She normally wore it up in a ponytail or bun for work, but she looked much softer with her hair down, brown eyes sleepy.

"When my grandfather went to prison, my dad became president of the True Destroyers. My dad was a jackass. I do not have one pleasant memory of those eight years I spent living under his roof. He hit my mom, hit me. Would have hit my baby sister if I hadn't taken the punches for her."

"You were a baby yourself," Sid whispered. The kettle on the counter began to beep, and she poured the bubbling water into the teapot.

"One night, my dad came home from a club meeting drunk off his ass. He started getting rough with my mom. Cops were called—probably by a neighbor—though most of our neighbors were afraid of my dad, so who knows. Either way, two cops came out. I can't tell you what happened next because I don't really remember. I heard the cops saying that if my mom didn't smarten up and leave my dad, they were going to call child protective services and take her kids away from her. That made me really mad. My mom was an amazing mom. She did the very best she could in the situation she was given."

"She didn't have any family she could go to?" Mel asked, thanking her wife for the mug of tea.

Isaac thanked Sid as well but shook his head. "They were all terrified of my dad. She knew she couldn't go to any of them because he'd find her, find us. She'd been socking money away since Natalie was born with the plan to get out. But he found her stash one night and—" He sipped his tea. It was too hot, but the burn on his tongue was a welcome distraction from the pain in his chest and gut. "He beat her so badly when he found that money, she needed ten stitches under her eye."

Sid pulled a chair out from under the island and sat next to her wife. "Was that the same night you ..."

"No. The night the cops came—though it wasn't the first time they came—he'd come home drunk and found a few dishes in the sink. Natalie and I were already in bed, but he started yelling anyway. But when I heard the cops say that Natalie and I could be taken away from our mother, and the one cop had even said that siblings didn't always stay together, I freaked out. My dad showed me where he kept his gun—*one* of his guns, I should say. A 9mm Glock. He showed me how to load it. He thought it was a bonding moment between father and son. Not that I needed to load it, because it already was."

"Stupid fucker," Mel muttered over the rim of her mug.

Isaac simply lifted both brows. "I can't tell you what happened next, because I don't remember. I just know I grabbed the gun, stepped into the kitchen where everyone was, and the next thing I know, one cop is dead on the floor, my mom is screaming, sister is crying and my dad is being arrested."

"You were scared," Sid said, stepping off her stool and coming to stand behind him. She looped her arms around his shoulders and hugged him from behind, resting her chin on his shoulder. "You were just a little kid. Forced to grow up way too early. To be the man of the house because your father was nothing but an abusive drunk prick."

"But I killed a man," he said, the tears stinging his eyes, emotion and the harsh reality of what he'd done clogging up his throat. "I killed Lauren's dad. That cop was Lauren's dad. I killed the woman I love's father."

"But you didn't know her at the time. She was like, what, five? Six?" Mel said, her expression gentle. "You were both children. You should never have been able to get access to that gun. You should never have been in that house with that man—that monster—in the first place." Her expression shifted from gentle to angry. "You were a baby."

"A baby with access to a gun," he said with a head shake, raking his fingers of one hand through his hair. "Fuck, thank God that Natalie never found that gun. She could have fucking killed herself."

"Okay, I have to ask the question that's begging to be asked," Mel started, her eyes serious. "Are you sure of what happened if you can't remember it?"

"Good question," Sid murmured, still holding Isaac, her chin now resting on his shoulder.

"I remember enough to know that a cop—Lauren's father —is dead because I walked into that kitchen with a gun. I've exhausted all other options in my head and I can't come up with one that points to someone else pulling the trigger. It had to be that *he* was the cop to make the threat about taking Natalie and I away from our mother and splitting us up. I probably got angry at him and lashed out." *Just like his old man used to.*

"Even so, you were a *child*," Mel said with emphasis. "A scared, child who never should have had access to a firearm. You can't still blame yourself."

"You said your grandfather murdered her grandfather, and your dad her uncle?" Sid said, stepping away from him to take a sip of her tea.

The laugh that fought its way up his chest was one forged out of disbelief. "Yeah. Her grandfather was a cop too. He went on a raid, was stabbed in the neck by the club president."

"Your grandfather?" Mel said, shaking her head.

"Yep. Good ol' gramps was a real stand-up guy. They didn't call him *Havoc* for nothing. Man wreaked it wherever he went."

"And your dad?" Sid asked.

"Steve? Or *Vo* as they called him."

Mel lifted a brow. "Vo?"

"Stevo ... Vo. I don't fucking know. Anyway, he was in prison for what I did, along with a million other charges. But he was still President of the Destroyers, and they were still running guns and drugs all through Omaha and the surrounding counties. An undercover cop was sent in to try to get a bead on what was going on, figure out how my dad was still running things from the inside. My old man was a psychopath for sure, but he wasn't stupid. He knew the smell of a cop a mile away. I don't for one second doubt it was him who stabbed Lauren's uncle-cousin or whatever, or at the very least put a hit out on him."

"But you don't know that for sure," Mel said, cupping her mug in both hands and tapping her fingers against it.

He shrugged. "Either way, I *do* know that I killed her dad and my grandfather killed her grandfather. The web is already tangled so tight, it's strangling me."

He felt like a royal dick leaving her in the middle of the night the way he had, but he couldn't stay there knowing what he'd done. What his father and grandfather had done. He *was* the curse. His family was the scourge that had destroyed Lauren's family. Taken men from them. Taken fathers, husbands away from the people they loved.

How could he face her again? Face Ike? Did they have a future together?

"You have to tell her," Sid said, squeezing him once more

before wandering out from behind him to stand next to her wife. "If you don't, it will eat you up inside and destroy your relationship."

Yeah, he knew that.

The memories of what he'd done still ate him up inside. The knowledge that he'd murdered a cop was like a tattoo on his brain he would never be rid of. Whether he was a scared kid or not when it happened, it didn't take away from the fact that he'd killed a man. A man who also just happened to be the father of the woman he'd fallen in love with. He knew that talking about it triggered the dreams and the warped thoughts as he lay in bed. What would happen to him now that he knew the name of the man he'd killed? That he knew the daughter he'd left fatherless. That he loved her.

"What do you need from us?" Mel asked, sipping her tea. "Do you want us to be there when you talk to her? We can do that."

Shaking his head, he buried his face in his palms. He didn't know what he wanted. Except to find a time machine and go back twenty-seven years to that night and tell his eight-year-old self to put down the gun.

But then how much longer would Steve have continued to beat him and his mother? Until one of them didn't wake up from their injuries? Until he killed his family in a fit of blind, drunken rage?

His phone in his coat pocket began to chirp.

He already knew it was Lauren.

She probably woke up to feed Ike and realized he was gone.

"You gonna answer that?" Mel asked, her green eyes soft but still no-nonsense.

He swallowed, pulled out his phone and hit the green button. "Hey," he croaked.

"I woke up to feed Ike and you were gone. Everything

okay?" Her voice was groggy, but he couldn't mistake the worry in her tone.

"I just ..." He couldn't tell her over the phone. That would be sadistic. "I just started having some bad dreams, and I didn't want to put you through that, so I thought it best if I left. I'm sorry I didn't let you know I was leaving. I didn't want to wake you. I know your sleep is precious."

"Yeah, but you had me worried."

Encouraging nods and grim smiles from the women in front of him had him pushing forward. "I'm sorry. I didn't mean to worry you. I'm okay."

"You can always talk to me, you know. I'm pretty open-minded, and I've been told that when I finally stop talking, I can be a decent listener." Her throaty chuckle sounded just as forced as his own.

"I know. I'm just ... not ready."

"Okay." Her words were faint. "When will I see you again?"

When I can bring myself to face you. "I work day shift tomorrow."

"And then I have wine night. Sunday?"

That gave him a little over twenty-four hours to get his shit together and figure out how to tell the woman he'd fallen in love with that he'd killed her father.

"You still there?"

Clearing his throat, he took a sip of his lukewarm team. "Yeah, sorry. Uh, Sunday sounds good. I'll text you."

"Or just come over when it works for you. You *do* have a key, you know."

"Right, a key. Sure."

"I can keep Penny until Sunday if you need me to. Sabrina keeps asking when she can kitten-sit again."

Right, Penny. What a stand-up cat dad he was turning out

to be. He forgot he'd left her there. Was she better off with Lauren anyway?

"She's welcome to watch her whenever she wants," he said.

Mel and Sid both made whirly motions with their fingers and mouthed the words "wrap it up." He needed to get off the phone with Lauren before he spilled the dead dad beans and ruined everything permanently.

"I'll let you go," she said, sounding a million miles away. "Take care of yourself, okay? I'm worried about you."

"Nothing to worry about, babe," he said, wiping a tear from the corner of his eyes before it sprinted down his cheek. "Just need some time to compartmentalize is all."

"Okay." She didn't sound convinced.

"Kiss Ike and Penny for me, and I'll see you Sunday."

"Okay, see you Sunday."

He took a deep breath. "I love you."

She sighed. "I love you, too, Isaac."

He disconnected the call and stared at his friends. Their expressions mirrored the way he felt. At a complete and total loss of what to do.

They'd only been together for a little over a month. Were they strong enough to get past something like this? Was she forgiving enough of a person to understand that he'd been a kid himself, scared of losing his mother and sister, angry at his dad and the cops who threatened to break up his family?

Would she understand that he thought about her father every day of his life and would continue to do so until his dying breath? That that was *his* curse?

"I'll make up the guest room for you," Sid said, not bothering to ask him if he wanted to stay over and simply heading toward the stairs.

Mel glanced at him curiously. "You're thinking about your own fate. What if you *hadn't* killed her dad that night? How much longer would your family have had to endure your father's wrath? Which one of you would have died before he was finally brought to justice?"

A tear dropped onto the counter as he nodded. He lifted his head. "Does that make me a terrible person?"

She shook her head. "No. It makes you human. Even as police officers, it's human instinct to protect ourselves first. Until you're a parent, I'm told. Then that instinct shifts to your children. But you were protecting yourself, your sister and your mother. You'd been protecting them from your father—the person that *should* have been protecting you—for years."

Yeah, he had been. He remembered the first time he'd stepped in front of his dad to protect his mom. He'd been five and half. Built like his dad, Isaac had always been big for his age. He looked three when he was one; five when he was three; eight when he was five; eleven when he was eight.

He'd bypassed the gangly teenager stage and just went straight from pimple-faced teen with bulk to a young adult man with height, breadth and muscle.

Meanwhile, Natalie took after their mother and was tiny for her age. Still was at thirty-two; she was a petite thing. She never would have been able to survive one of their father's kicks or punches.

Would he have lost his baby sister to one of their father's rampages if Steve wasn't sent to prison because of that night? Isaac wouldn't always have been around to protect her or his mother. Would he have come home to a murder scene and no family one night because Joan forgot to wipe the kitchen counter after dinner or pick up Steve his favorite twelve-pack?

He shuddered to think what could have been.

"It's not your fault, Isaac." Mel's voice brought him out of his thoughts. Her new blonde bob was smooshed in on one side of her head from where she'd been sleeping on it, and she still had a pillow crease across her cheek. "You need to keep reminding yourself that. It. Was. Not. Your. Fault."

Yeah, his therapist said the same thing to him every session. His mother refused to talk about it, but he and Natalie discussed it from time to time. She'd only been five, so her memory of the night was fuzzier than his. But she did say that it wasn't his fault.

And deep down, he knew that it wasn't.

Didn't make the nightmares go away though.

It didn't abolish the guilt that followed him around like a balloon tied to his beltloop.

Didn't make the fact that he killed a police officer—Lauren's father—any less true.

Sid bounded down the stairs and ran her hand down the back of her wife's head. "Guest room is all ready for you."

One side of his mouth lifted into a half smile of thanks.

"Maybe you should make an emergency call to your therapist," Mel suggested. "See if he can squeeze you in tomorrow. Take the day off. I don't think you should be working with what's going on in your head anyway. It's only going to be a distraction."

She was probably right about that.

A distracted cop was a dead cop.

They all knew that.

"I put fresh towels in the guest bathroom if you want to have a shower," Sid said. "Might help clear your head a little."

He nodded, but he wasn't really listening.

"We're going to go to bed." Mel stood up and linked fingers with her wife. "Let us know if you need anything though. We work night shift tomorrow, so we'll be around all day."

He nodded again, thanked them for the tea and letting him stay over but didn't lift his head.

"Turn the light out when you're done in here," Sid said.

He nodded again and stared into his empty mug. A few loose tea leaves stuck to the bottom.

Wasn't there some ancient Asian practice of reading tea leaves?

Did it predict the future? Or explain the past?

What did his leaves say about him?

Was he doomed? Was his relationship, his future with Lauren doomed to fail because of one night twenty-seven years ago? Was his past going to haunt his future forever? Tear apart the only hopes and dreams he had for a life and a family with Lauren and Ike before it'd ever really started?

Growling, he pushed the mug again and reached for his phone.

Mel and Sid had been helpful. They were two of his best friends, but they were also newer to the police force than he was. Neither of them had seen a person die—yet—and they had no idea what was going through his head. Where his thoughts were going and how dark they had the potential to get.

But he knew a couple of guys who did.

He knew a couple of guys who had not only served but had done the hard shit, the impossible shit not just any average Joe had the stomach for.

Just like he did, they knew how to compartmentalize. How to live their lives, be with their wives and kids, enjoy life, without letting the trauma and the memories of what they'd done and seen rule their every waking moment.

He picked up his phone and sent out a joint text message to Aaron and Colton.

They'd told their women a lot of what they'd done and seen overseas. They said it made it easier for them to step away when they were triggered. Their women knew when to let them be, when to give them space so they could go to their dark place. They also knew when and how to go and drag their men back out to the light before the abyss crushed them.

Maybe, just maybe they could help Isaac figure out a way to tell Lauren the truth. Though he really doubted there was a perfect way to tell the woman you loved that your family was single-handedly responsible for destroying hers.

18

"HE JUST LEFT?" Celeste asked Saturday afternoon as she and Lauren sat in the doctor's office waiting room for Lauren's appointment to get her IUD.

Lauren nodded. "Yeah, it was so weird. And then when I called him, he sounded strange too. The guy's got some demons, that's for sure."

Celeste had Ike in her arms and was making silly faces at him as he stared at her with wide-eyed wonder. In the last few days, his mouth had started to make what looked like a smile, and of course, Lauren had close to a thousand pictures of those sort of smiles on her phone.

"But you don't think those demons are a danger to you or Ike?" Celeste asked.

"He said they're not. That he's not violent in his dreams. His dad was abusive, so he made a point of telling me he'd never ever hurt us. That he's determined not to repeat history."

"Well, that's good at least. Though it still seems weird that he won't tell you what's bothering him. I don't like secrets in a relationship. And starting a new one with so many unknowns ..." Celeste shuddered. "He's hot and sweet, but is he too damaged? I mean, you've got a lot on your plate. You don't need to add *fixing* Sergeant Foxy McBigHands to it."

"He says he'll tell me his triggers when he's ready. I mean, he also served overseas, so maybe some of that stuff is triggering him? Maybe he has PTSD?"

"Then he needs to go to counseling."

Lauren nodded in agreement just as her name was called by the medical receptionist.

"You want me to stay out here with him?" Celeste said, glancing back down at Ike and opening her mouth wide before pursing it into a raspberry.

Lauren shook her head and grabbed the diaper bag from the floor. "No, come with me. If he gets fussy, it'll be easier for me to just nurse him right in there."

Celeste nodded and stood up, following Lauren and the receptionist down the hallway to the doctor's office.

"Now, are you sexually active?" the young, beautiful, barely legal nurse asked. She had long, camel lashes, flawless skin and gorgeous auburn hair down her back. Lauren felt like a hot pile of steaming garbage standing next to her. She'd put makeup on for the first time since New Year's Eve and was wearing clean yoga pants and a cute long cardigan over a black shirt, but compared with Miss Washington State next to her, she was a train wreck covered in spit-up.

Swallowing, Lauren nodded. "I am, yes."

"Since having the baby?" Was that surprise in the woman's eyes, or was Lauren just hypersensitive to her appearance these days?

Clearing her throat and struggling to smile, she squeaked out, "Yes."

"Is there any chance you could be pregnant?"

"We ... we use condoms, but, I guess, maybe. I don't think

I've ovulated since he was born though, and I thought breast-feeding decreased the chances of conception."

They were all standing on the threshold of the doctor's office. Which was incredibly uncomfortable, given the topic of conversation. People were walking by: patients, doctors, nurses and technicians. Why didn't she wait to ask Lauren once they were *in* the office and the door was closed? Wasn't that typical protocol? Privacy and all that jazz.

The nurse's smile was as white as snow, and she batted those long lashes so it looked like a gang of spiders was attacking her face. "Nothing is one hundred percent besides abstinence. I'm going to need you to take a pregnancy test before we can proceed. We can't insert an IUD if you're pregnant."

She set down an orange-lidded sample cup on the counter inside the exam room

"There's a bathroom two doors down the corridor on your right. When you're finished, just open the mirror and set the cup on the shelf behind it. I'll take it from there, and the doctor will be in to visit you shortly."

Inhaling deeply, Lauren nodded and grabbed the cup from the counter. Celeste and Ike were already settled on a chair in the exam room playing a riveting game of peek-a-boo. "Be back in a minute," she said with a grumble.

"Good luck," Celeste called, tickling Ike's feet.

Five minutes later, she was back in the exam room, sitting with Celeste and Ike. Her gut was in her throat, her palms were sweaty, and her knee would not stop bouncing.

"What if I'm pregnant?" she said.

"You're not pregnant," Celeste said, shaking her head.

"But what if I am?"

"You're not. You're like *two* months postpartum. Your body is still in recovery mode from the first baby. No way would it be ready for occupancy again so soon."

"But what if I am? Like the beauty queen said, *nothing is one hundred percent besides abstinence.*"

Celeste snorted. "Yeah, but abstinence isn't fun for anybody. That's why birth control was created. Because many years ago women were like, 'Hey, I'd like to get boned but not always have it result in a baby. Let's figure out a way for me to get mine without getting knocked up, too.'"

Lauren snorted.

"And then guys were like, 'You mean I won't have to pull out anymore? Huzzah, let's do it.' And voila, the birth of birth control."

"Well, I was *on* birth control, and Ike's here."

"Yeah, but you weren't taking it consistently. Which is why we're here getting you an IUD. Stick it in and forget about it for the next five years or until you want to have another baby. Easy peasy." She booped Ike on the nose. "Your sperm donor might have been a jerk, but you, sir, are a cutie patootie."

Lauren wiped her sweaty palms on her pants. "But what if I *am* pregnant?"

Celeste rolled her eyes. "You're not."

The knock on the door had them both sitting up straight and Lauren holding her breath.

Dr. Finton stepped inside, her laptop open in her hand. "Well, we won't be inserting an IUD today, I'm afraid. You're pregnant."

"No fucking way," Celeste breathed next to her.

Spots clouded Lauren's vision, and she reached out and grabbed Celeste's arm.

Dr. Finton closed the door and sat down on a small round, rolling stool, bringing it so she was in front of Lauren. "Judging by the fact that you're here for an IUD, I'm going to say this is unexpected news."

Uh, yeah, just a little.

"The HCG level was still quite low, so you're not very far along. If you're okay with it, I'd like to do a quick internal ultrasound to see how far along you are and that everything is okay, since you're only two months postpartum." Dr. Finton stood up and drew the paper down over the exam table. She reached into a drawer below the table and pulled out a robe. "I'll step out for a moment so you can get changed."

Lauren was barely able to nod, let alone stand up and do as she was supposed to.

She was pregnant.

Again.

Another oops baby.

Only this time, it was with a man she'd only known for a month—not three months—but she was also in love with him and he was in love with her.

It was better than the last time she got pregnant, right? Because she hadn't loved Tucker, but she definitely loved Isaac.

Had she thought about a life, a family and a future with Isaac? Of course she had. She wanted more children. She wanted children with Isaac. Little ginger cuties running around, hanging off their father's muscular arms as he hoisted them up and played with them in their backyard.

She saw it all.

She wanted it all.

But they'd only been together for a month.

Ike was only two months old.

She would have two under two.

Only crazy people did that, right?

Dr. Finton stepped out, closed the door behind her, and Lauren turned to Celeste. Her friend was as white as a ghost.

"I ... I'm sorry?" Celeste said, her expression hesitant, like she was waiting to see how Lauren felt about it all before she truly reacted. "I feel like I jinxed you."

Blinking, Lauren stood up and grabbed the robe from the table. She pushed her arms into it before pulling off her pants and underwear. Climbing onto the table, she rested her hands on her belly. It still had a pooch from the last time a baby was in there.

"You okay?" Celeste asked, shifting Ike to her shoulder and standing up to take Lauren's hand as she reclined back onto the table.

"Would you be?"

Her friend's smile was grim. "I'll support you no matter what you decide to do."

She squeezed her eyes shut. There was a knock at the door again, and Dr. Finton walked in. "We okay?"

Lauren swallowed, nodded and put her feet in the stirrups.

Dr. Finton's kind gray eyes pinned on Lauren, and her lips formed a flat line. "You're in shock."

"That's putting it mildly."

The doctor went about preparing the wand used for internal ultrasounds. Lauren stared at the ceiling and waited for the cool gel and the invasive probe.

Celeste's hand tightened around hers.

Gel. And ... wand.

The screen to her right flicked on.

"All right, let's see what we're dealing with," Dr. Finton said. She moved the wand around inside Lauren, and within minutes, a little blob appeared on the screen. "I'd say you're about three weeks along. Not enough to detect a heartbeat. But there's a sac there and cells."

Lauren's gaze flew to Celeste's face. Her friend's nostrils flared, and her mouth remained flat. "We're here to help you. All of us. And Isaac's not going anywhere. He's not like Tucker. He loves you. He loves Ike, and he's going to love this baby."

She knew all of that. But it was still a huge shock.

She'd struggled to tell a man she'd been seeing for only three months that she was pregnant. How on Earth was she going to tell a man she'd only been seeing for a month that she was having his baby?

Dr. Finton removed the wand, handed Lauren a small towel and pushed away from the exam table. "We've been through all this before, so you know the drill. Prenatal vitamins, ASAP. Folic acid. I don't see any reason for me to see you sooner than twelve weeks because that's about the earliest we can detect a heartbeat. Unless of course you are experiencing unusual cramping or bleeding or something— then, by all means, come in sooner." She stood up and came to stand next to Celeste, her gray eyes sympathetic and understanding. "I get the shock, but it'll wear off. You know I'll support you with whatever decision you make, but this *Isaac* guy sounds like a winner."

"He's the guy who helped her deliver Ike in that gridlock," Celeste said. "He's a good guy. A keeper."

Dr. Finton nodded. "I'm glad. You deserve to be happy, Lauren." She patted Lauren's leg, then left Lauren, Ike and Celeste in the room alone. Well, not *alone*. There was that clump of three-week-old cells in her belly too.

Isaac's clump of cells.

His baby.

Her baby.

Their baby.

How would he react? Would they survive this? Or was this all just part of the curse? Fall in love with a cop. Marry him. Have his children, and then he dies.

"Looks like we're back to just wine for two for the next nine months," Celeste said, patting Ike's butt.

A tear slipped down Lauren's temple and into her ear, and

she muffled a sob with her hand over her mouth. "I hadn't even thought of that."

SWEAT DRIPPED into Isaac's eyes as he swung another right hook into the punching bag. Aaron stood behind it, absorbing the force so that it didn't swing away with each punch.

Neither Aaron nor Colton had messaged him back until Saturday morning, but they'd been of like mind. Isaac needed to hit something.

Colton had suggested The Rage Room—a place downtown where you could pay to go into a Plexiglas room full of dishes, furniture, old printers and appliances while wearing protective gear, and with a baseball bat or tire iron, let out your frustrations.

He frequented The Rage Room with a bunch of fellow officers. The last Wednesday of the month, first responders could go for fifty percent off. But Aaron didn't think The Rage Room was what he needed. People didn't need to see his pain. Because even though he was angry, he was hurt and in anguish more than anything.

Colton tipped up a beer bottle to his lips, then muttered, "Good, good. Let it out."

Aaron lifted a brow in Colton's direction but didn't say anything.

They'd been in Aaron's garage for over an hour, and Isaac had barely taken a break for more than a minute to squirt some water in his mouth. He was exhausted, sweaty, but for the first time since he put all the puzzle pieces together, his head didn't feel like it was getting ready to explode.

Aaron encouraged him to explain his story as he

punched, to let each feeling out and transfer it into the bag. He'd done just that, and it helped.

All his anger toward his father and grandfather. How much he hated his old man and the shit he'd put Isaac, his mom and sister through.

Who did that to people they supposedly loved? Who hit their own children? Blood of their blood. Who hit their woman?

Joan Beauchamp was one of the most soft-hearted, quiet, kind women he'd ever met. Steve had charmed his way into her pants when they were sixteen, and then they were married at twenty. Isaac was born only a couple of years later.

His mother had never had a boyfriend before Steve.

And they all knew there was no way in hell Steve was faithful to her in their twelve years together. The man didn't have a loyal bone in his body.

But Steve's way of life scared his mother's family, and they withdrew from Joan's life, going so far as to move to the other side of the state, away from the True Destroyers and their nefarious clutches.

So Joan had nobody.

Nobody but Steve, Isaac and Natalie.

Was he angry with his mother for not getting them out of that hellhole sooner? Sometimes. But in his line of work, he went out on enough domestic disturbance calls that he knew it wasn't as easy as people thought to leave an abusive partner. The threats, the purse strings, the rage. They were all a deterrent to flee.

Joan did the very best she could by Isaac and his sister when they finally moved to Arizona. She worked her butt off to provide for them—working days at a bank and evenings at a call center. By the time he was ten, Isaac was mowing lawns, walking dogs and doing any other odd jobs he could to earn money to help his mama out.

They became the Three Musketeers. They didn't need Steve. They didn't need Quaint or anybody from there. They managed just fine on their own in Phoenix. And best of all, nobody was having to figure out a way to explain a black eye to their boss or the school principal anymore.

With a loud grunt, he landed a hard left hook into the bag, the sweat from his brow flying across the garage.

"I think we should take a break," Colton said, reaching into the bar fridge and pulling out a San Camanez Ale. He popped the cap and handed it to Isaac. "You need to hydrate."

"Water is best after a workout like that," Aaron said, opening up the fridge again and pulling out a bottle of water. "You want this instead?"

Shaking his head, Isaac accepted the beer from Colton and took a long pull off it. It was cool, crisp and so fucking refreshing he thought he might cry.

Of the two of them, Colton was the talker. His wife, Mercedes, had a tough time ever shutting up, and their daughter, Portia, although only six months old, was most likely going to be just like her mother.

Aaron was a grunter. He spoke when he had to. Otherwise, he seemed content just standing around drinking beer in silence.

Which, at the moment, suited Isaac just fine.

"You want us to come with you and help you explain shit to Lauren?" Colton asked, his dark brown eyes pinning on Isaac as he sipped his beer.

He shook his head. Sid and Mel had already offered that, but he didn't think it would be fair to show up with a cavalry. Lauren might feel like she was being ganged up on or something. Like if she didn't forgive him for murdering her father, all the people he brought with him would judge her.

He couldn't do that to her.

Aaron ran a hand through his red hair—a darker shade

than Isaac's—and blew out a long, slow breath. "You don't have any triggers from when you served?"

He shook his head. "Not really. I mean, I think about some of the shit I did and saw, and I don't feel warm and fuzzy about it, but it doesn't haunt me the way the other thing does."

"Because you're able to compartmentalize," Colton said. It wasn't a question. They all did it. It was how they survived the day-to-day. Their time serving their country—the things they did and saw—were put into a box inside their brains, and that box was put on a shelf in a deep, dark corner. They opened that box when they had to, but they did it in a safe space and didn't pull everything out of the box all at once.

Some vets were better at this than others.

Some vets, like Aaron and Colton, had families who helped them get through the day-to-day with joy, rather than spending all their time thinking about the past.

Isaac did that with his job.

As a cop, he was protecting, serving and putting away the bad guys—like his father. And now he had Ike and Lauren to help him get through the day-to-day. He wasn't opening that box on the shelf as much anymore.

"But you're not able to compartmentalize the shit that happened when you were a kid?" Colton leaned against Aaron's truck in the garage and crossed his ankles. Even though it'd been years since he'd served, he still kept his dark hair close-cropped.

"Makes sense," Aaron said, grabbing a wooden stool, handing it to Isaac before pulling one out for himself. "You were a kid. You compartmentalized it in a haphazard way back then. The best way you knew how. The *only* way you knew how. But it wasn't the *right* way. It didn't go into a box. It just buried itself in any and every dark corner it could find. It was never contained. Never properly processed. And if you're still fuzzy on the details, your brain is trying to fill in the blanks but doing so in a shitty-ass way."

Spot on.

Plus, he was an eight-year-old murderer. Seeing a man drop dead in front of you because you pulled a trigger was not something you forgot—ever.

"You need to speak to a professional," Colton said. "I can go with you to the veterans' center if you want."

"I have a shrink," he said, guzzling his beer. "Thanks."

"Maybe he should talk to Iz. She could work some of her voodoo magic on him." Colton chuckled.

Aaron's blue eyes narrowed. "She's not a witch. She's just a very sensitive person. An empath. Feels people's feelings as strongly as they feel them themselves."

Colton snorted and shrugged. "Seems like sorcery to me."

Aaron set his empty beer bottle down, reached into the fridge and grabbed another one, his fully tattooed arms bunching and flexing as he twisted off the lid. "But Tessa might be someone to talk to. She's an *actual* therapist. I know you have your own shrink, but she specializes in trauma and has dealt with loss. Her own as well."

Tessa was with Atlas, another one of the single dads. She was an art therapist who specialized in children who had experienced trauma, but she also worked with adults. Isaac had only met her once—at the New Year's Eve party—but she seemed nice.

He wasn't sure if he wanted people in his "circle" knowing his business though. Unless he told them, he didn't want just anybody knowing he was a murderer. Not that Tessa would tell anybody, but still. If they all started frequenting more of the same gatherings, he'd feel her scrutiny from across the room.

"Just let us know what you need, man," Colton said. "This isn't easy, no matter how you look at it. You've got an uphill battle ahead of you, but we've got your back to help you climb it if you need us."

Isaac grabbed a towel from his duffle bag and wiped his face. "Thanks." That's when he saw his phone flashing. It was on silent, but Lauren was calling. He picked it up and stared at it.

"That her?" Aaron asked with a grunt.

He nodded.

"You gonna answer it?" Colton asked.

Swallowing, he sipped his beer, answered the phone and put it to his ear. "Hey."

"Hey." Her voice was soft, scratchy and shaky. Like she'd been crying or something.

Was she crying because of him?

"You okay?"

"Um ... I know you're working right now—I didn't even think you'd answer— I was just going to leave a message— but do you think you could come by tonight after work?"

Shit. Was she dumping him? Did Ike's dad show up?

A million thoughts raced through his brain at what could have her so upset.

Did she figure it out on her own? Did she know he came from a long line of cop-killers and was a cop-killer himself?

"You're not going to wine night?"

Was that a laugh?

"I'm going ... probably. I just ... I really need to tell you something. I don't want it to wait. When you're done work, could you pop by, please? I won't keep you if you're tired or *whatever*."

The way she said *whatever* hinted at why he'd left her bed the night before. If he was tired, triggered, haunted. Whatever.

"Where are you now?"

"I'm at home. I just got Ike down for a nap. I was going to lie down too. I'm really tired."

Was she sick?

Pulling his phone away from his head, he checked the time. It was two o'clock. He didn't like that he was essentially lying to her because she still thought he was at work. He could leave Aaron's place and head straight over to Lauren's. But she was going to lie down. Ike was asleep. He didn't want to bother them.

He also needed more time to figure out what he was going to do. How he was going to handle telling her the news.

He couldn't go about their lives, about their relationship —if she wasn't calling him to break up with him—without telling her. He had to tell her now. It'd eat away at him like acid in a barrel if he kept it from her.

"I'll be by at five," he said. He'd tell her the truth about where he was and why he wasn't at work when he saw her.

The truth was always best.

The truth shall set you free.

"Okay. I'll see you at five." She was quiet for a moment. Like she was holding her breath or trying to contain a sob. "Stay safe, please, Isaac. You have people in this house who really love you."

He took a deep breath to loosen the cables that were squeezing around his heart. "I will," he finally said. "I really love you two, too."

"Two ... right, two," she whispered. Though it sounded like she was saying it to herself than him. "I'll see you soon."

"Get some rest, babe." He disconnected the call, released the breath that had been trapped in his lungs and glanced at Colton and Aaron.

"Well, at least she's not preparing to dump you," Colton said. "At least not by the sounds of it."

Isaac finished his beer. "Yeah, not *yet* anyway."

19

AT FOUR FIFTY-EIGHT, Isaac parked his truck in Lauren's driveway. He'd gone another round on the punching bag at Aaron's before heading home. Aaron and Colton gave him some solid advice on how to explain things to Lauren. Both their women, Isobel and Mercedes, knew a lot of their triggers and what they witnessed overseas, so the guys coached him on how to tell Lauren. He went home, had a shower, put on his big-boy underwear and drove straight over to Lauren's.

The light in the living room was on, and even though he had a key, it just didn't feel right entering without knocking. He didn't know why, but using his key before she knew the truth felt wrong.

He wasn't sure if Ike was sleeping again or not, so he knocked gently and waited a moment. He knocked again, a bit more forceful this time, and within moments, her figure appeared through the glass in the door.

When she opened the door, her expression held a melee of emotions: surprised, grim and almost slightly irritated. "You have a key. Why didn't you use it?"

"I, uh ..." He stepped into the house. "Sorry."

"I just got Ike down for another nap. The one earlier didn't last long. He's been fussy today since I got back from my appointment."

Right, her appointment. She was getting her IUD put in today.

Because she loved him. Trusted him and was in this relationship one hundred percent.

As he hung up his coat, Penny scampered into the entryway and meowed as she wove around his feet. He picked her up. "Hey, Penelope the Magnificent. How's my girl? Did you miss me?"

"I think she did," Lauren said, retreating to the living room.

He followed her with the kitten in his hand.

"She's been hanging out by the door a lot today, I think waiting for you."

His eyes followed Lauren as she sat down on the couch, her fingers knitting together in her lap, eyes laser-focused on her hands, lip between her teeth.

Setting Penny back down on the floor, he went to Lauren and sat across from her, taking her hands in his.

"I have something to tell you," he said.

"I have something to tell you, too." She lifted her head. The dark blue around her pupils seemed darker than ever, but it was the redness in the whites of her eyes and the blotchy skin beneath that told him she'd been crying.

Crying about what?

Him?

He squeezed her hand. "You first." She'd called him over here to tell him something. The least he could do was give her the floor first. Delay dropping his bomb just a little longer.

She shook her head. "No, you. I can wait."

So could he.

"I'm worried about you, Isaac. Worried about us. I know it's only been a month, but what I feel for you is real. Tell me we're going to be okay. That this is going to work and you're not going to keep leaving in the middle of the night. Leaving *us*."

"I ..."

Her chin trembled. "Just tell me."

"I know who killed your father." The words tumbled out of him.

Shit. This was already not happening the way he'd planned.

She pulled her hands free from his and reared back, distancing herself from him. "What? How?"

He released a breath through thinly parted lips. "It was an eight-year-old boy."

Her head began to shake. "What? No. That's not right. That doesn't make sense."

"Your dad was called out to a domestic disturbance, right?"

She nodded, her eyes gaining a wild look about them.

"Well, there was a little boy at the house. He was scared. Scared for his mother. For his sister. He knew where his dad kept his gun ..."

Her head was shaking again. "How do you know this? How, Isaac? Why are you telling me all of this?"

"Because ... *I'm* from Quaint. On October twelfth, my father was close to killing my mother. He was drunk, angry and violent."

Lauren's entire body began to shake. She stood up, maneuvered around the coffee table and began to pace in front of him. Her head shaking, hands twitching.

"Around ten o'clock, the police were called to my house. I wasn't in the kitchen of our trailer, but I was awake and listening in the hallway."

"But ..."

"My father was president of the True Destroyers. Just like his father before him."

Her eyes grew wide in horror. She stopped pacing just to stare at him, her face draining of any color.

"My father had a gun, several, actually. The True Destroyers were gun runners. Fed most of the supremacists in the area their artillery. I got confused. I got scared. I got angry. Angry at the cops for not doing anything sooner to get rid of my dad. Angry at my dad for hurting my mom. For hurting me. For trying to hurt our family. I took his gun and ..."

"Shot *my* dad." She sank down into the reclining chair, her face long, hands falling to her sides.

"I was eight. I was scared. I was angry. I don't really remember *what* happened. I remember taking the gun from his nightstand drawer, walking down the hallway toward the kitchen, and then the next thing I remember is hearing screaming and crying from my mom and sister and seeing a police officer on the floor of our kitchen, a big pool of blood around his head. My father was in handcuffs with the other officer, and neighbors from the trailer park were in our kitchen, trying to revive the fallen cop."

"My father, you mean. Trying to revive my father. Because you shot him."

He swallowed hard and dropped his gaze to his lap. "Yes. I think so."

That was the last time he'd seen his dad, but his mother refused to talk about it. Natalie couldn't remember much, since she was only five, and Isaac had blocked out a big chunk of that night.

"When did you figure this out?" Out of the corner of his eye, he saw her stand up and begin to pace again.

"Last night. When we were talking and you mentioned

the True Destroyers and Quaint. Then you mentioned October twelfth as the day your dad died. You said how your dad, grandfather and cousin's husband were all killed, and I put all the pieces together."

"You're telling me *you* killed my dad. Your grandfather killed my grandfather and ... who killed my cousin's husband? You got an uncle who likes to kill cops too?"

Her ire was justified. Her pain tangible. He could feel it in the air around him like a smothering fog. She was hurt, confused and devastated. But that didn't take away the sting of her words. Of the enormous cracks forming in his heart from the way she was looking at him.

"I don't know for sure who killed your cousin's husband, but the timelines make sense. My dad would have been in prison at the time, and if the cop was undercover, going in to find out how the Destroyers were still running guns, then chances are my old man killed him—or hired someone else to. He'd always had a sixth sense about who was a cop and who wasn't. Could smell them a mile away."

She snorted. "So what, you decided to become a cop to prove you were better than him?"

He lifted his head completely, chose his words carefully but spoke them clearly. "I *am* better than him. I'm nothing like my father."

Her jaw had grown tight, and a muscle ticked just below her ear. The look she gave him was enough to melt steel. "I think you should go, Isaac."

He'd been expecting her to kick him out at some point, but the fact that she'd actually done it was no less gut-wrenching. No less of a surprise.

Maybe in the back of his mind, he'd been hoping that she wouldn't look at him like a cop killer. Like the man who murdered her father but instead like the man who helped her bring her son into the world, who loved her and her little boy like he'd never loved anyone before.

With tears stinging the backs of his eyes, he swallowed, nodded and stood up. "I'm so sorry, Lauren. I couldn't keep this from you, but I never meant to hurt anybody. I was a kid. Please know that. I was scared."

Her tear-stained cheeks and red-rimmed eyes had his insides growing hot and twisting up, like someone had stuck a red-hot poker into his belly and was spinning it around his organs.

"I was just a kid too. You hurt a lot of people. Destroyed a lot of families." She forced out a strangled laugh. "But what do you expect from the son of a True Destroyer? It's in your blood."

That wasn't fair. Anger struck him like a bolt of lightning. "I may have Steve's blood coursing through my veins, but I am *nothing* like him."

She didn't say anything. The searing pain in her eyes said enough.

But he couldn't leave well enough alone. He couldn't leave with her thinking he was no better than his old man, than his grandfather—a cop killer.

"Would you like it if everyone compared Ike to *his* father for his entire life? It's not all about blood. My mother raised a good man. I'm not perfect, but I'm not a bad guy."

"Leave my son out of this," she whispered, seething.

His chin trembled and he gnashed his molars together to keep himself in check. With a curt nod, he made for the door, scooping up Penny as he went. "I'll just grab her stuff and leave you alone."

She stood in her living room with her hands on her hips, watching his every move as he packed up Penny's toys, food dish and bed and stowed it all in her bag.

She hadn't moved from her spot when he stopped next to

the wall leading to the entryway. "I love you, Lauren. You *and* Ike. I know this thing between us happened fast. I know I pushed for us to be more than just friends. But it's not a curse like you thought."

"No, your family just likes to kill my family." Her eyes closed and she dropped her head so all he could see was the top of it—blonde strands tucked up in a messy topknot with tendrils coiling down next to her temple. She was the most beautiful woman he'd ever met, and he'd hurt her more than anyone ever had.

His shoulders drew back and he sucked in a deep breath. She was trying to hurt him. Trying to push him away to make it easier to end things.

He wouldn't let her. He wanted to fight for them. For what they had. For what they could be.

"We were good together. No. *Great* together. I'm a good man. A good cop, and I live with what I did every damn day and will continue to do so until I die. That's my punishment." He hadn't been a bad kid that day. He'd been caught up in a bad situation. At least that's what his therapist told him nearly every visit. He wasn't bad; the situation was what was bad. His father was bad. Isaac was not a bad kid, and he wasn't a bad man now.

Her derisive scoff had him bracing his hand against the wall in preparation for more vitriol. But when she lifted her head, all he saw was anguish. She was crying now. Her lips were drawn down in a deep frown, her eyes ravaged by plump tears. "And my punishment for falling in love with a cop is finding out he killed my dad."

Like a mallet to a porcelain vase, his heart shattered. Sharp shards of his broken heart struck his chest from the inside, embedded inside his lungs and strangled his throat. He tightened his grip on the wall as the pain increased and he struggled to breathe.

He needed to get out of there before she killed him. Before her words and the agony in her eyes tore what little remained of his beating heart clean from his chest.

Curling his fingers around Penny's bag, he took one last look at Lauren. "We're not done. We're meant to be, Lauren. I'll give you space, time to cool off, but I'm not walking away. I don't walk away from something—from *someone*—I know I'm meant to be with. I will fight for you, fight for us."

He turned the corner, grabbed his coat off the hook and opened the front door, glancing back into the house with hope she was standing there watching him.

She wasn't.

"I love you," he called into the house before shutting the door.

He loaded Penny up into his truck, climbed in behind the steering wheel and fixed his eyes on the living-room window. She was standing there, with the curtain pulled back, watching him.

That's when it hit him—she never had told him what she needed to say. What she'd called him over there for to begin with.

Should he go back inside and demand she tell him?

The curtain fell, and he held his breath that she was moving through the house, the door would fly open and she'd race to stop him from leaving.

She didn't.

He turned over the ignition, let the truck warm up for a moment and then pulled out into her complex, hoping with every cell inside of him that this was not the end. That this was not the last he'd ever see of Lauren. That they could get past this and still have a future together.

A pipe dream?

Perhaps.

But at the moment, it was all he had.

Penny meowed in the passenger seat, and he scratched the top of her head.

A pipe dream and a kitten. That was all he had left.

At least he had something.

———

Lauren sat on Bianca's couch later that night, her face in her hands as the tears continued to fall. She'd been crying ever since she arrived home from the doctor's office, unable to turn off the tap. And after the atomic bomb dropped by the man she loved, the tears had doubled in size and volume.

She figured for sure she would have run out of liquid in her body by now and the tears falling would be no more than dust.

But, alas, they continued to fall in hot, stinging droplets.

Her friends sat on either side of her, their arms around her, rubbing her back, murmuring words of comfort and encouragement, though she wasn't really listening and couldn't remember everything they said.

A tissue was tucked into her palm, and she lifted her head to find Bianca smiling sympathetically.

She blotted her eyes and wiped her nose. "Thank you." She sniffled.

Bianca nodded and rubbed her back. "What did he say when you told him about the baby?"

Shaking her head, Lauren crumpled the damp tissue in her hand and twisted her fingers in the hem of her long cardigan.

"You didn't tell him?" Celeste asked, holding Ike and patting his butt. He'd fallen asleep on her shoulder ten minutes ago, but she was unwilling to relinquish him.

"I was just too stunned. Too hurt. Too ..."

"Shattered," Bianca filled in the last word.

Lauren nodded.

"You know he was just a kid when it happened." Celeste carefully sipped her wine using her free hand, her other hand not missing a beat against Ike's butt.

Yes, she knew that. She knew he'd only been a few years older than she was when it happened—a baby, really.

But it'd still happened.

Her father was still dead, and it was at the hands of Isaac.

Bianca grabbed Lauren's glass of sparkling water off the table and handed it to her, picking up her own wineglass in the process. "His family also imploded that day, too, you know. His dad went to prison. His mom became a single mom like yours. They moved across the country to start over. Something I know you can understand, since you and your mom moved to Utah after your dad died. It was an accident, Lauren. One that should never have happened if his father had been more responsible, but it was still an accident."

She knew all of that.

She knew in the deepest depths of her heart that Isaac was a good man. That they were good together and he had just been a scared little boy, worried about his family being torn apart. But she couldn't see past the fact that her father was dead because of him. That her family was torn apart because of him.

At five years old, she knew better than to touch her father's guns. She knew that guns were dangerous unless handled properly by grownups.

At eight years old, she would think Isaac would know better.

But then, she'd been raised by a good man. Isaac couldn't say the same.

He'd turned out decent though. He'd turned out to be a wonderful man who loved her and her son, like Ike was his own.

"He needs to know about the baby," Bianca said gently. "Not right away. You can wait a little. See if the pregnancy sticks if you need to, but he has a right to know his child."

She knew that.

She knew beyond a shadow of a doubt that Isaac would be an incredible father, that he would be there for their child —and Ike—and her. He'd been there for her when she needed him—needed anyone—the most, and he'd stuck by her ever since. Pushing to be more, because he knew they could be something great.

And they had been.

Fleetingly.

"A part of me wishes he'd never told me," she said, sipping her water. "That I could live blissfully ignorant, have his baby and we could live happily ever after."

"But that would eat him up inside," Celeste said. "And ultimately affect your relationship, even if he chose to never tell you."

She knew that, too.

If the shoe was on the other foot, she wouldn't have been able to keep quiet either. She'd been taught to be honest, particularly with those she loved.

And she loved Isaac.

So much.

Which was why everything hurt with the intensity that it did. Like he'd thrust his fist into her chest and yanked out her heart. Sawed off her lungs so every breath came out shallow and strangled.

She felt betrayed, even though he hadn't betrayed her.

She felt like her family—for the second time—had been ripped apart. But they weren't a family—not yet. They hadn't even gotten the chance.

"Take a few days," Celeste said. "You don't have to react now. Not when everything is still so fresh. I mean, today has been *the* day of days when it comes to getting information dumped on you. First the pregnancy, and then the information about your dad, your grandfather and your cousin's husband."

"What are the odds," Bianca said, shaking her head. "Like seriously. I'm still trying to wrap my head around the whole thing. You and the sexy cop that rescued you on the highway having such a warped connection. I mean, it could have been *anybody* beside you on that interstate, and yet it was him."

"If you ask me, I'd say the fates wanted you to meet," Celeste said softly. "He was *meant* to be there to help you with Ike. Not just to help you, but for you two to become close and for you to learn the truth about your father. Like the universe was helping him make amends for his past. He took your father from you, but he helped you bring Ike into the world. A life for a life."

A life for a life.

Fuck.

Lauren wasn't sure she believed in *fate*, but it was seriously fucked up that Isaac of all people had been the one who helped her in that gridlock.

"Do you love him?" Celeste asked, sipping her wine. Ike was out cold. He'd also started using a pacifier recently, and the *suck suck* noise coming from him every so often pulled at the last remaining strings of Lauren's heart.

Taking a deep breath, she strummed her fingers on her drinking glass. "I do love him. More than I think I've loved anyone in a long time. It's crazy, I know, because it hasn't been that long, but—"

"But it started off intense with him helping with Ike, then the friendship formed, followed by the romance," Bianca finished. "I get it."

"The heart wants what the heart wants," Celeste said. "I'm

proof of that. I fell for my daughter's teacher. Not ideal, but we're making it work."

Setting her water down on the coffee table, she reached to take her son from Celeste. She needed his warmth, his breath against her neck, his scent filling her nostrils and his heart beating against hers. Ike grounded her. That heavy dose of oxytocin to the brain when her baby was in her arms was the only thing getting her through today. When she pressed her nose to his head and inhaled his goodness, her nerves settled, her heart mended and her breathing steadied. Ike was a drug like no other.

"Feel better?" Bianca asked, her smile knowing.

Lauren nodded and leaned her cheek against her son's head, closing her eyes. "I'm not sure I can bear to look at Isaac right now. At this point, if he knocked on my door tomorrow morning, I'd probably start screaming and throwing things."

"And you're allowed to have those feelings," Celeste said. "For now. But your dad has been gone for a while now—twenty-seven years. You are a different person. Isaac is a different person. But you're two people who are *good* together."

"You're also having a baby," Bianca added. "If you choose to ... you know."

Yeah, she knew.

She'd be lying if she said the thought of not having this baby hadn't crossed her mind. Particularly after Isaac left. Could she raise a baby—even platonically—with the man who killed her father? Did she want to be a single mother to two children less than a year apart?

"Take the week," Celeste said, topping up her and Bianca's wine, which only caused new tears to brim Lauren's eyes. "Take the week to think on things, calm down and process everything. This time next week, you may have a different outlook on it all. Maybe talk to your mom?"

She shook her head.

Her mother would be of no help.

It would just upset her.

Bruce Cameron had been the love of Emily Russo's life. His death had nearly killed her, and it'd taken her a long time to pick up the pieces of her demolished heart and move on. Talking to her mother about it, even after all this time, would be like picking at an old scab just to watch the fresh blood pool.

She also wasn't sure her mother would offer the words of wisdom and guidance she needed. Because she wanted to be with Isaac. She wanted to forgive him, move on and have a blissfully happy life together.

But if she told her mom the truth, Emily would only get angry. She'd never be able to look at Isaac without hatred in her eyes. And that made Lauren worry if that hatred would spill over to their child.

No, Emily could never know the truth. No matter the outcome to all of this, Emily had to remain in the dark. If not to protect her heart, but Lauren's, Ike's, Isaac's and the baby's hearts as well.

Because even though she knew right at that moment she wouldn't be able to look at the man without wanting to hit him, Lauren loved Isaac, and she wanted a future with him.

She just had to figure out if that was even possible without wanting his head on a stake at the same time.

20

HE GAVE HER A WEEK.

The longest fucking week of his life.

And then he showed up on her doorstep.

Only, nobody answered.

He wasn't sure if she was home and ignoring him or if she really wasn't home.

He knew she needed time to cool off, but he was growing antsy having not seen or spoken to Lauren in a week.

She needed time to wrap her head around the bomb he dropped and decide whether she could look past his mistake from twenty-seven years ago.

Could she see him for the man he was now? The man who loved her and wanted to build a life with her? Or would she only ever be able to look at him as the man who killed her father?

So he gave her another week.

He dropped off a box of chocolates and a bouquet of flowers on her doorstep on Valentine's Day, but he never heard a word from her whether she got them, or perhaps some miscreant in the complex snatched them.

It was now fourteen days since he dropped the bomb on her—the longest they'd gone since this whole thing between them started—and he hated being without her.

It felt unnatural.

Wrong.

He'd texted her every day to let her know that they weren't over.

That he was going to fight for them until she outright told him to stop.

So far, she hadn't told him to leave her alone.

She hadn't responded to him once, though, either.

So he kept messaging her.

They were the longest, worst two weeks in his entire fucking life. And he'd been through basic training, war and the police academy. He'd gladly do all three over again than bear the torture of not seeing Lauren or Ike for another second.

He called his mom and the police department in Quaint.

He needed more information about that night.

Maybe, just maybe he had it all wrong. Perhaps his memory was playing tricks on him and he wasn't the one to pull the trigger that night.

Maybe.

In the meantime, he was left to do more waiting.

Waiting for his mother to call him back.

Waiting for the detective in Quaint to check his messages.

According to his sister, their mother was on some Amazonian jungle trek with her new husband, and they didn't have cell service.

The receptionist at the Quaint police department told him that she'd have the detective call him when he had a moment. That was three days ago.

He wasn't holding his breath that he'd hear back at all.

At least not from the cops in Quaint.

Hopefully, his mother could shed some light.

For the last twenty-seven years, she refused to talk about that night, but Isaac figured if he laid all that he had to lose out on the table for Joan, she might help him out and fill in the gaps.

Maybe.

At Sid and Mel's suggestion, he'd gone back to his therapist to talk through some shit, and even though he still didn't have Lauren, speaking with a professional did help.

The shrink basically told him that he could hope and pray all he wanted for Lauren to "get over" the fact that Isaac killed her dad, but at the end of the day, that was Lauren's decision and he needed to respect it. Especially since, as much as he tried to convince himself otherwise, Isaac wasn't over killing Bruce Cameron either.

That night still haunted him. Still fucked with his head, messed up his dreams.

Which was why, when he wasn't working, seeing his therapist or sleeping with Penny curled up next to his head, he was at the gym.

Sweating out his frustrations.

Which was precisely where he was Saturday morning alongside Aaron and Mason.

Working out.

Getting his sweat on to clear his head, and after his session with his therapist Friday night, he needed to clear his head more than ever.

"You heard from her yet?" Mason asked, his tattooed forearms bulging with veins as he did a shit-ton of chin-ups on the bar. The man had barely broken a sweat and wasn't even out of breath. It made Isaac wonder if he was even human when he did this kind of shit.

Isaac set his weights down on the ground between reps. "No. I text her every day to see how she is. To make sure she's okay and say that I'm here if she needs to talk, but so far she hasn't responded."

"Hard line to walk," Mason said with a grunt. "Being caring and attentive without coming across as needy or demanding."

Truer fucking words had never been spoken.

Raised by a single mom and having a little sister, Isaac liked to think of himself as a sensitive man. A feminist. He was all about female equality and abolishing the patriarchy. But while supporting women and their rise to power, he didn't want to lose his own masculinity.

A hard line to walk indeed.

"If you were in my shoes, what would you do?" he asked, leveling his gaze on Aaron.

Aaron had lost a lot in his life, too.

His sister.

His parents.

He'd been raised in foster care.

He'd been to war.

Had done things for the "greater good" that would fuck him up for the rest of his life. He, more than any of the other guys, understood Isaac's situation, his life.

Not that Mason wasn't a great guy, but he came from a nuclear family full of joy and happy memories. He didn't understand where Isaac's head was the way Aaron did.

Aaron set his own weights down on the bench. "I'd wait another week. You called your mom, right?"

Isaac nodded.

"I'd wait to see what she has to say. Press that department in Quaint for more info. Fuck, go there if you have to. Get the lowdown on *exactly* what happened that night, that way when Lauren comes to you with questions, you will have the answers."

Mason nodded in solidarity. "Honesty, bro. Best way to go about it."

"It's honesty that got me into this mess," Isaac muttered.

"And it's honesty that will get you out of it," Mason said.

Isaac made to reach for his weights again when his phone in his pocket started to vibrate and chirp. He grabbed it. It was his mother.

Shit.

Lifting his chin at Aaron and Mason to watch his stuff, he took off to an empty corner of the gym and connected the call.

"Hey, Mom."

"Hey, baby," his mother greeted him. "How's my favorite son?"

"Getting better-looking by the day. And you?"

"Had to turn down *yet* another modeling gig. Why won't they let me retire in peace?"

It was their go-to greeting for each other. Always some complimentary comment about their looks.

Chuckling, he lifted the hem of his shirt and wiped his face. "How was your trip into the jungle?"

"Full of bugs. Jorge didn't get bit once—because they all filled up on my blood. I swear I came out of there half a pint lighter."

"You took your malaria pills, right?"

"Took everything, honey. All the shots, all the pills. I'm fine—besides all the itchy bites."

"Did you have a good time though, despite the bugs? See any of those pink dolphins or monkeys?"

"Saw everything, darling. It was wonderful."

"I'm glad, Mom. You deserve to live retirement in peace."

"And what about you, baby. How's your life? Peaceful?"

Joan Fox-Jimenez was an intuitive woman. She could

usually tell just by the tone of her children's voices whether they were calling simply to chat or to vent.

"What's going on, Isaac?"

Taking a deep breath, he raked his fingers through his sweaty hair and stared out the window at the fat flakes falling out of the sky. "I know you hate talking about this, Mom. In fact, you *refuse* to talk about it, but something has happened."

The sharp inhale of his mother's breath said she already knew where he was going next.

"I met a woman. An amazing, smart, funny, beautiful, kind woman. She is *the* one. I know it."

His mother's voice shook. "That's great, honey, but what does this—"

"It was her dad that was shot in our house that night."

Aaron and Mason probably heard his mother's gasp, it was so loud.

"I need to know everything that happened that night, Mom. I remember bits and pieces, but you need to help me fill in the gaps. Did I kill Officer Bruce Cameron?"

"H-how did you meet her? Did she come find you? Was she looking for her father's killer? What does she want from you?" His mother's words came out fast, frantic and fearful. Like she was on the lam on a burner phone and couldn't talk long before the law caught up with her.

"We met on a gridlocked interstate. She went into labor and I helped her deliver her baby in the back of her car. Then we became friends. Then we became *more*. She told me about her dad, that he was part of the Quaint police department, how and when he died, and I put the pieces together."

"Does she know?"

"Of course she knows. I couldn't keep something like that from her. I love her. I want a life with her. She named her son after me."

"Oh God, Isaac."

"I need to know what happened, Mom. Please. Lauren won't speak to me now. But I can't let it end like this. She deserves answers, and frankly, so do I. It's been twenty-seven years and I still dream about it. It haunts me more than anything I did as a marine. Please, help me."

"If she ended it, maybe it's for the best, honey. I'm not sure how you two can make it work—"

"Mom!" he barked, causing a few heads in the gym to turn his way. He brought his voice down. "I need to know. I *deserve* to know. It's been nearly three decades. Tell me. I've already got a call into the Quaint police department. I'll fucking fly there if I have to, to get the facts. Easier if you just tell me though."

His mother was quiet on the phone for a while, to the point where he wasn't sure if she'd hung up on him or not. But when a muffled sob echoed through, followed by labored breathing, he realized she was crying.

"You came down the hallway, cocked the gun and had it pointed on your father," she whispered.

On his father?'

"You said you weren't going to let him hurt me, you or your sister again. That the cops kept coming when they got called, but they never did anything, and then Dad would just hurt us again."

He squeezed his eyes shut, and memories started to flash through his brain like an old movie reel. At the very most, whenever the cops came to his house, his dad would get handcuffed and hauled away in the cop car, but then Steve would be back angrier than ever the next day. He'd keep his fists to himself for a week or so, sometimes he even disappeared for several days. Rumor around the trailer park was that Steve went off to a nearby county after he got out of prison and whored it up, drank until he passed out and spent what little money he did have on a fuck-ton of blow. Then, he'd show up back at home out of the blue, drunk off his ass, and it was lather, rinse repeat all over again.

In his eight years with his father, he could only remember one instance of Steve going to jail. He father spent six months in county for breaking and entering and assault with a weapon.

Those were the best six months of Isaac's childhood, until they moved to Arizona at least

His father never paid for his crimes. Not really. Not like a true criminal should. *"Steve Fox has more people in Quaint on his payroll than there are people in Quaint,"* he used to hear people say.

"The cops tried to get you to put down the gun," his mother went on. "You were crying. You had a cut lip from the day before when your father hit you, bruises on your arms, and a cracked rib. He'd gone after Natalie, and you'd landed a good punch on him, which was why he had a black eye."

More memory flashes.

He remembered the sound of his sister's screams when their dad came after her because she was laughing too loudly at a television show and Steve was hungover on the couch.

"You said you weren't going to let him hurt us again; you didn't care if you went to jail because with Steve gone, your sister and I wouldn't need you to protect us."

Now that his mother mentioned it, he remembered having thoughts like that. He'd thought a lot about killing his old man. The consequences be damned. His own future be damned if it meant his mom and Natalie were safe.

The hair on his arms stood up, and his gut churned. He felt close to puking. But he needed to hear all of it. He'd come to his mother for the truth, and she was finally, after all this time, giving it to him.

"You pulled the trigger, but I lunged to stop you, redirecting your aim to—"

"Lauren's dad," he breathed out, all the blood draining from his upper body until he swayed and was forced to sit down on a workout bench.

The last glimmer of hope that he hadn't been the one to shoot her dad vanished into the air like a puff of smoke.

"Yes, honey. Lauren's dad. Officer Bruce Cameron."

He swallowed down the taste of bile on his tongue and took a deep breath. "Thank you, Mom. I know that couldn't have been easy."

"I wanted to spare you, baby. Spare you the knowledge of knowing that you'd gone after your father, that you'd killed a police officer, and that—"

"You'd intervened. You were saving yourself, too, by not telling me the truth. Saving yourself from what Natalie and I would think of you if we knew you tried to save that bastard."

His mother's inhale was sharp.

"Admit it, Mom."

More silence.

"Mom! Admit it!"

"Yes, okay. Yes. As horrible as your father was, I didn't want you to be saddled as a boy who killed his father."

"Just a boy who killed a cop?"

"I didn't mean for the cop to get hit." She was sobbing now, her voice a high-pitched screech in his ear. "I didn't mean for anybody to get hit. I just ... *lunged.* It was instinct. To protect our family."

"Steve wasn't *family.* He was a monster. You might be dead right now if I hadn't stepped in and taken some of those punches for you. And we know Natalie wouldn't be here if I hadn't taken them for her."

"I didn't care about your father. I cared about you and what killing your father would do to you!"

"But instead I killed a cop."

"I thought you knew it was an accident. I thought you

knew I lunged at you. Have you been thinking all this time that you went into the kitchen with the purpose of killing the police officer?" Horror came across in every syllable of his mother's words. "Isaac ... I had no idea. Oh God." She gasped, and murmurs in the background interrupted her sobbing, followed by static.

"Hello? Isaac?" It was Jorge, his stepdad. His thick Spanish accent had him saying Isaac's name more like *Ee-sack*.

"Where's my mom, Jorge?"

"She is too upset to speak now. I think it best if you two try later. I understand you want the truth, but telling you that truth has exhausted your mother. She thought you knew it was an accident. She needs time to rest."

He had to hand it to Jorge. The man loved Joan implicitly. Spoiled her rotten, took care of her.

Taking a deep breath, he hung his head, the pulsing headache in his frontal lobe a new sensation in the last minute or so but a blinding one. "Fine, Jorge. Please tell my mother that I love her, no matter what. We'll talk again soon. Also, thank her for finally telling me the truth." *Albeit late.*

"Will do, son. You take care." Jorge hung up.

Squeezing his eyes shut, he massaged the bridge of his nose with his finger and thumb before lifting his head and turning around. Aaron and Mason were standing behind him, their faces grim, concerned.

"You got your answers?" Aaron asked, already knowing the answer.

Isaac nodded and stowed his phone in his pocket just as Colton bounded forward, all smiles. "So I guess you and Lauren are okay, then? And I should offer up congratulations." He thrust his hand forward.

Isaac shook his friend's hand, not knowing why, though.

"What do you mean?" Aaron asked, stepping aside to make room for Colton. "Congratulations?"

Colton's smile dropped like a stone in a pond, and he let go of Isaac's hand. "Shit. You don't know?"

What the fuck was he talking about?

What didn't he know? Was Lauren okay?

"Know what?" Mason asked.

"Mercedes didn't tell me you didn't know. Damn woman and her gossip." Colton took a deep breath, his head shaking and a muscle ticking in his jaw. "Apparently, Lauren's pregnant."

21

She needed this.

Friends. Babies. Chocolate. A distraction.

She thought she knew what she needed—to be alone with her son and her thoughts—but then they showed up on her doorstep with babies in tow, snacks and understanding smiles.

She needed it more than she knew.

News traveled fast through their ever-growing circle of friends, so when Aurora with Dawson and Lowenna with Wyatt, Warren and a box of chocolates knocked on her door, she knew they knew.

Bianca and Celeste were her friends, but they also had a tendency to seek advice from their "family," and by doing so, they apparently let the kitten out of the bag.

She should have expected it.

She wasn't angry that they showed up unannounced, just tired.

Tired of feeling so betrayed. So hurt. So broken. So confused.

Because she was broken inside. Her heart had splintered

into a million pieces. Her soul felt ripped from her body and like it was being pulled in every direction but back inside her. And although it was still early in the pregnancy, she was nauseous, exhausted and so freaking lost.

She loved Isaac. She loved how good he was to her. How much he loved her son. How he wanted the picket fence, house in the suburbs and matching rocking chairs on the porch with her.

But that noose around her neck, that dark cloud hanging over her head, that painful throbbing at the back of her skull kept reminding her that their relationship was cursed.

And not in the way she thought it had been.

Not because he was a cop and Russo women who married cops doomed those cops to death. It was a different kind of curse. One she wasn't sure she could break, especially now that she was having Isaac's baby.

It was tummy time for the little ones. They had all four babies on the floor in a circle on a blanket in Lauren's living room. Four little heads wobbled and eight legs and arms flailed.

One of Lowenna's twins, Warren, was the first to get fussy, and Lowenna scooped him up to settle him. "How's Ike sleeping these days?" she asked, bouncing Warren on her knee and making silly faces at him.

It wasn't Ike's sleep she was worried about. It was her own. He woke three times a night to feed. Almost like clockwork now. Her breasts would wake her up leaking and throbbing sometimes before Ike stirred.

But that was when she actually managed to fall asleep. She wasn't doing much sleeping as of late, despite how tired she was.

Sipping her tea, Lauren forced a smile. "He's sleeping better than before. Did some reverse cycling for a bit and then was up with gas, but we seem to have hit our stride."

Aurora crossed her fingers and bit into one of Lowenna's chocolates, her brown eyes serious but playful. "Until the next stage, right? Things get good, we figure them out, and then *bam!* They move on to another developmental stage and we have to learn them all over again. I feel like just as soon as I figure Dawson out, he changes things up. Keeps me on my toes."

Lauren nodded.

Aurora booped her baby on the nose and smiled down at him. "He's just lucky he's so cute. And that his big brother and sister are so helpful."

"Aiden and Tia all over him?" Lowenna asked.

Zak had two children from a previous marriage. Tia was ten and Aiden twelve.

Aurora nodded. "They love him so much. They get upset when they have to go to their mom's house and then beg to come back to our house early. And Dawson adores them too. They've both been really helpful. I definitely miss them when they're with their mother."

"Your parents are in the apartment over your garage though, right?" Lowenna asked. "Do they help much?"

Aurora's expression said she wasn't entirely keen on just *how* close her parents lived to her and her family. "Perhaps a little *too* much sometimes. My mother is *obsessed* with Dawson, and sometimes I feel a little smothered. Hence why I'm out of the house right now. Needed a break from the mothership, who has her own set of *ideas*. I'm not complaining. I love my parents and that they moved across the country to be closer to me and my family, and how much they love my kids and help out. But ..." She sighed. "Right now it just feels like too much. Does that make me sound like a bitch?"

Lowenna shook her head. "Not at all. Motherhood is exhausting and when too many opinions are being thrown at you it can drown out your own instinct which isn't good. He's *your* baby, you need to listen to *your* gut."

Lauren fought back the surge of jealousy at how much help Aurora had around her. Stepchildren, parents, a loving husband.

She knew Aurora was probably dealing with her own issues and feeling overwhelmed in her role as mother to a newborn, but Lauren couldn't stop the feelings of envy that twisted through her like an invasive ivy vine. She would love to have people around her like that. People who loved her and Ike and wanted to help.

People like Isaac.

Sure, she had Celeste and Bianca, but they had their own children to take care of. They had jobs, and Celeste had a budding relationship with Max. Bianca also had her parents and brothers in town. She had family she could lean on and spend time with.

Lauren had nobody.

Her friends were there for her, but not in the same way.

Not in the same way that Isaac had been.

Pain ripped through her as she thought about him, about how fast and furious their passion had burned when she finally gave in to temptation or, more accurately, gave in to his decision that they were going to be together.

A smile broke through the frown on her face as she remembered when he helped her bathe Ike after one of his massive blowouts. They'd hosed off his tiny butt together, laughing. Isaac stepped right into the shitstorm without hesitation. Just like a hands-on, good father would.

She missed him so much, and even though Ike was just a baby, she could tell he missed Isaac too.

"You okay?" Lowenna asked, sinking down onto the floor with Warren and laying him down on his back next to his brother. The twins were fraternal, so it was easy to tell them apart. Her silver-gray eyes slid to Lauren's face, concern filling them.

Inhaling through her nose and letting it out the same way, Lauren nodded. "Just tired."

"And sad," Aurora finished for her. "You miss him."

So damn much.

"Look," Lowenna started, "we don't know what happened between you two. All we know is that you are"—she glanced at Lauren's belly—"and the two of you split up. We're here if you need to talk. If you need anything."

Lauren smiled through the tightness in her face and swallowed through the harsh lump hanging at the back of her throat. Unshed tears stung her eyes, and she nodded. "I know. And I do miss him. I just don't know if we can—"

KNOCK! KNOCK! KNOCK!

"Lauren! I know you're home. Open up, please."

Lowenna's phone vibrated on the table. "Shit," she said, staring at it. "It's a message from Mason. He just said Colton spilled the baby beans and Isaac knows."

Crap.

"Man, Mercedes is a gossip," Aurora muttered.

They were all gossips.

"I know about the baby, Lauren. We need to talk."

Double crap.

Prying herself off the couch, she glanced at her friends and their grim faces before she made her way around the corner and into the entryway.

"You've got this," Aurora called to her. "We've got your back."

It wasn't her back she was worried about. It was her heart. And the man behind the door currently held the demolished pieces of it.

The remaining fragments of her heart began to thump more heavily in her chest, and her breathing turned shallow at the thought of seeing Isaac after two weeks apart. After she asked him to leave. After the things she'd said to him.

Because she had said some hurtful things. She knew she had. She'd been angry. In pain. In shock. And those emotions came out in the form of harsh words and accusations.

Taking a deep breath and holding it, powering through the cramp in her chest, she opened the door. Air fell from her lungs in a mighty *whoosh* when she saw him and just how wrecked he was.

· A mirror image of her own feelings. Of her own miserable, melancholy, broken soul.

Lost without the other person but incapable of finding her way back even though she was standing right in front of him.

It was raining and windy. Fitting for how she felt. Dreary, weary and devastated.

But she was also really glad to see him. The tingle in her chest and the way warmth filled her when he lifted his head and pinned his gaze on her bolstered her hope that maybe they could get through this and have that picket fence and house in the suburbs.

"Someone here?" he asked, glancing behind him at the two extra vehicles in the driveway.

"Aurora with Dawson and Lowenna with the twins." Thankfully, her foyer was located around a corner down a small corridor from her living room. The women might be able to hear them, but they wouldn't be able to see them.

They needed more privacy.

She stepped over the threshold and shut the door behind her so they were now out on her stoop alone.

"I know about the baby," he said, blinking through the rain. The eaves over her stoop did nothing to protect him as the wind just pushed the droplets sideways.

Slowly, she nodded. "I was going to tell you that day but—"

"I dropped the first bomb."

"And it kind of pushed my bomb onto the back burner." A strong gust of wind had her wrapping her arms around herself for warmth.

Without hesitation, Isaac shed his big winter coat and wrapped it around her, stepping back and shoving his hands in his pockets. His lips flattened into a thin line. "How far along are you?"

Swallowing, she zipped up the jacket and thanked him for it, grateful for the warmth and his scent that encircled her.

"How long, Lauren?" he probed, unwilling to allow her distraction to let his question go unanswered.

"About five weeks."

His sapphire eyes widened. He blew out a breath and raked his long, nimble fingers through his damp hair. "Five weeks. So ..."

"The shower?"

It was the only time they hadn't used a condom from the get-go. So it was the only time she could think of that it happened.

The man had some seriously determined swimmers, and she was apparently dropping eggs like the Easter bunny with an overflowing basket.

Understanding dawned on him, and his expression turned somber. "Right. Shit."

Shaking her head, she glanced up at him, fear swirling inside of her like a cyclone. "I can do this on my own. I don't need anything—"

"I'm not walking away." Anger infused his tone. He pointed at her stomach. "That's *my* kid. I'm not fucking walking away. Even if you don't want anything to do with me,

I'm not abandoning my kid. I'm not abandoning either of them. I'm not abandoning you."

Either of them.

He meant Ike.

I'm not abandoning you.

And that's why she loved this man standing in front of her so damn much it hurt. Because he was a *good* man. An honest man. A man who was fighting for her, for them and for their child. For her child with another man, a child he had grown to love like Ike was his own.

"I would never keep you from your baby," she said quietly.

"What about Ike? Would you keep me from him?" His jaw was tight, his nostrils flaring.

She squeezed her eyes shut. "No."

"And you? Are you going to keep me from you?"

"Isaac—"

"I've given you space, Lauren. I've given you time to cool off. To wrap your head around what I told you. But I've also called and messaged you every day so you knew I didn't walk away. I'm going to fight for us with everything I have until you tell me to stop."

Opening her eyes, she lifted her head.

"You telling me to stop?"

A hot tear slid down her cheek.

He stepped into her space, cupped the back of her head and tilted her neck so she was forced to look up at him. With his big, warm thumb, he swept the tear from her face. "Are you telling me to stop fighting for us?"

She shut her eyes again. It was too hard to look at him. She could feel her resolve crumbling. All she wanted to do was melt against him, let him take away the hurt, take away the past they shared and promise her a beautiful future.

"Lauren?"

"No," she whispered. "Don't stop."

She felt him relax, the breath he'd been holding hitting her lips in a warm puff.

"I didn't aim the gun at your father," he said, his mouth now inches from hers, his forehead against her forehead.

She blinked open her eyes again and stepped back, out of his embrace. "What?"

"I called my mom and demanded she give me the truth about that night."

"And?"

"And I came out of my parents' room with a gun, but I aimed it at *my* father, not yours. I was angry at him for hurting our family, for going after my mom and my sister the way he did. I wanted him gone for good. The police had been called out to our house before, but nothing would happen. The Destroyers ruled Quaint, so chances are he had one cop or another on his payroll."

"Not my father," she said defensively.

He shook his head. "No. Not your father. I didn't care what happened to me. I just wanted my mom and sister to be safe. I wanted Steve out of our lives, and even at eight, I knew the only way to do that was for him to die."

"But my dad ..."

"My mother lunged at me when I pulled the trigger, and your dad was hit by the wayward bullet. She didn't want me to be saddled for life with the knowledge that I'd killed my own father. It was a complete accident. One that should never have happened, but an accident nonetheless."

"An accident," she breathed. Somehow, she wasn't entirely sure why, but that made it easier on the last remaining pieces of her heart.

"I never meant to hurt your father. I didn't go into that kitchen looking to kill a cop." Pain flooded his eyes. "I would never."

But he went into that kitchen with the intentions to kill somebody. Which meant he was still a killer, didn't it?

"He'd gone after Natalie the day before. She was being loud, and Steve was hungover and angry about the noise. I stepped between him and my sister. That was the first time I swung back, too. Gave my old man a black eye. But then he got even something fierce. I had a split lip, bruises on my arms and a couple of cracked ribs."

Lauren's hand covered her gasp.

"I was eight, Lauren. Natalie was five. I wasn't always going to be there to protect her or my mom, and I was worried one day when I wasn't home and able to defend them, he'd kill my baby sister or my mom."

"So you figured you'd shoot him in front of the police?"

He lifted a shoulder. "Maybe in the back of my mind I didn't believe I'd go through with it, but the cops would see how bad it really was and either haul Steve off to jail for longer than a day or remove us from the house."

"But you pulled the trigger." It wasn't a question.

They both knew the answer.

Her father knew the answer.

"That night is fuzzy. My mom says I did." His head shook. "I mean *obviously* I did. But I never meant to hurt—" He cleared his throat. "To *kill* your dad. To the disappointment of my father, I idolized the police. I always wanted to be a cop. To be one of the good guys. He wanted me to follow in his footsteps with the club, but I had no desire. I wanted to help people, not hurt them."

Which was exactly what he did now. His dream of becoming a man in blue with a badge came true. He helped. He served. He protected.

"I love you, Lauren. More than I think I've ever loved anybody. And I love Ike, and I already love this baby, even though it's no bigger than a peppercorn."

She wrinkled her nose and lifted a brow.

A peppercorn?

His boyish, lopsided smile stole every last molecule of oxygen from her lungs. "I did some quick Googling before I came over here."

That made her love him even more.

"I know we have an uphill battle here and that it's going to take you some time to *not* look at me as the person who—"

She pressed her fingers to his lips. "We've said it enough. We know what happened. We don't need to say it again."

Nodding, he swallowed. "Okay."

Tears spilled down her cheeks. "I'm sorry for the things I said. For how awful I treated you when you told me. I was just ..."

"Shocked. Angry. Sad. Confused."

Nodding, she wiped her finger beneath her eye. "All of that." And more.

He reached for her again, wrapped his arms around her waist and cupped the back of her head, angling it again until she was forced to look up at him—not that it was a chore. "We're doing this. I'm not going to let you get away. I'm not going to let the past rule the present or the future, because, baby, we can have a really great future. A wonderful life together, I just know it."

His thumb swept away more tears and landed on her lips, prying them apart. Her tongue darted out and grazed the calloused pad, tasting her salty tears.

"You're not getting rid of me that easily, Lauren." His voice was a gruff rumble that made her body turn molten hot. "If you want to end this, you're going to have to tell me to leave and slam the door in my face, otherwise, I'm not going anywhere."

A rattled sob shook her chest, but she smiled through the tears before biting his thumb playfully.

His smile dissolved the last of her indecision, and she wrapped her arms around his waist, buried her face in his chest and hugged him tight, letting his love, his kindness and his dedication to their family envelop her. Heal her broken heart and retrieve her lost and darkened soul. This man had been there for her when she needed somebody—anybody— the most. And he hadn't handed things over to the midwife and jumped back in his truck. He stuck around, supported her when she had her baby, let her lean on him. And then he reappeared at a moment in time where she was feeling extra alone, and he saved her again. Saved her from her thoughts, from her loneliness and the endless loop of being a single mom. Their friendship had blossomed because of Isaac. Because of his persistence, his desire to know her, know her son, and be a part of their lives. She'd fallen in love with him long before he declared them "more than just friends." She was simply too afraid to admit it.

He was an impossible man not to love.

An impossible man not to forgive.

An impossible man not to want to build a future with, despite the tormented past they shared.

She held onto him even tighter, pushed her hands beneath his sweater so she could grip the soft fabric of his shirt. The hard, warm muscles of his back bunched beneath her fingers, and she held on even more, pulled him into her.

She was never letting this man go again. Not for anything.

"I'm sorry, baby. I'm sorry for everything," he murmured against the top of her head, planting a kiss there. "And I'll spend the rest of my life apologizing every damn day if you need me to. If that's what it takes to be with you. I'll do whatever it takes. More counseling, couples counseling. Whatever, just say the word."

Lifting her face to look at him but not pulling away, not even an inch, she shook her head. "I know you are. I forgive you. Just love me, love our children every day, and that will be enough. You're an incredible man, Isaac Fox, and I love you with all my heart."

Dipping his head until his mouth hovered just above hers, he whispered, "And I love you and our children with all that I am."

EPILOGUE

One year later ...

LAUREN SHUT off the tap for the shower—albeit reluctantly—and opened the door. She paused for a moment, tuned in to the noises in the house and let out a sigh of relief. This was probably the first shower she'd had in two months where she didn't shut off the water only to be bombarded with the sound of children crying.

Wrapping her hair up in a towel, she tossed another one around her body and stepped onto the plush white bathmat, scrunching her toes in the cushy material.

It was a mundane act, but as the mother of two children under two, she was quickly learning to appreciate the simple joys in life.

The simple *child-free* joys in life.

She took her time brushing her teeth, slathering on some facial moisturizer and plucking her brows, all to the blissful sound of—nothing.

Pure, exquisite, soul-cleansing silence.

But as she spat into the sink, she started to wonder if maybe all that silence wasn't so golden as it was ominous.

Was Isaac okay with *both* children?

Maybe they had knocked their father out cold with a frying pan and were currently painting her hallway walls with his blood.

With panic replacing the serenity she'd had, she rinsed out her mouth and flung open the door.

More silence.

Surely, if the kids had knocked their father unconscious and were rampaging the house, they wouldn't be so silent about it. A fourteen-month-old and four-month-old didn't have stealth mode.

But you think they're capable of maiming their father and painting the walls with his blood?

Yeah, she was tired.

Really freaking tired. So tired, she was coming up with ludicrous scenarios that painted her children as overly capable psychopathic beasts.

Shaking her head at her own stupidity, she stepped into her bedroom only to be attacked from behind, have the towel ripped from around her and her body flung to the bed, belly down.

Big, strong, warm hands gripped her by the ankles, and she was pulled down to the end of the bed until only her upper torso remained on. Her toes dug into the rug at the foot of the bed, desperate for purchase.

"The kids are asleep," he purred.

She craned her head around in disbelief. "Both of them?"

He looked hurt. "You think I'm incapable?"

"I think your nipples are useless."

"Ah, alas, they are, but my singing voice by far makes up for my inept nipples."

That was true. He did have a lovely singing voice.

"Where's Ariel?"

"Hallway, asleep in her bassinet."

"And Ike?"

"In his crib in his room." He palmed her inner thighs, spread them and dipped his head between her legs. She spasmed when his tongue found her clit.

"You're a miracle worker," she breathed, settling down onto the bed more comfortably and spreading her legs.

"With the children or on your clit?" He flicked it again, and she squirmed.

"Both."

"And Penny?"

"Curled up at Ariel's feet, purring. Now shush, woman. Let me eat."

Sighing, she sank into the bed and shut her eyes. It'd been way too long since they'd been intimate. Not that they hadn't tried, but the kids were major cockblockers. One or both of them seemed to have a sixth sense about when their father tried to stick it in their mother. Like they were worried another sibling was going to be made.

Not freaking likely.

Not anytime soon anyway.

Lauren had the doctor put in an IUD right after Ariel was born. She was protected and in the clear.

Isaac slid two fingers into her slit and pumped them, his thumb replacing his tongue on her clit.

She shivered when he circled her tight rosette. Poked the tip of his tongue against her hole, making her pucker and bear down on his thumb as it fiddled relentlessly against her swollen, slippery nub.

"Gonna take you here tonight, baby," he purred, spreading her cheeks apart and burying his face there, devouring her until her legs shook and she thought she might pass out.

Thrusting back into his face, she sank down on his fingers, pushing them deeper inside her, relishing the way he so effortlessly brought her to climax. He knew her body so well. What made her tick. What made her come.

That blissful, tingly warmth began to swirl in her lower belly, worming its way through her extremities with each pump of his fingers, each prod of his tongue and flick of his thumb. She was scaling the mountainside. Digging her fingers into the jagged rock bluff and hoisting herself upward. It didn't matter than she was afraid of heights; onwards and upwards when the reward was so breathtaking.

So close to the summit now, she was getting lightheaded and could feel the air thinning around her. Spots began to cloud her vision, and her pulse thundered hard in her ears.

She was barely able to discern the loud, rapid beat of her heart from the buzzing sound behind her until she felt Isaac press something cool and slick against her anus.

She went off like a rocket.

Leapt off the cliff.

But there was no falling here.

She took flight and flew straight up to the stars, which only competed in brilliance with the stars bursting behind her closed lids.

When the climax finally began to recoil from her limbs, pulling back into her center, she relaxed on the bed, panting, satiated and really fucking happy.

"No rest for the depraved, baby," Isaac said, his mouth next to her ear, the hard length of his cock pressing against her lower back as he hovered over her. "Idris and I are going to double-team you."

She had zero control over the shiver that wracked her body at the thought of being so full.

They hadn't done that in a *long* time. Not since before Ariel was born.

Not only did she love Isaac because he was the most lovable man in the world, but she had to admit it was nice having somebody around to help satisfy her insatiable sexual appetite while pregnant. He also helped her with her vibrator when her belly got too big for her to do it herself.

The man came in handy, she wouldn't deny that.

Still hovering over her, he slid his hands along her outstretched arms to where she gripped the duvet cover. "I've missed this," he whispered, nipping the shell of her ear. "Missed taking you whenever I wanted."

"Since when was that possible? We've had a baby or babies our entire relationship."

His lips traveled over her neck, and his fingers linked with hers. "True, but there was that wonderful blip in time when Ike was six months old and slept through the night for four weeks straight."

Ah, simpler times, indeed. And then the eight-month sleep regression hit, and they were up with him multiple times a night again.

With his lips trailing a warm, wet path down over her shoulders and back, he released her hands and raked his knuckles across her skin, from the back of her neck to the base of her spine, goosebumps chasing his caress. He cupped her ass before gripping her hips tight. The head of his cock pressed against her slick, swollen folds, and he dipped it inside, both of them sighing when he powered deep.

"Just a couple deep fucks, baby. Just to get my dick wet. You know how to soak it until it drips."

"More than a couple," she begged, tightening her pussy around him as he straightened up and began to move.

She gripped the bedspread tighter, ground her clit down on the bed for some friction and pushed back against him so he could go deeper.

Every draw, every plunge had her quivering just like

earlier, when his tongue was on her anus, his thumb on her clit and his fingers inside of her. He always knew how to get her to the mountaintop faster than anybody—even Idris.

But just as she started to feel that euphoric tingle begin to bloom in her belly once more, he pulled out.

Bereft of him inside her, filling her, she whimpered.

"You won't be empty for long," he said with a chuckle, sliding a finger up her crease. That familiar buzzing sound filled her ears, and she felt Idris probe her soaked center. Isaac pushed the vibrator in, turning on the sucking feature at the same time. Reaching beneath herself, she adjusted it until her eyes threatened to roll back into her head when the suction latched onto her clit *juuust* right.

Involuntarily, her hips pressed into the bed, fucking Idris, riding his sleek, ribbed, bulbous length.

"Wait for me," Isaac said, squirting lube out of a bottle and running it between her cheeks.

She lifted her hips, breathed out slowly and pushed out with her muscles as his cockhead notched at her tight hole.

Gently, he eased his way inside, pausing every so often to give her time to acclimatize to his girth, to relax around him and welcome him in deeper. He was also fighting for space in her body with Idris, so he had to go slower than usual.

"Jesus, fuck," he breathed when he was finally buried all the way inside of her.

"Yeah."

Tightening his hold on her hips, he started to move. First slowly, then faster, deeper, harder. She encouraged him to go harder, pushing back into him, mimicking his hip movements but increasing the speed. It didn't take him long to pick up on what she was putting down and take it up a notch—or two. Soon, every thrust of his cock into her ass pushed the air from her lungs, and as soon as she'd suck in another breath, he'd hammer it right back out of her.

She was so full. So utterly consumed.

Her pussy fucked, her clit sucked, her ass full of the man she loved. Was there a greater sensation than this?

Hunching over her, but still moving, Isaac pressed his lips to her shoulders. His breath was hot and ragged in her ear as he powered forward and into her, filling her, taking her completely.

She adjusted Idris beneath her again, trembling when her clit was sucked harder.

She wasn't going to last long.

Reaching for her hands, Isaac intertwined their fingers and spread them out in front of her on the bed like a starfish.

Now, all his power came from those hips of his. She could feel his balls slapping her ass, the sound of damp flesh against damp flesh the only music in the room, aside for their heavy breathing and grunts and moans of passion.

He surged forward again, driving deeper, harder into her. "Not gonna last long, baby. You close?"

Boy, was she ever.

"Yeah," was all she managed to get out before the climax crashed into her like a tidal wave. Unlike the first orgasm, which bloomed from her clit, this one came from multiple sources. Every erogenous zone triggered went off at once, causing the climaxes to cannon around, crash into each other and ricochet through her like a bouncy ball in a rubber room. She shook beneath him, cried out, and tightened her fingers in his until her knuckles ached and she thought she might snap off his pinky.

But as powerful as it was, as hard as it came on, it quickly became too much. She wriggled beneath him until the clit sucker broke free of its grasp, allowing her to breathe more than just shallow pants.

Idris still vibrated inside her, and Isaac continued to buck.

"You okay, baby?" he asked, slowing down but continuing to drive deep.

"Yeah." She shut her eyes. "Just got to be too much."

"Just about there, baby. Fuck, this feels so good. *You* feel so good. Hugging my dick with your tight hole." His teeth fell to her shoulder and raked a painful but electrifying track down her arm and up again.

She continued to move into Isaac, enjoying Idris still inside her but knowing she didn't need him. Even without Idris present and Isaac just in her ass, she'd still get off. Isaac was enough.

"Fuck ..." His words came out as more of a grunt as his teeth clamped down on her shoulder once more and he stilled behind her.

His cock pulsed inside of her, filling her with his liquid heat. She clenched her butt cheeks and pressed her hips down against the bed, squeezing him tighter inside her as he came. Idris inside of her, Isaac in her ass sent another mini orgasm spiraling through her out of the blue. Her eyes flashed open, and she moaned, pressing her face into the mattress to muffle her whimpers, her pants shallow and ragged as her pussy clenched and throbbed around the vibrator.

She rode out her orgasm, milking his cock with her ass until she had every last drop from him and he collapsed against her back with a loud, shuddered sigh.

Their skin was slick with sweat, their breathing out of control.

Isaac released her fingers and brushed her hair off her face. She opened one eye and smiled up at him. The grin that met her gaze was one of the most beautiful things in the world. Lazy, satisfied and all fucking hers.

Fisting one hand in her hair, he pulled her head back enough until he could take her mouth in a hard, smacking kiss. "Fucking beautiful, woman. You, freshly fucked. Most gorgeous thing I've ever seen."

Her chest compressed to the point where it became difficult to breathe.

She must have made a face, because he lifted up off her, pulled out and retrieved Idris from her. She rolled over to her back, welcoming him down to her again with her arms outstretched.

With that same grin as earlier, he covered her body with his, his thumb rubbing across her bottom lip, prying her mouth open as he cupped both sides of her face. "I love you, Lauren."

Tears began to burn a path down her cheeks from just how damn happy she was.

All she could do was blink and smile.

"I love our life. I love our family. I love that Ike is *mine*. That you're *mine*. That Ariel is *mine*."

"A bit possessive, aren't we?"

"Of the people I love, damn straight."

Her heart swelled at his words. Because she knew how true they were. Two months before Ariel was born, Isaac officially adopted Ike. He was now Isaac Bruce Cameron Fox. And their daughter was Ariel Hope Fox.

Lauren was kind of feeling left out that she lived in a house full of Foxes but was still a Green herself.

But he said they didn't have to get married if she thought it was part of the curse.

Though that conversation had taken place over a year ago, and her opinion on the curse had changed.

They believed it best not to tell her mother that Isaac was the one to shoot her dad and instead just said he was a police officer and let her mother's disapproval land where it may. No need to stack even more odds against her man than they needed to. Plus, they were all in a good place now—including her mother with her stepfather—no need to open old wounds.

Blinking up at the man she loved more than anything, she cupped his face with hers. "I love you. And I love that you're so possessive, so protective and passionate about all of us. Your children think the world of you, and"—she shrugged —"so does their mother."

He lifted a brow, and his lips curled into a devious smile. "Do you think the world of me enough to marry me?"

Lauren's eyes widened at the same time he levered over on one elbow, opened his nightstand drawer with a grunt and pulled out a black velvet box. "I was going to do this on Valentine's Day, but—"

"We all had the flu," she finished.

His nose wrinkled. "Yeah. Didn't think that was the right time to pop the question, when we were ankle-deep in toddler vomit."

Her stomach churned from the memory. "Good call."

"I make them from time to time." Settling on his side, rather than back over top of her, he rested his elbow on the bed, his head in his hand and the velvet box on her chest between her breasts. "Like knowing you were the best thing to happen to me in fucking forever and fighting for us and what I knew was the real deal."

More tears pricked her eyes. She opened the box and was nearly blinded. A dazzler sparkled back at her, and a sob clutched the back of her throat, making it tough to breathe.

With a gasp, she swung her gaze to his face. "Isaac ..."

"Don't say anything about the size of the diamonds. I wanted to. I could afford to. Plus, you deserve it." With his free hand, he picked up the ring from its velvet bed and waited for her to hold up her hand. "Lauren Cameron Green, will you ditch the last name of Green already and join us Foxes in our burrow? Become my vixen? You're already the love of my life, the mother of my children and the best cook and lay I've ever had. Let's make it legit."

A laugh fought its way through her tight throat. "Did you rehearse that?"

Smiling like an idiot, he gruffly grabbed her hand and slid the ring onto her finger. "I did, and I happen to think it's a great proposal. Cute, funny and romantic. You don't?"

She pushed herself up to sitting on the bed, reached for his hand and pulled him to sitting too, then she stood and led him to the bathroom. "It was perfect. Now, let's celebrate our engagement with a *loooong,* sexy shower. Because I'm sweaty and gross, but I'm also not done fucking you, not by a long shot."

Slapping her ass and making her squeal, he followed her into the bathroom. "Baby, we're going to fuck for the rest of our lives. Forever and ever, picket fence, suburbs, matching rocking chairs, side-by-side burial plots. We're in it for the long haul."

Smiling and waiting for the water in the shower to warm up, she looped her arms around his shoulders. "Nothing would make me happier than to be your vixen."

"Good, because the ring is on your finger. There's no backing out now." He took her hand and pulled her into the shower, his cock having already grown hard again. He took it in his fist and stroked it. "Besides, can you really say *no* to *this?*"

She shook her head. "Nope. And I don't plan to. Not ever again."

HOT FOR THE HANDYMAN - SNEAK PEEK

THE SINGLE MOMS OF SEATTLE, BOOK 3

Chapter 1

"I don't care if you don't have matching socks, I am leaving this house in two minutes," Bianca Dixon called up the stairs to her six-year-old twins, Hannah and Hayley. "In other words, get your scrawny asses down here," she muttered under her breath.

"Scawnyass," Charlie, her two-year-old son echoed, sitting on the stairs heading down to the garage, kicking his feet and poking the eyeballs of his dinosaur stuffed animal.

Bianca grabbed her purse, her kids' backpacks for school and daycare, and her lunch bag, hoisted Charlie onto her hip and headed down to the door to the garage.

"I mean it, girls. Get your butts down here."

Stomps and growls, followed by thundering size-one youth feet rumbled the foundation of the house as her bickering twins descended the stairs.

"You can't leave without us, Mom," Hannah said with impatience. "The whole reason we're even leaving is so

Hayley and I can go to school." She sat at the top of the stairs and pulled on her running shoes.

Her identical twin sister, just with a shorter haircut, joined her and pulled on her matching shoes. "Yeah, Mom. We're *only* six. You can't leave us home alone. Otherwise, you'll get in trouble."

Bianca rolled her eyes. "In trouble with whom?"

The girls looked at each other, smiled and turned back to their mother with triumph in their brown eyes.

"Nana," they both said.

Bianca rolled her eyes again, placed Charlie on the ground beside her and opened the door to the garage. "Get your asses down the stairs, or you *won't* be going to Nana's soon."

That was a big ol' lie. No way in hell was Bianca giving up her child-free moments and denying her parents and children time together without her as a referee.

Hannah and Hayley's mouths dropped open.

"Mom said a bad word," Hayley whispered to her sister.

"We can tell Nana when we see her. Just be good so we can see her," Hannah replied.

"Get down here!" Bianca yelled, heading into the garage to load up her Honda Odyssey.

She had just got Charlie into his car seat and was closing the sliding door to the van with all her children strapped in with socks, shoes and combed hair when her cell phone began to warble in her purse.

"Fuck," she murmured as she swung in behind the steering wheel.

"Duck," Charlie repeated. "QUACK!"

She dug around in her purse and found her still ringing phone.

Of. Fucking. Course. It was her cheating-ass ex.

She canceled the call, hit the button to open up her garage door, and turned over the ignition. He could wait.

The last thing she wanted was to talk to the lying, cheating, wimpy, small-dicked douche. Particularly with her children within earshot, because then she'd have to remain pleasant with the fucker.

Glancing at the clock on her dash, she took a deep breath. She still needed to run by the property she managed to check in on the handyman before she took the girls to school. Charlie didn't start daycare until nine-thirty, so she had a bit of leeway there.

A huge delivery of kitchen cabinets was arriving today and Rod—the handyman—hadn't answered the last three of her text messages or the last four of her calls.

She needed somebody at the house to receive the delivery and she couldn't guarantee that they wouldn't be delivered at nine sharp. She had to make sure Rod—her sixty plus, round-bellied, chain-smoking, misogynistic handyman was there and aware and didn't dick off to the hardware store or something.

From the moment she'd met him she had reservations about the guy. He looked down on her. Spoke down to her and smoked like a chimney with nothing but plastic and green leaves in the hearth below.

But her last three contractors had left mid-project. One because he hurt his back, another because he got a job with another company across town, and then the last one moved to an entirely different state.

So she took pity on her kids' piano teacher's brother, out from Idaho, down on his luck, and apparently good with tools. Rod had been "working" for her for the past ten days, but so far, the guy wasn't worth the four grand they'd agreed on for him to get the first two units where she needed them to be. The guy hadn't earned five hundred in her opinion.

How long did it take to paint one bedroom?

She painted the kids' room, her room and both upstairs bathrooms in two days. And that was *with* children running around like jammy-hand meth-heads.

"What did you pack us for lunch?" Hannah asked, as Bianca turned out of their townhouse complex and onto the main road. Hannah was her loud, type-A, alpha-child. She had no problem voicing her opinions, taking charge and ruling any roost she set foot in.

Except Bianca's roost of course.

Only one hen ruled that house. Only one *queen*. And her children knew it. As hard as Hannah tried to run the show, Bianca pushed back enough that her child was finally—after six *long* years—learning her place.

"I packed all three of you turkey bacon, cheese and pickle sandwiches, a yogurt tube, a banana each, some cucumber and pepper slices and one of those coconut bars you like."

All three kids cheered.

"Yay! Candy bars!" Hannah screamed.

They weren't candy bars. They were coconut and cocoa flavored bars made by some local health-food company and geared toward children who were picky-eaters. Somehow, the creators had managed to jam spinach, dates, carrots, chia and hemp hearts into the bars without tainting the flavor. Her kids thought they were getting candy, when in truth they were getting two servings of vegetables and two tablespoons of coconut sugar.

In your picky-eating faces, you little crotch demons.

"Thanks for such a great lunch, Mom," Hannah said. "That sounds so good."

Hayley made a noise of agreement. "Yeah, so good, Mom. I love those sandwiches."

She could serve up turkey bacon, cheese and pickle sandwiches for every meal of every day and her kids would devour them. At least it hit all the major food groups—kind of. Pickles were still considered vegetables, right?

"*Shake off*," Charlie called out. "*Shake off.* Pwease."

Rolling her eyes, she turned on the music in the van and located Taylor Swift's *Shake it Off* from the playlist on her phone.

As soon as the upbeat, peppy tune started, all three kids began to dance in their booster and car seats.

And she had to admit, when Taylor told her to *Shake it off*, her foul mood from earlier did slough off.

"Dance, Mama," Charlie said. "Dance."

They were only about two minutes from the property now and stopped at a red light, if she left the kids in the van with the door open, ran up to the front door, left that open too and spoke quickly to Rod for under two minutes, she could run back to the car and still get the girls to school on time.

"Dance, Mama!" Charlie ordered.

Bianca rolled her eyes again. "Okay, okay." Her torso jostled and twisted, then when the "Shake it off" part started she batted invisible dirt off her shoulder, only when she glanced beside her, the man on the motorcycle in the adjacent lane was grinning at her. His long nose wrinkled, he bobbed his head and gave her a jolly thumbs up just before the light turned green and he sped away.

Her face burned with embarrassment and she turned the volume down.

"Up, Mama. Up," Charlie ordered. "Loud-ah."

"Why'd you turn it down?" Hayley asked. "Was it because that man on the motorcycle was smiling at you?"

Ignoring her children's demands and how astute her six-year-olds could be, she turned down the street where the soon-to-be affordable off-campus student housing would be.

Two developers up in Canada—James Shaw and Justin Williams—bought up old, run-down houses in university districts, then they renovated them, turned them into multi-unit dwellings and offered them as affordable housing to students. They'd done it several times over in the Seattle already—three of their properties Bianca already managed—as well as in Vancouver and Montreal in Canada and Eugene and Portland in Oregon. If the students moved out over the summer, she rented them as Airbnb's or to locum doctors or whoever needed short-term housing. So far, it'd been working like a dream.

She slowed down when the van approached the house, and thankfully, Rod's beat-up old Nissan truck was parked out front. At least he was there.

Turning off the ignition, she went to unbuckle her belt when Charlie yelled, "Shake off, again ... pwease."

"Can you leave the music on, Mom?" Hannah asked. "It'll keep him happy."

Nodding, Bianca shoved the key back into the ignition, turned the music back on, but kept it low so she could still hear her children if they suddenly started choking on their own spit. She unrolled her window and made her way to the front door of the unit Rod had been assigned to work on.

She went to open the door, thinking Rod wouldn't have locked it if he was working inside, but it was locked.

Odd.

He'd never locked it before when she went there to check on things.

Though, she hadn't been by that early in the morning since he started working for her. She usually popped by after she dropped the kids off at school and daycare. Maybe he had earmuffs on and was using a power tool and didn't want to worry about anybody breaking in.

It wasn't a *huge* unit. But it was a decent size. Two bedrooms with a small living room, kitchen, dining area and a bathroom. Perfect for two students, or three if they got along. An identical unit was next door, and two one-bedroom basement suites would go in below.

She'd had the job managing the rentals for almost a year, and vetted tenants hard in order to eliminate the potential for headaches down the road.

So far, no headaches.

Except for Rod. He was proving to be the biggest headache out of everything.

If only she could find a decent handyman. A Jack of all trades to get the house ready for school in August. It was early May. They didn't have much time left.

Fishing her property keys out of her purse, she slid the key into the lock and opened the door only to be greeted immediately with the loud, obnoxious grunts and groans only heard when two people were having sex or moving heavy furniture.

What. The. Fuck?

There was no furniture in the house yet. So that only left one source for noises like that.

With her keys still hanging in the door, she followed the noise.

That's when she found Rod, laying on a blow-up mattress in one of the bedrooms, his boxers down to his ankles while a woman with faded pink and blonde hair bounced up and down on his lap. She looked as bored as Bianca was shocked.

"What the *fuck* is going on here?" Bianca yelled, slamming her hand on the wall and turning on the light.

The woman on top of Rod shrieked and spun around. She looked young enough to be his granddaughter.

Rod was pushing seventy—for sure. Though, you really can't tell when people smoke several packs a day. He could have been younger than Bianca who was thirty-seven.

Not fucking likely though.

The little pink-haired thing on his lap still had that baby-faced peachy glow to her skin and wide-eyed innocence. Though Bianca didn't think she had any of that innocence left, she just played the part well. Well enough to get customers.

Pink-hair clambered off Rod and pulled her skirt down over her crotch. She went on the hunt for her top.

Rod didn't even seem embarrassed. He lazily tucked his wrinkly old man sac and condom-covered knob back in his boxers and stood up. "Why are you here so early?"

Blinking hard enough she saw spots and shaking her head, Bianca found herself at a loss for words. "Wh-hy am *I* here so early?" she sputtered. "That's the first thing you have to say to me. Why am *I* here so early?"

He nodded, reached for a pack of smokes from his duffle bag and went to light up.

"No fucking smoking in here, you sick pig."

He reared his head back, jowls wobbling. "What the fuck, bitch? What crawled up your ass this morning?"

"Don't *what the fuck me*. I've texted you three times and called you four times to see what is going on and if you'll be here today to accept a delivery and you never got back to me. You haven't done *half* the things on the list. You take dozens of smoke breaks. There are burn marks everywhere because I *know* you're smoking inside, and now I come here and find you with—" She pointed at the pink-haired girl who had found her shirt and tugged it over her tits. She was now lacing up big combat boots.

Rod shrugged. "What the fuck do you want from me?"

She was in the twilight zone.

This was not happening.

They didn't make people as horribly ignorant, disrespectful and repugnant as this, did they?

"How about a little respect," she finally said.

He shrugged again. "Fine, you have it. Now can I finish my smoke and go grab a coffee?"

Bianca scoffed. "Dude, you are fired. Get your shit, give me your keys and get the fuck out."

He rolled his eyes and reached into the pocket of his jeans that were lying on the floor, the movement causing the head of his flaccid cock to poke out the hole of his boxers and the condom to fall off and onto the floor.

She averted her eyes and struggled not to gag.

Pink-haired girl finally got her boots laced, gathered her items, but then stood there like she was waiting for Rod or something.

Bianca turned to her. "Can I help you?"

The girl nibbled on her lip and glanced down at her feet.

"Yes?" Bianca asked with impatience.

"He needs to pay me."

Grunting, but not hustling to vacate the premises like any normal person would, Rod grabbed his jeans again, pulled out his wallet and lifted two bills from inside. He held them out for the girl.

Sheepishly, she stepped forward and took it. Her mouth opened when she counted it. "I—it was one hundred for the night."

Rod snorted and closed his wallet. "Yeah, but we were interrupted so I didn't finish this last time. Forty."

This last time.

Bianca was going to be sick.

The girl's sad, pale gray eyes shifted to Bianca. "I—"

As angry as she was, Bianca's heart went out to the girl. She couldn't be more than twenty-five, was clearly down on her luck and had taken to selling her body to feed herself.

The question was: how much of that money would end up in her pocket, and how much went to *someone* else? And if she didn't show up with the full hundred, was she going to pay for it in other ways?

Lunging forward, Bianca grabbed Rod's dingy jeans from the floor where he'd already stowed his wallet. She opened his wallet and found the remaining sixty bucks.

"Don't touch my fucking money." Rod made to take the wallet back from her, but she shot him a look she would have hoped caused him to evaporate into the ether, but at the very least back the fuck off. She spun around, grabbed the money and handed it to the girl. "You need to go."

Relief filled her face, but her gaze shifted to Rod behind Bianca before landing back on Bianca, concern in her eyes. "You'll be okay here?"

Bianca nodded, her sympathy for the young woman growing, along with her appreciation that, despite how she looked, the woman held concern for Bianca's well-being. "I will be. You go get something to eat, okay?"

The girl didn't need to be told twice and ran out of the room.

Even through the white-hot fury inside her, it broke her heart. That young woman was somebody's baby. Somebody's daughter. She had parents out there who could be wondering where she was, worried.

She said a silent prayer that she didn't do anything to her children as she raised them that drove them from her arms and to the streets selling their bodies. No matter how old they were, her babies could always come home to Mama.

She headed over to the corner where Rod's bag was, picked it up and shoved the blankets, pillows and clothes into it haphazardly. "You've been living here?"

He didn't say anything.

She found his laptop in the corner, the video option engaged.

Fuck, he was filming himself with the prostitute.

Jesus, fuck. What kind of a monster had she hired?

She closed his laptop and shoved it into his bag, marched through the house and tossed the entire bag out onto concrete walk-way. "Get the fuck out of my house, now!"

Rod, still in his boxers, with a heavy layer of white scruff on his jaw and a holey off-white, stained wife beater covering his beer belly stood in his socks on the front stoop. "My computer was in there."

Clearly, this man was a psychopath if not even his computer being ruined phased him.

"I don't care. It shouldn't have been in the house. *You* shouldn't have been in the house unless it was to work. You definitely shouldn't have been fucking a damn prostitute in the house."

He stepped down the walkway and grabbed his bag, he glanced at the open window of her van where her three children stare at them. "You talk like that in front of your kids? In front of your *daughters*?"

"What the fuck does daughters versus sons have to do with a damn thing?" She planted her hands on her hips and glared at him. The pink-haired girl whizzed by behind him in a seen-better-days brown Chevy Sprint.

Rod snorted. "Teaching some real *class* to those girls. Mother of the Year right here, everyone!" he announced pointing at Bianca to anybody in the neighborhood that cared. Nobody was around. And she really didn't think they'd balk at her use of profanity over his current state of undress and what he'd just been doing in the house he was supposed to be working in, not *living* in and whoring around in.

"I'm teaching my children to stand up for themselves, you useless waste of skin. Teaching my girls to be warriors. Get the fuck out of here, Rod."

He shrugged. He actually shrugged. "Then pay me."

"I'll go through the house, see what's been done and

pay you for services rendered. I'll also be deducting damages and if anything is missing. I'll give the money to your sister when I've figured out what your ten days of *work* is worth."

Shaking his head like an arrogant son of a bitch, he lit up a cigarette from a pack he grabbed from his backpack. "You like who you are? You like your life?"

"I fucking love my life and who I am. You like your life, Rod? Like who you are? Cheating people, lying, damaging property, hiring hookers to get you off?"

Pinching his cigarette between his thumb and forefinger he took a long, lip-puckering inhale which caused his eyes to form thin slits. "I like who I am. It's you who needs to calm the fuck down."

Scoffing, she shook her head. "That's fucking sad. If had your life, I'd have killed myself by now."

With a sneer, his eyes traveled her body. "Ever thought of going on a diet?"

She resisted the urge to laugh. She'd been under a hundred pounds when she arrived in Seattle almost a year ago. She was skeletal after the stress of her divorce and what Ashley put her through. She felt like the only control she had left in her life was what she did or *didn't* put in her mouth. It'd taken her a long time to put the weight back on. And yeah, she had a bit of plush now. A squishy middle and an ass that filled out her jeans and then some, but at least her family didn't look at her like she was going to die of a heart attack at any second.

"Did you just call me fat?" she asked with a laugh.

He shrugged again. "I'm not leaving without my money."

"And I'll call the fucking cops if you don't. You are trespassing. Hand over your keys, now. Or I will call the police and have you arrested." She'd been walked on before by a man, treated like less than she was worth, and although Rod wasn't a romantic partner, he was still a man who thought he could treat her like dirt.

That was the problem with men of a *certain* generation. Her father's generation—not that her dad was anything like Rod—but they had a hard time being *beneath* a woman young enough to be their daughter. To take direction and be given orders by someone of the weaker sex—and a millennial to boot. His fragile ego and his arrogance blinded him to progression and the ability to shut up, put his head down and do the fucking job he'd been hired to do.

No, he figured with age came wisdom and with a penis came immunity.

The former wasn't always true, and the latter was never true.

Why was it so difficult for men to understand that a mushy bit of flesh hanging between their legs does not immediately garner them respect, nor does it grant them the license to treat others like crap?

"I'm not leaving. Call the cops then." He pulled on his jeans, reached into the pocket and tossed the keys on the ground in front of her. "I've done nothing wrong."

Bianca thought her head might explode.

Done nothing wrong?

Done nothing wrong!

He was using his place of work at a place to stay and a place to bring hookers. What kind of mental-case had she hired?

Fuck Lorene, the piano instructor and her *reference* for her brother. She was either equally fucked in the head as her brother, pulling a fast-one on Bianca, or had no clue who she was related to.

Either way, Bianca would be giving Lorene and earful when she got the chance.

Pulling her phone free from the back pocket of her denim

capris, she glanced at the time before she went to call the non-emergency line for the police.

Damn it.

The girls were going to be late for school.

Fuck. Fuck. Fuck.

Shaking her head, she glared at Rod before turning around to go and lock the house. She'd have to come back and deal with everything once the kids were in school and daycare.

Fuck. She could not catch a damn break.

Not bothering to look at Rod, she climbed back behind the steering wheel of her van, turned the ignition on and backed out, nearly causing the backend to fishtail.

Somehow, by grace and by God, she managed to get mostly green lights and was only eight minutes late dropping the girls off at school.

With Charlie on her hip, she ran behind her twins, murmuring, "Quick, quick like bunnies," through the parking lot.

"We're going as fast as we can, Mom," Hannah said, turning around fixing her mother with a look Bianca only saw on her friend's sixteen-year-old.

"No time for attitude, Han, just go as fast as you can."

It was early May, but already hot as the surface of the sun and Bianca's dark brown hair that had escaped her messy bun flew around in front of her, only to get plastered to her sweaty face as soon as she stopped in front of the girls closed classroom door. She set Charlie down on his feet and opened the door earning herself a lifted eyebrow from Ms. Beatrice the first-grade teacher.

Fuck off, you childless, judgemental bitch. You have no idea the morning I've had, or the morning I'm going to continue to have.

Ignoring the teacher she was glad her daughters were going to be rid of in a few weeks, she ushered them toward the coat closet and cubby area, assisting them in changing into their inside shoes and removing their sweaters. They didn't need sweaters, but when she sent them to school without sweaters last week for A SINGLE DAY—a very warm day—she received a strongly worded, condescending email that evening from Ms. Beatrice.

A quick kiss to her girls, followed by an "I love you" she patted their butts and sent them toward the carpet where the rest of their class was listening to Ms. Beatrice read a story.

Ms. Beatrice gave her another scolding look as Bianca, with Charlie back on her hip, exited the classroom and quietly shut the door behind her. She was halfway to freedom, halfway down the hall to the exit when a shrill *"Oh, Bianca!"* Made her blood turn icy and her whole face cringe. Her asshole puckered too.

"Oh, Bianca, I'm so glad I caught you. I thought for sure I would see you during drop-off, but it would seem your girls are late today ... again." It was Gwynyth—yes *two Y's*—Charlamagne, a fellow mom in Hannah and Hayley's class. Her daughter, Duchess, was the same age as the girls, and her son, Duke was two years ahead of the girls. No need to slag on the woman's name choices. The universe would do that for her.

"Yes, Gwynyth, I had an issue come up at work I had to deal with which is why we're late. I have to head back there now, actually. After I drop Charlie off at daycare." Which she was also going to be late doing.

She only hoped Rod didn't go full psycho and light the house on fire.

"I don't know how you do it, Bianca," Gwynyth said, flipping her blonde hair behind her with her perfectly French manicured nails. "A *working* single mom to three kids. I feel like I'm losing my mind most days and I only have two kids, a husband and I don't work. I certainly wouldn't want your life."

Bianca's smile was forced and brittle as she hoisted a hefty, pancake-loving Charlie onto her hip a bit better. She loved his tummy and baby chunk, and wouldn't trade an ounce of her little boy for the world, but when she had to hold him for more than five or ten minutes her biceps started to scream at her. "Everyone's Everest is a different size. I do it because I have to."

Gwynyth pursed her lips. "Well, anyway, I'm glad I caught you. We need somebody to organize the end of school joint class-parent gift for Ms. Beatrice, and I figured since you have two children in her class it would make sense if that was you."

What. The. Fuck?

She fucking hated Ms. Beatrice and Ms. Beatrice hated her.

Thankfully, the woman seemed to be professional enough not to take her dislike for Bianca out on Hannah and Hayley. Those two raved about their teacher and how wonderful she is.

Gag.

She switched Charlie to her other hip and he promptly shoved his tiny finger into her ear. She swatted him away. "I'm not sure I'm the best person for the job, Gwynyth. I have a full-time, demanding job and three children. Plus, if you haven't noticed, I'm not exactly Ms. Beatrice's favorite parent. Why can't you do it? You just said you don't work and noticed how full *my* life already is. Why are you asking me to do it? Can't you just take the bull by the horns and get it done?"

She had zero patience for this woman—for most of the moms she'd met in the pickup line. So many of them looked down on her because she was a single mother. A few of the women she also knew from way back when in high school, and she's pretty sure her brother Scott had scorned at least two of them.

Thanks, Scottie.

Gwynyth's eyes glittered with a mischievous twinkle that made the hair on the back of Bianca's neck stand up. "I'm simply much too busy. And Ms. Beatrice loves all the parents, don't be silly. Just like she loves all the students. It's not a big job. Just email the parent list and ask for suggestions on gifts. Take the top ten gift suggestions. Create a poll. Send the poll to all the parents, and then the top choice is the gift. Then get everyone to e-transfer you their child's share of the money. Then go buy the gift. You of course, will pay two shares as you have two children in the class." Gwynyth's smile was so white Bianca's eyes hurt.

"Of course," Bianca said blandly. "Easy peasy."

"Exactly. Now, I have to run. These thighs aren't going to spin themselves bikini-season ready if I don't get them to the gym." She tittered at her own stupid joke and took off in the opposite direction of Bianca—thank God.

Growling, which only caused Charlie to growl too, Bianca stepped up her pace and booked it down the rest of hallway and burst free into the fresh air as if she were a prisoner finally released after a life-sentence.

IF YOU'VE ENJOYED THIS BOOK

If you've enjoyed this book, please consider leaving a review.
It really does make a difference.
Thank you again.
Xoxo
Whitley Cox

ACKNOWLEDGMENTS

There are so many people to thank who help along the way. Publishing a book is definitely not a solo mission, that's for sure. First and foremost, my friend and editor Chris Kridler, you are a blessing, a gem and an all-around terrific person. Thank you for your honesty and hard work.

Thank you, to my critique groups gals, Danielle and Jillian. I love our meetups even if they're only video chats right now (Thanks, COVID) where we give honest feedback. You two are my bitch-sisters and I wouldn't give you up for anything.

Kathleen Lawless, for just being you and wonderful and always there for me.

Author Jeanne St. James, my alpha reader and sister from another mister, what would I do without you?

Megan J. Parker-Squiers from EmCat Designs, your covers are awesome. Thank you.

My street team, Whitley Cox's Fabulously Filthy Review Crew, you are all awesome and I feel so blessed to have found such wonderful fans.

The ladies and gents of Vancouver Island Romance

Authors, your support and insight have been incredibly helpful, and I'm so honored to be a part of a group of such talented writers.

Author Cora Seton, I love our walks, talks and heart-to-hearts, they mean so much to me.

Author Ember Leigh, my newest author bestie, I love our bitch fests—they keep me sane.

Ana Rita Clemente, the first "fan" I ever met in person. Thank you for proof-reading this one.

My parents, in-laws and brother, thank you for your unwavering support.

The Small Human and the Tiny Human, you are the beats and beasts of my heart, the reason I breathe and the reason I drink. I love you both to infinity and beyond.

And lastly, of course, the husband. You are my forever, my other half, the one who keeps me grounded and the only person I have honestly never grown sick of even when we did that six-month backpacking trip and spent every single day together. I never tired of you. Never needed a break. You are my person. I love you.

ALSO BY WHITLEY COX

Love, Passion and Power: Part 1

mybook.to/LPPPart1

The Dark and Damaged Hearts Series Book 1

Love, Passion and Power: Part 2

mybook.to/LPPPart2

The Dark and Damaged Hearts Series Book 2

Sex, Heat and Hunger: Part 1

mybook.to/SHHPart1

The Dark and Damaged Hearts Book 3

Sex, Heat and Hunger: Part 2

mybook.to/SHHPart2

The Dark and Damaged Hearts Book 4

Hot and Filthy: The Honeymoon

mybook.to/HotandFilthy

The Dark and Damaged Hearts Book 4.5

True, Deep and Forever: Part 1

mybook.to/TDFPart1

The Dark and Damaged Hearts Book 5

True, Deep and Forever: Part 2

mybook.to/TDFPart2

The Dark and Damaged Hearts Book 6

Hard, Fast and Madly: Part 1

mybook.to/HFMPart1

The Dark and Damaged Hearts Series Book 7

Hard, Fast and Madly: Part 2

mybook.to/HFMPart2

The Dark and Damaged Hearts Series Book 8

Quick & Dirty

mybook.to/quickandirty

Book 1, A Quick Billionaires Novel

Quick & Easy

mybook.to/quickeasy

Book 2, A Quick Billionaires Novella

Quick & Reckless

mybook.to/quickandreckless

Book 3, A Quick Billionaires Novel

Quick & Dangerous

mybook.to/quickanddangerous

Book 4, A Quick Billionaires Novel

Hot Dad

mybook.to/hotdad

Lust Abroad

mybook.to/lustabroad

Snowed In & Set Up

mybook.to/snowedinandsetup

Hard Hart

mybook.to/hard_hart

The Harty Boys, Book 1

Hired by the Single Dad

mybook.to/hiredbythesingledad

The Single Dads of Seattle, Book 1

Dancing with the Single Dad

mybook.to/dancingsingledad

The Single Dads of Seattle, Book 2

Saved by the Single Dad

mybook.to/savedsingledad

The Single Dads of Seattle, Book 3

Living with the Single Dad

mybook.to/livingsingledad

The Single Dads of Seattle, Book 4

Christmas with the Single Dad

mybook.to/christmassingledad

The Single Dads of Seattle, Book 5

New Years with the Single Dad

mybook.to/newyearssingledad

The Single Dads of Seattle, Book 6

Valentine's with the Single Dad

mybook.to/VWTSD

The Single Dads of Seattle, Book 7

Neighbours with the Single Dad

mybook.to/NWTSD

The Single Dads of Seattle, Book 8

Flirting with the Single Dad

mybook.to/Flirtingsingledad

The Single Dads of Seattle, Book 9

Falling for the Single Dad

mybook.to/fallingsingledad

The Single Dads of Seattle, Book 10

Hot for Teacher

mybook.to/hotforteacher

The Single Moms of Seattle, Book 1

Hot for a Cop

Mybook.to/hotforacop

The Single Moms of Seattle, Book 2

Upcoming

Hot for the Handyman

Mybook.to/hotforthehandyman

The Single Moms of Seattle, Book 3

Lost Hart

The Harty Boys, Book 2

Torn Hart
The Harty Boys, Book 3

Dark Hart
The Harty Boys, Book 4

Quick & Snowy
The Quick Billionaires, Book 5

Doctor Smug

Raw, Fierce and Awakened: Part 1
The Dark and Damaged Hearts Series, Book 9

Raw, Fierce and Awakened: Part 2
The Dark and Damaged Hearts Series, Book 10

ABOUT THE AUTHOR

A Canadian West Coast baby born and raised, Whitley is married to her high school sweetheart, and together they have two beautiful daughters and a fluffy dog. She spends her days making food that gets thrown on the floor, vacuuming Cheerios out from under the couch and making sure that the dog food doesn't end up in the air conditioner. But when nap time comes, and it's not quite wine o'clock, Whitley sits down, avoids the pile of laundry on the couch, and writes.

A lover of all things decadent; wine, cheese, chocolate and spicy erotic romance, Whitley brings the humorous side of sex, the ridiculous side of relationships and the suspense of everyday life into her stories. With single dads, firefighters, Navy SEALs, mommy wars, body issues, threesomes, bondage and role-playing, Whitley's books have all the funny and fabulously filthy words you could hope for.

YOU CAN ALSO FIND ME HERE

Website: WhitleyCox.com
Twitter: @WhitleyCoxBooks
Instagram: @CoxWhitley
Facebook Page: https://www.facebook.com/CoxWhitley/
Blog: https://whitleycox.blogspot.ca/
Multi-Author Blog: https://romancewritersbehavingbadly.blogspot.com
Exclusive Facebook Reader Group: https://www.facebook.com/groups/234716323653592/
Booksprout: https://booksprout.co/author/994/whitley-cox
Bookbub: https://www.bookbub.com/authors/whitley-cox

JOIN MY STREET TEAM

WHITLEY COX'S CURIOUSLY KINKY REVIEWERS
Hear about giveaways, games, ARC opportunities, new releases, teasers, author news, character and plot development and more!

Facebook Street Team
Join NOW!

DON'T FORGET TO SUBSCRIBE TO MY NEWSLETTER

Be the first to hear about pre-orders, new releases, giveaways, 99 cent deals, and freebies!

Click here to Subscribe
http://eepurl.com/ckh5yT

Manufactured by Amazon.ca
Bolton, ON

26292902R00206